THEY WERE GALLANT, COURAGEOUS, DE-
FIANT—AND CAUGHT IN A DESPERATE
STRUGGLE TO SURVIVE. . . .

FRANK KESSLER—A Special Forces Master Sergeant. No fighting man in the world was better with a
weapon or hand-to-hand . . . but the odds were
against his getting out of Russia alive.

ADRIAN DULANEY—An ex-Marine. Still in love
with a woman he'd last seen ten years before, he might
die trying to be with her again.

HANA CERNIKOVA—A Czech Olympic skater. She
was now hiding the information the CIA would risk a
war to get . . . and she would risk her future to keep.

CROSSFIRE

"The plot [is] so believable it prompted a friend of
mine, a living legend in the [Special Warfare] community, to growl enviously, 'I'd love to have that operative.'"

—G. Gordon Liddy, *U.S. News & World Report*

"All the important elements of a riveting suspense ride
are here."

—*Publishers Weekly*

By J. C. Pollock

CROSSFIRE

—— J. C. POLLOCK ——

A DELL BOOK

Published by
Dell Publishing
a division of
Bantam Doubleday Dell Publishing Group, Inc.
666 Fifth Avenue
New York, New York 10103

This is a work of fiction. The names, characters, incidents, places and dialogues are products of the author's creativity and are not to be construed as real. Any resemblance to actual events or locales or persons, living or dead, is entirely coincidental.

ISBN: 440-11602-3

Reprinted by arrangement with Crown Publishers, Inc.

Printed in the United States of America

July 1990

10 9 8 7 6 5

RAD

For Al and Jo Hart—
for being there when I need them.

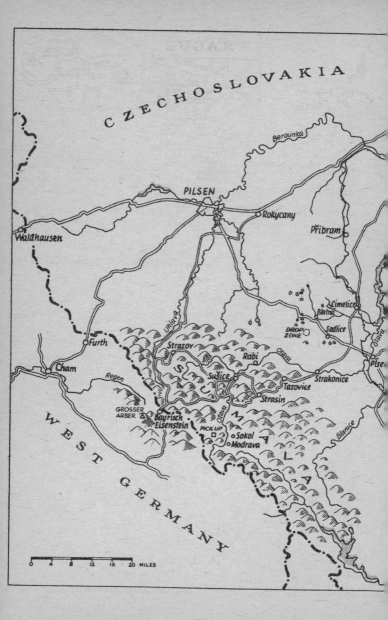

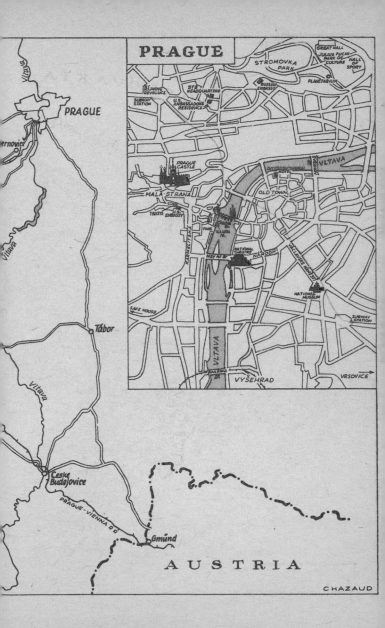

CROSSFIRE

Prologue

*Tyuratam Space
Launch Center and
Missile Test Site
Republic of
Kazakhstan, Soviet
Central Asia
July 19, 1984*

�֍ THE SPRAWLING COMPLEX OF modern structures loomed on the desert horizon like an alien mirage—an aberration in the heart of the vast desolate stretches of windswept, arid wasteland. Missile test silos pockmarked the ground, and squat concrete bunkers and high-rise assembly and support buildings broke the monotony of the flat terrain scored by roadways and railroad tracks. Prefabricated housing for the growing population of scientists and technicians now stood on the harsh, barren land where once seminomadic Kazaks had camped with their herds of sheep en route to summer grazing lands at higher elevations. The steel frames of space-launch towers and the smooth metal skins of propellant storage tanks glistened in the brilliant sunlight, their shapes distorted from a distance by the scorching summer heat that rose in shimmering waves from the ancient dried-up riverbeds and cracked, cobbled clay of the desert steppe.

Inside the launch control center where engineers and technicians sat before rows of computer terminals and electronic consoles the air was cool and the light subdued. The pace had quickened in the final hour of the countdown and an atmosphere of restless anticipation permeated the room as upgraded data flashed on the display screens and a colorful array of lights glowed from the consoles.

General of the Army Vladimir Tolubko—Commander in Chief of the Strategic Rocket Forces of the Soviet Union—accompanied by the missile design project director and a small entourage of deputy commanders and aides—sat quietly in a glass-enclosed room above the floor of the control center watching the activities below and listening to the countdown on the intercom. The general's broad, solemn face and emotionless eyes showed no signs of the eagerness he felt about having the testing completed and the new SS-X-24, with its greatly improved accuracy and reliability, ready for operational deployment. The scene in the control room pointedly reminded him of how far Soviet missile technology had advanced since the day in October 1960 when a test missile had blown up at this very spot, killing Chief Marshal Nedelin and over three hundred other officers and key scientists, and a near identical tragedy in 1972 when hundreds more had been killed, including fourteen high-ranking military officers, when a giant booster rocket had exploded on its pad.

The launch director, his normal prelaunch anxiety increased by General Tolubko's presence, monitored the engineers' status reports on the readiness of the major components and subsystems of the missile poised in an underground silo a quarter of a mile away. This was the eleventh in a planned series of eighteen tests of the SS-X-24. The first eight missiles had been fired from launch pads at the Plesetsk rangehead in northern Russia between Moscow and Murmansk—three had had major malfunctions and five had developed minor problems that were later corrected. The last two had been tested under realistic operational conditions and successfully fired from silos. The site for the remaining tests had been relocated to Tyuratam in an effort to confuse American intelligence-gathering efforts.

For the past three days the preparation for the launch had proceeded smoothly. The telemetry instrumentation packages had been thoroughly tested, as were the downrange monitoring and radar-tracking facilities for the later stage of the missile's flight on its trajectory to the impact area four thousand miles away on the Kamchatka Peninsula.

As the countdown neared the point where the computer-controlled automatic launch sequencer would take over, the test conductor listened to the engineers respond to his ready-report questions.

"Propulsion?"

"Ready."

"Hydraulics?"

"Ready."

"Pneumatics?"

"Ready."

"Range safety command?"

"Ready."

"Propellant utilization?"

"Ready."

"Flight control?"

"Ready."

"Telemetry?"

"Ready."

"Electrical?"

"Ready."

"Launch director?"

"Ready."

At T minus nine minutes, the guidance engineers entered the final data into the missile's on-board guidance computer. The computer responded, confirming that the missile was positioned at 337 feet above sea level on lines of longitude and latitude that corresponded with the Tyuratam Space Center. A further check was made of the electronic packages of the integrated flight-control system that commanded and controlled the navigation, guidance, altitude control, sequence of events, and telemetry and data management functions.

A response from the range safety officer confirmed that the ground-controlled destruct system was armed and ready in the event the missile had to be destroyed in flight.

At T minus five minutes a quick series of hydraulic-pressure checks were made, verifying that the systems were functioning normally. And in a final test, the main engines and vernier engines were gimbaled into a preprogrammed series of movements that caused the missile to tremble and stir in its silo. The tension in the control center heightened as the automatic launch sequencers took command.

Three minutes later the compressed-gas generators at the bottom of the silo strained under the tremendous pressure waiting to power the piston mechanism that cold-launched the missile. At the automatic launch command, explosive charges on the silo door detonated, driving the door off to the side on its rails. The sabots around the girth of the ninety-five-ton, seventy-foot-long ICBM kept it aligned as the enormous pressure the generators had created was released and the missile was forcefully ejected from beneath the earth. The sabots dropped off as it cleared the silo and at the critical point—twelve feet above the ground—the on-board sensors instantly detected a slight decrease in the cold-launch acceleration and simultaneously transmitted the command to start the first-stage engines.

The missile growled ominously as the igniters at the top of the solid-fueled engines sent concentrated bursts of flame into the core of highly combustible powdered-aluminum propellant. A booming, crackling noise followed a split second later as the flames spread throughout the fuel, sending white-hot pressurized exhaust gases thundering through the engine nozzles and out the exit cones. The sudden eruption of four hundred thousand pounds of thrust shook and rocked the missile sideways for an instant as it roared upward on a fiery, brilliant yellow white column of flame and exhaust.

The earth-shaking noise and blinding light resonated and flashed across the desert floor as the sleek projectile climbed rapidly, accelerating to three times the force of gravity within seconds. Four hundred feet above the ground the main engines responded to the pitch-program commands of the on-board computer and pitched the missile over from its vertical position. The vernier engines swiveled and adjusted their thrust, making minor course corrections and rotating the missile on its axis to properly align the guidance system to the trajectory path.

Inside the control center all eyes were on the tracking radar and instruments that monitored the missile's telemetry reporting systems as it headed downrange. Computers processed the raw data being received in analog and digital form, transposing it to enable the engineers to read at a glance the hard copy the chattering strip-chart printers spewed out at the rate of a foot a second. The guidance engineers riveted their attention on graphs projected on computer display modules and blips on radar screens simulating the missile's trajectory. One screen displayed the flight path and another the course. One set of lines on the graph indicated the ideal trajectory while a second set showed the acceptable limits.

At two minutes and seventeen seconds into the flight—52 miles downrange at an altitude of 37 miles and a velocity of 5,398 miles per hour—the preprogrammed first-stage engine cutoff occurred. Activated by the on-board computer, explosive charges blew apart the connecting bolts, sending the now inert first stage of the missile tumbling back to earth. A sudden, but brief, deceleration was followed by another crackling roar and flash of white light as the second-stage engines ignited.

At three minutes and twenty-seven seconds after launch, the flight was proceeding smoothly. The missile was 164 miles downrange and had reached a speed of 6,823 miles per hour and an altitude of 380,000 feet.

An abrupt change on the radar tracking display screen made the launch director stiffen. His brow furrowed as he quickly glanced at another screen and confirmed what was happening. The intercom suddenly came alive with engineers reporting the malfunctioning of their instruments monitoring the flight. Their equipment had gone dead. The on-board telemetry packages had stopped transmitting. The tracking radar indicated erratic behavior. A rapid decrease in velocity was followed by the missile straying beyond the acceptable limits of its course and flight path.

The range safety officer, seated at a console in a glass-partitioned area separated from the control center, stared at the large display screen on his wall. The plotting mechanisms showed the same radar tracking data being received by the launch director. Glancing over his shoulder he caught the director's eye and acknowledged the frustrated nod of his head. Flipping a toggle switch, he sent the destruct signal to the errant ICBM now tumbling out of control above the earth's atmosphere. The shaped explosive charges on board the missile detonated, enveloping the second stage and the postboost vehicle containing the dummy warheads in a huge fireball.

The project director's face paled as General Tolubko got to his feet and cast a withering, icy stare in his direction. The general slowly shook his head in disgust before turning on his heel and leaving the room in ominous silence, his deputies and aides in tow. The director slumped in his chair, confused and dejected by the outcome of the test. Within minutes he would send salvage crews out to scour the desert to find what remained of the missile after it had reentered the atmosphere in pieces and fallen to earth to be scattered in a wide radius from a point two hundred miles northeast of the test site. Within the hour, he would assemble a panel of scientists and design engineers and they would back out and analyze the test data and review the telemetry stored on the magnetic disks in an attempt to determine the cause of the failure. He took small comfort in his well-founded belief that the design of the missile was sound, and would be proved so by the completion of the planned series of tests.

※ ※ ※

Xinjiang Ulghur Autonomous Region People's Republic of China

Nine hundred twenty-five miles east of the Tyuratam Space Launch Center, beneath the permanently snow-capped peaks of China's Tian Shan mountains, the fate of the Soviet ICBM had not gone unnoticed. This virtually uninhabited backwater area had once been an invasion route for the Mongol hordes, and a path of contact with the outside world where the ancient Silk Road passed through the province on its northern route through Central Asia to Europe. Small groups of nomadic Chinese-Turkic herdsmen still occasionally camped in the hidden valleys and foothills for brief stays—their dome-shaped yurts, framed with wooden lattice and covered with felt, dotting the grassy slopes, the aroma of their rancid butter tea clinging to the clear mountain air.

Far above one of the quiet, remote valleys, in the deep pine forests at the edge of the treeline, a broad alpine meadow opened among the draws and ravines to reveal a scene a century removed from the pastoral society below. A double row of ten-foot-high cyclone fencing topped with coils of razor wire and patrolled by armed guards and attack-trained dogs secured the outer perimeter of the meadow as closed-circuit television cameras scanned the inner compound. Low-slung buildings housing an operations center, power station, and quarters for the personnel were dwarfed by an extensive array of signal-gathering and radar-tracking antennas—the electronic eyes and ears that had witnessed and recorded the failed Soviet missile test. Huge silvery white geodesic radomes enclosed towering dish antennas forty and sixty feet in diameter, protecting them against the brittle arctic air and heavy snow of the brutal winters brought from Siberia by the prevailing northeast winds. The United States Central Intelligence Agency's top-secret intercept station —built with the approval of the Chinese government in exchange for an intelligence-sharing agreement—was situated on the China-Soviet border for the specific purpose of gathering intelligence information on the Soviets' eastern test range.

Three weeks prior to the ICBM test, an increase in the communications traffic to and from the Tyuratam test site had alerted the CIA to the early signs of preparation for a launch. Reconnaissance satellite photographs of a missile canister being brought in by trailer and loaded into its silo added further confirmation. Two days before the test, real-time transmission of television photographs, instantaneously beamed from another satellite to a ground station, revealed a series of indicators showing that the test was imminent.

Seconds after the missile was ejected from its silo, the intercept station's tracking radar had locked on to it, and the signal-gathering antennas began eavesdropping on the telemetry being transmitted back to the Soviet control center from instruments on board the missile. The intercepted transmissions, recorded for later analysis, would tell how true the missile's trajectory was to the preprogrammed instructions in the guidance system's memory: the number and degree of the on-board computer's correctional commands, and the missile's response to those commands, would reveal the accuracy and efficiency of the new Soviet missile.

In the operations center control room, their faces bathed in a soft red glow from the radar tracking screens, the CIA personnel had quickly realized that the missile had been destroyed when the sudden interruption of signals occurred within four minutes after lift-off. The CIA communications officer on duty immediately radioed a report of the failure of the test to the intercept platforms waiting downrange to eavesdrop on the later stage of the missile's flight. In response to that report, an operations officer at the Shemya Air Force Base in Alaska's

Aleutian Islands recalled an RC-135W electronic intelligence aircraft, and also informed his technicians on the ground operating the Cobra Dane radar that surveyed a two-thousand-mile corridor of the Soviet test range that the bird was down. Out at sea, the United States Navy ship *Observation Island,* its aft deck and superstructure bristling with radome antennas and a Cobra Judy phased-array radar turret, changed course from its position fifty miles off the coast of the Kamchatka Peninsula, its mission prematurely ended. An air force ground station in California radioed a command to turn off the recording instruments in an orbiting SIGINT satellite, its sophisticated surveillance sensors positioned to intercept, from a different angle, the very-high-frequency and microwave signals used by the Soviets.

Activity in the control room at the intercept station on the China-Soviet border returned to normal. Signals analysts and telemetry specialists removed their headsets, now filled only with a static hiss, and relaxed at their consoles. Before the end of the day, the recorded telemetry and other information garnered from the test flight would be transmitted to CIA headquarters at Langley, Virginia, where signal conversion officers and other specialists would decode, analyze, and interpret the captured data.

At the rear of the operations center, isolated and secured from the rest of the building behind a cipher-locked steel door, a warren of offices and storage areas branched off a narrow hallway. In a small electronics laboratory at the end of the hall, a man sat hunched over a computer console, his eyes rapidly scanning the data on the visual display. He had arrived at the Yining airport the day before the Soviet missile test and made the uncomfortably long journey by jeep over the deeply rutted dirt roads and the narrow, rock-strewn trail that switchbacked up the steep mountainside to the intercept station. The security guard driving the jeep had occasionally glanced at the aluminum cases that cradled and cushioned the man's highly specialized equipment, but asked no questions of his silent passenger, who insisted on carrying the heavy cases himself.

The credentials the intense, wiry, middle-aged man presented to the officer in charge of the intercept station identified him as a CIA research analyst. CIA headquarters had cabled the station about his arrival, mentioning nothing of his purpose, stating only that he was to be given whatever cooperation and facilities he required. The man was not, in fact, a research analyst, but a highly skilled computer scientist and communications specialist with the Central Intelligence Agency's Directorate of Science and Technology—Office of Special Projects.

A trace of a smile passed briefly across his tightly drawn, owlish face as he studied the data on the screen before him and prepared to carry out the final phase of his assignment. He cared nothing about the intelligence information the intercept station had gotten from the Soviet missile test concerning its accuracy and efficiency. His interests lay only in the fact that the test was a failure: not simply that it had failed, but the precise moment at which the missile had begun its erratic behavior, and each minute detail of the pattern of that behavior until it was destroyed. This particular test in the series had been carefully selected—the missile's development having reached a crucial stage where his superiors at CIA felt certain the Soviets would not falsify telemetry or cause deliberate malfunctions as they sometimes did in early tests to throw off American intelligence assessments of their progress.

Glancing at the data sheets he had brought with him from CIA headquarters, the special-projects officer switched on the instruments on an electronics console and selected a frequency on a transmitter. Activating the transmitter, he sent out a command signal spread over a spectrum that made it virtually undetectable as it disappeared into the background noise.

Twenty-two thousand three hundred miles above the earth's surface a Defense Support Program satellite hurtled through the cold, black silence of space at seven thousand miles per hour. Attached to its hull was a small instrument package piggybacked into geosynchronous orbit with the satellite when it had been launched from the space shuttle. The function of the instrument package was unrelated to that of the DSP satellite, and upon receiving its second command signal within twenty-four hours from the CIA ground station on the China-Soviet border, it was detached and jettisoned away from its host by rocket thrusters that dropped it into a lower orbit where, within a few weeks time, it would reenter the atmosphere and burn up, its mission completed.

1
September 25, 1985

✖ ANDREI VOLODIN PLACED A small white pill on the tip of his tongue and swallowed it with a quick gulp of water. In a few minutes his breathing became more even and the tightness in his chest eased. Standing at the window of his corner room on the ninth floor of the Prague Intercontinental Hotel, he pulled the drapes aside and watched the first thin trace of a pale yellow dawn backlight the spires and gabled roofs of the ancient city. He had been awake for nearly twenty-four hours; his thoughts were dominated and tormented by the decision he had made, and the reasons he had made it. He tried to focus his mind on his plan of action, but past events forced their way to the surface as he stared at the broad expanse of the Vltava River, its smooth-flowing water changing from dark gray to shades of blue and green as the morning light grew on the horizon.

His double life had begun thirteen years ago, in 1972—a heady period for American-Soviet relations. Détente had relaxed the tensions between the two superpowers and exchanges on business, cultural, and educational levels reached an unprecedented peak. He was then a doctoral candidate at Moscow University, and the future seemed filled with possibilities of new freedoms and opportunities. The American who had befriended him, an exchange student doing graduate work in physics, had encouraged him to apply for the exchange program at MIT, promising to do what he could to see that his application was accepted. His own government's approval was given without delay, and the year he spent studying in the United States had served to expand his knowledge in his field of physical and mathematical sciences while permanently altering the course of his life in a way he could never have imagined.

Upon reflection, the method the Central Intelligence Agency had used to recruit him was patently obvious, but at the time the subtle nature of its application had seemed perfectly natural in the context of his growing friendship with the MIT graduate student he had met in Moscow. His occasional semicritical remarks about the Soviet Union—telling comments that revealed his deep-seated doubts about his country's system of government—led to philosophical discussions about the advantages of the American system. Convincing arguments, supported by reminders of the history of American-Soviet relationships, that the United States had no designs on the Soviet Union, were followed by long, thoughtful talks about what small contributions he and his newfound friend might make toward bringing about a higher standard of living and greater freedoms for the Soviet people and a better understanding between their two governments.

Their friendship deepened—carefully nurtured, he realized later, by his American "friend" working as a contract agent for the CIA—and his remarks became more candid and open. He told him about friends and acquaintances, fellow students and colleagues, dissidents who had spoken out against the system and were branded as enemies of the state, arrested, and disappeared into the gulag. A few months before it was time for him to return to the Soviet Union, he was introduced to a man who readily identified himself as a CIA case officer, and who further convinced him that his purpose in helping them would be worthwhile, his goal noble. He had agreed to work for them, setting the hook himself, by meeting secretly with the case officer and undergoing the necessary tradecraft training to carry out his future assignments. To this day, though he had no regrets, he never fully understood why he had agreed to betray his country.

With his expertise in microelectronics, he advanced to the position of project manager on a computer design team specializing in the internal architecture of microprocessors. The military applications of his work were of considerable interest to American intelligence, and he had been carefully protected and used sparingly by his CIA case officer in Moscow. In the last three years, however, with his design team at the Zelenograd Center for Microelectronics assigned to work with one of the Strategic Rocket Forces missile design bureaus, his position had taken on monumental significance. His contacts with his case officer became more frequent and risky. The demands and pressures of his duplicity increased to the point of affecting his health. He had gained forty pounds and his consumption of vodka had grown from an occasional drink to debilitating quantities. The added weight and the effects of the alcohol had worsened his heart condition, and he began to find it near impossible to function under the constant stress and fear of being discovered. A circular madness sometimes gripped him, an imagined pounding at the door waking him from a fitful sleep. Did they know? Were they simply waiting for the opportune moment to arrest him, to send him to a prolonged living death at the hands of brutal guards in a Siberian slave-labor camp?

His anxiety had increased as two months passed with no action taken on his request for immediate arrangements to get him out. His case officer, whom he no longer believed in, had tried to assure him that the arrangements were being made, but he could wait no longer. They would never go back on their word, he reassured himself, even if he did act without their approval. The information he had in his possession was vital; their operation could not succeed without it. They had promised him asylum in the United States; to allow him to live out his life in peace and comfort after completing his present assignment. All that remained was to turn over the final data, something he had no intention of doing until he was safely on American soil.

His invitation to present a paper and participate in panel discussions on computer technology at the Eastern Bloc scientific conference in Prague had provided him with the opportunity to take matters into his own hands. He had a close friend in the city: Jan Marcovic, a professor of physics at Charles University whom he had known since his student days. He visited him on his summer vacations—staying at his small cottage on a central Bohemian lake—and they met yearly at various conferences in other Eastern European cities. Marcovic had agreed to help, using his contacts among the Prague dissident community.

Summoning his courage, Volodin pulled on his raincoat and took only his briefcase as he left his room. Exiting the elevator, he entered the lobby and walked through the lounge. At seven o'clock in the morning it was already crowded with guests bused in from the rural areas for a few days sightseeing—workers' rewards for reaching or exceeding quotas in factories or on collective farms. Coarse, strong faces filled with wide-eyed anticipation gaped at the opulence of the modern hotel. Poorly dressed, some comically so, in bright plaids combined with equally garish checks and stripes, they sat awkwardly in the overstuffed armchairs and sofas, tugging at their ill-fitting clothes with thick, callused hands, their gruff voices lowered in awe as they waited for their tour guides. Small, scattered groups of men and women, better dressed and more at ease, stood about the lobby—Czech Communist Party members, civil servants from the hinterlands, gathered for a three-day district meeting being held in the hotel conference rooms.

Volodin's nervous eyes scanned the lounge, finally spotting the man he was looking for sitting near the information desk at the far end of the lobby. The KGB officer, his chair positioned to provide a clear view of the bank of elevators, looked bored and tired from his night-shift vigil. Volodin pretended not to see him, avoiding the narrow, hooded eyes that instantly recognized him. He was relieved to see that his lone surveillant was the same man who had followed him each morning since he arrived in Prague. The smallest member—and obviously the most junior judging from his constant night duty—of the rotating team assigned to him and the four other Soviet scientists attending the conference. The man waited until Volodin turned into the corridor at the end of the lobby, then got up slowly and fell into step, following him past the shopping arcade on the way to the dining room at the opposite side of the hotel.

The KGB officer waited outside the restaurant's only entrance as Volodin brushed past a milling group of impeccably dressed Swedish trade delegates and was seated by the hostess at a table along the glass wall overlooking the river. Built on the banks of the Vltava, the hotel was a modern excrescence of concrete and glass that contrasted badly with the buildings in the Old Town section of the city. The only true luxury hotel in the country, it served as a government showplace for foreign visitors where no expense was spared to impress them, providing the finest in food, service, and accommodations. Volodin's attention was drawn to the reason for the delay in seating the Swedes. Their Czech government escort was seeing to the final details at the group of tables set aside for them—properly aligning the small Swedish flags placed by the waitresses at each setting, and officiously examining the silverware, scowling at the hostess as he quickly polished those he found stained with water spots. After a cursory inspection of the steam tables at the breakfast buffet—the white-gloved attendants removing the gleaming steel covers for his approval—the government escort motioned to the hostess and the Swedes were paraded in.

Staring at a distinguished-looking gray-haired man at an adjacent table, assuming that he was British by the cut of his suit and his shoes, Volodin sipped the cup of coffee placed before him and concentrated on the details of his plan. He was too nervous to eat, and didn't bother going through the buffet line. His thoughts briefly turned to his wife, and how she would react when told of his defection. He would not miss her, nor she him. It was a childless marriage that existed only for convenience. Her life and professional career as an anthropologist would suffer little past the initial interrogation, and she would, he had no doubt, successfully divorce herself from his disgrace as she had from his affections.

Glancing at his watch, he drank the last of his coffee and got up from the table. It was time, and he steeled himself against the nervous tension that soured his stomach and brought the familiar tightness to his chest. Leaving the restaurant, he exited through the hotel's side door into the crisp September morning and crossed the street, past a line of empty tour buses parked at the curb, and stepped up to the sidewalk above the river. The sun was well over the horizon, sparkling off the water, and the air was unusually clean and fresh, cleansed by yesterday's brief but heavy rain. He walked slowly, avoiding the sections of black, sticky macadam negligently applied the previous day to fill the patches where the concrete had broken and crumbled. A quick look confirmed the presence of the KGB officer following at a discreet distance, making no effort to conceal his presence. Maintaining a steady pace, Volodin headed in the direction he had purposely established for the past three days as the route for his walk each morning before the conference convened. He wondered if the slight change in his routine—taking his briefcase with him as opposed to returning to the hotel for it after his walk—had been noticed. Judging by the KGB officer's relaxed attitude and the casual attention he was paying to an old man rowing a small boat out into the river, he guessed not.

Another glance to the rear made him lengthen his stride. Timing was critical. A city bus pulled out from the traffic light at the hotel and headed down the narrow street in his direction, fouling the air with its diesel fumes. A crowd of people on their way to work stood beneath the trees at a bus stop on the corner of one of the dozen bridges that spanned the river. As Volodin drew closer the crowd began moving toward the curb, jostling for position. He listened to the sound of the approaching bus, casting nervous glances over his shoulder, displaying an intentional interest he hoped the KGB man would notice. He timed his arrival perfectly. Wading into the middle of the crowd as the bus screeched and rattled to a stop, he was out of the line of sight of his surveillant, lost among the crush of people squeezing and elbowing their way into the already crowded bus. Turning quickly to his right, he ran down the steep steps leading to the quay at the river's edge, and darted under the bridge into the dark shadows along the wall beneath the arch.

Pressing a hand to his chest in response to the increasing pain, he leaned back against the cool dampness of the moss-covered stones and waited. If he had been successful, the KGB officer would panic at having lost sight of him, and would assume that he had boarded the bus, leaving him no option but to chase after it to the next stop six blocks away in the opposite direction from Volodin's intended destination. The roar and clatter of the diesel engine filled the air as the bus pulled out, the sound trailing off as it continued along its route. Volodin stared at his watch, waiting a full three minutes before leaving the shadows under the arch and walking along the quay. Going beneath the bridge to the opposite side, he cautiously climbed the steps leading back up to the street level, and entered a narrow strip of trees and grass that overlooked the river. Stopping to collect himself, he sat on one of the benches, using his handkerchief to mop the perspiration from his face and neck as he glanced about the small park, searching for the man he hoped he had eluded.

Ten yards from where he sat, the sight of a familiar figure leaning against a tree at the edge of the sidewalk took his breath away. The KGB officer stared back at him through menacing eyes, a humorless grin fixed on his thin, angular face. Volodin's head slumped to his chest. He felt as though he had been kicked in the stomach, and cursed himself for having been foolish enough to believe he could outwit a professional. But there was no turning back; a report would be filed, he would be put under heavy surveillance because of his actions, and questions would be asked if he returned to Moscow, all culminating in an investigation that would inevitably lead to his exposure. There was even the possibility that he would be taken into custody upon returning to the hotel and escorted back to Moscow immediately, denying him another chance to escape during the remaining two days of the conference.

His mind raced aimlessly until his thoughts settled with startling clarity on the only course of action available. Drawing a deep breath of resignation, he got up from the bench and began walking slowly out of the park, crossing the street and heading toward Old Town Square. The KGB officer was now alert, following close behind. A spiderweb of narrow, crooked streets and alleys set in medieval patterns, intersecting from every angle, fed into the square that was once an ancient marketplace and now one of the major tourist attractions in the city. Ornate gables and elegant spires adorned the Gothic, Baroque, and Renaissance buildings that surrounded the broad open plaza. Tour groups beginning their day of sightseeing trailed after their guides, and Volodin angled toward the largest of the groups in front of the Old Town Hall as he entered the square.

He was painfully aware that he was out of his element, but his advantage in height and weight bolstered his wavering courage. With the sole exception of a childhood scuffle—a brief shoving match with a bully who had taunted him—he had never struck anyone in anger, and had never physically harmed another human being. Edging his way through the crowd of tourists, he looked back to see the KGB officer respond to the potential danger of losing him by closing the distance between them. Leaving the group behind and moving quickly along an arcaded walk, Volodin again looked back to see the familiar face bobbing and weaving among the tourists to keep him in sight. A narrow, cobbled alley led off the square, winding its darkened way through a solid maze of buildings, the eaves of their tiled roofs nearly touching, forming a near-perfect canopy that allowed only thin shafts of sunlight to penetrate the deep shadows along the walls. Clutching his briefcase under his arm, Volodin turned into the alley. Breaking into a run, he stumbled over the rough paving stones, his eyes searching the dark recesses in front of him for a place to hide and lie in wait. Rounding a corner, he tripped over his own feet and fell, scrambling upright only to hear the sharp staccato echo of heavy footsteps from the direction he had come.

Recovering his composure, he stepped inside the archway of a building, pressing his back against a carved wooden door. He could barely hear the approaching footsteps over the sound of his own labored breathing, but instantly caught sight of his pursuer as he came around the corner. Grasping the handle of his briefcase firmly, he swung it with a strength born of desperation, hitting the KGB officer squarely in the face, knocking him flat on the ground where he lay momentarily stunned by the forceful blow. Getting to his knees, he reached inside his jacket for his pistol, but Volodin reacted swiftly, rushing from the doorway, flailing alternately with briefcase and fist; his attack clumsy and unbalanced, but effective. His opponent tried to fend off the blows, but Volodin continued the windmill attack, pummeling the KGB officer without mercy until he lay unconscious at his feet.

Surprised by the ease of his victory, he stepped back and stared for a long moment at the trickle of blood coming from the corner of the KGB officer's mouth. Volodin breathed a sigh of relief when he heard the man groan, thankful that he hadn't killed him. Glancing in both directions, he ran to the end of the deserted alley, slowing to a walk as he emerged onto a busy street. Stopping momentarily to look back, he quickened his pace, eager to reach the apartment house only a few blocks away.

⁜   ⁜   ⁜

Professor Jan Marcovic opened the door of his third-floor apartment the instant the buzzer sounded, peering out into the hallway as Volodin stepped inside.

"Was there trouble?" Marcovic asked, noticing Volodin's ashen face and grim expression.

Volodin nodded as he crossed the small living room to the window overlooking the street.

"Were you followed to this building?"

Volodin shook his head. "I had to take more drastic measures than expected," he said, leaving the window and sitting heavily on the hard-cushioned sofa against the wall. "I left the man following me unconscious in an alley a few blocks from here."

"How long ago?"

"Ten minutes."

Marcovic's deeply lined expressive face showed his concern. Had the KGB officer been in doubt about whether he had lost Volodin at the bus stop due to his own negligence, or by design, they would have had two precious hours before the conference convened and Volodin's absence caused the incident to be reported. "Then we must leave the city immediately," the professor said, "before the state security police begin to search for you."

"Have the arrangements been made?"

"Yes. Someone is waiting outside to drive you to my cottage at the lake where you will spend the next two days. The dissident community has made arrangements for some of their people to take you across the Austrian frontier."

"But they will have sealed the borders by then."

"They know how to deal with that. They will get you across, my friend. Do not worry."

Volodin looked skeptical. "Have they contacted the Americans?"

"I do not know."

"I could call the American embassy," Volodin said, getting up from the sofa and crossing the room to the small telephone table near the door. "Believe me, they will not let the KGB get me."

Marcovic grasped him firmly by the arm. "Andrei, you are not thinking clearly. Their telephone lines are monitored by our state security police. What could you tell the American CIA . . . that you are here in my apartment . . . where they can meet you? Relax, my friend. The people who are making the arrangements will notify the Americans in Vienna. They will meet you when you cross the frontier. You said yourself that they might only try to stall you again if you contacted them here in Prague."

"Perhaps you should just drive me to the American embassy. I could request asylum."

"We have discussed this at length, Andrei. It is highly probable that the VB guards outside the embassy would stop you before you got inside. But even if you did manage to get into the embassy, the Americans would then have whatever it is you are carrying in your briefcase, and you would have no guarantee that they would not simply release you to the KGB over the protests of your country."

"They would never do that; it would negate all that I have done for them."

Marcovic glanced at his watch. "It is now out of the question. We must assume that the man who was following you has recovered and reported to his superiors. The Czech guards across from the embassy will be notified immediately and their numbers doubled; they will seal off the street. You would be arrested on sight."

"But two days at your cottage," Volodin protested. "The KGB will have no trouble discovering that you and I are friends. It must be in my records. They will know you helped me. We will both be arrested."

"They are the best arrangements I could make with only two days notice, Andrei. And do not worry about me. Friends will be watching my apartment. If the police come to see me, I will deny any knowledge of your defection. If I am arrested, your companion at the cottage will be alerted and you will be moved to another location. It has been well thought out."

"Forgive me," Volodin said. "I am too frightened to think rationally."

"I understand," Marcovic said. "But there is no longer any time to question or change plans. You must leave at once."

"Defect with me," Volodin said. "Your state security police will suspect you have helped me even if they can't prove it."

Marcovic shook his head. "I have no desire to live in the West. I have important work here. Besides, your defection is a Soviet matter. My government will investigate to appease their Soviet masters, but it will be pursued halfheartedly. Now come, the driver is waiting."

Volodin embraced the much smaller man, smothering him in his arms. "You are a true friend, Jan Marcovic. I will always be grateful."

"If what you have in your briefcase for the Americans helps weaken the Russian bear, I am the one who will be grateful to you."

"It will do that and more," Volodin said with a nervous smile as he followed Marcovic through the doorway. "It will emasculate him."

2

QB SALVATION REPORTS ON URGENT BASIS 1:08 P.M. LOCAL TIME TODAY. APPARENT DISAPPEARANCE SOVIET SCIENTIST ATTENDING PRAGUE CONFERENCE. ANDREI VOLODIN REPUTED EXPERT COMPUTER SCIENCE. SUSPECT DEFECTION BUT AT THIS JUNCTURE HAVE NO WAY OF KNOWING CAUSE OR PURPOSE OF DISAPPEARANCE. MARSHALING RESOURCES TO DETERMINE. POSSIBLE SOME OF OUR ASSETS COMPROMISED RESULT CZECH/SOVIET FULL COURT PRESS. DAMAGE BEING ASSESSED. FURTHER DETAILS AS THEY OCCUR.

TOM DYER SAT AT his office desk on the seventh floor of CIA headquarters in Langley, Virginia, grinding his teeth as he reread the cabled message from QB SALVATION—the cryptonym for the CIA's Prague station chief. The cable had come into the operations center only five minutes earlier. Its external tags had classified it as "operational immediate," and it had been brought directly to his office by the Soviet Bloc Division chief to whom it had been routed. As Deputy Director for Operations, in charge of all Agency covert activities, Dyer was accustomed to crises and invariably handled them in a calm and efficient manner, but at this moment, with the realization of the stakes involved, he was rattled by the far-reaching implications of the message before him.

He regretted the abrupt manner in which he had dismissed Paul Davidson, but although the Soviet Bloc Division chief was aware of Volodin's activities as an agent and the nature and value of the intelligence information he was passing on, he knew nothing about the details of Operation Trojan Horse. The "bigot list" for the top-secret operation was the most limited of any in Agency history. For security purposes, only select members of the National Security Council knew of its existence. The NSC special group—5614/3—was formed to handle highly sensitive, close-hold operations, and consisted of the President and his assistant for national security affairs, the secretaries of State and Defense and their deputies, the chairman of the Joint Chiefs of Staff, the Director of Central Intelligence, and the Deputy Director for Operations. Dyer, as DDO, had been involved from the beginning, and during the initial planning stages had structured the special security compartmentation on a strict need-to-know basis.

Checking the time, he decided against calling the Director of the Central Intelligence Agency on his mobile phone. A man of precise habits, the DCI would be in his office within ten minutes, enough time for Dyer to get Volodin's file and start thinking about a plan of action. If they could find him and get him safely out, their operation would be secure. The Soviet and Czech "full court press," as the Prague station chief had put it, was understandable. Volodin was a middle-level scientist with limited access to strategic military intelligence information. His defection, planned from the beginning, would do nothing to compromise Trojan Horse. The KGB would simply consider him a defector who had possibly taken top-secret documents with him, but they would have no way of clearly determining, or for that matter suspecting, that he had been a CIA agent. But Dyer knew that if the information he was certain Volodin was bringing out with him fell into Soviet hands, they would not only know that he was an agent, but they would have the thread to unravel his specific mission.

Opening his private safe, Dyer removed Volodin's file, brought to his office only three days ago as plans were being developed to bring him in. TS-SI-TH was stamped across the cover in bold red letters—the designation translating to Top Secret—Special Intelligence—Trojan Horse. Skimming the recent reports from the Moscow station, he found no mention of the Prague conference, guessing that it was an invitation Volodin had received after their last contact with him. Flipping through the pages, he paused to read an assessment of their most valuable agent's present mental and physical condition, and of his marital difficulties. Dyer muttered to himself, cursing the inept handling of the situation by the Moscow case officer. Turning to the biographical information in the file, he searched for anything that might give him a clue as to why Volodin had chosen Prague to defect. Finding nothing, he read the periodic reports from his case officer, noting brief mention of three previous conferences Volodin had attended there in the last eight years. A footnote had been added at the bottom of one of the reports, and as Dyer read it, he had the answer to his question. Volodin had spent seven summer vacations out of his last ten in Czechoslovakia. The DDO had ordered no surveillance of him during these periods, not wanting to alert other stations to his importance and risk exposing him; consequently there was no information on where or how he spent his time. A friend, Dyer thought. Male or female, but definitely something more compelling than the scenery had made him return to Prague that often.

The latest report from the Moscow station, the details still fresh in Dyer's mind, explained why Volodin had jumped the gun. Two months earlier, he had used an emergency means of communication and mailed an innocuous letter under a pseudonym to a drop address in East Berlin that was backstopped by the Agency. The letter had been processed chemically, revealing the hidden message. Volodin wanted out. Immediately. He no longer trusted his case officer and was beginning to panic. He had pointedly, and needlessly—as a desperate man's veiled threat—reminded them of the importance of the information he was bringing with him. Apprised of the letter, Dyer had instructed the Moscow station to tell Volodin to sit tight, and reassure him that arrangements to bring him in were in the final stages.

The intercom on his desk buzzed, and his secretary announced that the Director had just left his private elevator and gone into his office. Dyer placed the cabled message inside the file folder and slipped on his suit jacket. Turning left in the corridor, he passed the Deputy Director's office, nodded to one of the security guards inside the glassed-in room across the hall, and entered the Director's suite. Walking briskly through the anteroom unchallenged, he went directly into the inner office.

John Stevens looked up from the papers stacked neatly in the center of his desk, his alert, intelligent eyes immediately taking in the file folder tucked under Dyer's arm and the stern look on his face. "I hope this isn't as serious as you look," the Director said, flashing a quick half smile as he motioned the DDO to a chair in front of his desk. He patted the stack of intelligence summaries before him. "This is what we're going to spoon-feed to the honorable congressmen today," he said with more than a trace of sarcasm. "Waste of time. They won't authorize another cent for the Honduras operation."

Dyer removed the cable from Volodin's file and handed it to the Director. "This isn't going to improve your mood."

Stevens read partway through the message and glanced up, the defector's name not immediately registering. "Volodin?" the DCI asked, trying to place him among the myriad of names and operations stored in his prodigious memory.

"AR-BANDIT," Dyer said, using Volodin's cryptonym.

"Trojan Horse," Stevens said after a brief silence, the tone of his voice changing as he made the connection and read the rest of the cable. "How the hell did this happen?"

Dyer squinted against the bright sunlight streaming into the office through the floor-to-ceiling glass wall beyond the Director's desk and shook his head. "I don't know. We had some warning that he was beginning to panic, but we thought we had him under control."

"Does he have a contact in Prague?"

"No. No one at the station knows anything about him," Dyer said. "We were planning on getting him out from Budapest next month while he was attending a seminar."

"Was there any indication he was in danger of being compromised?"

"None. He held up fine until the operation was completed. Then he started to come apart at the seams. The pressure got to him—he just wanted out. His case officer thought he had him calmed down enough to wait until we were ready. Apparently he was worse off than we thought."

"Any idea who he'd turn to for help in Prague?"

"According to his file, he's made frequent trips there for extended stays. My guess is he's got a friend, or a relative, somewhere in the city. With a little luck, someone the Prague station can locate through their agents."

"Cable the Prague station chief and tell him to find him. Priority one. Damn!" Stevens said, glancing at the cable. "If the KGB gets to him first it's all over. Four years of work down the drain. The finest operation this agency's ever put together."

"If we locate him," Dyer said, "we've got another problem."

Stevens's eyes bored into him, his face now showing the anger growing inside him. A political appointee and close friend of the President, the DCI had a shallow knowledge of the intelligence profession and virtually no experience in paramilitary operations—relying completely on the DDO's expertise gained from twenty years in the clandestine services. "What problem?"

"Getting him out. We have a limited immediate-action capability for paramilitary operations into Czechoslovakia. Less than we'd need to guarantee success of the mission if things get rough. That's why we chose Budapest."

"What about our special operations people?"

"It would take too long to put the right group together. We've got to be ready to move immediately." Dyer paused before continuing, still arranging the details in his mind. "I was thinking along the lines of someone with current in-depth knowledge of the country and the necessary muscle if we have to use it."

"I'll get you whatever you want. Just spell it out."

"The Army's Tenth Special Forces Group," Dyer said. "They have a battalion in Bad Tolz, Germany. Twelve operational detachments—A-Teams—whose areas of operation in time of war are Eastern Europe. The detachments assigned to Czechoslovakia are area specialists. They know every inch of the country; they're well-trained, fluent in the language, and they know how to get in and out without a ripple. They're exactly what we need."

"They're hot-war troops, Tom," Stevens said.

"Exactly. They're ready to go on a moment's notice. And when we find Volodin, which could be in a matter of hours, we've got to be prepared for an immediate response."

"What about the Prague station chief's local agents and assets?"

"According to the cable, he's afraid some of them have been burned. Apparently the Czechs and the Soviets are really applying the pressure. The ones who haven't been picked up have probably broken off contact and gone to ground. They aren't about to surface until the heat's off. And the station only has four case officers; the KGB and Czech State Security are going to be on them like white on rice. Their capability for getting Volodin out once they find him has got to be crippled at best."

"How do you plan on using the Special Forces troops?"

"When Volodin is located, we can use one of our indigenous deep-cover agents to get him to an extraction site near the border, then send the Green Beret team in to bring him across."

"We'd have to have complete control over them," Stevens said, well aware of the international repercussions if they were caught. "And they'd have to go in sterile, nothing that can peg them as our military. Under those conditions, the army's going to mewl and puke about handing them over."

"The chairman of the Joint Chiefs is on the bigot list for Trojan Horse. He knows the stakes; he can smooth out the bumps."

"I'll have to go to the President on this, but I'm sure we'll get a green light; he's counting on Trojan Horse being fully operational within the next six months. Go ahead and start getting things cranked up. I'll see him within the hour."

"I thought to expedite matters I'd cable the Bonn station chief and tell him what we need. He can send his Special Forces liaison man down to Bad Tolz immediately. If the President approves it, he'll be in position to get things under way. We can move the team to one of our launch sites, brief them on the mission, and have them on stand-by alert and ready to go as soon as we have Volodin under wraps."

Stevens glanced at his watch. "What's the time difference?"

"Five hours ahead of us," Dyer said. "It's twelve thirty in the afternoon in Germany. We can have someone at Bad Tolz in an hour."

3

LT. COL. PAUL KITLAN swung his jeep onto the apron in front of the small, weather-beaten operations building at the Flint Kaserne airstrip. Pulling up to the edge of the steel-matted runway, he cut off the engine and sat watching the horizon. His eyes were drawn to the south, to the austere beauty of the steep limestone walls and jagged snow-capped peaks of the Bavarian Alps that rose dramatically above the gently rolling meadows and deep pine forests of the Alpine foreland. Small farming villages dotted the landscape, their onion-domed churches and brightly painted houses with low sloping roofs and wooden balconies adding splashes of color and texture to the lush, green valley.

A faint, pulsating sound in the distance drew the colonel's attention away from the scenic view. Stepping out of the jeep, he shielded his eyes with his hand, scanning the cloudless cobalt-blue sky in the direction of Bad Tolz. A small speck entered his vision, growing in size as it drew closer, flying low over the small resort town on the banks of the Isar River. Making a straight-in approach over the military base, the helicopter settled noisily on the runway a short distance from where the colonel stood—the rotorwash tugging at his camouflage fatigues.

A tall, blond-haired man, in his mid-thirties, dressed in a

business suit and carrying a suitcase, exited the aircraft. Ducking his head until he was clear of the rotors, he gave a short wave to the pilot and the helicopter lifted off, rising swiftly and banking into a steep turn.

"Sorry about the mystery, colonel," Peter Bailey said, walking over to Kitlan and extending his hand, "but it isn't something we could discuss on the phone."

"It never is with you people," Kitlan said, shaking Bailey's hand and motioning him into the jeep. He had never met the CIA's Special Forces liaison officer but had seen him in the company of his commanding officer on two previous occasions. And although he had no personal animosity toward him, he did resent the Agency's intrusion into his domain, and the unholy alliance that he had learned from personal experience inevitably undermined and abused the Special Forces mission and purpose. As a young Green Beret lieutenant, he had served with the CIA-controlled Special Operations Group in Vietnam, and he was familiar with the Agency's methods of operation. The call he had received only two hours ago from the CIA's chief of station in Bonn, advising him of Bailey's arrival, had not brightened his day.

"Where's Colonel Thompson?" Bailey asked, wondering why the senior Special Forces commander had not been there to meet him.

"He's on leave."

"Well, as battalion commander you're the man he would have sent me to anyway."

"I was afraid of that," Kitlan said, the remark confirming his suspicion, after seeing the suitcase and the dismissal of the helicopter, that this visit was more than what he had first thought: a simple request to provide unit evaluations and other intelligence information gathered during the joint field-training exercises his men were scheduled to participate in with NATO unconventional warfare troops.

"This one's important," Bailey said, a forced smile on his intense, handsome face. "We need your help."

Kitlan gestured toward the suitcase on the floor of the jeep. "I take it you plan on staying a while."

"I prefer to discuss it in the war room if you don't mind, sir."

Kitlan nodded, making no reply as he turned the jeep around and headed back toward the main compound. Passing beneath a broad archway, he drove into a large open quadrangle surrounded by a sprawling three-story concrete building with a faded, red tile roof. The building was the heart of the Flint Kaserne military base, containing the administration offices and various post facilities. Now the home of the First Battalion of the Tenth Special Forces Group and the Seventh Army NCO academy, the post had a checkered past. Built by the Nazis in 1936, it had been the training academy for German SS officers during World War II. Following the war, General Patton had made it his headquarters, and following that, it had served as the headquarters for various United States Army units until the Tenth Special Forces Group took up permanent residence in 1953.

Kitlan parked at the entrance to the administrative offices and led Bailey into the building and along the polished tile hallway past the hand-carved wooden statue of a Special Forces soldier surrounded by flags and brass plaques honoring the men of the Tenth Group who had died in Vietnam. Continuing up a stairwell to the third-floor classified briefing area known as the war room, Kitlan opened the padlock on an iron grille and the two men walked down a long, dimly lit tunnel to a steel door blocking the opposite end. Deftly opening the combination lock, the colonel escorted Bailey inside, closing the door behind him and turning on the lights as he crossed the wood-paneled, windowless room to the briefing platform.

Sitting in one of the overstuffed leather chairs on the raised platform, he gestured to Bailey to take the chair opposite him. "Let's hear it," he said in a tone that left no doubt he was less than eager to hear what the CIA case officer had to say.

Bailey glanced about the room, taking in the rows of empty seats and the large-scale wall maps of West Germany and the Eastern Bloc countries. Pointing to a map of Czechoslovakia, he said, "We have a problem in Prague. A defector we have to get out. I can't tell you much about him; at this point all I know is his name—Andrei Volodin—and that he's a Soviet scientist who was attending a conference. We believe he defected this morning. I do know that the DCI wants him safely out at all costs."

"You 'believe he defected'? You're not sure, or you're not sure that it was this morning?"

"The chief of station Prague reported his disappearance this morning. The Deputy Director for Operations is proceeding on the basis that it is a defection. I can assure you, he wouldn't do so without hard evidence that it is precisely that."

"For your sake, I hope so. Otherwise you're talking about kidnapping a Soviet scientist."

"He's a defector, colonel," Bailey said evenly, ignoring the sarcasm evident in Kitlan's remark. "And I'm here to enlist the services of you and one of your teams whose area of operations is Czechoslovakia. We want you to help us bring him in."

Kitlan bristled at the use of the word *enlist,* knowing that the voluntary nature the word implied was virtually nonexistent when used by the Agency. "You seem to have skipped over the obvious solution to your problem. You have your own paramilitary people. And with the little I know about your operations, even I'm aware of the fact that you have any number of agents and assets inside Czechoslovakia."

"The short answer is that what we need isn't readily available. We've got to have qualified people ready to go, possibly as soon as tonight. And there's no one more qualified than your men."

Kitlan rose from his chair and walked to the edge of the raised platform, his eyes fixed hard on Bailey. "Your local Czech agents and assets, unless they're incompetent morons, have got to be able to bring your man to the border and get him across. This doesn't hunt, Bailey. What aren't you telling me?"

"The chief of station Prague has reason to believe that some of his local people have been compromised," Bailey said, pausing to carefully choose his words. "We received an updated cable from Langley before I left Bonn; the Soviets and Czechs want Volodin as badly as we do. They're hauling in everyone they've ever suspected of being connected with the dissident movement and the underground. Those who haven't been arrested have dropped out of sight, so we're temporarily denied use of them until we can reestablish contact. We're trying to determine the extent of the damage, but without knowing who's been compromised, we can't depend on any of them. When Volodin is found, we have to be ready to move immediately with American assets we can trust." Bailey avoided Kitlan's gaze and braced himself for the reaction the Bonn chief of station had told him to expect from the tough, no-nonsense combat veteran who had spent his entire military career in Special Forces.

"You believe that some of your Czech agents have been compromised," Kitlan said, a sharp edge to his voice. "But you don't know how many or which ones. And it stands to reason that you can't risk using any of the Prague station's case officers; the Czechs and Soviets will be all over them. So that means you've got to use at least one local agent to get your man to an area where we can extract him for you. A local agent who could damn well have been compromised and turned. And you want me to send my men into a situation like that—a possible setup. You're out of your goddamn mind."

Bailey retained his composure and responded calmly. "We have deep-cover agents in Czechoslovakia who are totally unknown to any of the underground cells in Prague. They can't be compromised by the people who have been picked up for questioning. As soon as the Prague station locates Volodin, they'll contact one of them and have him bring Volodin to an extraction site as close to the border as possible."

"Why can't he just bring him out himself? There're a dozen ways of getting across that border for someone who knows what he's doing."

"The Czech State Security has put out a full alert. The border patrols have been beefed up and reinforced by Czech and Soviet army troops that have moved into the areas along the West German and Austrian borders. If we run into trouble we'll need more than one local agent to handle it."

"Bailey, let me explain something to you," Kitlan said, making an effort to control his volatile temper. "My men are not potential kidnappers; they are not bodyguards; they are not cold-war spooks; and most of all, they are not an armed volunteer rescue squad at your agency's disposal. What they are, without any doubt, are the finest unconventional warfare troops in the world. And they did not train and study to reach that stage of excellence to be sacrificed on some harebrained, half-assed operation that has nothing to do with their mission."

"Colonel, if you'd listen to . . ."

"No. You listen," Kitlan said, jabbing a finger toward Bailey. "I have a dozen twelve-man operational detachments here. They are extremely valuable soldiers. They're experts in advanced parachuting and SCUBA techniques; they can infiltrate anywhere under any conditions. In the event of war their mission is to conduct raids deep into enemy territory—East Germany, Bulgaria, Poland, Czechoslovakia, even Russia. They have preselected targets all throughout the Eastern Bloc. They can provide us with intelligence information about troop movements; they can destroy hardened supply points, highway bridges, railroad trestles, and airfields, and interdict lines of supply and communications. They're force multipliers who can evade capture and contact local partisan forces, and support and train them to commit sabotage and carry out guerrilla raids on small enemy units and isolated base camps.

"To put it graphically, Bailey, if the Russians make an all-out move on Western Europe, they'll go through Germany like shit through a goose. My men can make the difference between victory and defeat in a conventional war on this continent. They can harass the hell out of the Russians behind their lines and cause a massive bottleneck in their supply lines that would leave most of their troops stranded. They can slow down the Russian attack and give our military the time we'd need to bring in reinforcements and to stage a counterattack. Not to put too fine a point on it, we're the best chance Western Europe has for not ending up like their neighbors on the other side of the wall. And I'm not about to hand even one of my men over to you for the type of operation you're proposing. The days of the handshake operations with you people ended with Vietnam."

Bailey reached inside his coat pocket and withdrew an envelope that he handed to Kitlan. "I'm afraid you have no choice," he said somewhat apologetically, his tone of voice indicating a genuine respect and understanding.

"It's not my choice to make," Kitlan said, tearing the envelope open. "I'm the operational commander of this battalion, but there's a full bird colonel at Fort Devens, Massachusetts, who commands the Tenth Special Forces Group. I take orders from him, not the Agency. And I'll strongly recommend to him, and anyone else, that they refuse this mission."

"Please read the letter you have in your hand, colonel."

Kitlan unfolded the single handwritten page, slowly shaking his head as he read. The letter was from the Commander in Chief, United States Army, Europe. The last paragraph brought an ironic smile to Kitlan's craggy face. He read it a second time, hearing in the written words the low, rumbling drawl of his former group commander in Vietnam.

I know you won't like this, Kit, but the order comes directly from the chairman of the Joint Chiefs, so bite your tongue and play ball with these folks. Give them your fullest cooperation and complete control over the men they require for their mission.

The smile faded as Kitlan looked up from the letter. "You push the right buttons and you get what you want," he said, reluctantly resigning himself to the situation. "A *possible* defector can generate this kind of clout, huh? My ass! Who the hell is this guy?"

"I don't know any more than I've already told you," Bailey said. "But I agree with you, he's not just any defector."

"Does the commander of the Tenth Group know about this?"

"It's my understanding that he's been told we need some of your men, but he's not been briefed on the mission; that's on a need-to-know basis. Do I have your full cooperation, colonel?"

"I'm a professional soldier, Bailey. I do not disobey the orders of my superiors."

"Fine. We want you on board to plan and run your end of the operation."

"What's your military background?" Kitlan asked.

"Limited. No combat experience," Bailey said without apology. "Three years with naval intelligence after the Vietnam War. As I'm sure you know, as the Company's liaison officer for Special Forces, Europe, I'm a war planner; I don't run agents." Seeing the look of skepticism on Kitlan's face, he quickly added, "The deputy chief of station in Bonn will exercise operational command and control over the mission. He'll coordinate our efforts inside Czechoslovakia with you. I'm here to make sure you get everything you need."

"You're not a Yale man, are you?"

"Penn State."

"There is a God," Kitlan said, flashing a civil smile in the spirit of cooperation. "How much time do we have?"

"Only until we locate Volodin. And if we find him today, we'd want to bring him across tonight."

"Where's the extraction site?"

"We thought you might want to choose the area."

"If the level of activity along the borders is as heavy as you say it is, it's too risky to go in on foot."

"What do you have in mind?"

"A hay-ho infiltration," Kitlan said, pronouncing the military acronym. "A night operation."

" 'Hay-ho'?" Bailey repeated. "I'm not familiar with the term."

"H-A-H-O. It's an acronym for a new parachuting technique. A high-altitude, high-opening jump." Kitlan stepped off the briefing platform and crossed the room to the large-scale wall map of Czechoslovakia. Pointing to a rural area in western Bohemia, he said, "We can insert the team deep, behind the heavy troop concentrations along the border."

"What's the advantage of the high-altitude, high-opening jump?" Bailey asked.

"The aircraft doesn't have to enter Czech airspace; consequently if their radar operators pick it up along our side of the border, they won't attach any special significance to it. A team can exit a plane at thirty-five thousand feet on the West German side, deploy their chutes immediately, and with the right wind conditions they can conceivably reach a drop zone thirty miles or more inside Czechoslovakia."

"Won't the Czech radar pick up the parachutes?"

"They'll pick up some blips for a few minutes. But there are gaps in their coverage," Kitlan said. "Places on their side where their radar doesn't overlap; in some of the rural areas just inside their territory it's a mile-wide corridor. Their coverage right on the border is tight—an aircraft couldn't penetrate it for any distance without compromising the mission. And with the Czechs on alert, even flying under the radar it would stand a good chance of being spotted from the ground. But if your people can provide a diversion—a little unscheduled air activity along the border to draw their attention away from the sector where my men will exit their aircraft—they can slip through and stay in the gaps."

"How will your men get past the border troops when they bring Volodin out?"

"They won't. Considering the importance of your defector, it's too risky to try." Pointing to a mountainous area on the Czech–West German frontier, Kitlan said, "My men will get him to an extraction site within two miles of the border, maybe less if they're lucky. They'll try to work their way around the Czech and Soviet troops into one of these remote valleys. When they're in place, they'll transmit a signal and we'll send in a helicopter flying nap-of-the-earth to pull them out. If it's spotted, we'll be back on our side before they can react. I don't care if they know we've been there, but I sure as hell don't want my men compromised on the way in. That's how you get people killed."

"You make it sound like a simple surgical procedure, colonel," Bailey said, impressed by Kitlan's expertise and the mechanics of the operation.

Kitlan's face twisted into a grim smile. "That's before we factor in Murphy's law."

"Where do you want our agent to bring Volodin?"

"I haven't decided," Kitlan said, "but I don't want him anywhere near the troop concentrations along the border. My men will get him in close. You just have your people put him where I tell you. And I'll need a constant update on the weather conditions until we launch the mission, and the present positions and any redeployments of Czech and Soviet troops."

"The chief of station Prague is keeping us informed," Bailey said. "And the deputy chief of station from Bonn will have three case officers with paramilitary experience from the Frankfurt station with him at the mission support site on the border advising him on the arrangements being made inside Czechoslovakia. We'll hold up our end."

Kitlan grimaced at the optimism of the inexperienced man before him. He restrained himself from pointing out all of the things that could go wrong in this type of operation—all of the things that had gone wrong with similar CIA-run missions he had been on in Vietnam. "You tell your people that I want a reception committee and as much security on the drop zone as you can provide. I don't want my men going in there with their asses hanging out."

Bailey nodded his understanding. Conscious of the time, he asked, "Do you have a team in mind?"

"Yeah. We don't need a full operational detachment," Kitlan said. "Too many people to move around undetected. A half team, six men, can handle the mission." Picking up the telephone on a table across from the podium, he dialed the battalion sergeant major. "Zabitsky, locate Master Sergeant Kessler

45

for me and have him report to the war room immediately."
Kitlan glanced at his watch. "Check the team house first—there
was a training jump scheduled for this morning; he should be
back from it by now." Hanging up the phone, he turned to
Bailey. "I'd like my executive officer and my operations and
intelligence officers in on this."

"Sorry, colonel. My instructions were that only you and the
team you select are to be briefed on the mission. Everything else
will be handled through the deputy chief of station and the case
officers assigned to the operation."

"You're hamstringing me, Bailey. This isn't some goddamn
boy scout picnic we're putting together."

"Any operational intelligence you require will be at your disposal, and the deputy chief of station is, in effect, your executive
officer for your end of the mission."

"What about weapons and equipment?"

"We'll provide them; all sterile. Just tell us what you need
and we'll have it ready for you."

"And if my men are caught?" Kitlan asked.

"You know the rules, colonel. We'll deny them; sell them
short and trade for them later," Bailey replied sheepishly. "But
we'll do everything possible to make sure that doesn't happen."

"The more things change the more they stay the same,"
Kitlan said bitterly.

"Why did you send for the master sergeant?" Bailey asked.

"Master Sergeant Kessler will be the team leader."

"An enlisted man? Why not an officer?"

"Because that's how it works in Special Forces. On certain
types of missions the most experienced man commands the
team. And for this one, I'm going to let Kessler handpick his
men."

"What are his qualifications?" Bailey asked.

"Nineteen years in Special Forces. Five combat tours in Vietnam running recon with the Special Operations Group. He's his
team's operations and intelligence sergeant, and a master parachutist with more hay-ho jumps than anyone in the battalion. If
that's not enough, he's the best damn soldier I've ever known."

"I wasn't questioning your judgment, colonel," Bailey said.
"I guess I have a natural bias, being a former officer."

"Most of my A-Team officers are young men in their mid-
twenties. On the average they've only been in SF four or five

years. They're well trained, and they're good men, but when it comes to this type of operation they'd be the first to tell you that they have no problem taking orders from a combat veteran with Kessler's experience and expertise."

Both men turned in response to a loud hollow knock on the steel door to the war room. "Enter," Kitlan called out.

M. Sgt. Frank Kessler entered the room and came to attention, casting a quick appraising glance at the civilian seated on the briefing platform. "Sergeant Major Zabitosky said you wanted to see me, sir."

"At ease, sergeant. This is Peter Bailey," Kitlan said as Bailey got to his feet. "Our CIA liaison officer."

"Sergeant," Bailey said, shaking Kessler's hand and staring into the calm, steady eyes set in a tough, leathery outdoor face made up of equal parts of self-confidence and determination. At six feet tall, Bailey was less than an inch shorter than the man standing before him, but he appeared much smaller next to Kessler's solid, well-muscled two hundred and thirty pounds that was densely packed on a broad-shouldered, heavy-boned frame. He reminded Bailey of a grizzly bear, both in size and countenance.

"I want you to choose a six-man team, including yourself, for a special operation," Kitlan said to Kessler. "A night hay-ho infiltration into Czechoslovakia; to bring a defector across the border."

"Where's the exercise being held, sir?"

"Czechoslovakia. And it's not an exercise, it's a mission."

Kessler's light brown eyes narrowed as he glanced at Bailey and then back to the colonel, correctly reading the mood of his commanding officer. He paused briefly before speaking, his face betraying none of the surprise he felt. "If it's my choice, sir, I'd want sergeants Thornton, Pitzer, Teodozio, Shumate, and Lieutenant O'Neil."

"O'Neil?" Kitlan said, unsure why Kessler would choose the young lieutenant who had only been with the team a few months.

"Yes, sir. He's a good officer, with a cool head. And he's as good at hay-ho jumps as anyone on the team."

Kitlan nodded in agreement. "I'll have the sergeant major notify them."

"They're all at the team room, sir. Putting away their gear."

"For the integrity of the operation," Kitlan said, "you and your team will be kept in the isolation quarters here on the third floor until we leave the base. Your wives will be told you've been sent on a classified training exercise. You'll be briefed on the mission when we arrive at the mission support site the Agency has set up on the border." Glancing at Bailey for confirmation, he said, "I assume that's where we'll launch from." Bailey responded with a nod.

Picking up on Kitlan's deference to Bailey, Kessler held the colonel's gaze with a questioning look.

"What is it, sergeant?" Kitlan asked.

"Who has operational command and control of the mission, sir?"

"The Agency's deputy chief of station from Bonn," Kitlan replied flatly. "We'll plan and run our end of the mission for him, but he has command and control."

Kessler nodded his head slowly and said nothing. His eyes came to rest on Bailey, leaving no doubt in the CIA officer's mind how he felt about the change in the command structure.

"Do you have a problem with that, sergeant?" Bailey asked.

Kessler's eyes shifted to his commanding officer who, more than familiar with Kessler's outspoken nature and their similar views on CIA-run operations in Vietnam, warned him off with a barely perceptible shake of his head that went unnoticed by Bailey.

"No problem," Kessler said. "We're ready when you are."

4

✖ THE AMERICAN EMBASSY IN Prague is a large, stone seventeenth-century palace on Trziste Street in the Mala Strana (Little Quarter) section of the city among the Petrin Hills on the west bank of the Vltava River. The palace—referred to as Schoenborn Palace after its last titled owner, Count Carl Johann Schoenborn—contains over one hundred rooms and was built in four wings around three courtyards. It was sold by the count in 1919 to Richard Crane—the first American minister to Czechoslovakia—who in 1924 sold it to the United States government.

Behind the palace are terraced gardens and seven acres of orchards rising steeply to the top of a hillside with a panoramic view of the city and the river. The palace has several hundred feet of frontage on Trziste Street, a narrow cobbled lane in the heart of what had been a lively trade center in the early Middle Ages. Situated near the Prague Castle, the present seat of the Czech government, the area had also been the residence of the bishop of Prague, and later, near the end of the Middle Ages, a fashionable residential district for the Czech nobility, where their private parks and gardens descended from the gently rising hills to the banks of the river. The district eventually expanded to include burgher's houses and the modest homes of merchants, and at the beginning of the twentieth century parts of it had deteriorated to slums, coinciding with the founding of the Czechoslovak Republic and the land reforms that resulted in the confiscation of the aristocratic estates and the decline in the fortunes of the wealthy nobility. Some of the old palaces have since been renovated by countries that have purchased them to house their embassies and legations, while others are maintained and used as cultural institutions and luxury apartments for privileged Party officials. The majority, however, have been converted to crowded state-owned workers' apartments in an attempt to solve the city's housing shortage. Despite the impoverished Czech government's benign neglect, evident in the various stages of disrepair suffered by most of the buildings, the area still retains much of its charm and atmosphere in its shops and cafés and winding cobbled streets and small open squares and public parks.

Trziste Street and the area surrounding the American embassy have changed little in the last two centuries; neither have the machinations of opposing governments. On the third floor of the west wing of the embassy are the offices of the political section. Adjacent to those offices, separated from them by a cipher-locked steel door, is another suite of rooms, ostensibly part of the political section, but in reality a transparent cover for the offices of the CIA's Prague station.

Adam Purcell, a CIA case officer assigned to the station for the past five years, turned away from the large street map of Prague on the wall above his desk. He stared out a corner window from the rear of one of the smaller offices, absently watching two sweatsuit-clad Marines from the security-guard detachment tossing a football on the lawn of the terraced gardens behind the embassy. He was biding time, his mind on other matters—the route he would take to his clandestine meeting with one of his resident agents. His day had not gone well. The initial information received from his fringe agent at the Intercontinental Hotel alerting him to Volodin's defection was all he had been able to learn about the Soviet scientist. He had spent the morning and most of the afternoon eluding the Czech surveillance teams and trying to contact his local support agents, checking his dead drops for messages. There had been none. Danger signals at most of the drop locations warned him not to approach (a danger signal being the absence of a safety signal), leaving him to suspect that more than a few of his agents had been compromised. His three fellow case officers at the Prague station, and the local pavement pounders they had put out, were having similar problems, coming up empty and reporting that large-scale arrests were being made by the STB—the Czech state security police—directed and reinforced by their KGB advisers.

Purcell was alarmed and surprised at the speed with which many of the station's local agents had been picked up, revealing how thoroughly their organization had been penetrated. The willingness of the Czech state security to reveal the extent of that penetration underlined the importance placed on Volodin, and the pressure the Soviets were applying. But Purcell knew that the structure of his agent organization precluded the possibility that all of his cells had been compromised. Each case officer at the station ran one or more resident agents, who in turn maintained supervisory contact over principal agents who directed the activities of support and action agents—the action agents being at the end of the line in contact with the target of the intelligence-gathering effort. The organization was cellular in structure, offering multiple coverage of single targets or multiple targets of related interests. Many of the cells were linked—series cells with communication between them secured by a cut-out known only by sight and operating as a courier between agents, with dead drops and live drops used as further means of securing the lines of communication. Some of the agents in each cell were known to each other, but they had no direct contact, with the result that the compromise of one agent did not necessarily contaminate the entire series cell.

Agent–case-officer meetings were called for only when a communication link had been broken, or the agent's assignment needed to be explained and the methods of achieving it discussed. A case officer's lines of communication with his agents were never direct, filtering up through the cellular structure to the resident agent and ultimately reaching him by secure means. But in the event of emergencies, when the exchange of information through drops proved too slow and uncertain, direct contact, though highly dangerous, was necessary. With the immediate need to locate Volodin, and no time to get his agent to neutral territory in Budapest or East Berlin where a clandestine meeting could be more easily arranged and carried out, Purcell was left no option but to set up a personal meeting in the city with one of his resident agents. If Volodin was indeed a defector, he would have to make contact with the Czech underground or dissident organizations if he intended to get to the West, making it inevitable, Purcell had reasoned soundly, that someone in his agent organization, or those of the station's other case officers, had to learn of it when he did.

That morning, utilizing the special communications equipment provided for the resident agent he needed to contact, Purcell had left a message for the man to meet him at a location established in case of such emergencies. He had parked his car across the street from the agent's apartment building and, using a remote-control device, activated a miniature transmitter/receiver linked to a high-speed tape recorder concealed in the apartment. The agent's recorder had been modified to transmit a thirty-minute message in a single "burst" of ten seconds. If intercepted by the STB, the signal would appear to be only normal static noise, but when received by Purcell's compatible unit, the message was made intelligible when played back at normal speed. The agent's recorder was further equipped with two small lights that were controlled by Purcell. One light being lit informed him that his message had been received by Purcell and he could erase the tape. Both lights being lit was a danger signal, warning him neither to use the equipment again nor to initiate any contact until he received further instructions through an alternate means. Finding no message left for him on the agent's recorder, Purcell then transmitted his own message, instructing the agent where and when to meet him, knowing that the recorder would be checked in ample time when the agent, following his established end-of-the-week pattern, came home early from work.

The need for the CIA's Prague station to locate the Soviet scientist and take over the task of getting him safely to the West, putting a stop to any local arrangements being made to help him, was of paramount importance in light of headquarter's urgent cable and the dissidents' dismal record of failed attempts at getting people out of the country. The STB and their KGB advisers were well organized and competent—even more so than Purcell had suspected given the day's revelation of their depth of penetration of his agent organization—and the operational environment in Prague was, at the best of times, difficult. With the STB on full alert, it would require all of his tradecraft skills and a great deal of luck and timing to elude them on his way to the meeting site with the resident agent.

The plan he had formulated in his mind hinged on a diversionary tactic against the surveillance teams he knew were waiting for him the moment he set foot outside the embassy. He had managed to shake them earlier that day when the cable instructing the station to find Volodin had been received from the DDO, and he and the other case officers had left the embassy in concert, confusing and dividing the surveillance effort by presenting them with multiple targets going in different directions. But he had returned to the embassy alone to clear his improvised meeting plan with the deputy chief of station—the senior operations officer in charge of coordinating the efforts to locate Volodin—and this time, with his fellow case officers still out trying to establish contact with their agents, he was on his own, with no one to assist him in implementing the extensive countersurveillance procedures usually used for a high-risk meeting.

Checking his watch, Purcell left the office and skipped quickly down the three flights of stairs to the ground floor. He felt certain, because of his earlier success, that the number of STB agents would be at least doubled—applying pressure not only in the hope of being led to Volodin, but also watching for him, in the urgency of his mission, to inadvertently reveal the carefully protected upper echelon of his agent organization. The present situation did not allow for the subtleties of his tradecraft training; after losing him that morning, the STB would make no attempts to disguise their efforts, changing their tactics if all else failed to those of overt harassment in the hope of preventing him from making any contact, or forcing him into reckless behavior.

He had decided on a bold and somewhat dangerous move to break free of the surveillance teams upon leaving the embassy grounds, before following a circuitous route to the meeting site to filter out any of the opposition who had managed to stay with him. Leaving the building, he crossed the cobbled courtyard and climbed the broad stone steps leading up to the first garden terrace. Getting the attention of the two Marine guards, he summoned them to him, catching the pass the squat, barrel-chested corporal tossed as he jogged over to his side.

"What can I do for you, Mr. Purcell?" the corporal asked.

"I need your help, Murphy," Purcell said. "And yours, too, Burton," he added, nodding to the taller of the two Marines. "When do you go back on duty?"

"A few hours," Murphy answered cautiously, aware, as was most of the embassy staff, that Purcell's position in the political section was strictly a cover given to him as a CIA case officer.

"This won't take long," he told the young Marines. "I want you to run interference for me on my way out of here."

"Is this official or unofficial, sir?" Murphy asked.

"Officially unofficial," Purcell said with a smile. "But I'll make sure you don't take any heat because of it."

Murphy gave a questioning glance to Burton, who shrugged his agreement. "You'll square it with the sergeant?" he asked Purcell.

"Absolutely."

"What do you want us to do, sir?" Murphy asked, now eager for a break in his monotonous routine.

Purcell motioned for them to follow him, leading them down the steps into one of the three inner courtyards just inside the main entrance where a number of cars were parked.

"Murphy, you'll drive me in the Volvo. Burton, you take the Audi; I want you to pull out of here first and head down to the bottom of the hill. If I'm right, before you get to the end of the street, a car with two men in it will try to block access to the intersection to slow us down until the other Czech surveillance teams can pick us up one at a time. I want you to do whatever you can to get us through and prevent them from following Murphy and me until we have a few minutes lead time. Bottle up the intersection if you can, just leave enough room for us to get by."

"You care if a few fenders get crumpled?" Burton asked.

"That's the least of my worries. Just keep yourself in one piece."

"You got it, sir," Burton said, flashing a broad grin.

Across the street from the embassy the VB—the Prague city police—have a static observation and guard post. Its stated purpose is to aid in directing traffic and to protect the American embassy from demonstrators or vandals; its unstated and more important purpose is to report on the comings and goings of the embassy staff, particularly the defense attaché and his staff and the CIA personnel, and to prevent any Czech national from entering the embassy without authorization from his own government. Twenty-four hours a day at least one VB guard is seated in a small glass-fronted guardroom built into the face of a building directly across from the embassy entrance. Upon seeing anyone of interest leaving the embassy, a guard immediately telephones the information to his superiors who in turn notify the STB surveillance teams waiting on-station nearby. Another guard, sometimes two, stands at the sidewalk ready to intercept any unauthorized Czech citizens and to assure the orderly flow of traffic out of the embassy into the crowded, narrow street.

The VB guard crossing the street toward the embassy in response to the sound of automobile engines in the inner courtyard was almost run down. He jumped back, with only inches to spare, as the Audi sedan suddenly appeared and roared through the tunnel entrance, swerving on the slick cobblestones as it turned sharply right and raced toward the intersection a few hundred yards away at the bottom of the hill. Following immediately behind Burton, Murphy momentarily lost control of the Volvo, narrowly avoiding a collision with a van parked at the opposite curb as the Volvo's tires squealed and skidded in the right turn before gripping firmly and propelling it forward.

Speeding down the hill toward the broad, busy street, Burton caught a brief glimpse of a short, stocky man in a leather jacket flicking a half-smoked cigarette to the sidewalk and bolting from the corner where he had been casually leaning against a building. The man scrambled into the front passenger seat of a dark green Skoda sedan waiting at the curb near the intersection and facing in the direction Burton was traveling.

The driver of the Skoda, spotting the Volvo behind Burton, started his engine and pulled slowly out into the street, intent on blocking access to Karmelitska, the larger, main thoroughfare that intersected with Trziste—its flow of traffic uncontrolled by a signal light. The man who had jumped in beside him spoke excitedly into a radio microphone and glanced nervously over his shoulder at the fast-approaching Audi.

As the Skoda edged farther out into the street, Burton saw his chance and took it. Braking to lessen the impact, and bracing himself for the collision, he angled to his right, aiming for the front of the much smaller and lighter Skoda. Striking it a hard glancing blow across its grille, he spun it into a quarter turn, knocking it up over the curb and across the small sliver of sidewalk into the side of a building, severely jolting the two men inside. Regaining control of the Audi, Burton cut the wheel hard to the left and said a fast Hail Mary as he skidded out into the busy intersection. The screeching of brakes and the howling of tires accompanied the deafening, metal-crunching chain reaction that followed.

Halfway up Trziste Street in the Volvo, Murphy hit the brakes, reacting to the scene below him. "He's turning it into a goddamn demolition derby."

"Stay with him," Purcell said. "Watch for an opening."

Two broadside collisions in rapid succession unseated Burton, slamming him into the opposite door. The drivers of the cars had reacted instantly and braked hard, decreasing their speed considerably before colliding with the Audi. Uninjured and only slightly shaken, Burton slid back behind the wheel and quickly surveyed the chaotic scene. He had just missed hitting a huge red-and-white tram car that had been rear-ended and bounced off its rails by a truck that had swung wide into the opposite lane to avoid the Audi. Fortunately the afternoon rush hour had not begun and the tram was nearly empty, revealing only a few frightened, disconcerted faces through its grimy windows. Glancing about, Burton saw that he had successfully gridlocked the intersection, bringing traffic from both directions to a virtual standstill.

"Which way?" Murphy shouted to Purcell. He had again slowed the car and was looking for a way through the tangled mass of vehicles.

Purcell's eyes scanned the intersection. The traffic had been light, and the pile-up was only three or four vehicles deep, with others now coming to a safe stop behind those involved in collisions. Looking to his right he saw that the dark green Skoda was temporarily out of commission; the two STB men were outside the car, struggling to pull the left-front fender away from the tire.

"To your right," he told Murphy. "Up on the sidewalk. There's an opening behind that truck. Once you're past it we're clear."

Purcell braced his hands on the dash as Murphy accelerated rapidly and climbed the curb. To the wide-eyed horror of the pedestrians who dove into doorways and flattened themselves against the sides of buildings, he made the turn on to Karmelit-ska using most of the sidewalk for another fifty yards before caving in the trunk and smashing the taillight of a parked car as he pulled back out into the street.

The Volvo was equipped, as were most embassy staff cars, with two rearview mirrors mounted on the windshield: one for the driver's normal use, and one for the passenger to watch for surveillance vehicles. Purcell was familiar with how the STB teams worked. There were always at least two men in each vehicle—one to drive and one to get out of the vehicle and proceed on foot if the target parked and left his car. The green Skoda that Burton had rammed was only one of two vehicles positioned to follow from behind. And there were others, one a few blocks ahead and one to the left and right on each of the streets paralleling him, effectively boxing him in. They were all in radio contact coordinating and orchestrating their moves. Ordinarily the surveillance vehicles would exchange positions to keep from being spotted by drawing attention to one particu-lar car behind their target, but given the circumstances and the fact that they had lost their man once that day, not losing him again had taken precedence over any attempt to conceal their presence.

Using his rearview mirror, Purcell watched the street behind him and spotted a white Skoda with two men inside working its way around the edge of the traffic snarl. "There's number two," he said to Murphy.

Burton, sitting calmly in the Audi in the middle of the clogged intersection, saw the same car, and its passenger with a radio microphone in his hand. Recognizing it as an STB surveil-lance vehicle, he reacted quickly. The white Skoda was directly behind him, using part of the sidewalk to get through the inter-section. Another damaged car—a small station wagon—par-tially blocked Burton's path. Putting the Audi in reverse, he pressed the accelerator to the floor. The tires spun for a brief second before gaining traction and driving the rear of the Audi into the side of the unsuspecting car behind him. The force of the impact drove the station wagon sideways across the street and into the white Skoda, locking bumpers and pinning it against the side of a building.

"Good move," Purcell said with genuine admiration, and

turned his attention to Murphy and the direction in which they were heading.

The street began to slope off gradually as they sped away from the intersection. Purcell had not yet spotted the surveillance vehicle he knew was somewhere ahead of him, but he hoped that his next move would neutralize it, along with one of the cars on a parallel street.

"Which way, sir?" Murphy again asked, his attention riveted on the oncoming traffic that was slowing down and creeping toward the clogged intersection.

"A hard left at the next cross street," Purcell said, keeping watch for any vehicle parked at the curb with two or more men in it.

Murphy cut sharply at the corner and careened into a narrow street that led down a steep hill toward the river.

"At the bottom of the hill, go straight across the bridge," Purcell said, watching his rearview mirror to see if another car had picked them up. He breathed a sigh of relief at the sight of the empty street behind him. The forward surveillance vehicle, he reasoned, must have been stationed past the point where they had made the turn.

Purcell had planned the route carefully. Once he drove on to the bridge two of the three remaining STB cars would be out of position. The one on the parallel street to his right and the one in front of him would have no choice but to change directions and follow behind if they wanted to stay close. If they tried to stay in front of him or on a parallel street, they would have to continue moving away from the direction in which he was traveling and use the next bridge, a half mile away, putting themselves too far out of position to continue the surveillance. Purcell smiled to himself; he had broken out of the box. With what he had planned next, they would not have time to reestablish it on the other side of the river.

As Murphy drove on to the First of May Bridge and headed toward the Stare Mesto (Old Town) section of the city, Purcell spotted the faded red mini-van that pulled out of a side street and fell in behind them. It was the surveillance vehicle that was guarding the parallel street to his left, and the only vehicle he now had to contend with—the others were still out of position and no longer a threat to him if things went according to plan.

Luck was with him as they reached the other side of the

river. The signal light turned red just as Murphy entered the intersection and continued on to Narodni—the broad avenue leading off the bridge. The mini-van had no alternative but to come to an abrupt halt as a bus pulled out and blocked the street.

The STB driver thumped the steering wheel with his fist, and as the bus passed, he ran the light, edging out into the cross traffic to the din of honking horns and the shouts of angry drivers. He had lost less than fifteen seconds getting clear of the intersection, and he caught a fleeting glimpse of the Volvo as it turned off Narodni and entered one of the side streets that led into the labyrinthine network of winding cobbled streets and lanes that ran through the old section of the city. The STB driver cursed under his breath; he knew he would eventually find the Volvo and its driver, but by then the passenger would be gone, having left the car and disappeared into the heart of the city.

Purcell reached into the back of the Volvo and grabbed the tan raincoat lying on the seat. He quickly pulled it on, watching his rearview mirror as Murphy slowed to a sensible speed to negotiate the twisting lane ahead of them.

"Turn left at the next corner," he told Murphy, who was still caught up in the excitement of the chase. "Slow down, but don't stop. I'll get out just after you make the turn."

"Yes, sir," Murphy said. "Then what do I do?"

"Go directly back to the embassy. If Burton is having any trouble with the VB, tell your sergeant that I'll get the deputy chief of mission on it as soon as I get back. If they stop you en route, just place the blame on the car that pulled out in front of us. We were simply trying to avoid an accident."

Murphy nodded his understanding and turned left as instructed, into an even narrower street barely wide enough for two cars, and slowed to a near stop.

"Good work," Purcell said, and he jumped from the car, moving away quickly and disappearing into an arcaded walk between two buildings.

Making two sharp turns down narrow alleyways not much broader than his shoulders, Purcell exited onto a busy street, slowing his pace to that of the pedestrian traffic. Two blocks farther on, he entered Vaclavske Namesti, commonly called Wenceslaus Square after the "Good King" of the Christmas carol who ruled Bohemia a thousand years ago. It is less a square than a broad boulevard, the center of the city's shopping district. In all but the coldest winter months the sidewalks and island rest areas in the middle of the boulevard are always crowded with Eastern Bloc tourists and window shoppers and absentee workers lounging on benches or aimlessly wandering about. The crowds rival those of New York City's Fifth Avenue, but only in number, not in energy and purpose. Purcell blended in with the throngs of faceless people wistfully staring into shop windows at inferior merchandise they could not afford, and walked casually past the busy sidewalk cafés and ice-cream and sausage stands toward the impressive Neo-Renaissance façade of the National Museum at the head of the square.

Crossing to the center island at the statue of Saint Vaclav, he left the flow of street traffic and descended the broad stairs to the subway that ran beneath the square. Weaving his way through the rush of passengers streaming to and from the trains, he crossed to a newsstand adjacent to the turnstiles and bought a pack of cigarettes. He stood watching the entrance and exit stairs to the street and observing the movements and actions of the people walking through the concourse. He was studying the rhythm of the crowd, watching for anyone who broke the random pattern. He knew that he had disrupted the STB team's concerted surveillance effort, and in all probability lost them, but was not so sure that a radio call had not gone out to perhaps another team waiting nearby in the Old Town section, giving them the location where he was last seen. If they were searching for him, they would be far more obvious than a team who had him spotted and was organized to follow him.

He waited and watched until the next train had come and gone, and, having seen nothing that stood out against the normal flow of movement, he ducked into the men's room next to the newsstand and entered a stall. Reversing his tan raincoat—designed for that purpose—to its muted plaid side, he put on a pair of nonprescription steel-framed eyeglasses and completed the change of appearance by pulling on a short-visored black leather cap kept in the inside pocket of the coat. Waiting to leave the men's room with two men who had been using the urinals when he entered and had taken no notice of him, he came out of the stall as they finished washing their hands at the sinks and followed them through the door, merging with the crowd and climbing the exit stairs to the street level where he quickly crossed the square and boarded a bus.

Before heading to his intended destination, Purcell changed buses and directions twice. Confident that he was no longer under surveillance, he boarded another bus, taking it to the Vysehrad section of the city, where he walked the remaining distance to where he had instructed his resident agent to meet him.

The location he had selected was a lonely, deserted section of the quay beneath a railroad bridge that crossed the river at the western edge of the city near the industrial suburbs. He had never used the site before; in the parlance of the profession it was known as a "place of conspiracy"—used only for control meetings or other urgent matters when a communication link has been broken or an operative has been isolated through the capture or compromise of his immediate superiors. In an emergency, with no other way of contacting his case officer, the operative would visit the preselected site at the same time each day until he had reestablished contact.

Without hesitating or breaking his stride, Purcell removed from his mouth a piece of gum he had been chewing and, unnoticed by the few people on the sidewalk in front of the run-down apartment buildings across the street, he used it as a safety signal for his agent, sticking it to the side of a lamppost at the top of a stairway leading down to the quay. Continuing down the steps, he turned left and walked toward the railroad bridge, staying close to the wall and brushing past the overgrown waist-high weeds and bushes along the river's edge. The water had risen over the banks, and he kept to what remained of a narrow footpath where an occasional late-blooming wildflower poked through uneven paving stones that were partially matted with a colorful array of fallen leaves. Away from the more attractive parts of the city—its vistas of smokestacks and tumble-down shacks and rusting, empty warehouses lining the opposite shoreline—the quay was seldom traveled and well suited for its intended purpose.

Purcell checked the time. He was twenty minutes early. A short distance from where the bridge passed overhead, he stopped, out of sight of anyone on the street above, and sat on a small bench set in a grottolike arch cut into the stone wall along the bank. He breathed deeply, taking in the musty smells of the ancient river, and listened to the gentle flow of the water and the occasional muted sounds of traffic from the street. The late afternoon sun dropped quickly below the horizon, bringing a sudden chill with the autumn twilight. Turning up the collar of his raincoat and shoving his hands in its pockets, his eyes came to rest on the reddish-orange glow that was mirrored in the shimmering surface of the river and backlighted the city skyline, silhouetting the gabled roofs and spires in the distance.

The failing light deepened to somber shades of purple and gray, and with the rapid drop in temperatures came a thin, wispy fog that rose from the water, drifting slowly ashore, enveloping the quay and the street above in a gossamer veil of mist that left Purcell's face damp and cold. His thoughts as he waited for his agent were of Ann, his wife. Despite the fact that Prague was considered hardship duty by the Agency and the State Department—as was a posting to any of the Soviet Bloc countries—Purcell loved the city and his work and was less than enthusiastic about his transfer to Stockholm in the coming spring. Ann, however, expecting their first child, was eagerly counting the days. The role of an intelligence officer's wife was antithetical to her ingenuous, friendly, and trusting nature. She loathed living a lie, and a life of restricted movement and constant security precautions, and was put off by the lack of warmth in the members of the diplomatic community whom she saw as pretentious and aloof. Purcell suspected that her discontent went even deeper—to the cloistered life in embassy apartments and the constant schedule of diplomatic receptions, dinners, and cocktail parties where she suffered through the inane, guarded conversations of people who considered her an outsider as a CIA wife, and were, by necessity of their profession, too circumspect to talk of anything in more than superficial terms, always aware that what they said was probably being recorded to be scrutinized later by those who played what Ann referred to as deadly children's games.

For her sake, Purcell had not requested an extension of his time in Prague, hoping that living again in the West and enjoying the basic freedoms she took for granted would raise her spirits and outlook to the point where she would cease her subtle but persistent arguments for him to leave the Agency and take the position offered him by a prestigious Washington law firm. Her periods of depression, something she had never experienced before coming to Prague, were becoming more frequent, partly attributable, he thought, to her pregnancy and her lack of social contact with her family and friends back home. And even now, in the fall, her favorite time of year, she took no joy in the beauty that surrounded her. She seldom left the apartment, and had reduced even the vibrant color of the autumn leaves to a depressing analogy—telling him at breakfast that morning that the falling leaves reminded her of the repressive brutality of the Soviet system and what it had done to the people of Czechoslovakia: the dying leaves, their chlorophyll fading, their cells breaking down, living their last days in a deceptively beautiful phase before their source of nourishment is cut off and they tumble to the ground to begin the cycle of decay.

Purcell's thoughts were jolted back to the present as a commuter train rattled and clattered noisily across the bridge overhead. The street lights had come on with the last of the twilight retreating into darkness, and he stood up and moved away from the wall into the deep shadows at the edge of the overgrown brush where he had a clear view of the top of the stairs, now bathed in the soft glow from the lamplight. The street above was quiet, only the occasional passer-by hurrying home from work.

He heard his resident agent before he saw him. Walking briskly along the sidewalk, Anton Nemecek's hollow footsteps echoed out across the river as he approached from the opposite direction Purcell had used. Pausing briefly at the lamppost, he spotted the safety signal and quickly descended the stairs to the quay.

Nemecek had been a valuable agent for the past ten years. Recruited and made operational while a low-level staffer at the Czech embassy in Washington, he had, upon his promotion within the Czech Ministry of Foreign Affairs and his reassignment to Prague, been turned over to the CIA's Prague station and initially used to gather intelligence information and target potential recruits for the Agency. With time, he became a resourceful and competent operative, and was personally responsible for recruiting two secretaries within the STB and numerous agents and assets among the low- and middle-level personnel from the Ministries of Interior and Foreign Affairs, skillfully organizing them into a productive series cell. Purcell recalled from reading his file that, despite his treason, Nemecek considered himself a patriot. Unlike the typical greedy or disgruntled official seduced or coerced into working for the Agency, his actions, he had told the case officer who recruited him, were witting and intentional, directed against the Soviets and their puppets who controlled his country and bled it white, and not contrary to the best interest of his people or his homeland.

Standing deep in the shadows, Purcell watched the tall, lonely figure approach to within a few yards of his position before stepping out into view. He startled the handsome, distinguished-looking Czech, who stopped abruptly and glanced nervously about.

"This is highly dangerous," he said without greeting, his expression grim and a hint of anger in his voice.

"I know," Purcell said apologetically. "But I need some information, and I need it fast."

Nemecek nodded his head. "Volodin. The missing Soviet scientist."

"Yes. I need to know who he went to for help. And how I can get to him."

At the sound of an approaching car on the street above, Nemecek stepped quickly, and unnecessarily, into the shadows along the wall until it passed.

"When I received your message requesting the meeting, I assumed that was what you wanted. His defection has the state security thugs out in force, with the KGB cracking the whip at their heels."

"Were you able to learn anything?"

"I would not have come to this meeting if I hadn't," Nemecek said flatly. "I contacted one of our support agents in the dissident community. A friend of his is involved with the group that is arranging Volodin's escape to the West."

"Where are they hiding him?"

"The weekend cottage of a professor from Charles University. It is on a lake near the village of Blatna, thirty-five kilometers south of Pribram." Nemecek reached into his pocket and handed Purcell a slip of paper. "These are the specific directions to the cottage."

Purcell was familiar with the weekend cottages, a paradox under the Communist system. The majority of the people in Prague have a cottage in the countryside; unlike their apartments in the city, it is the only form of real estate they can own privately and sell or pass on to their heirs. Little more than crude cabins built with their own hands on small plots of ground, they are a much needed reprieve from crowded apartment life in the city and the ever present totalitarian regime. The government allows them only for their own purposes—realizing their value as a way for the owners to express their individuality, providing the illusion of freedom, and as a safety valve in times of economic difficulties or more stringent social reforms.

Purcell slipped the paper into his pocket. "I want you to contact your support agent again, as soon as you leave here. Tell him to inform the dissidents not to make any attempt to get Volodin out. Our people will take over. Under no circumstances are they to move him before we get there unless there's a direct threat of his being arrested."

"Then I would advise that you act immediately," Nemecek said. "The STB will have little difficulty learning what I have just told you. They have arrested hundreds, many of them dissidents. With the KGB conducting the interrogations, it will not take long."

"We'll have someone there as quickly as possible. Probably before midnight. I'd also appreciate a damage assessment on how many of your agents were caught in the net. I'll check your recorder within the next few days."

"I'll do what I can." Turning to leave, Nemecek added, "What about the professor—his name's Marcovic, by the way—who helped Volodin. His complicity will be discovered."

"He's not our problem."

Nemecek smiled humorlessly. "Please, no more of these emergency meetings. I would not stand up well under interrogation."

"I had no choice," Purcell said. "The request for this one came from the top. But don't worry. I took every precaution."

"I always worry, my friend. Even in my sleep I worry."

Purcell watched him leave, disappearing quickly into the thickening fog. Waiting a full fifteen minutes before following, he continued along the quay, returning to the street level only after he was well past the stairs he had used on his arrival. Glancing at his watch, he decided against returning to the embassy; the chief of station would be at the ambassador's private residence attending a dinner party, and would want to be briefed immediately and in person. Leaving the back streets and alleys, he entered a broad avenue and boarded a tram back to Wenceslaus Square where he took a taxi to the Bubenec section of the city, hoping that he would arrive before the guests were seated for dinner.

※　※　※

The private residence of the United States ambassador to Czechoslovakia is a neoclassic stone mansion on an eight-acre parklike estate in a small but exclusive residential district set aside for the diplomatic community and high government officials on the west bank of the Vltava River. The well-manicured grounds of the estate contain a swimming pool, clay tennis court, and two smaller homes built for the original owner's parents and sister (one now occupied by the deputy chief of mission, the other converted into apartments for the embassy's secretaries). The estate was once the property of a wealthy and prominent Jewish banker and industrialist who, in the mid-1930s, disturbed by the rise and stated intentions of the Nazis and fearing for the safety of his family, sold his home and his vast holdings and emigrated to the United States. Other formerly wealthy and prominent families in the area were not as prescient or fortunate—along with their financial holdings, their stately and elegant homes were confiscated at the end of World War II by the newly enforced Communist regime and sold to various countries as residences for the upper echelon of their diplomatic staffs.

The private homes of the Cuban and Soviet Bloc diplomats, and the Soviet embassy compound with its schools and other facilities occupying a dozen buildings, are concentrated at the eastern edge of the residential area. Directly across the street from the American ambassador's estate is another, quite different, compound, its function far removed from that of the diplomatic corps. Occupying an entire square block and enclosed by an eight-foot-high concrete wall, the dreaded headquarters of the Statni Bezpecnost (State Security), known as the STB, serves as a constant reminder of the iron will and ruthlessness of the repressive system responsible for its existence. Within the walls of the austere, imposing compound, surrounded by the administration buildings and private offices, is a separate and tightly secured gray stone monolith well known to the Prague dissident community—the STB's private detention cells and interrogation rooms. Of those who are arrested and brought there, some are never seen or heard from again, and those fortunate enough to be eventually released do not speak freely of what they endured.

Adam Purcell took note of the lights burning late in the offices inside the STB compound as his taxi stopped near the main gate. His driver yielded to a black Tatra sedan—the luxury car used by Czech government officials—that sped out of the inner courtyard into the street and headed in the opposite direction. Discharging the taxi at the entrance to the ambassador's estate, Purcell flashed his identity card to the polite but hard-eyed Marine guard stationed at the gatehouse. Recognizing Purcell, he bade him good evening and motioned him through. Continuing up the long, gracefully curved driveway to the mansion, Purcell climbed the steps sheltered by a colonnaded portico and entered the spacious, high-ceilinged foyer.

A Bach violin concerto played softly in the background against the laughter and lively chatter coming from a large drawing room to his right where drinks were being served before dinner. The diplomatic community thrives on its daily social life: the endless invitations to receptions, dinners, and cocktail parties that are the life blood of diplomatic relations and a primary source for the intelligence-gathering efforts of the CIA station. The Agency keeps extensive biographical files on all foreign diplomats of interest, including those of Western allies as well as Soviet and Eastern Bloc officials posted to Prague. Each new observation and piece of information is noted and filed for possible later use. Contacts are made and nurtured, possible recruits are targeted and evaluated, and the most promising pitched, often resulting in a new agent or asset.

Entering the ornately decorated drawing room, Purcell angled his way through the milling crowd of guests dressed in formal evening wear—the Eastern Bloc diplomats conspicuous in their more egalitarian dark business suits. He nodded to the West German and British ambassadors who had paused in their conversation, offering pained expressions that suggested their disapproval of his less than proper attire. Removing his raincoat, its plaid pattern clashing badly with his tweed sportcoat, he noticed he had drawn the attention of a Czech he immediately recognized as the head of the Ministry of Interior's political intelligence service, and a Soviet cultural affairs officer he knew to be a KGB agent. Aware of Purcell's true affiliation, they expressed more than a passing interest in his presence, continuing to watch him as he proceeded across the room.

Jordon Palmer, the Agency's chief of station, stood near the massive marble fireplace at the far end of the room talking to the East German defense attaché and the Norwegian deputy chief of mission. Purcell spotted him and moved forward, returning the smile of the East German Army colonel, a man he had targeted as a possible recruit, given his ego and excessive curiosity about the affluent life styles in the United States. Palmer had agreed with his assessment and was in the process of further evaluation.

Palmer excused himself and withdrew from his conversation when he saw Purcell approaching, making eye contact with him and motioning with a nod of his head toward a door adjacent to the fireplace. Under the wary gaze of the American ambassador, who had taken notice of him, Purcell followed the chief of station through the door leading into the ambassador's private study. Crossing the thickly carpeted chestnut-paneled room, the two men remained silent as Palmer opened a sliding partition recessed in the paneling, revealing another, even smaller room that was little more than an enclosed alcove providing sufficient space for two people and the small pedestal desk and two leather chairs it contained.

Closing the door and securing the lock, Palmer sat behind the desk and opened the bottom drawer. He removed what to the uninitiated would have appeared to be a deeply disturbed engineer's unreasoned and illogical creation of two oxygen masks fitted with earphones and connected to each other for some obscure reason by a thin cable. It was, however, a cleverly designed secure communications device used by the Agency when away from the more elaborate security precautions available to them at the embassy. The esoteric equipment provided the capability to discuss classified business in locations where it was known or suspected that listening devices were concealed. The American ambassador's residence was, as were all foreign embassies and residences, a prime target for electronic eavesdropping equipment surreptitiously installed by the local Czechs employed as domestic servants—all loyal Party members who were vetted and trained by the Czech Intelligence Service before being made available for employment.

Purcell took the chair across the desk from Palmer, adjusted his mask and headset, and activated the switch for the miniature battery-powered internal amplification system. When they began to speak, none of the sound vibrations of their slightly muffled voices would escape the device, foiling any attempt, no matter how sophisticated, to listen in on their conversation.

"We've got him," Purcell said, handing the chief of station the slip of paper with the directions to the cottage where Volodin had been taken.

Palmer read the directions carefully, then put the paper in his inside coat pocket. "His contact was with the dissidents?"

Purcell nodded. "A professor from Charles University."

"You instructed them not to make any attempt to get him out?"

"Yes. But Nemecek suggested we move immediately. I think he's right. The STB can't be too far behind us."

"A cable from the DDO came in an hour ago. There's a team of Green Berets from the Tenth Group at Bad Tolz ready to come in."

"How are they going to infiltrate?"

"High-altitude, high-opening parachute drop."

"It's going to be dangerous trying to move Volodin closer to the border," Purcell said. "It might be best to inform the infiltration team to get as close to the cottage as possible. The sooner they take over, the better."

Palmer nodded in agreement, remembering the information he had received that morning: Soviet Colonel General Levchenko, commander of the Central Group of Forces—the five Soviet-controlled Czech Army divisions stationed in Czechoslovakia—had been ordered to commit two battalions of his infantry to aid the border troops in sealing off the frontier and the roads leading to the West.

"We'll select a drop zone within a mile of the cottage that will put them well to the rear of the troop concentrations and limit the distance Volodin has to be moved before the team can protect him. I'll cable the location and the time for the rendezvous to the DDO."

"It would be best to let the commander at the mission support site choose the DZ and the time," Purcell offered gingerly. "He's got a lot of things to factor in. He can cable the estimated time of arrival at the drop zone to us before they launch, and give us the frequencies on which the agent can contact them if necessary."

"I'll get a cable off immediately. As soon as we get a reply we'll move. Unfortunately, once I've given the agent the time and location of the infiltration and sent him to get Volodin, he'll have no means of further contact with us or the mission support site."

"He has no emergency communications capability, no way of scrubbing the mission if there's trouble?"

"He doesn't have the necessary equipment on hand, and we can't risk direct contact to get it to him."

"With your permission, I'd like to make the contact with Volodin and get him to the drop zone," Purcell said. "I spent two years as a company commander with the Eighty-second Airborne; I know how to secure a DZ. And I can take a radio with me."

Palmer shook his head. "None of us can go near Volodin. They know we've been trying to locate him. If they see you, or anyone from the station, leave the city they'll know we've found him. They'd put every available man on us—our chances of losing them would be remote."

"The same could be true of any of our Prague agents," Purcell said, pressing for the assignment. "We still don't know how many of them have been compromised. I shook my surveillance twice today; I can do it again."

"No," Palmer said emphatically. "The man I have standing by is a deep-cover agent from Pilsen. He has no Prague connections. I can have him at the cottage within two hours. He'll secure the DZ and provide transportation to get the team and Volodin closer to the border. The DDO's cable said they have their own arrangements for getting them across."

"Does your man have other agents or assets to help him?"

"He works as a singleton."

Purcell held Palmer's gaze. "A one-man reception committee with no security for the drop zone and no radio communications capability?"

"It's all we've got to go with, given the operational environment and the short notice. I don't like it any more than you do, but the DDO wants him out, and he wants him out *now*. I know the agent well—he's experienced, competent, and he knows every back road, farm track, and gully in Bohemia. He'll get the job done."

"With all due respect, sir, considering the emphasis placed on getting Volodin out safely, it would make more sense for us to put him on ice ourselves until we've had more time to make proper arrangements."

Palmer's eyes hardened. He had had enough criticism from his junior case officer. "I don't make policy, Purcell. And the cable I received from the DDO wasn't a suggestion thrown out for discussion—it was an order." His tone of voice made it clear that his decisions were also not open to further discussion.

"Sorry," Purcell said. "Old habits die hard. I'm just concerned about the safety of the airborne infiltration team."

"Understood," Palmer said. Then, changing the subject: "If the ambassador tries to buttonhole you about our progress, stonewall him. He knows about Volodin and our attempts to locate him, but my instructions are to tell him nothing about the mission. He's supportive of us, and my relations with him are good, but not good enough to keep him from bellowing loud enough to be heard in Washington if he finds out that what we're involved in could loosely be interpreted as an act of war."

5

Classification: TOP SECRET

Copy No. 1 of 2 Copies
Company A, Operational Detachment A-204
PT937929 Bad Tolz, Germany
28 Sept. 85

Operations Order—01-54
Reference: Map Series K424, Czechoslovakia, 1:50,000

1. SITUATION
   A. *Enemy Forces:* Heavy enemy traffic and activity along
   Czechoslovak borders with Austria and West Germany.
   Reconnaissance satellite intelligence reveals approximately two battalions of Soviet and Czech infantry forces
   have been detached from main units to reinforce Czech
   border patrols in these areas.
   Forecast: High-pressure system dominating target area.
   Thin, scattered cloud cover at 12,000 ft., otherwise, clear
   skies. Dry, cool air. Projected temperature range: 58 degrees F—42 degrees F.

   Quarter moon: 33% illumination

   Sunrise: 0657 hours. Sunset: 1659 hours
   (1) *Terrain:* The terrain is rolling hills. On the high
   ground the terrain is open with tall pine forest ar-

eas. In the low ground it is open farmland and night movement will be easy.

(2) *Identification:* The enemy is Czech and Soviet troops with probable STB and KGB elements.

(3) *Location:* See map overlay—Enclosure #1

(4) *Activity:* The enemy is currently reinforcing the border guard units and setting up roadblocks on main routes leading to the border areas.

(5) *Strength:* Indeterminate, but all indications suggest border forces at least triple normal strength.

B. *Friendly Forces in Target Area:* None.

(1) *Fire Support Available for the Detachment:* None.

2. MISSION: Operational Detachment A-204 (Half Team) will conduct infiltration to contact local agent on DZ, take control of defector, and escape and evade to extraction site. (See map overlay—Enclosure #1)

3. EXECUTION

A. *Concept of Operation:* ODA-204 (Half Team) will conduct the operation in two (2) phases.

Phase I: Airborne Operation—night HAHO infiltration to DZ to link up with local agent and defector.

Phase II: Escape and Evade with defector to extraction site.

B. *Coordinating Instructions:*

(1) Time of departure and return:
Depart: 28 Sept. 85–2100 hours
Return: 29 Sept. 85–0500 hours
(However, mission has priority)

(2) *Infiltration Route, Escape and Evasion Route, and Coordinates of DZ and Extraction Site:* See Enclosure #1

(3) *Rally Point:* See Enclosure #1. The Detachment Leader will designate the Rally Point—to be used only when separated or disorganized.

(4) *Actions on Enemy Contact:* As per Detachment Field Standard Operational Procedure.

(5) *Actions at Danger Areas:* As per Detachment Field SOP.

73

(6) *Actions at the Objective:* Take control of defector and escape and evade.

(7) *Prisoners:* None will be taken.

(8) *EEI (Essential Elements of Information):* None

(9) *OIR (Other Intelligence Requirements):* None

4. SERVICE SUPPORT
   A. *Supply*
      (1) *Rations:* One (1) day's rations will be carried.
      (2) *Arms and Ammunition:* As per Special Requirements—see Enclosure #2
      (3) *Uniforms and Equipment:* As per Special Requirements—see Enclosure #2
      (4) *Method of Handling Wounded:* Walking wounded will accompany Detachment. Critically wounded will be cached until mission is completed when recovery attempt will be made.
      (5) *Method of Handling Dead:* Bury (shallow), mark grave, record grid coordinates, and report at debriefing upon completion of mission.

5. COMMAND AND SIGNAL
   A. *Signal*
      (1) Signals to be used by the Detachment will be hand and arm signals.
      1. *Detachment Code Names:*
         Lt. O'Neil—K-20   SSG Shumate—M-11
         MSG Kessler—C-24   SFC Thornton—A-21
         SSG Pitzer—B-12   SGT Teodozio—S-22
      2. *Code Words:*
         MISSISSIPPI FLOOD—Have taken control of defector and proceeding with escape and evasion.
         ALASKA EARTHQUAKE—Have reached extraction site.
         PRAIRIE FIRE EMERGENCY—Mission has been compromised. To be followed by Situation Report ASAP.
      3. CHALLENGE *and* PASSWORD *at* RALLY POINT: Any combination of 21—Phrase is "Green Mountain Boys."
   B. *Command*
      (1) *Chain of Command:* Kessler—Pitzer—Shumate—O'Neil—Thornton—Teodozio

ADDITIONAL ENCLOSURES: Map overlays of radar gaps and checkpoints along airborne infiltration route to target area. Required time and altitude at each checkpoint. Photograph of subject (defector). Code Name for local agent at DZ. Communication frequencies.

DEBRIEFING: Detachment will be debriefed upon completion of mission by CIA Deputy Chief of Station–Bonn at isolation area.

Ten miles northwest of the town of Regensburg, West Germany, at the end of a remote, tightly secured airstrip that appeared on no aeronautical charts, the powerful turboprop engines of a Lockheed C-130 Hercules shook and roared to maximum power as it began its takeoff roll and lumbered down the runway. Steadily gaining speed, its throttles fire-walled, the huge transport rattled and creaked, threatening to come apart at the seams as it rotated, lurching its broad bulky frame into the night air and climbing slowly away from the retreating lights of the CIA isolation base and staging area.

Banking into a slow turn as it gained altitude, the aircraft headed due east before following a southerly course over the mountainous region of the Bavarian forest that formed the West German frontier with Czechoslovakia. The course had been precisely planned to track a narrow corridor above and parallel to the commercial airline routes in that area; the takeoff time of 8:30 P.M. coinciding with a period of heavy commercial air traffic. The effort to divert the attention of the Czechoslovakian radar operators away from the flight path of the C-130 would soon be augmented by elements from the United States Air Force base at Frankfurt. Resulting from a request by the director of the Central Intelligence Agency routed through the proper channels, two formations of jet fighters were scheduled to arrive in the border area at the same time as the C-130. Their mission—its true purpose unknown to the pilots—was to conduct high-speed night maneuvers a few miles north of the release point where the Special Forces team would exit the transport aircraft for their HAHO parachute jump.

M. Sgt. Frank Kessler sat on a nylon web seat on the starboard side of the aircraft, the vibrations from the deck plates traveling up through his entire body. The sound of the engines was muffled by the helmet he was wearing, and he listened to the rhythm of his own breathing through the demand regulator attached to his oxygen mask. His thoughts were of the mission. The details of the Operations Order were burned in his memory, along with countless other details he would have to call into play before the long night ahead was over. He glanced down the row of seats at the five other members of his team: all lean, sinewy, finely honed soldiers, superbly conditioned by a constant regimen of hard training. With that training had come deep reserves of sheer will power and a shared sixth sense—acquired through months of working closely together—each man knowing how the other would react in a given situation.

There had been no false bravado or tough talk about the mission, just a silent self-confidence and professional ease. But, to a man, they were grateful for the reprieve from their often boring, monotonous training schedule. The few apprehensions they had about the haste in which the mission was planned, and the fact that the Agency exercised command control as opposed to Lieutenant Colonel Kitlan, were overcome by an eagerness to participate and contribute. Kessler, along with Pitzer and Shumate, had seen action before, each having served multiple combat tours in Vietnam. The others had no operational experience other than field training exercises, but had conducted countless similar infiltration missions during their months of training with the team.

Kessler's eyes settled on Tuggle, the CIA paramilitary man seated on the opposite side of the aircraft. Tuggle had been chosen by the Agency to act as oxygen safety man and jumpmaster for the HAHO jump. Kessler had questioned him at length following the briefing at the isolation base, and was satisfied that he was more than qualified to handle the tasks assigned him—having made over two thousand jumps and been through jumpmaster's school while in the army.

With a nod of recognition to Kessler, Tuggle got to his feet and moved toward the team, his attention on the oxygen console strapped down in the aisle of the cargo hold. The console contained a large high-pressure oxygen bottle mounted in a welded tube frame, and an oxygen regulator and flow indicator for each jumper, with a pressure-reduction valve system in between to control the flow from the bottle to the regulators. Flexible hoses connected to the console ran to each man's oxygen mask. Tuggle repeatedly glanced from the console to the face of each team member; he was monitoring the flow indicators and watching for any signs of hyperventilation from stress or symptoms of hypoxia—the lack of sufficient oxygen in the body tissues as a result of the high altitude. The team had been prebreathing pure oxygen for thirty minutes prior to takeoff, and would continue to do so for the thirty-minute flight to the release point, saturating their systems for the jump. Any indication that a member of the team was not getting sufficient oxygen and suffering from hypoxia would require immediate action. Prolonged hypoxia can result in unconsciousness, brain damage, and death, and at thirty-three thousand feet—the altitude to which the aircraft was climbing—hypoxic effects could occur within thirty to sixty seconds.

The noise of the aircraft and the use of helmets and oxygen masks required that all aircraft procedures and jump commands be given by arm and hand signals rather than verbally. The time warnings to the release point—informing the team of the time remaining to the drop—were communicated in this manner by the jumpmaster, whose oxygen mask and helmet were fitted with a microphone and headset that were plugged into the aircraft's intercom system, allowing him to communicate directly with the aircraft's navigator and relay information to the team.

Tuggle stepped back from the oxygen console and pointed to his wrist, indicating that he was about to give a time warning. Opening and closing both hands twice, he signaled that twenty minutes remained. Conducting an oxygen check, he directed a thumbs up to each team member making certain that the signal was returned, signifying that there were no oxygen problems. Completing the twenty-minute warning procedure, each jumper removed the arming pin from his automatic opening device and held it up for Tuggle to see. Their main parachutes were now armed to open automatically at twenty-five hundred feet in the event that any of them became incapacitated and were physically unable to deploy their chutes after exiting the aircraft.

Relaxing until the next time warning, Kessler and his men concentrated on the visual images crammed into their brains during the hours of briefing at the isolation base. They had been impressed by the thoroughness and awed by the state-of-the-art technology used to prepare them for the HAHO jump. The CIA's Area Specialists had drawn on their extensive files of satellite photographs taken of the earth's surface. The photographs, converted to simulation imagery, were stored in computer programs capable of manipulating a computer to display an image of any piece of terrain, seen from any angle, illuminated by an imaginary sun or moon at any time of day or night. Upon being told where the *observer* is, the computer can then place the observer at any altitude from sea level to forty thousand feet.

The team had sat in a specially equipped room to view the computer-generated three-dimensional imagery of the Czechoslovakian landscape they would cross during their mission. The primary area-of-interest was displayed on the central portion of the screen, showing the terrain that corresponded to the jumper's line of sight, while the remainder of the curved screen, displayed at lower resolution, corresponded to their peripheral vision. Each town, village, and terrain feature—ridgelines, valleys, lakes, and rivers—its vegetation, and manmade obstructions such as power lines, bridges, railroads, and highways, appeared in vivid, realistic detail, precisely as they would when illuminated by the available moonlight. The visual effect, with its frontal and downward viewing angles, was the same as the team would experience during the actual jump from thirty-three thousand feet through their descent to the drop zone twenty-eight miles inside Czechoslovakia. The film had been shown repeatedly for three hours, providing each man with a lasting mental image of the ground reference checkpoints they would need to guide them to the drop zone.

Kessler's concentration on the terrain features in his mind's eye was interrupted by Tuggle, who again moved to the center of the aisle and stood before the team. Opening and closing both hands once, he gave the ten-minute warning and conducted another oxygen check. The aircraft had reached thirty-three thousand feet and was now fully depressurized to the outside air pressure in preparation for the opening of the tailgate at the next time warning.

Despite the inefficiency of the heater in the cargo bay, the team was well insulated from the cold air. Upon arrival at the CIA isolation base, the men had turned in all of their clothing and personal effects, including all items of identification. They were issued forged Czech identification papers, the equivalent of fifty dollars in Czech crowns, and the sterile (bearing no mark of manufacture or origin) and untraceable clothing and equipment stored at the site for their mission. East German–made boots, socks, underwear, and thermal longjohns were worn beneath Czech-made civilian slacks and shirts and parkas. A one-piece insulated jumpsuit—light gray in color—and gloves, worn as the outer layer, provided the additional protection that would be needed against the fifty-degree-below-zero temperature and sixty-miles-per-hour winds they would experience when exiting the aircraft at thirty-three thousand feet. The helmets, goggles, and oxygen masks, completely covering the face and head, would leave no skin exposed to be frostbitten by the high-altitude temperatures and the wind-chill factor as they descended under canopy.

The team's primary weapons—German-made H&K sound-suppressed nine-millimeter submachine guns—were secured to their sides on the outside of the jumpsuits for ready access, and the Walther twenty-two-caliber sound-suppressed automatic pistols, also of German origin, provided as backup weapons were carried in shoulder holsters beneath their civilian parkas. Extra magazines of ammunition were stored in the bellows pockets of the parkas, along with one packet of freeze-dried rations, and two mini-grenades per man to be used to break contact in the event of an ambush. Kessler carried a sophisticated satellite relay radio in a padded rucksack strapped beneath his main parachute, and each member of the team wore an illuminated panel board—containing an altimeter, stopwatch, and compass—attached to the harness strap across his chest. Once on the ground, the jumpsuits would be stripped off, and all of the equipment used for the jump would be discarded and concealed before the team, dressed only in civilian clothes, left the drop zone.

The tension and adrenaline flow increased as the team saw Tuggle give the six-minute warning. Pulling down their goggles, they responded to another oxygen check and saw the red lights go on over the tailgate. The huge cargo bay resonated with the high-pitched whine of hydraulic motors as the tailgate was lowered to its horizontal position, forming a ramp on which the jumpers could stand. Frigid air filled the rear of the aircraft and a gaping black hole opened to the night sky.

Four minutes later, their senses heightened, their eyes clear and alert, they received the two-minute warning—the start of the jump commands. In response to the first command (Tuggle raising an outstretched and an open hand upward), the team got to their feet, conducted an equipment check, and prepared to disconnect from the oxygen console.

At the one-minute warning, the men activated their individual oxygen systems—the "bail-out bottles" that would sustain them through their descent to ten thousand feet, where they could safely breathe the available air. The steel bail-out bottles, stored in the compartment on the side of the parachute pack tray, were actually two small high-pressure canisters specifically designed for high-altitude jumps to provide a demand-regulated thirty-minute supply of pure oxygen with virtually all of the moisture removed to prevent the oxygen-mask valves from icing. Upon disconnecting the flexible hoses that connected them to the on-board oxygen console, the team remained standing, responding to another of Tuggle's oxygen checks to verify that the individual systems were functioning properly.

When given the command, the team moved in unison to the rear of the aircraft. Huddled together and standing three feet from the end of the ramp, they were positioned for a coordinated exit that would get them out fast and limit their lateral dispersion. Switching on the secure-voice interteam radios—the headsets built into their helmets and a voice-activated microphone attached to their throats—the men could now communicate with each other from a distance of up to three miles during their descent.

All eyes were on Tuggle as he keyed his microphone and spoke to the navigator, who was now constantly updating him on their position relative to the fast approaching release point. With ten seconds remaining, the *stand by* command was given, and with it came the sharp stab of fear that each man, no matter how experienced, feels before a jump. The fear passes instantly, upon exiting the aircraft, but serves the purpose of putting the senses on full alert for the task ahead.

Giving a thumbs-up signal to indicate they were ready, the team moved to within four inches of the end of the ramp, their eyes still riveted on Tuggle, his arm raised and bent at the elbow; a single finger pointing upward. The coiled tension set every nerve on edge as the jumpers glanced quickly at their altimeters to verify the altitude and waited for the *go* command. The green lights came on and Tuggle instantly relayed the command from the navigator, thrusting his extended finger vigorously toward the exit.

Each man activated the stopwatch on his panel board as he stepped off the tailgate into the black void. They were at first caught and pulled along in the slipstream of the C-130, the force of the propwash momentarily tossing them about like windblown leaves before they assumed a stable face-to-earth body position. They hesitated a full five seconds, not wanting to deploy their parachutes until their forward momentum had slowed from that of the aircraft—all of them aware of the fate of a former team member who had deployed immediately during a training jump; the impact from the opening shock dislocating his knees.

Prior to takeoff, the air crew had checked the prevailing winds aloft at three-thousand-foot intervals up to thirty-three thousand feet, and computed the weighted average to determine the distance the jumpers could travel under canopy. The present conditions allowed for a distance in excess of that required for the team to reach the drop zone, giving them a small margin for error. The pilot of the C-130 had released the team into the proposed wind line on the West German side of the border, and maintained a constant airspeed, not slowing down for the drop as he would have under normal conditions—aware that any decrease in airspeed would have alerted an enemy radar operator that a parachute drop had occurred.

Frank Kessler pulled his ripcord and felt a slight tug at his back as the small pilot chute deployed and inflated, pulling his canopy from its bag and extending the suspension lines. His canopy blossomed two seconds later; his harness straps firmly gripping the inside of his thighs as a solid bone-jarring jolt abruptly slowed his fall. A brief upward drift, a feeling of buoyancy, followed as he swung in his harness and began a slow, controlled descent with a forward speed—combining the flying speed of the canopy and the tailwind at that altitude—of eighty miles per hour. The sound of the aircraft trailed off in the distance, leaving an unearthly silence broken only by the rhythm of his breathing and the sound of the wind flapping his insulated jumpsuit. Slipping his gloved hands into the nylon steering loops, he glanced at the illuminated compass on the panel board strapped to his chest and made a five-degree course correction as he turned to the proper heading.

"High man, give me a count," he said, the voice-activated microphone at his throat transmitting his order on the scrambled frequency to the other members of the team.

"I see five," came the reply from Shumate, who was above the other men. "Approximate dispersion twenty meters." The team would maintain the close proximity throughout their descent, enabling them to land as a tactical unit, prepared to react as a team.

As low man it was Kessler's responsibility to guide the team to the drop zone. His eyes swept the moonlit landscape far below, appearing as grid lines on a map as opposed to the distinctive patchwork pattern seen from jumps at lower altitudes. From his present position he could see the curvature of the earth, and off in the distance, sixty miles to the northeast, the densely concentrated lights of Prague. Glancing again at his compass, then at the stopwatch and altimeter mounted beside it, he continued to hold his present heading, and began watching for his first ground-reference checkpoint; a soft glow from the crescent moon reflecting up at him from the thin, scattered layer of clouds at twelve thousand feet.

The high-glide, deep-penetration mission parachute used by the team was the same gray color as their jumpsuits—proven as the color of least visibility against the night sky. Highly maneuverable, the square, MT-2 Ram-Air canopy—resembling a hang glider more than a conventional parachute—required only a light touch for steering. At times, simply shifting his weight or rotating his body in the harness was enough for Kessler to make minor course corrections. The steering/control loops attached to the risers above his head were extended to help alleviate the problem of a restricted flow of warm blood to his fingers. Under the conditions of the jump, without the nylon extension loops his hands would become numb and useless if held above his head for the thirty-two minutes it would take the team to reach the drop zone. The extended steering loops allowed a jumper to keep his hands below his heart while flying the parachute over long distances, switching to the higher loops for more positive control during landing.

The team's forward speed slowed in direct proportion to the decrease in the tailwinds at the lower altitudes. Their rate of descent, due to the wing design of the canopy, remained constant, unaffected by the increasing density of the atmosphere.

At fifteen thousand feet, through breaks in the scattered cloud cover, Kessler had his first checkpoint in sight: the village of Rabi on the Otava River. The lights from the small cluster of houses and the reflection from the moonlit surface of the water were clearly visible below him. He studied the surrounding landscape for the triangulation points that would verify his position and course. Off to his left, he spotted the three small lakes north of the village, and to his right, the sharp bend in the river and the lights of the town of Strakonice. The sightings confirmed his position as being on course and in the center of the radar-gap corridor.

Checking his panel board, Kessler saw that his stopwatch indicated he was within thirty seconds of his estimated time of arrival for the first checkpoint, and the altimeter showed him to be five hundred feet above the planned altitude. Both readings were within acceptable limits, and he continued to hold the steering loops at the "no brakes" position, getting the maximum thrust from the canopy. Keeping his eyes on his compass, he made a slow turn and "crabbed" the canopy at a slight angle while still running with the wind—the rest of the team following suit as he announced the new azimuth over the interteam radio. The planned course change would keep him well within the corridor and headed in the direction of the next checkpoint.

Descending through a dense patch of clouds among the mostly thin, wispy, scattered layer at twelve thousand feet, Kessler made no maneuvers, holding steady on his course in a controlled drift—any lateral movement or change in course while in the clouds could result in a collision with another jumper unable to see the man below him. Condensation formed on Kessler's goggles, the warm moist air fogging them and obstructing his vision. Once through the clouds, his goggles cleared and he began again to scan the sparsely populated countryside below him, its features now more clearly defined and easily recognizable at the lower altitude.

Locating the second checkpoint—a small farming village—he sighted the unique pattern of intersecting roads northeast of the village, and the horseshoe-shaped ridgeline to the south. A quick glance at his altimeter and stopwatch told him he had arrived within an acceptable time frame, but he was now nine hundred feet above the planned altitude.

"High man, give me a count," he said again, to verify that the rest of the team had cleared the clouds and were still closely grouped.

"I see five," Shumate responded as before. "Approximate dispersion twenty meters."

"Applying full brakes," Kessler announced. "Decreasing altitude by seven hundred feet. Acknowledge."

The team, following above and closely behind him at the same rate of speed, stated their names in reply to the warning and prepared to duplicate the maneuver that would keep them evenly spaced and prevent them from gaining on, and possibly colliding with Kessler.

Pulling down on the steering loops, Kessler brought the canopy to the "full brakes" position, on the verge of a stall. Rapidly decreasing his forward motion, while increasing his rate of descent, he held the position until his altimeter showed that he had bled off most of the excess altitude, leaving himself a two-hundred-foot margin for error.

Kessler's arms were beginning to tire as he descended through ten thousand feet. Moving a gloved hand to his face, he unsnapped his oxygen mask, letting it flop to one side. He was now breathing the ambient air, and he could feel the cold wind on the exposed skin beneath his goggles. When his altimeter indicated five thousand feet, he began looking for the checkpoint that would tell him he was approaching the target area. A large reservoir came into view, nestled in a valley surrounded by low, wooded hills. The ruins of an ancient castle, defined by the soft light reflected off the water, commanded the crest of a hill near the overflow, confirming the checkpoint. He felt the mist rising from the reservoir as he passed overhead, and a strong updraft while crossing the ridgeline on the far side.

Checking his altimeter, he announced another decrease in altitude to the team, and a crabbing maneuver, in the opposite direction, to put them back on course, correcting for his slight overcompensation at the last checkpoint. The terrain changed to rolling farmland broken by patches of forests and hedgerows. A power line ran north to south along a road that intersected with narrow, unpaved farm tracks leading to occasional clusters of small houses and barns. The terrain features all corresponded to the visual images he had retained from the computer simulation at the isolation base. He was closing fast on the target area.

The CIA officer in command of the mission had told them at

the briefings that his agent on the drop zone would be informed of their estimated time of arrival, and advised them of the signal the agent would use to alert them to his situation on the ground. Kessler's eyes moved quickly back and forth across the terrain. He was now at two thousand feet, low enough for both ends of the horizon to be visible in his peripheral vision. Judging from his movement across the landscape, he estimated his forward speed at thirty miles per hour.

His attention was on the area dead ahead, watching for the agent's signal that would guide him to the drop zone. Out of the corner of his eye, he saw the final checkpoints that fixed his exact position: a series of five small lakes northeast of his line of descent, and two miles to the south, just off to his right, another group of even smaller lakes with a broad stream emptying into the one closest to him. The lights from the village of Blatna and the highway leading north to Pilsen and south to Pisek lay directly in front of him. He was precisely on course—the drop zone located three miles short of the tiny rural village and the highway.

As he descended across a deserted secondary road, a deeply shadowed patch of open ground that had gone unnoticed suddenly became the focus of his attention. A bright, flashing strobe light pierced the night sky from the small clearing in the isolated section of woods. The evenly spaced pulses of white light, channeled through a funnel attached to the strobe, were directed upward, visible only within a narrow arc from above. The agent on the ground, informed prior to the mission of the heading on which the team would approach, had directed the light toward them.

Kessler moved his hands to the high steering loops and homed in on the beacon. He felt the tension drain from his body; had the agent suspected the drop zone was not secure, or that he was in danger of being compromised, he would have attached a red filter to the strobe, signaling danger. The team would then have had to abort their approach and disperse, getting as far away from the planned target area as possible before landing—leaving them in the position of having to regroup, and escape and evade through hostile territory without completing their mission, with the added probability of the enemy being aware of their presence.

The agent, using night-vision goggles, had spotted the team

minutes before. He had attached the strobe light to a small steel rod and planted it firmly in the ground, pointing it at an angle along the path of their descent. Moving from his place of concealment inside the treeline at the edge of the clearing, he quickly broke open the fluorescent chemical sticks he removed from his rucksack. Pouring the liquid contents along the open ground, he formed an arrow ten yards long, its tip pointed into the wind. Seeing that the team was only a few hundred yards from the drop zone and in position to see the arrow, he returned to the strobe light and switched it off.

Kessler immediately spotted the lightning-bug-green fluorescent glow of the wind direction indicator. Studying the ground as he passed overhead, he estimated the size of the open area at forty square yards. Executing a one-hundred-eighty-degree turn downwind of the drop zone, he was now facing into a ten-knot wind that drastically reduced his forward speed. Descending at a forty-five-degree angle, he noticed he had dropped lower than intended during the turn and that his present angle of glide would land him in the trees short of the clearing. Holding both steering loops at the "half brakes" position, he slowed his rate of descent until reaching the edge of the drop zone. Upon clearing the trees, he applied "full brakes," stopping all forward motion and dropping swiftly toward the ground. Ten feet above the grassy field, he deftly worked the canopy, almost having to force the huge parachute down as he glided to a standup landing, stalling it at the last moment. The rest of the team followed him in, landing in rapid succession near the center of the clearing, touching down within five yards of each other.

Kessler pulled his quick-release devices, shrugging off his pack tray and stepping out of his harness as he gathered in his suspension lines and canopy. Glancing over his shoulder as he moved toward the treeline, he caught a quick glimpse of the other men heading in his direction, their parachutes bundled in their arms, hurrying to get off the drop zone.

A sudden flash of brilliant light flooded the clearing, turning night into day. The team froze in midstep for a brief second before reacting instinctively and dropping flat onto the ground in the ankle-high grass, unslinging their weapons as they fell. Kessler had reached the edge of the treeline and crawled on his stomach into the underbrush. The other men, caught in the open, began crawling toward him in an attempt to reach the woods and get under cover.

The glare of the floodlights concealed their source at the far end of the clearing, forty yards away. But the voice, amplified by a bullhorn that shattered the silence left no doubt in Kessler's mind that he had dropped into a well-organized ambush. The harsh words were muffled by the helmet he was wearing, but still clearly heard.

"Lay down your weapons and walk to the center of the field with your hands raised," the high pitched, heavily accented voice ordered. "There is no possibility of escape. Do as you are told or you will be killed."

The fact that the voice had spoken in English was not lost on Kessler. It told him that they were expecting Americans. Cursing under his breath, he scanned the opposite end of the field. Squinting into the lights, he determined that they were arranged in a half circle just inside the woods, and he suspected that the troops were deployed in the same manner, providing them fields of fire that, while covering the entire clearing, would not endanger their own men. Spotting the rest of his team, now within ten yards of his position at the edge of the woods, he was reminded by the muttered curses he heard through his headset that their interteam radios were still on.

"Keep moving straight ahead," he said. "I'm directly in front of you."

The silence was broken again, this time by a single short burst from an automatic weapon. One of the Czech soldiers on the left flank of the half-circle formation had broken fire discipline. Others, assuming the shots were a signal to open fire, joined in. The night air was filled with the sharp, staccato sounds of automatic weapons as a chain reaction from the enemy troops sent a flurry of rounds storming across the clearing, cracking through the underbrush and spouting small fountains of soil and debris from the ground around the team. Kessler heard two distinct cries of pain.

"I'm hit!" Pitzer said. "In the leg."

"Oh, shit!" It was Teodozio. "I can't move, Frank. I can't move."

Kessler scrambled quickly off to his left, crashing through the woods to a position where he could return fire without hitting his own men. He wondered why the agent and the rest of the reception committee had not opened fire in their defense. Extending the stock on his submachine gun, he took careful aim, directing short, accurate bursts at the floodlights, knocking out two of them on the enemy's right flank. The lights from the opposite end of the half-circle illuminated the objects he had hit: two sets of floodlights mounted on scout cars parked at the edge of the clearing. Aiming for the lights in the center, he took out another set before dropping his fire to the brushline to cover for his men who had now jumped to their feet and were running the final ten yards to the safety of the woods where they could regroup and get away from the ambush.

Changing magazines, Kessler continued laying down covering fire as the team struggled toward him. Pitzer was limping badly as he ran, and Shumate's progress was slowed as he dragged Teodozio along the ground by the collar of his jumpsuit. They were clearly visible targets for the heavy barrage of enemy fire that was concentrated on them as they raced for cover. Tracer rounds streaked across the open ground, their telling fiery red trails increasing the accuracy of the enemy soldiers. Pitzer and Shumate went down first, followed by O'Neil and Thornton. Kessler saw no signs of movement and heard nothing through his headset as he called out to the men.

The shooting stopped in response to repeated commands shouted over the bullhorn by a different voice—deeper and angry, speaking his native Czech language. At the far end of the field, Kessler spotted small groups of soldiers advancing in short rushes toward his position. Startled by something brushing against his shoulder, he spun around to see the shadowy figure of a man kneeling beside him. Reacting instantly, he clamped a huge, powerful hand on the man's throat and pinned him to the ground.

"Raven!" the man managed to say in a raspy, choking voice as Kessler tightened his grip. "Raven," he gasped again, using the code name as the chief of station in Prague had instructed him.

Kessler stopped short of crushing the desperate man's windpipe. "You son-of-a-bitch! You *stupid* goddamn son-of-a-bitch. What the hell are we up against?"

"I don't know. I swear, I don't know."

Kessler released the terrified man from his grasp and returned his attention to the advancing soldiers, who were within twenty yards of where he knelt in the underbrush. Grabbing the rucksack that contained the satellite-relay radio, he slung it over his shoulder and got to his feet. Jerking Raven up with him, he dragged him into the woods, out of the range of the floodlights.

"They must have been watching the cottage," Raven said as they stopped and stood silently among a stand of pines.

"Shut up! And get down," Kessler snapped, shoving the agent to the ground where he knelt beside him. He tried again to contact his team.

"Walt . . . Fuzzy . . . Nick . . . Dan . . . lieutenant. Acknowledge," he whispered repeatedly into the throat microphone, but there was no response, still no movement where he had seen them fall, and none of the awful sounds of wounded men that he knew too well. The soldiers had reached the treeline and were now between him and the rest of the team. Removing his helmet and the microphone, he tossed them aside and pulled Raven along with him as he edged deeper into the woods.

After going only a few yards, he stopped abruptly and dropped to one knee. He had heard movement in the brush ahead and the faint sounds of urgent voices coming from the direction in which he was heading—troops deployed to approach the drop zone from the rear. Cupping his hands around his ears, he listened carefully, then veered quietly off to his right where he had heard nothing. Shoving Raven in front of him, he slid down a shallow embankment and followed a narrow gully to a dense thicket of underbrush. Dropping to the ground, he pulled the agent under cover with him, his eyes intently scanning the woods.

"Where are the rest of your men?" he whispered.

"I'm alone," Raven said.

Kessler's entire body tensed as he stared hard at the darkened face within inches of his own. The agent was clearly frightened and confused.

"Where's the Russian?"

"Dead. He had a heart attack at the cottage where he was being hidden."

Kessler fought for control over his rage, to keep from striking out at the agent. Five men who had been his friends as well as his teammates probably dead. For nothing.

"I had no way to call off the mission. It happened after my last contact with your people."

Kessler heard the sound of footsteps in the underbrush nearby. "Follow me," he told Raven. "And stay close. Try to escape and I'll kill you."

"I am not your enemy," Raven said.

Crawling backward out of the thicket, away from the direction of the approaching footsteps and the stalking silhouettes he glimpsed in the distance, he slowly got to his feet and, using the cover of the trees, moved silently through the forest. He doubted that any of his team had survived the ambush, and if they had, they were wounded and prisoners of the Czechs. But, adhering to the mission plan, he headed for the rally point two miles due south of the drop zone: the preselected site where they were to regroup in the event they were separated.

Reaching the edge of a large field, he stayed inside the tree-line, skirting the open area while working his way to the other side. Stopping to get his bearings, he saw the prominent terrain feature that told him he was near the rally point—a steep, pyramid-shaped hill, selected because it could be easily located from the ground without using a map. Upon arriving at the base of the hill, a member of the team was to wait thirty minutes, using the challenge and running password to identify anyone who approached.

Kessler signaled Raven to stop in a narrow clearing on the bank of a confluence of two small creeks. Taking a position off to the right in the thick, tangled bushes, he pulled the agent down beside him where he could whisper into his ear. "If you give me one answer that even sounds like a lie, you're a dead man."

Raven's voice didn't waver. His light blue eyes, set in a narrow, sharp-featured face, stared back boldly. "I am not responsible for what happened here," he protested. "I simply followed orders. They should have given me more men . . . more time to prepare for the operation."

Kessler calmed himself, determined to salvage what he could of the mission. "My orders were to escape and evade with the Russian and any documents he had in his possession. What did he have with him when you found him at the cottage?"

"Nothing. There was a briefcase, but the dissidents had removed it before I got there."

"Removed it to where? Didn't they know you were coming for him?"

"They were amateurs," Raven said. "They panicked when they heard the professor who had helped the Russian in Prague had been arrested. It was his cottage where they were keeping him. Before he died, the Russian told them that the documents must not fall into the hands of the KGB."

"Where's the briefcase now?"

"A girl, the professor's niece . . . the girlfriend of one of the dissident students at the cottage . . . took it back to Prague. The Russian died before the dissidents learned of the professor's arrest. The girl was returning the briefcase to her uncle when she saw him being taken from his apartment by the STB. She was frightened . . . she is only eighteen . . . a member of the Czech national figure-skating team. She took the briefcase to a close friend, her coach . . . a woman named Hana Cernikova. Then she contacted her boyfriend and told him what she had done and about the STB taking her uncle. He and the others at the cottage had been waiting for instructions on what to do with the Russian's body; they left immediately when they learned of the professor's arrest. I arrived as they were leaving. I did not have time to get to Cernikova in Prague to retrieve the briefcase and get back here in time for your arrival."

"Does the skating coach still have the briefcase?"

"Yes. I will contact her and get it to your CIA in Prague as soon as we get away from here."

Kessler's anger flared again as the searing image of his teammates being cut down flashed in his mind. "How the hell did you miss spotting that ambush at the DZ? I counted four scout cars. And there must have been at least a company of troops. Didn't you reconnoiter the area before you brought us in?"

Raven nodded his head. "I saw nothing. They probably followed me from the cottage and moved into position after I checked the perimeter."

Kessler sat silently, assessing his situation, listening to the sounds of the forest and the rippling water in the nearby creek. His swift, appraising eyes gleamed with a feral alertness as they moved constantly across the densely wooded terrain.

"Are you armed?" he asked Raven.

"I have a pistol."

"Keep watch," Kessler said.

Drenched in perspiration, he unzipped his insulated jumpsuit and pulled it off. He continued undressing down to his thermal underwear, which he shed before putting his civilian clothes back on. Opening his rucksack, he removed the satellite-relay radio. The ultrasophisticated piece of equipment, no larger than a standard dictionary, was designed for both continuous-wave and voice transmissions, and capable of encoding and sending messages over thousands of miles, across entire continents and oceans in a matter of seconds. A recorder built into the radio allowed the operator to record a message of up to fifteen minutes in length which was then automatically encoded before being compressed into a burst of only a few seconds duration when transmitted—defeating any attempt by the enemy to locate his position with direction-finding equipment.

The communications room at the CIA isolation base in West Germany had a twenty-four-hour monitor on the radio frequencies assigned for the mission. The three coded messages contained in the operations order for the mission were stored in the radio's memory. By simply switching the unit on and pressing a coded memory key, the operator, even while on the run, could transmit an emergency message in a minimum amount of time.

Kessler turned on the radio. The ready light glowed as he extended the four-foot telescoping antenna. Pressing the memory key for PRAIRIE FIRE EMERGENCY, he transmitted in a split second the message that informed the mission support site that the team and the mission had been compromised. He stared blankly at the radio for a long moment before punching the off button and retracting the antenna.

The sharp crack of a fallen branch breaking underfoot raised the hair on the back of his neck and sent a jolt of adrenaline through his body. He dropped to a prone position, his weapon at the ready. Raven followed his lead, lying close at his side. They heard the sound of hesitant footsteps coming from the direction they had used to approach the rally point.

The dark outline of a man carrying a weapon appeared from among the trees. Partially hidden from view by the thick underbrush, he stopped and stood motionless. Hoping it was one of his team, Kessler strained to see more clearly, but to no avail. The man slowly turned his head, his eyes sweeping the woods around him. Kessler was about to call out the challenge when he saw the silhouettes of three more figures appear to the left of the first man, who was now moving again in concert with the others. The way the men moved indicated that they could not possibly be his teammates. None of the figures he saw were limping or being supported by another man. The distinct outline of a uniform cap on one of the men became visible, confirming his judgment.

Pulling the highly classified radio to his side, he felt for the destruct button on the front panel. The button, when depressed, activated a timing mechanism—set for a thirty-second delay—on an explosive charge inside the radio. The charge was powerful enough to destroy the radio and anyone standing within three feet of it. His orders had been explicit: if the probability of capture or death existed, the radio was to be destroyed; under no circumstances was it to be allowed to fall into enemy hands intact.

"Don't open fire until I do," he whispered into Raven's ear.

Kessler lay still, watching the woods and listening, determining that the men in front of him were not all he had to contend with in the immediate area. He heard two more men approaching on his right flank. They were all advancing slowly, directly toward him, now less than twenty feet away. Tapping Raven on the shoulder, he pointed to the two shadowy figures on their right, indicating that the agent should fire at them. Raven nodded and quietly shifted his position.

Kessler opened up with his submachine gun, killing two of the men in front of him. The remaining two dove to the ground, returning the fire. Their aim was wide, off to Kessler's left, his sound-suppressed weapon denying them a fix on his location. Raven rose to his knees and fired, missing his targets. One of the soldiers reacted expertly, spotting the muzzle blast from the pistol and getting off an accurate burst that riddled the agent's chest, killing him instantly.

Pressing the destruct button on the radio, Kessler placed it against Raven's body, then crawled quickly away. Getting to his feet behind the broad base of a large spruce tree, he slung his weapon over his shoulder and tore at the snap fasteners on the cargo pockets of his parka. Removing his two mini-grenades, he pulled the pin on one of them, holding the spoon firmly in place as he peered around the tree to see four crouched men cautiously approaching the spot where Raven lay dead. Counting softly under his breath, he estimated within two seconds the moment when the intense orange-white light flashed briefly through the forest as the radio exploded into lethal shards of metal. Two Czech soldiers, kneeling beside Raven's body, screamed as they were lifted into the air and tossed backward—absorbing the full force of the shrapnel and the blast.

Kessler had closed his eyes in anticipation of the bright flash of light, retaining his night vision. Less than thirty feet away from the explosion, he stepped from behind the tree and tossed the mini-grenade at the remaining two soldiers, throwing it underhand to avoid hitting the low-hanging branches of the trees. Immediately pulling the pin on the second grenade, he threw it in the same manner, ducking back under cover before the four-second time-delay fuse set off the charge of the first grenade. The Dutch-made V40 mini-grenade was only one and a half inches in diameter and weighed just four ounces, yet within ten feet from the point of impact, the casualty rate was one hundred percent. Its steel casing, prenotched on the inside, insured maximum fragmentation. Upon detonation, it disintegrated into four hundred incapacitating tiny pieces that shot outward at a velocity of six thousand feet per second. The thick underbrush around Kessler's targets sharply reduced the effective burst radius, but his aim had been good enough to cause multiple disabling wounds to the legs of the two men standing beside their fallen comrades, knocking them to the ground and preventing them from pursuing him any farther.

Kessler began running, staying along the base of the hill on the level terrain. Fast and agile for a big man, he darted swiftly in and out of the trees, crashing through the underbrush with his powerful stride. Reaching a flat stretch of deep pine forest, he quickened his pace and headed due south, intent on putting as much distance as possible between himself and the site of the attack on the Czech soldiers before other troops drawn by the sounds of the battle could reach the area. He knew that the Czechs would concentrate their search for him toward the West German and Austrian borders, expecting him to head in that direction. His instincts and experience told him he could beat them at their own game and get across the frontier, slipping past them before they had time to fully deploy. But his sense of mission and professional responsibility focused his mind in another direction. To Prague, and the briefcase that had cost the lives of five of his teammates.

Stopping to catch his breath, he spotted a place to hide and collect his thoughts. Climbing partway up a rise, he sat on his heels beneath a rock ledge, positioning himself where he was out of sight of anyone approaching from the rear, and had a clear view of the flat, moonlit terrain directly below and on both flanks. He began sorting through his options and organizing a plan of action. He needed transportation. His clothes were no different from those worn by the locals, but with the Czech soldiers searching for him, even though they would not expect him to go north to Prague, he could not risk walking the forty-two miles to the city cross-country in daylight, and it was imperative that he get to the skating coach as quickly as possible, before the STB learned of her involvement. The small van that Raven had been instructed to bring to the drop zone to drive the team and the Russian closer to the border was out of the question, even if he could backtrack and locate it. The Czechs had undoubtedly staked it out, if not put it out of commission.

He had kept track of the direction and distance he had traveled as he ran and was aware of his location. The village of Blatna was two miles northeast, and Sedlice less than a mile and a half to the south. He knew the Bohemian countryside well, having studied it thoroughly and extensively during his frequent classroom training. It was his team's area of operations behind enemy lines in the event of a Soviet invasion of Western Europe.

Searching his memory, he concentrated on the details of the immediate area. The town of Cimelice was only seven miles from his present position. He recalled that a branch of the main rail line from Vienna to Prague passed through the town—the railroad bridge spanning the river to the north was designated as one of their secondary targets to interrupt the flow of Soviet supplies to the south during a war. There was a railroad station near the center of the town with early morning and late afternoon trains to Prague every day.

Reaching into the inside pocket of his parka, he withdrew a clear plastic moistureproof packet. Tearing it open, he removed his Czech money, and a small red imitation-leather-bound booklet the approximate size of a passport. The booklet was a forged copy of the internal passport Czech citizens had to carry with them at all times. Kessler's photograph and a fictitious personal history, including date of birth, names of parents, employment records, and place of residence, complete with official stamps, had been expertly inserted. The CIA had issued them to the team only as "flash cover" identification—good enough to get a bearer with excellent language skills through a cursory check if stopped by the police, but not able to withstand close scrutiny.

Kessler's language skills were polished to perfection at the Defense Language School in Monterey, California, and kept finely honed by classes three times a week with his team at Bad Tolz. But his true strength lay in the foundations of his knowledge of the Czech language. His father was a Sudeten German; his mother a Czech national. They were "rucksack" immigrants from Grazlitz, located in what had been the German-annexed Sudetenland in northwest Czechoslovakia. They had come to the United States at the end of World War II, in July of 1946, after the territory had been returned to the Czechs. Kessler, born the following year, in Trenton, New Jersey, had grown up, at the insistence of his parents, speaking Czech and German as well as English. His command of the Czech language was consummate not only in his verbal ability, speaking without a trace of a foreign accent, but in his understanding and recognition of the subtle nuances of tone and inflection that expressed the mood and attitude of the speaker. During the four years he had been stationed at Bad Tolz, while on leave and traveling as a civilian, he had visited Czechoslovakia as a tourist with his wife and children on six occasions and knew the city of Prague and the surrounding area well from these trips and his classroom studies.

Shifting his position until he found a smooth spot on the rockface behind him, he settled back, cradling his weapon in his arms. He pulled up the sleeve of his parka and strained to see the face of his watch, the luminous dial barely visible. It was eleven fifteen. He was exhausted, and by the time the sun rose, he would have been awake twenty-five hours. He decided to rest for a short period before making his way under the cover of darkness to the outskirts of Cimelice, where he planned to hide until early morning, then enter the town and take the train into Prague. He reached for one of the timed-release amphetamine capsules in his shirt pocket, but thought better of it, realizing he might need them more after contacting the skating coach and making his way back to the border. By then, if he still hadn't slept, he would require all the help he could get to stay awake and alert.

He soon discovered that the amphetamines would have been unnecessary. The images that dominated his thoughts denied him sleep in a far more painful manner. He saw again the deaths of his teammates, and envisioned the moment of confrontation with their wives and children, all of whom were friends. He dreaded the thought of seeing their suffering and tears, and deeply resented the fact that he would not be able to tell them what had really happened to their husbands and fathers; how they had lost their lives on a dangerous mission for which they had volunteered. He would be given a backstopped cover story to tell them by the Agency: lies . . . an accident during a parachute training jump . . . a helicopter crash . . . anything but the truth. There would be a logical explanation for the sealed coffins—weighted to give the impression to pallbearers that the bodies were indeed inside. No detail would be overlooked. He smiled sadly at the mental image of his wife's face, then those of his two daughters, and hoped that no one would have to tell the same lies to them. Getting to his feet, he began moving slowly through the woods in the direction of the town, silently vowing to complete his mission and get back to those he loved and needed.

✳ ✳ ✳

Eighty-seven miles west of the darkened forest where M. Sgt. Frank Kessler trod softly across a carpet of pine needles, Lt. Col. Paul Kitlan paced the hardwood floor of the brightly lit communications room at the CIA isolation base near Regensburg, West Germany. The PRAIRIE FIRE EMERGENCY message had confirmed his worst fears.

"Don't evade the question," Kitlan demanded, his face tight and drawn. "How much security did you have on that DZ?"

Elliot Simpson, the CIA's deputy chief of station from Bonn, and the man exercising command and control over the mission, avoided Kitlan's angry gaze. "The truth is, I don't know if the Prague station was able to provide the necessary manpower."

Kitlan started toward him, his anger now manifested in his threatening posture. He stopped himself short and threw his half-empty cup of coffee across the room, shattering it against the wall.

"Your exact words at the briefing were 'the reception committee on the drop zone will provide adequate security.' And now you're saying you don't know if they did."

"The Prague station's orders were to see that the DZ was secure to the extent they were able to do so under the circumstances."

"You sound like some goddamn politician. C.Y.A.," Kitlan said in disgust. "Cover your ass. At all costs. Well, I know my men, and the mission wasn't compromised by anything they did, or failed to do."

"We don't know to what extent they've been compromised," Simpson said. "They may still be operational."

"They wouldn't have sent that message unless they made contact with the enemy and were under fire. Kessler chose PRAIRIE FIRE EMERGENCY for the code because it's one we used on Special Operations Group missions in Vietnam. It meant they were under heavy enemy fire and needed immediate extraction from the area of operations."

Simpson gave Kitlan a blank look. "We have no way of extracting them, they—"

"They're aware of that," Kitlan interrupted. "It's their way of telling me that they're on the run. It's been forty-five minutes since they transmitted the message. They would have followed up with a brief situation report by now if it was simply a case of being spotted and still being operational."

"At least we know they're still alive and haven't been captured."

"We know one of them was alive when he transmitted the message. And that's all we know."

"I've cabled the Prague station, advising them of the situation and requesting any information on the fate of the team. They'll contact their agents and get back to us as soon as they have something. I hope to God your men don't panic and attempt to seek refuge at the embassy," Simpson added. "The DCI and the President will have us all for breakfast."

"My men are professionals," Kitlan said pointedly. "They don't panic." Turning his back to Simpson, he abruptly left the communications room. Continuing down the hall to the briefing room, he sat and studied the large-scale wall map, updated with the most current intelligence information on the deployment of the Czech and Soviet troops. If his men were alive, he reassured himself, they could make it out, despite the full alert. Leaning his chair back against the wall, he propped his feet up on a table and lit a cigarette. The memories of other missions flooded his mind. The hot, still jungle nights, the frayed nerve ends and endless cups of coffee and the hours of half sleep in the radio room waiting for a team "over the fence" deep in enemy territory to make contact . . . remembering the many times he had waited in vain, hoping against hope. Entire reconnaissance teams disappearing without a trace, their fates forever unknown.

6

STRENGTH AND AUTHORITY—AND the will to use them when provoked—emanated from Josef Masek in a palpable aura. His strength was evident in his physical bulk. A broad, Slavic face, framed with high cheekbones and a strong jawline, sat squarely on a thick, short neck appearing as one with his massive, sloping shoulders, giving the impression of a man made from the mold of a concrete block. His authority was derived from his position as Chief of Regional Political Counterintelligence, Prague, holding the rank of colonel in the STB's Third Department.

Masek's abilities and singleness of purpose had earned him the respect of his superiors, and had placed him next in line to succeed the chief of his department. A dedicated and relentless worker, his only interests outside his profession were his wife and teenage daughter whom he adored and doted upon, spending the time away from his job and all his vacations in family activities and providing for them the material things and special privileges accessible to him through his position. A Party member in his youth and an excellent student, he had joined the STB in the mid-1950s upon graduating from Charles University. It was a time of reorganization of the Czechoslovak intelligence services under strict Soviet supervision—their organizational principles, methods, and objectives aligned in a mirror image of their Soviet counterparts. He had attended the compulsory two-year intelligence course at a special school on the outskirts of Moscow—housed in a small palace formerly the home of Russian aristocracy. He found it a waste of time, its curriculum largely duplicating what he had learned at the Czech intelligence school. But he was intuitive enough to recognize its value: a way to assure rapid career advancement for those who excelled in the areas the Soviets considered of greatest importance. Masek realized soon after arriving in Moscow that those areas were far from what he had expected. Individuality and originality of thought were not highly valued, but considered ideological deviation. Strict conformity to Soviet approaches, and a thorough mastery of the dogmatic indoctrination in Marxism-Leninism as well as the tradecraft of intelligence were the way to approval and advancement. He saw the school for what it was: a way to evaluate the Czech students, noting their personality traits, strengths, and weaknesses, to be used throughout their careers to manipulate them for Soviet purposes. He learned to play the game well, while also learning to despise the Soviets for their domineering and insidious ways—thoughts he kept to himself, sometimes exercising great restraint in order to do so.

The events of the last few hours had not gone as he had hoped or planned. With his hands deep in the pockets of a leather trenchcoat stretched tightly across his chest and biceps, he stood at the edge of the forest in the beam of the headlights of a troop transport parked off to the side of a narrow, unpaved farm track a few hundred yards from the clearing where the Special Forces team had landed. His formidable presence and menacing demeanor intimidated the uniformed officer standing at attention before him to the point where the young man involuntarily took two steps back from the barrel-chested, squatty giant who was voicing his anger in a low but emphatic tone.

The young Czech army captain looked at the ground, avoiding the unyielding stare from Masek's perceptive onyx eyes that warned of the intelligence behind them. The captain offered no excuse for his failure to control the troops who had opened fire on the drop zone against orders to do so only at Masek's command.

"I wanted the Americans alive, captain. They are useless to us now."

The captain remained silent. In his peripheral vision he could see the last of five body bags being carried from the woods to the rear of the canvas-covered truck.

"Look at me when I speak to you!" Masek commanded.

The young captain's eyes snapped upward. "Yes, sir," he answered in as firm a voice as he could manage.

Masek's attention was diverted to a fast-approaching vehicle that skidded to a halt a few yards from where he stood. A Czech army major jumped from the open scout car before it had completely stopped and walked quickly toward the two men.

"If you will please come with me, sir," the major said to Masek, gesturing toward the vehicle.

Masek accompanied the major to the back of the scout car and watched silently as he removed the equipment and articles of clothing from the rear seat.

"We found these in the woods near the clearing," the major said, holding up Kessler's helmet and throat microphone and pointing to the parachute and harness still on the seat. "And the jumpsuit and insulated underwear three kilometers to the south."

Masek glanced at the parachute and clothing, and examined the helmet and microphone. "Have you killed him?"

"No, sir. He ambushed one of my patrols sweeping the area east of the drop zone. We found the body of the agent who aided them during the infiltration . . . and unfortunately the bodies of four of my men who were killed at the site . . . and two more who were badly wounded."

Masek reacted inwardly to the news of the agent's death. "The American has escaped?"

"He cannot be far away, sir. I have concentrated the search in the immediate area. We will find him, if not before daylight, shortly after. I have taken the added measure of having all local police forces in the direction of the Austrian and West German borders placed on alert."

Masek said nothing, again picking up the helmet and holding it to the headlights to get a closer look, intrigued by the integral earphones and the connecting plug for the voice-activated microphone. "He eliminated six of your men?"

"Two of the dead men had limbs partially severed from an explosion," the major said. "The two who survived reported that the American had hand grenades and some sort of antipersonnel-mine booby-trapped beside the dead agent's body."

An army sergeant crossed the road from the rear of the troop transport in which the bodies of the team had been placed. He saluted the major smartly and handed him the Czech currency and forged internal passports taken from the dead men. The major gave them to Masek who flipped through each one, slowly nodding his head as he studied the photographs.

"At least two of them are not CIA paramilitary," he said to the major, showing him the photographs of O'Neil and Teodozio. "They are too young."

"American military?" the major asked.

"Perhaps. The CIA has been known to use them in special circumstances."

Masek put the documents in his pocket and took notice of a black Tatra sedan that pulled up behind the scout car, immediately recognizing the tall, lanky man dressed in civilian clothes who got out of the rear seat. Masek's eyes remained fixed and expressionless as he watched the senior Soviet KGB adviser to the Third Department approach.

The STB is a state within a state, numbering in excess of thirty-five hundred personnel—disproportionately large for the size of the country—and possessing the power to eliminate anyone for its own narrow interest and purpose. It is, however, far from an autonomous organization. There are those within it who are willing to betray their own country for their Soviet masters. Josef Masek was not one of them. He believed in the Communist system, but not in the Soviet domination of his people and the rape of his country. Each department of the STB has several Soviet advisers who offer not only advice, but have the authority to usurp power and command operations. They are in turn commanded by a Soviet KGB general whose operational influence is pervasive; nothing is undertaken without his stamp of approval. Daily activities are closely monitored, and each department and division's objectives are tailored to Soviet requirements without regard for Czech interests. Masek had learned to deal with the ever present advisers and their imperious ways, mastering his tradecraft and extending his influence through his exceptional abilities, making himself indispensable to his superiors, who were often less capable. The man walking toward him from the black sedan was more intelligent and experienced than most of the Soviet advisers, and therefore more dangerous in Masek's judgment. He had little daily contact with him, dealing primarily with his deputies, but he was aware, as was everyone in the Third Department, of the Russian's ruthless ambition and his constant intrigues aimed at undermining his fellow advisers and improving his own position within the KGB hierarchy in Prague.

Stopping short of where the three men stood, Viktor Rudenko stared silently until Masek, unable to ignore his intrusive presence, dismissed the major and the sergeant and walked over to him, nodding a silent greeting.

"You have captured the other American?" Rudenko asked, his coarse, flat features exhibiting no trace of any recognizable human emotion.

"Not yet, comrade."

"And the dissidents whom you observed running from Professor Marcovic's cottage?"

"My men were able to identify only one of the three men they saw. He was arrested when he returned to Prague. He will eventually tell us who the others are."

"Why did you not arrest them all when you arrived at the cottage?"

"I thought it best not to reveal our presence until I had established that Volodin was there. My objective was to prevent your scientist from escaping to the West, not to divide my men over a minor task that can be easily accomplished later."

Rudenko swept an open hand across his forehead, brushing back an unruly shock of thick black hair. He looked down on Masek through narrow, suspicious eyes. "Volodin was already dead. Was he not?"

Masek recounted his actions in an icy monotone. "When I learned of the professor's involvement through an informant, I immediately dispatched six men to the cottage. They had just gotten into position to observe when the man we believe to be a CIA agent arrived and the dissidents began leaving. I was en route to the area with additional men when those watching the cottage radioed me for instructions. I ordered them to stay in place until Volodin was sighted. I did not know he had died until the CIA agent we followed to the infiltration site had left the cottage alone and we discovered the body. I considered the activities of the agent to be more important than those of the dissidents. They will be caught. The CIA operative was obviously a deep-cover agent experienced enough to be entrusted with the assignment to guide the American infiltrators. Had we been able to capture him alive, he could have provided us with valuable information."

"But you have not captured him alive."

"No," Masek said, glancing at the young captain who was still standing at attention on the opposite side of the road, not certain if he had been dismissed.

"And the briefcase Volodin had in his possession?"

"None of the dissidents, or the agent, were seen leaving with it, and it was not found in the cottage."

"The briefcase must be found!" Rudenko said, his facial expression calm and dispassionate in contrast to his harsh and demanding words. "We suspect it contains defense secrets vital to the security of my country. You will use all of your resources to locate it and return it to me. The chairman of the KGB has issued the order himself."

Masek controlled a primal urge to reach up and snap the arrogant Russian's neck like a twig—a feat he was capable of accomplishing with ease. "I will find it, Comrade Rudenko."

Turning and walking toward his chauffeur-driven car, Rudenko made his parting remark without looking back. "And *we* will help you," he said.

Masek stared after the impeccably polished car as it slowly bounced and swayed over the deeply rutted surface, the red glow of its taillights disappearing into the forest as it rounded a sharp bend in the road. His thoughts returned to the American who was still at large. The men who had infiltrated his country were not ordinary airborne troops, he felt certain. Probably members of an elite, highly trained unconventional warfare unit assigned to the CIA for the mission of extracting the Russian defector. He wondered if the remaining American was indeed headed for the border as the army major believed. He would be dressed in the same manner as his dead comrades, indistinguishable in appearance from countless other Czech citizens, and no doubt fluent in their language. He would have money and credible, though somewhat limited, identification. If the documents in the scientist's briefcase were military secrets, then were they not equally as important as Volodin himself? And, if possible, would the American not first try to fulfill his mission before attempting to escape? Masek suspected that he would.

He further reasoned that the briefcase the KGB valued so highly had to have been in the scientist's possession—his assurance of acceptance and reward from the Americans—and at the cottage until he died. Perhaps removed by someone prior to the arrival of his men and returned to one of the dissident leaders. But if the CIA agent had access to it or knowledge of its location, why had he not simply delivered it to the American parachutists, or arranged to get it to the CIA station at the embassy in Prague? Perhaps Volodin's untimely death had set off a chain of events beyond his control. The agent did not have it with him when he left the cottage, therefore, if he knew where it was, his intentions must have been to retrieve it for the American infiltrators. And if, before he was killed, the agent told the surviving parachutist where to find the briefcase. . . . The questions required immediate answers, at this point available only from those under interrogation at STB headquarters.

The manpower and facilities at Masek's disposal were extensive. The chief of his department had given him broad, sweeping powers in response to the Soviets' demands to find and apprehend Volodin and return any documents in his possession. He decided to alert the Prague city police—the VB—to the possibility of the American's presence, and instruct the STB Second Department, in charge of counterintelligence against foreigners in Czechoslovakia, to increase surveillance on American citizens in the event the surviving infiltrator tried to contact them. He had already coordinated his efforts with the Fifth Department, requesting that they use their vast network of informants at all levels of Czech government and society to help him locate and arrest known and suspected subversives and members of the dissident community. Of those so far arrested and detained, he had ordered the interrogations concentrated on university faculty and students who were believed to be acquaintances or associates of professor Marcovic and the dissident arrested after leaving the professor's cottage.

The more Masek went over in his mind the events and circumstances of Volodin's attempted defection and the CIA's bold, extraordinary effort to extract him, the more he was convinced that the man who was still at large would go after the briefcase. And his gut-level instincts from years of experience told him that this man would be difficult to find and would not easily be taken alive.

7

THE BRIGHT EARLY MORNING sun heightened what little color remained in the faded, peeling yellow paint on the railroad station in the small provincial town of Cimelice. Frank Kessler stood outside on the waiting platform, away from the shaded area beneath the overhang. He could feel the sun's warmth drawing the chill from his bones and the stiffness from his muscles as he squinted against the reflection off the glittering dome of a nearby church that towered above the tiled roofs of the small cluster of sixteenth-century buildings. He had reached the outskirts of Cimelice hours before dawn, hiding in a dilapidated barn on an abandoned farm until sunrise, when he made his way along a wooded path to the edge of town. Twice during the cold and sleepless night he had heard the faint, distant voices of men moving through the forest, heading south, away from his intended destination. His submachine gun, now useless due to its size and his inability to conceal it beneath his civilian clothes, lay buried with his extra magazines of ammunition in one of the old horse stalls in the barn—the freshly disturbed soil carefully raked over and covered with moldy straw. His backup weapon, the sound-suppressed twenty-two caliber Walther automatic pistol, was secured snugly under his left arm in the shoulder holster beneath his parka.

He reached the station only ten minutes prior to the scheduled arrival of the train, waiting until a small group of people had gathered inside before approaching the counter and purchasing his ticket to Prague. He ignored the occasional questioning look from the locals, knowing that it was unlikely they would consider him anything more than a curiosity—someone visiting a relative in the outlying rural district. His eyes carefully watched the area around him and the faces of the recent arrivals who left the station and walked out onto the platform, casting impatient glances down the tracks. The train was fifteen minutes late. Kessler was watching for the local police and soldiers, or anyone expressing more than a casual interest in his presence. His nerves were on edge, and he overreacted to the approach of a station attendant, reaching inside his half-zipped parka and placing his hand on the grip of the Walther before realizing that the man only wanted a light for his cigarette. Kessler obliged with a curt greeting and a half smile.

He knew that the trip to Prague on the northbound train would present no problem if the search for him was still being concentrated to the south and west. All security checks and examinations of identification papers and travel visas of the passengers already on board would be completed by customs control and border guards when the train entered Czech territory after passing through the Austrian checkpoint at Gmund, seventy miles south of his present location. A thorough, hour-long search of the train by Czech officials and trained dogs would be conducted: every possible hiding place inspected, even the ceiling panels in the carriages, and each parcel and freight container sniffed by the dogs. Western newspapers and periodicals would be confiscated, with special attention paid to religious and news magazines and pornography—items considered undesirable and offensive by the Communist regime. The sexually explicit magazines would be appropriated by the guards, enjoyed, and later sold for ten times their Western price. Once the border checkpoint search was completed, the passengers would continue their journeys through Czechoslovakia without further controls or inspections.

Kessler heard the train before he saw it approaching, gradually reducing speed as it rumbled slowly through a maze of shunts, past empty flatcars and rusted machinery and deserted warehouse sidings in the rail yard adjacent to the station. Its brakes screeched in protest as it came to a stop alongside the platform, filling the crisp morning air with the pungent sting of diesel fumes. Boarding the first carriage, he took a seat to the rear near the exit, apart from the scattered group of en route passengers who glanced indifferently at him as he walked down the narrow aisle. Sitting against the window, he watched for any last-minute boarders who seemed out of place with the locals. He saw only the people he had previously observed, and settled back in his seat when the car jolted and lurched forward as it pulled away from the station. Fighting off his mind's increasing demand for sleep, he teetered on the razor edge between deep relaxation and unconsciousness as the train clattered and swayed rhythmically over the rails. The straight-line distance from Cimelice to Prague was forty-eight miles, but the train's route extended it to just over sixty miles, which Kessler estimated would take approximately an hour and a half with the intermediate stops. He gazed trancelike at the scenery, nodding in recognition as they passed over the railroad bridge north of town—remembering precisely where the explosive charges were to be placed on a wartime mission. Teodozio had been the team's demolitions expert, and his cry of pain as he was shot echoed poignantly in Kessler's memory of the disaster that had happened only hours ago yet seemed infinitely removed from the present, perhaps distanced by his need to force the anger and sorrow from his mind and concentrate on what he now had to do.

The picturesque Bohemian countryside, a land of hills and forests and streams and meadows, passed before him. Lush, rolling pastureland, broken by hedgerows and peat bogs and dense stands of fir and beech, was coursed by the winding ribbons of gravel roadbeds that led off the main routes to isolated villages and tiny farmsteads, their Baroque gables evoking the atmosphere of earlier times. Occasionally, on the crest of a terraced hill above a fast-flowing stream, or on a precipice with a commanding view of the surrounding terrain, Kessler spotted the ruins of ancient castles and chateaus and monasteries, many dating from the fifteenth century, left to the ravages of time and the elements. He thought of the winter nights of his youth, spent with his mother in the warmth of the small kitchen in their apartment above his father's bar, listening to her tell about her native land and the history of her people. She had told him that it was important he know and understand the heritage that would define and shape him.

She had been a gifted storyteller, capturing the drama and reality of the past, explaining cause and effect without distorting them through any personal prejudice. He had listened intently as her soft, heavily accented voice brought to life the tales of the Slavic tribes from the north who had settled the land as early as the first century A.D., their empire flourishing until the tenth century, then dying with the thousand-year reign of the Hungarians, to be followed by two centuries of their own Bohemian kingdom before being engulfed by the Hapsburgs who ruled for three hundred years until 1918. She told him of how the Thirty Years War had drastically diminished the population of Bohemia from three million people to less than nine hundred thousand, and how between the two World Wars the new Czechoslovak Republic had emerged only to be taken over by the Nazis—a period she had personally experienced and which she spoke of with great emotion when recalling how his father had been torn between his duty to the country of his birth and his hatred of what the Nazis stood for and how they were destroying the fabric of life in the Sudetenland. He had served with the German army, fighting the Russians in Poland and back to Berlin where he lost three of the fingers on his right hand during the final battle for the beleaguered city. With the end of the war, the Czechs were once more independent, but no longer free, and Fritz Kessler returned home to his wife to emigrate to the United States before the Communists took complete control and sapped the strength and spirit of their country. It was a country that had once verged on becoming an industrial giant: a nation of only fourteen million people, one half of one percent of the world's population, accounting for fully two percent of the world's industrial production of high-quality steel, coal, heavy machinery, weapons, textiles, and chemicals. Diminished and decaying under the mismanagement and stifling monolithic control of the Communist system in the ensuing years, its resources were squandered and depleted by the harsh demands of the Soviet Union, its industries and technologies neglected to become outdated and uncompetitive, turning the socialist dream into a demoralizing descending spiral of false hopes and unrealistic promises.

Kessler's thoughts returned to the present when he saw the

Prague skyline in the distance as the train slowed and entered the industrial suburbs west of the city. He was still fighting to stay awake and alert, eager to get up and move about. He decided not to get off at one of the smaller suburban stations and waited until the train had crossed the river, using the more crowded Vrsovice station from where he could take a tram the short distance into the heart of the city and the safety and anonymity of the throngs. His body and mind began to respond to the challenge that lay ahead, tapping the deep reserves of strength and endurance gained from his endless training and conditioning.

He stepped off the train into a milling crowd of provincial tourists waiting to begin their journeys home, crossed the busy lobby, and entered a telephone booth. There were two listings for H. Cernikova. The first number he dialed was answered by an elderly woman who responded obediently when he identified himself as an employee of the telephone company wanting verification that she was still living at her current address and was the party listed in the directory. With that confirmation, judging from her aged voice, he dismissed her and dialed the other number, letting it ring unanswered until he was certain no one was home. Looking up the number for the Federation of Sport, the governing body for all organized athletics in the country, he called the switchboard and asked to be transferred to the personnel office. Speaking in a halting and confused voice, he informed the young woman who answered the phone that he had just been assigned to the maintenance crew at the ice rink used by the national figure-skating team and he had no idea where it was located or what time he should report there. In response to her question he told her that he was to work with the evening crew, not the early morning crew. In a less than polite tone the woman gave him the location and told him that the rink would be in use by the skaters and their coaches from 9:30 A.M. until 4:30 P.M., after which the crew would begin work on grooming and preparing the surface for the evening training by the national hockey team.

Kessler glanced at his watch. It was nine o'clock. Cernikova was probably on her way to the skating rink. He thought of calling the American embassy and asking for the security officer, simply giving his code name for the operation and the phrase PRAIRIE FIRE EMERGENCY, nothing more, and hope that the mysterious call would be reported to the CIA chief of station who would in turn recognize it for what it was and inform the mission support site that he was still alive and operational. But he knew that the telephone lines would be tapped, and that his call would run up a red flag that could possibly alert the STB to his presence in the city. Even if he were successful in getting the scientist's briefcase, he reasoned that he had no secure way of arranging a meeting with the Agency in Prague to make a transfer or a drop without compromising himself and the mission. He might succeed in getting inside the embassy grounds where he could deliver the briefcase, but if he was observed and photographed while entering, as he felt certain he would be, his presence would put the ambassador, and the United States government, in the untenable position of having to explain who he was and how he had gotten into Czechoslovakia without proper credentials or documentation when the time came to get him out. The integrity of the mission came first, and the further consideration of disavowing any connection with his government, in the event of his capture, was equally as important to avoid an international incident that could prove useful to the Czechs and Soviets in embarrassing his country. If the possibility of the disastrous turn of events during the infiltration had been factored into the mission plan, he would have been provided with a contact number in Prague where he could at least have placed the briefcase in the hands of the CIA before making his escape. . . . He forced the unproductive hindsight reasoning and logic from his mind, accepting the hard fact that he was on his own until he got back across the border, and any contact with the embassy was out of the question.

He purchased a street map of the city at a newsstand near the entrance to the station, and studied the public transportation routes to the rink. Leaving the building, he took a tram to the nearest subway entrance, a few blocks south of the National Museum, and continued on the subway to the end of the line where he exited onto a crowded street, across from the square commemorating the Russian Revolution. He consulted his map again and determined that he was less than a mile from the entrance to a huge, sprawling public park—formerly the private hunting and game preserve of the Czech nobility. At the opposite end of the preserve was the Julius Fucik Park of Culture

113

and Leisure where the Hall of Sport, containing the ice rink, was located.

Following a broad avenue lined with apartment and office buildings, Kessler kept pace with the pedestrian traffic, not wanting to draw attention to himself. He turned on to a narrow tree-lined street and proceeded through a residential district of elegant private homes and reached the entrance to the park where a large walled-in compound that occupied at least a dozen acres dominated the hillside overlooking the wooded preserve. A brass plaque on one of the entrance pillars identified the compound as the Soviet embassy, explaining the presence of the array of antennas bristling from the roofs of the numerous buildings. Two immaculately uniformed guards posted just inside the gate ignored him as he continued down the hill along a broad macadam path into the autumn-colored woods.

The park was quiet and peaceful, nearly empty except for an occasional pensioner walking a dog that seemed its owner's equivalent in age and infirmities. The path wound its way through the open forest, descending past a series of ponds and a small fish hatchery, at which point it leveled off and branched out in a number of directions. Kessler turned right and walked to where the Park of Culture adjoined the wooded preserve at the extreme eastern end. A small planetarium, with a sign announcing that it was closed for repairs, was situated outside the wooden stockade enclosing three sides of a large area containing an expansive plaza bordered by ornate exhibition buildings and the Hall of Sport. Kessler moved briskly along a tree-shaded cobblestone walk past the planetarium and the stockade fencing to the open end of the plaza located at the corner of a busy commercial intersection. A ten-foot-high chain-link fence at the main entrance barred access to the grounds, and the deserted plaza inside made it obvious that the exhibition park was closed to the public. Kessler noticed a small gate off to the side, in front of the ticket office, through which three men carrying lunch pails passed without being challenged.

A street vendor wearing a starched white smock had set up his serving cart on the corner, and Kessler was drawn toward the mouth-watering aroma of pork sausages cooking on a rotating spit over a charcoal grill. Though he had not eaten since the light lunch served at the isolation base, he had given no thought to food in the last twenty hours, realizing only now that he was hungry to the point of feeling enervated. Taking advantage of the opportunity, he purchased two of the sausages served on soft, steaming rolls and stood near the chain-link fence, away from the few people who had gathered at the vendor's cart. He quickly devoured the sausages as he observed the entrance used by the workmen. Seeing no one in the ticket office, he guessed that the small gate was left unlocked for the maintenance crews and the figure skaters training in the Hall of Sport.

His entire body tensed and stiffened when, out of the corner of his eye, he caught sight of a VB patrol car as it pulled up to the curb. Two uniformed city police officers got out and approached the sausage vendor. Kessler was in plain sight of the two men, who paid no attention to him as they followed their daily routine and purchased their morning snacks. One of the VB, his cheek distended by a mouthful of food, glanced in his direction, looking past him, then back again, this time making a more thorough appraisal. Their eyes made brief contact, and Kessler detected the man's growing suspicion as his gaze moved from the dark stubble on his face and fixed on the soiled spots on his trousers and parka. Before leaving his hiding place that morning, Kessler had brushed away what he could of the dirt and grime that had accumulated on his clothes during his escape from the drop zone and the night in the barn, but some of it was ground in and stubbornly remained on his knees and elbows. Reacting in a self-conscious manner he hoped would appear normal, he assumed a puzzled expression, then shook his head in mock disgust as he brushed at his clothes, noticing for the first time the small bits of straw clinging to the eyelets of his boots. When the VB officer who had been watching him nudged and spoke to his partner, Kessler knew it was time to act.

His first thought was to enter the exhibition park grounds and if challenged by the two VB try to bluff his way out of the situation by claiming to be on one of the maintenance crews. But he ruled out the impulsive, ill-considered thought; once inside the fence, he would be trapped, an easy target in the broad, open plaza if he had to run, and confronted with a high, smooth-sided stockade fence to climb behind the buildings at the end of all three avenues of escape leading away from the main entrance. Maintaining his composure, he decided on the best way to handle a possible confrontation with the two VB.

Moving away from the chain-link fence at a casual pace, he walked back toward the planetarium and the wooded park, resisting the overwhelming urge to look over his shoulder to see if he was being followed. Continuing slowly along the cobbled walk, he stopped briefly to feign interest in the "closed" sign posted on one of the columns at the entrance to the planetarium.

The voice that called out brought with it a rush of adrenaline that prepared him for what he had hoped to avoid.

"You!" someone shouted from behind him.

Kessler turned to face the two quick-stepping VB officers, his look of innocent surprise masking the deadly calm of resignation beneath the surface—an involuntary inner calm that took control of his thoughts and actions, allowing him to function almost mechanically. He had initially experienced the feeling as a twenty-year-old buck sergeant at the onset of his first firefight in Vietnam, learning to recognize and rely on it in the countless life-and-death situations throughout his five years of combat.

He had purposely positioned himself near the bottom of the steps leading to the planetarium, out of the line of sight of the sausage vendor and the pedestrian traffic a hundred yards away on the busy street corner. A quick glance revealed that the path leading back into the woods was deserted, and he ambled toward the two men, veering slightly off to his left where a small area of grass and trees separated the buildings from the stockade fence behind the exhibition park. Stopping in the middle of the grassy area, he waited until the two VB reached him.

"Your identification papers," the larger of the two men ordered. He was a husky man with small, close-set eyes and a hard, pockmarked face. His partner was younger, and inexperienced, judging from his wide-eyed expression and his nervous posturing. Kessler assessed him as the lesser threat.

Kessler shrugged and flashed a tolerant smile. "You must not be very busy today," he said, patting the pockets of his parka as though he had forgotten where he had put his internal passport. "What have I done?"

"Your papers!" the larger man said, this time using a more commanding tone as he unfastened the snap on the covering flap of his leather pistol holster. His partner did the same, placing his hand on the grip of a nine-millimeter automatic.

Kessler spread his palms open in an obeisant gesture and

removed the red booklet from a pouch pocket at the front of his parka. The smaller of the two VB took his hand off his weapon and glanced at the document as his partner studied it. If the VB accepted his documents as genuine there would be no trouble, but based on their conduct and the nervousness of the younger officer, he knew they had not stopped him without reason— suspecting that the Czech State Security had taken no chances, covering all bases in their search for him by putting out an alert that included Prague and its environs.

Kessler was now thinking in terms of reaction time—the split second it takes to start to move with the perception of danger. Experience and training had taught him that to act first is to win, to react is to lose. The time difference involved could be as little as a quarter of a second, but in the drawing and firing of a weapon that was often the difference between life and death. If you allowed your opponent to move first, especially at close range with no available cover, you gave him the advantage. By the time you detect his movement and fire your first shot, he will have already pointed his weapon at you and fired at least twice. Kessler began the preparation for the attack as he handed the VB officer his documents, taking an unnoticed step backward, giving himself an unobstructed sweep of movement between the two men. He watched, poised and ready, as the older VB officer flipped through the red booklet; his eyes riveted on the gun hands of both men.

"You will come with us to the car," the larger officer said, motioning with his head toward the distant corner.

"But I don't understand," Kessler said, attempting to engage the man in conversation—one of the methods used to slow an opponent's reaction time. "My papers are in order."

"You will come with us!" the man repeated.

"What crime have I committed?" Kessler said, his eyes quickly glancing to his left and right. The path leading into the woods was still empty, and neither he nor the VB could be seen from the street corner.

"We must verify your identity and your place of res—"

Kessler's shots cut the man off in mid-syllable. In less than a second, with cold, practiced precision, he had reached inside his parka, drawn his pistol into a firm two-handed grip, and, from a distance of less than eight inches, fired a rapid three-shot burst directly into the left eye socket of the larger man who shuddered momentarily then staggered two steps back and crumpled to the ground. His partner's head jerked in the direction of his fallen comrade, a shocked expression still on his face as Kessler immediately fired another three-shot burst into his ear canal at near point-blank range, killing him instantly. The highly accurate placement of the shots, penetrating the brains of both men, had more than compensated for the lack of stopping power inherent in the small-caliber weapon, and the subsonic ammunition and the silencer had reduced the noise to nothing more than the click of the bolt action and a light crack as the round left the barrel—neither sound could be heard twenty feet away.

Shoving the pistol in his pocket and picking up his ID papers, he grabbed both men by the collars of their tunics and quickly dragged them across the grass to the rear of the planetarium out of sight of any passers-by. Spotting a stairway leading to a basement entrance, he pulled them to the edge of the landing, using his foot to send them tumbling down the stairs, where their bodies sprawled grotesquely against the doorway. He replaced the magazine in the Walther with the spare attached to the strap on his shoulder harness and chambered a round before putting the pistol back in its holster. A short distance from where he stood, he noticed a canvas tarp covering a stack of roof tiles stockpiled for the repair work on the building. Retrieving the tarp, he carried it to the bottom of the stairwell and carefully covered the bodies of the two VB officers.

Leaning against the rear of the building, he took a series of slow, deep breaths, collecting himself as the shock to his nervous system subsided. The muscle tremors and hyperactive feeling had always followed the calm after the firefights. In the vernacular of Vietnam veterans it was known as coming down from a combat high, and he knew it would pass in a few minutes. He relaxed against the wall until he felt in control again, then walked to the front of the planetarium and headed back to the main entrance to the exhibition grounds.

※　※　※

Kessler's return went unnoticed by the sausage vendor, his attention focused on filling the orders of his waiting customers. Opening the unlocked gate near the ticket office, Kessler entered the Park of Culture, glancing at the wedding-cake architecture of the exhibition pavilions and the repeating mosaic patterns set in the cobblestones as he walked toward the Great Hall—the centerpiece at the head of the plaza used for Communist party rallies and meetings. A red-and-white banner was strung above the entrance instructing the faithful in bold letters to: WORK, LEARN, AND LIVE FOR THE PROGRESS OF THE SOCIALIST FATHERLAND. The large clock framed in the gilded dome atop the ornate glass-fronted arched façade had either stopped or was four hours slow. Kessler smiled inwardly at the irony.

As he drew nearer the Great Hall, he saw the Hall of Sport to his right, at the end of a macadam street leading off the plaza. It was obviously a recent addition to the park, its modern architecture a sharp departure from the other structures. The doors to the skating rink were unlocked, and he entered the deserted lobby, continuing past the turnstiles to an access corridor that led around the interior of the building. Passing through one of the many archways feeding off the main corridor, he emerged on the lower level of the arena and descended the stairs past row upon row of empty seats, stopping at the Plexiglas shield erected for the spectator's protection during hockey games. The recessed lights in the dome ceiling illuminated the skating surface, casting the seating area in deep shadows. In a corner at the far end of the rink, he saw a skater moving slowly across the ice, making figure eights, glancing over her shoulder to study the pattern she had etched in the frozen surface before beginning another, more intricate design. He stood stock-still, his eyes scanning the entrance ramps and aisles around the huge arena, but saw no one except the lone skater.

As he approached the area where she was practicing the school figures, he saw her leave the ice through an opening in the boards—the four-foot-high barrier enclosing the rink. She stopped briefly at a small table and lingered over what appeared to be a console of electronic equipment before reentering the rink to the sound of distinctly American rock music that reverberated loudly and clearly from the massive speakers strategically mounted in the corners of the ceiling. Kessler was momentarily startled, not just by the assault on the hollow, cavernous silence of the arena, but by the choice of music. As opposed to the romantic symphonies usually associated with skating exhibitions, the pulsating beat of Kim Carnes's recording of "Bette Davis Eyes" blared from the speakers.

Kessler stopped and watched in awe. He went unnoticed by the leggy woman dressed in a bright red, one-piece short-skirted costume as she skated past him. She was deep in concentration, at one with the music, moving sensuously, with a fluid, supple grace in perfect unison with the driving, up-beat tempo. Using the entire length of the rink, building speed with long, forceful, gliding strides, she exploded into a tremendous leap, straight up, high above the ice, her body perfectly upright, not tilted off its central axis, twirling with blurring quickness, twice . . . three times before landing flawlessly and then moving again with elongated strokes to gain momentum only to leap into another triple jump in combination with two double jumps, and when the mood of the music dictated, into gracefully executed intricate spins. The movements of her body were perfectly choreographed to blend with the music—even her facial expressions were representative of the emotions and lyrical message and not strained from the exertions of her performance. With her every move, the powerful muscles in her haunches and long, shapely thighs flexed and rippled from her loins to her knees. The thin, glossy stretch fabric of her costume clung to her skin, taut across her firm, round breasts, deep rib cage, and tightly knitted abdominal muscles that tapered to a narrow, tiny waist, revealing the details of her magnificent figure, perfect in its symmetry and proportion, sculpted from within by finely toned, superbly conditioned layers of muscle.

The tape was recorded to repeat the music without pause, and Kessler, despite his anxiety to complete his mission, found himself captivated by the dynamic, spellbinding performance. She showed no signs of tiring; if anything, she grew stronger, more relaxed, moving with incredible speed and balance, responding effortlessly to the demands of the strenuous seven-minute program. She was the synthesis of athletic power and aesthetic sensitivity, an elegant, charismatic performer with a natural grace and strength that made the efforts of others look labored. What Kessler did not know was the international reputation of the woman he was watching. Fifteen years ago, at the age of nineteen, she had risen to the top ranks of her country's national team, and for three years, until the age of twenty-two, had dominated the international women's figure-skating competition, setting new standards by which all future women skaters would be measured. She was the first woman to perform triple jumps, once the domain of only the strongest male skaters, and was unrivaled in both artistic impression and technical merit. The most popular athlete in her country's recent history, she had reigned as the women's national, European, and world champion for three consecutive years, retiring from competition at her peak after winning a gold medal at the 1972 Winter Olympics. Now, as a coach for the national team, the only performing she did was for her own enjoyment, coming to work early each morning, using the time to free-skate before her students and the other coaches arrived. Her time alone on the ice was the only consistent pleasure in her life, precious moments of freedom of expression, doing what she did best.

She concluded her performance in the center of the rink with a layback spin, swirling with dazzling speed, her body extended and her back arched to what seemed an impossible degree. Her program ended precisely with the music, and the arena fell silent as abruptly as it had come to life. Standing erect, she glided slowly across the ice toward the opening in the boards. Untying a ribbon that undid her ponytail, she held her head back and with an extremely feminine gesture shook her shoulder-length hair free; it fell softly about her broad, square shoulders and shimmered an iridescent black in the glare of the overhead lights.

Kessler moved from the shadows to the edge of the boards and called out. "Hana. Hana Cernikova?" hoping he had guessed right.

Hana's head turned toward the voice. She made a barely perceptible shift of her weight that set the edges of her skates and changed her course to a slow curve in the direction of Kessler. She stopped in front of him, perfectly balanced on the thin blades of steel, and gazed quizzically at the unfamiliar face. "Yes?"

Upon seeing her close up, Kessler was struck by her physical magnetism. A darkly handsome woman, her face contained no single remarkable feature, rather the composite forming a quiet, haunting beauty. There was a hint of olive tone to her skin, and beneath softly arched eyebrows a sense of sadness reached out from wide, gold-flecked, chestnut-brown eyes. He had the strange feeling that he was looking at an entirely different person from the one he had just seen skating. The bold, provocative presence of the performer had been transformed to a shy, vulnerable reticence in the woman before him; the alluring sensuality remained, but it was not forced or contrived, and she gave no indication of being aware of the effect she had on men, simply accepting without question or design that they responded to her. She shifted positions; the ridges along the front of her long, curving thighs rippled with the tension of a bent sapling, echoing from the demands made of them during the free-skating routine.

"My name is Frank Kessler," Kessler said in flawless Czech, aware that his open stare was beginning to make her uncomfortable. "I'm an American, and I've come for the briefcase that was given to you by one of your students."

Hana's response was to stare quietly back, her dark eyes opaque behind their reflective glow. A light dew of perspiration beaded her forehead, and her chest rose in rhythmic swells of controlled, even breaths. When she finally spoke, it was in a soft, dusky, alto voice. "I'm sorry, I'm afraid I don't understand."

"Miss Cernikova," Kessler said, the urgency of his situation in his tone. "I don't have time for any games or explanations. Just give me the briefcase and I'll leave."

"I am not playing games," she said with a directness that contradicted Kessler's initial impression of vulnerability. "I don't know what you are talking about. You speak our language very well for an American," she added with a touch of cynicism.

Kessler hesitated, watching her closely. He had no identification other than his forged Czech papers, nothing tangible that could prove he was who he said he was.

"The existence and importance of the briefcase the dissidents gave you is known only to the Americans and your STB. If I were with your state security police, I would ask you only once, then use other methods."

Hana brushed at an errant strand of silky, raven hair that curled softly across her temple, the single gesture that betrayed the anxiety and inner conflict behind the calm expression on her face. "I'm sorry, I can't help you."

"Goddamn it, listen to me. People are dead because of this. Friends of mine, and in all probability friends of yours among

122

the dissidents. I don't have much time. Just give me the brief-case."

"I don't know what you are talking about. I have no friends among the dissidents. I am a loyal citizen of my country. And what proof do I have that you are an American?"

Kessler was confused by the contradictory nature of her remarks. In one breath she had denied knowledge of the briefcase and in the next implied that she would give it to him if she was certain he was an American. There was an invisible barrier between them. She was lying, he was certain, but why? Was she frightened by the thought of being caught by the STB, or was he too tired to recognize something she was trying to communicate. He simply wanted to get the briefcase and get out of the country and was growing anxious about the situation outside the ice rink. The empty VB patrol car would draw attention, if it hadn't already, and eventually lead to the discovery of the bodies behind the planetarium, resulting in the area being cordoned off. He had no idea how much time he could spare, not knowing the routine of the VB patrols, how often they responded to radio calls or reported in.

He sensed that despite her calm demeanor, Cernikova was frightened, and perhaps intimidated by his physical size and intensity. Against his better judgment, he decided on the tactic of making her more afraid of him than the STB. He leaned menacingly toward her.

"I *want* that briefcase, Miss Cernikova. And I have no more time to waste. I'm an American and I mean you no harm, but if you don't give me what I want, I'll—"

"I don't believe you are an American."

Tears welled in her marvelous eyes, and Kessler shook off a conflicting instinctive reaction; an acute feeling of protectiveness toward her. Despite the tears, her face held firm in an expression of defiant determination as he racked his brain to try to understand her reasoning.

"Look, lady," he said, slipping into colloquial English with the distinctive accent of his native New Jersey; the tone and cadence of his speech changed drastically from that of the Slavic languages as he gestured emphatically with his hands. "I'm a goddamn American. What can I do to convince you of that? Look at me, for Christ's sake!" He pointed to his soiled, disheveled clothing and to his face—an exhausted mask of bloodshot eyes and black stubble topped with matted, unruly hair. "I spent the goddamn night in the woods. Just stop and think about it. Who the hell else would stand here and argue with you. The STB would drag your ass out of here in a heartbeat and you wouldn't look the same when you came back."

He saw a flicker of recognition in eyes that suggested they had learned not to expect too much of the world. Her guarded expression softened. Choosing her words carefully, she surprised Kessler by speaking in excellent, though heavily accented, English.

"I know an American."

"What?"

"I know an American," she repeated.

"So? You know an American. So what are you—"

"His name is Adrian Dulaney and he lives in Chadds Ford, Pennsylvania."

Kessler was on the verge of explosive anger. "I don't have time for this. What are you saying? What do you want me to do?"

"I would trust him," Hana said, her face now expressing a curious blend of fear and hope.

"I can't leave without that briefcase, Miss Cernikova," Kessler said, his patience wore thin. The United States is a big country. I don't know your friend; you'll have to trust me."

"I will trust *him.*"

Kessler tensed as he saw five teenage girls step onto the ice through the opening in the boards. They were accompanied by two adults who glanced in his direction. Hana had seen them too, and waved to the two coaches who returned their attention to the young girls as they began their stretching exercises.

"I must go," she said, turning back to Kessler.

"The *briefcase,* goddamn it!"

Hana made no reply but stood stolidly before him as though awaiting an answer to an unspoken question.

Kessler's desperation did not affect his sound judgment. There was nothing more he could do, nothing to be gained by further threats. He had fulfilled his mission to the best of his ability. He had no way of knowing where she had put the briefcase, or if she had passed it on to someone else. His exhausted mind could still not fathom her convoluted reasoning. She had in effect admitted that she had the briefcase, and in doing so

124

placed her trust in him. She could have continued to deny any knowledge of it, and yet she had not.

"Is there something you want in exchange? Is that it?" Kessler asked in a final desperate attempt, keeping his voice low as one of the young girls skated by and smiled at Hana. "I can arrange to have someone from our embassy here in Prague contact you and give you the assurances you need, whatever it is you want."

"No!" Hana replied adamantly. "I will talk to no one but Adrian Dulaney."

"Jesus *Christ!*" Kessler was at his wits' end. The two coaches were casting occasional glances in his direction. "All right. I'll relay your conditions to the proper people and they'll do what they can to find your friend. But if you do have the briefcase, don't tell anyone about it and keep it hidden until you're contacted." It was all he could do.

Hana simply nodded. Leaning across the boards to avoid any chance of being overheard by the students and her fellow coaches, she spoke softly to Kessler, lightly touching the back of his hand in what seemed a plea for help. "Please, when you speak with Adrian, tell him that my father died last year."

Kessler stared at her blankly. "That's it? That's all you want me to say?"

"Yes, that is all."

"Is there anything else you can tell me about him, in case he no longer lives in Chadds Ford?"

"He was in your Marine Corps . . . in Vietnam . . . and he was here in Prague in 1975. I have not seen him since." She hesitated, poised to say something else, but turned and skated quickly away, looking back at Kessler, her eyes holding his until she reached the group of student athletes.

Kessler stepped back into the shadows and took the steps up to the exit ramp two at a time. What the hell had he gotten himself into! Another goddamn CIA maze of pitfalls and mirrored rooms. Did Cernikova, a supposedly innocent victim, work for the Agency? How much of what had happened on the mission had they anticipated or known about and not told him? He was too tired and too angry to pursue the train of thought any further. He thought of Shumate and what the tough combat veteran he had served with in special operations in Vietnam had said about all Agency operations. "Clusterfucks, Bear.

That's what they are. Blindfolded clusterfucks where everybody gets screwed and nobody enjoys it or knows who did it or how or why." And now he was dead, the man who had named him "Bear" and been his friend for seventeen years, and survived four combat tours in the Nam. He would miss him. He grimaced in pain and anger as he glanced at the message in four languages—one being English—set in tiles on display boards at each end of the arena near the ceiling for all to see: PEACE.

Leaving the Hall of Sport, he dismissed the urge to exit the exhibition grounds by climbing the stockade fence behind the main pavilion, opting for a less conspicuous route and walking in a casual manner across the cobblestone plaza, using the gate at the ticket office. A quick glance confirmed that the unoccupied VB patrol car was still parked at the curb and the street scene around the sausage vendor and the path leading back into the woods appeared normal. Briefly consulting his map, he crossed the broad thoroughfare against the light just in time to board a tram headed back into the heart of the city. Collapsing into a rear seat, he reached into his shirt pocket and removed one of his amphetamine capsules, popping it into his mouth and swallowing it with a toss of his head. He needed a means of getting close to the West German border and was well aware that any use of public transportation in that direction would expose him to unacceptable risks. His thought processes were dulled, but he forced himself to relax as the tram car lumbered along the tracks, descending the hills through crowded, traffic-snarled streets and across the Svermuv Bridge. Getting off at the first stop on the other side of the river, he headed south, along the sidewalk above the quay. His senses began to heighten, brought back to life as the amphetamine cast its jittery spell. He thought of a possible solution to his problem of transportation, and continued walking for another three blocks to where the Intercontinental Hotel was located on the banks of the Vltava.

8

✂ Most of the semicircular driveway and the parking spaces beneath the portico in front of the Prague Intercontinental Hotel were filled with an assortment of Tatras, Mercedes, Volvos, and BMWs bearing diplomatic license plates from various Eastern Bloc and Western European countries. Taxis, their drivers possessing highly prized permits allowing them to pick up the hotel's guests (and consequently bargain with Western tourists offering more than double the official exchange rate for their coveted currency), took up the remainder of the parking spots. The small square directly in front of the hotel contained an entrance and exit ramp for the underground parking garage, used by those guests not influential enough to command the readily accessible above-ground spaces.

Kessler entered the square and without hesitation proceeded down the steep entrance ramp to the garage. Making a sweep of the partially filled parking spaces, he glanced at the license plates and makes of the cars in the dimly lit subterranean slots. The attendant's glass-enclosed booth was empty, and Kessler noted the pegged corkboard containing the car keys mounted on the wall at the rear. A small bay for washing cars was located adjacent to the exit ramp and the attendant, dressed in blue coveralls and black, knee-high rubber boots, was busy putting the finishing touches on a sparkling Mercedes sedan.

Kessler entertained the idea of simply selecting a fast car, removing the keys from the booth, and attempting to drive the car out of the garage unnoticed. The location of the washing bay diminished his chances of pulling it off. The attendant would have to be dealt with if he was going to get out of the city, let alone anywhere near the border, before the police were alerted to the theft of the car. He approached the front of the Mercedes where the man knelt on one knee facing away from him as he wiped a stubborn spot of grease from an alloy wheel. Glancing to the rear to make certain he was unobserved, Kessler used the knife edge of his hand to deliver a powerful blow to the base of the man's skull, knocking him unconscious and sending him sprawling face down in a puddle of water on the concrete floor. Tearing the cleaning cloths into strips, he quickly tied the attendant's hands and feet, stuffing a wad of the cloth into his mouth and securing it in place with another strip tied at the back of his head. The parking slot on the opposite side of the washing-bay wall was deep in shadows, and Kessler opened the rear door of a Volvo sedan bearing Yugoslav diplomatic tags and dragged the attendant from the brightly lit bay, shoving him into the back of the Volvo where he left him, still unconscious, on the floor.

The keys were in the ignition of the Mercedes, and Kessler reasoned that its West German license plates and rental car sticker affixed to its rear window would not draw undue attention to it when driven in the direction of the border. Turning out the overhead lights in the washing bay, casting the Volvo and the bound-and-gagged attendant into near total darkness, he got into the Mercedes and drove slowly up the exit ramp and away from the hotel. Heading south through the heart of Prague's Old Town section before crossing the river, he took the main route west toward the city of Pilsen, fifty miles away, and approximately half the distance to the border. The highway to the city famous for its brewery was a heavily traveled road, one of two main arteries from Prague through western Bohemia. Kessler had chosen it for the express purpose of being able to spot at a considerable distance any traffic backed up by a roadblock, giving him time to react and change course before reaching the checkpoint and the inevitable armed guards. Consulting his map as he drove, he searched for a secondary road that would take him south from Pilsen to an area of the Czech–West

German border with which he was familiar—one of the crossing points preselected for the team as an escape route during a wartime mission.

Driving without incident to within ten miles of the city, he decided not to press his luck by entering the urban area and risking a possible confrontation with local police if the garage attendant had already been discovered and the car reported stolen. Turning off the busy highway before reaching the outskirts of Pilsen, he headed south at the town of Rokycany and drove into the rolling Bohemian countryside. Carefully studying his map, he took an indirect route, trying to evaluate and avoid the main intersections of the secondary roads leading toward the border that would provide the most advantageous location for roadblocks.

The condition of the roads on which he was traveling deteriorated with each passing mile. Small villages lay tucked away in narrow valleys, their presence revealed by an occasional glimpse of red-tiled roofs and bulbous church steeples that rose above the rural landscape of meadows and streams. Kessler recalled what his mother had told him about the region. Before the Communist collective agriculture system, the Bohemian farmers had prospered greatly, producing an abundance of livestock and fruit, and perennial bumper crops of wheat, rye, sugar beets, and malting barley for the breweries. The privately owned farms were gone now, along with the pride and incentive of the peasant families who had farmed the land for generations, their individual efforts limited to what they could produce for their own consumption from the small state-permitted garden plots, with the government officials turning a blind eye to the common practice of selling the small amount left over to local markets. Farms that were once the most productive in central Europe were replaced with huge inefficient state-run collectives, some incorporating dozens of villages and as many as twenty thousand acres of confiscated land. In the years when even the ignorance and incompetence of the collective farm managers could not negate the richness of the soil and nature's benevolence, and large crops were produced despite the bungling efforts of the five-year-planners, the Soviets, to bolster their own failed agricultural programs, appropriated for themselves through inequitable, nonnegotiable trade agreements what rightfully belonged to the Czech people.

Kessler turned due west onto an even narrower gravel road and the terrain changed from lush, fertile farmland to long-neglected and overgrown fallow fields separated by stands of colorful deciduous forest that covered the low hills rising gently in the distance. Rounding a sharp bend in the road, he barely avoided smashing into the back of an ancient tractor taking up most of the roadbed as it crept along, swaying precariously onto and off of the soft shoulders, its driver oblivious to the near collision and the car behind him. He slowed Kessler's progress for what seemed an interminable period before turning onto a time-worn farm track, allowing the Mercedes to increase its speed as much as the rough, uneven surface would allow.

As Kessler drew nearer the border—now headed more south than west, on a direct route for the West German frontier—the trees gradually changed to the dark green of deep pine forests and the land rose quickly into steeper, heavily wooded slopes. His map showed that he was close to the only intersection within miles, and that the gravel road he was on was leading him directly to it. He considered himself extremely fortunate for not having blundered into any roadblocks up to this point, but he knew that the heaviest concentration of troops would be massed in the area he was now approaching. The West German frontier was less than twelve miles away, and unless he soon found an uncharted farm track leading in the direction he wanted to go, and away from the intersection, he would have to ditch the car and set out on foot. No sooner had he completed the thought than a narrow swatch cut out of the forest came into view. It had appeared so suddenly out of the thick undergrowth that he passed it by, having to back up in order to make the turn. The road proved only a brief reprieve, narrowing to the point where the Mercedes was literally forcing its way through tangled brush that encroached on both sides of what had become a wooded, rocky trail with a downhill grade so steep that Kessler had to maintain constant pressure on the brakes to keep the car under control. His good fortune ended when he heard the undercarriage scrape the high mound of earth in the center of the trail; a sudden jolt followed as the car bottomed out and came to an abrupt halt.

Leaving the now useless vehicle, he began climbing a steep slope leading away from the rocky trail. Following a footpath that led through the damp, pine-scented forest, he reached the crest of a hill that overlooked a deep gorge with a frothing stream flowing through its narrow trough. Sitting beneath a tree, he oriented himself to his position on the map, identifying the terrain features within his field of vision. To his left, a mile away and a few hundred feet below him in a quiet valley, he could see the rooftops of the village of Strazov, and from his excellent vantage point, he spotted something that raised his spirit: ten miles distant, on the West German side of the border, he could see the towering, five-thousand-foot peak of the Grosser Arber rising majestically above the treeline of the Bavarian forest. Using the village and the distinctive mountain peak as points of reference, he estimated he was approximately seven miles from the frontier.

As he walked along the ridgeline, looking for a less severe incline to make his way down into the valley, an intersection of two secondary roads west of Strazov came into view in the hazy distance far below him. The troop transports parked at the sides of the roads and the soldiers milling about and manning the roadblock looked like children's toys from his mountain aerie. He felt the adrenaline begin to rise in his system as he stopped on a rock ledge and again studied his map, selecting a line of march that would take him around the roadblock to a spot where he could wait until nightfall when he would attempt his escape—a spot that would allow him to observe the activities and routines of the border guards and soldiers in the immediate area where he intended to make his crossing.

The Czechs, unlike their East German neighbors, are not blatant about the extent of their security measures to keep their people from escaping to the West. At most of the border crossing points, they have an official border marked by striped boundary posts, and a few hundred yards away, an innocuous customs control checkpoint, usually a small building with a few administrators and guards armed only with pistols who examine passports and visas, exchange the required amount of currency, and search the vehicles and luggage of anyone entering or leaving the country. From the West German side of the frontier, this is all that is visible to the observer. Well out of sight, in many cases two to three miles inside their territory, is the Czech equivalent of the East German "death strip," comprised of a double row of ten-foot-high wire fence with an alarm wire woven into a mesh so fine and sharp that getting a fingerhold is impossible. Between the two parallel fences is a cleared strip of land approximately one hundred yards wide stretching the entire length of the border. The cleared land does not contain the ten-foot-deep cement antivehicle ditch or the deadly antipersonnel mines used by the East Germans, nor does the outer-perimeter fence have the automatic-firing machine guns activated by an electric eye. The area is, nevertheless, guarded by border troops with shoot-to-kill orders. Armed with submachine guns, they patrol in scout cars, or on foot with attack-trained German shepherds at their sides. Unlike the East German's grim steel-and-concrete towers topped with glass-enclosed observation posts complete with machine-gun ports, the Czech towers are wooden structures covered by a roof, but open to the elements on all sides. Spaced to provide intersecting fields of fire covering the cleared strip between the fences, the towers are equipped with floodlights and pedestal-mounted searchlights turned on each evening. The tower guards have radio communications with the foot and scout-car patrols and the nearby guard huts where additional border guards are ready to respond to an alarm in their sector. Though less secure and menacing than the East German death strip, it is more insidious. Anyone managing to get through the East German defenses, once over the final obstacle, steps immediately onto West German soil. With the actual Czech frontier in some areas as much as three miles beyond their border defenses, a successful escape over the fences and across the cleared strip gives the illusion of freedom, but the reality is quite different. The guards on patrol or in the huts, alerted by the alarm wires or the tower guards, still have ample opportunity to mobilize and track down and kill anyone attempting to escape.

Deprived of the aid and fire power of his team, Kessler had no intention of providing the Czech patrols with that opportunity. He had selected the area near the West German border town of Bayerisch Eisenstein for his escape. The road leading to the official Czech crossing point opposite the small resort town wound its way through the low mountains and wooded hills of the Bohemian forest. A lightly traveled secondary road—the crossing points at Furth-im-Wald and Waldhaus being used by the majority of travelers from the West—it was surrounded by dense woods of fir and spruce and steep mountainous terrain;

terrain that was Kessler's element, knowing as he did how to use it to his advantage.

For someone with his training and experience, the area provided a weak spot in the Czech border defenses. In an effort to conceal the presence of the death strip from passing motorists, the parallel fences and cleared strip of land ended twenty yards from the road and were screened by thick stands of evergreens at the point where they merged into a single six-foot fence of commercial welded wire that was barely visible where it cut across lightly wooded fields on both sides of the road until joining the support posts of a permanently manned barricade. A formidable red-and-white striped steel crossbar the thickness of a telephone pole was locked into position against equally sturdy posts—a crash barrier constructed to prevent any vehicle from ramming through it without sustaining massive damage. In the process of calling to mind the details of the barricade, Kessler was again haunted by the memory of his closest friend. "It ain't there to keep us out, Bear," Shumate had said with his humorous down-home wisdom for every occasion, "it's to keep them in. Nobody defects to the East except British homosexual spies." His remark had been in reference to the design of the barricade. The strong side of the crossbar, where it rested against the support post, was to the east, revealing to even a casual observer that its primary purpose was for internal security against the Czech people, effectively restricting the flow of traffic toward the easily breached official Czech border station on the West German frontier only a mile and a half away. The barrier was operated manually, swung open and closed by the armed guards stationed there to secure it and the small area of single fencing on either side.

It was to this permanently manned roadblock that Kessler was headed. Finding an old forester's trail that switchbacked down the side of the mountain, he stayed deep in the woods upon reaching the floor of the valley, circumventing the Czech army troops at the emergency roadblock hastily organized in response to the STB alert near the village of Strazov. He stayed well south of the intersection to avoid any patrols that might be combing the nearby area. Mentally alert from the amphetamine capsule he had taken, he was becoming physically exhausted by the demands of the rough terrain, still feeling the debilitating effects of the HAHO jump and the firefight at the drop zone.

Glancing at his watch, he saw that it was noon; he had now gone thirty hours without sleep. Perspiring heavily in the warm midday air, he stopped at a stream to drink and stripped off his parka, tying it around his waist as he continued forging through the tangled underbrush and climbing in and out of the isolated valleys. He promised himself a much needed rest when he reached the observation point he had chosen near the border defenses, estimating that he would cover the distance of four miles within the hour, giving him at least six hours to relax until nightfall when he would need what remained of his reserves of strength for the crossing.

Nearing the crest of a steep slope, he stopped to catch his breath and consult his map. Unable to locate any distinguishing terrain features in the midst of the dense woods, but sensing that he was drawing close to the death strip, he began to pause briefly every fifty yards and stand motionless to watch for signs of movement among the shadows and the shafts of sunlight that pierced the natural canopy and dappled the underbrush. He listened to the sounds of the forest, for the sudden whir of a bird taking wing, or a squirrel scampering to the safety of its treetop nest—things that could warn him of an approaching patrol in time to take evasive action.

A distant noise not of the forest made him drop to the ground and take cover. It was the distinctive sound of a car engine, coming from the other side of the mountain ridge. Crawling to the crest and out onto a rock ledge covered with low scrub brush, he peered down into the valley. Sixty feet below, at the bottom of the slope, a Czech scout car, bearing four border guards armed with submachine guns, drove down the center of a wide swath of open meadow cut through the forest. The sight of the guard towers and fences directly below him at the edge of the woods left no doubt in Kessler's mind that he had reached the death strip. The terrain beyond the fences changed to low rounded hills of evergreen and chestnut and birch trees and occasional swatches of open fields where the land leveled off toward the border before again rising dramatically into the mountains on the West German side. He watched the scout car move slowly away and come to a stop after descending a grassy knoll. The border guards shouldered their weapons and walked toward what Kessler could clearly see from his vantage point was the barricaded section of road he was looking for. Out of sight of the two tower guards within his field of vision, he crawled back off the ledge and moved cautiously along the ridgeline, closer to the road and to a place of concealment that provided an unobstructed view of where the death strip ended and the smaller, single fence enclosed the area leading to the steel-crossbar barricade. Crouching beneath the low-hanging, conical branches of a spruce tree, he positioned himself to watch the activities of the border guards sixty feet below and forty yards to his right. In front of him, over the tops of the low hills, he could see the Czech customs station a mile and a half to the west, its inspection bays spanning the road, and just beyond that, the evenly spaced blue-and-white striped Bavarian border posts set in a broad meadow coursed by a branch of the Regen River. The sight of the eastern edge of the small town of Bayerisch Eisenstein nestled in the Regen Valley on the West German side of the frontier bolstered Kessler's resolve as he settled back against the base of the tree to observe the routines of the guards and study the terrain.

By the time the sun disappeared behind the horizon, he had carefully considered his options and repeatedly gone over in his mind the route he would follow once past the barricade. Off to his left, the cleared area inside the fences was being heavily patrolled both by guards in scout cars and on foot. Within the past two hours, he had counted three two-man teams with attack-trained dogs entering the woods on the far side of the second fence. Their purpose, he suspected, was to be in position to track and pursue anyone who made it through the death strip. The dogs worried Kessler more than the guards did. Once he got past the single fence near the road, they would be somewhere between him and the border, able to sense his presence and alert their masters long before he could silence them.

With the last of the twilight's crimson glow fading into darkness, he zipped his parka against the cold mountain air, left his hiding place and moved slowly down the wooded slope toward the road. The usual force of six border guards at the barricade had been at least quadrupled from what he had been able to see of the men standing about the area and walking the single line of fencing. With the periodic arrival and departure of the scout cars, he had at times counted as many as thirty troops in the immediate area, and he had to assume that there was at least an equal number on the opposite side of the road in the sector he couldn't see from his present position. He attributed the heavy concentration of men and scout cars at the barricade to the probability that the garage attendant and the theft of the car had been discovered.

Reaching the bottom of the slope, he knelt behind a tangle of brush where the meadow met the treeline. A crescent moon illuminated the grassy open areas with a soft, gray light that occasionally darkened as scattered clouds scudded across the sky. Short stretches of the single six-foot fence were cast in deep shadows by the tall stands of pines that screened the border defenses from the road. Moving along the edge of the forest, he reached a spot opposite the border guard who was patrolling the section of fence that began where the death strip ended and included approximately fifty feet to where another guard stood watch over the section leading to the road. The rest of the troops in Kessler's vicinity were out of his field of vision, concentrated at the barricade, where they secured the roadblock while waiting their turn in the rotation of patrols.

He had selected his target and the area of approach with great care, taking into consideration the lay of the land and the sentry's lack of attentiveness to his duties. The grass leading to the fence was knee-high, providing excellent cover if he crawled on his stomach until reaching the three closely planted pine trees the man passed as he walked back and forth along the fence. He had studied the habits of the guard closely, observing that he had not once looked in any direction other than toward the distant lights of the border town, or back toward the men milling about the barricade. The other sentry, assigned to patrol the section leading up to the barricade, was equally inattentive, walking only part of his post, and lingering for long periods at the shoulder of the road to smoke cigarettes and exchange comments with his comrades manning the roadblock. Kessler had thought long and hard about using his sound-suppressed pistol to dispose of his chosen target, but had decided against it. The sound would not have been heard by even the closest guard, but in studying the man's habits, he had also noticed that he was barely out of his teens, and at least fifty pounds lighter and four inches shorter than he was. There was no need to kill him. Having silently eliminated a number of enemy sentries on prisoner-snatch missions in Vietnam, Kessler knew, with the self-confidence of a big man, that it would be a simpler matter to knock him unconscious, removing him as a threat for the period of time needed to clear the fence and get across the meadow into the wooded terrain and to the border beyond.

Keeping his head low as he crawled on his stomach, he reached the stand of pine trees without incident, rising slowly to his knees, then to his full height among the interwoven branches. Completely hidden from sight and within arm's reach of the sentry's path, he withdrew his pistol from the holster, grasping it by the barrel as he waited patiently, coiled to strike, the familiar icy, dispassionate calm overriding the tension of the moment. He could barely hear the conversation of the men standing near the barricade, and he parted the branches slightly to verify that the other sentry was still facing away from him. His target had reached the limit of his designated post and did an about face, unaware of the cold, calculating eyes that watched his every step while casting an occasional split-second glance in the direction of the man at the road.

Kessler moved with the speed of a synaptic impulse. Reaching out with his right arm, he cupped a bear-paw hand over the sentry's mouth, smothering his cry of alarm and lifting him off his feet as he pulled him into the thick of the branches and struck two solid blows to his temple with the butt of the pistol. The young sentry collapsed silently in his arms. Lowering him slowly to the ground, he took his victim's Soviet-made AKR submachine gun and slung it across his chest. Parting the branches again, he checked on the other sentry, who was still facing in the opposite direction talking to his friend.

Seizing the opportunity, Kessler covered the short distance to the fence with three powerful strides. His forward momentum and the strength in his heavily muscled legs propelled him off the ground to a height where his upper body reached the top of the six-foot fence, allowing him to swing over in one continuous fluid motion. Dropping into a crouch on the other side, he quickly glanced to his left and right and was surprised to see that neither the sentry standing at the edge of the road, nor any of his comrades at the barricade had seen or heard him. Even though the single line of fence was outside the death strip, he had expected it to have an alarm wire, yet there was no indication that one had been activated. The pedestal-mounted searchlights in the guard towers inside the death strip remained fixed in position, casting a bright yellow light across the area between the two fences, leaving the woods in darkness. Unslinging the compact weapon taken from the sentry and cradling it in his arms, he extended the folding stock, wishing he still had his own sound-suppressed submachine gun. Using the AKR would immediately give away his position and bring every border guard in the area down on him. He had taken it against the possibility of a worst-case scenario, but hoped to get by with his silenced pistol if the situation came to that.

His eyes moved slowly across the area in front of him. A narrow strip of grassy meadow was the only open ground he had to cross to reach the woods on his left. Before leaving the ridgeline where he had hidden until nightfall, he had memorized the terrain features, noting that the woods continued toward the frontier, broken only occasionally by small clearings until reaching the broad meadow covering the last hundred yards to the West German border. The grass in the meadow before him was waist-high, untrampled, and unattended, as opposed to the heavily patrolled path along the other side of the fence. Staying in a low crouch, he headed for the cover of the trees, estimating the distance to be no more than thirty yards. He paused repeatedly to listen and look back toward the barricade, still detecting no signs that the sentry he had removed had been missed.

Reaching the edge of the woods, he began moving warily in the direction of the border, pausing and listening as before. His attention was now on the darkened floor of the forest. In the pale glow of the moonlight that filtered through the trees, he could see the well-worn patrol paths that crisscrossed the ground. He thought of the dogs, and he slung the AKR over his shoulder, removing the silenced pistol from its holster and holding it at his side, the hammer cocked and ready to fire, his finger in position alongside the trigger guard. The ground rose and descended gently, dipping into shallow gullies and depressions, and he had covered half of the distance to the border when he heard the cries of alarm from the vicinity of the roadblock. He froze in position as the voices grew in volume and intensity.

"Over here! Over here!" someone was shouting. They had found the unconscious sentry.

Kessler heard the roar from the engines of the scout cars parked at the roadblock and saw their headlights flash briefly up into the night sky then back to the ground as they sped past the barricade and bounced over the shoulder of the road and down into the meadow he had just crossed. One of the cars was moving along the narrow strip of cleared land between the road and the edge of the woods. Two guards in the rear seat had their weapons trained on the trees while the man in the front passenger seat shined a spotlight into the woods, its bright halogen beam penetrating deep into the shadows. A second scout car, carrying four more guards, cut into the woods, taking a crude road that roughly paralleled the path Kessler was following.

He saw no further purpose in stealth. They knew where he had climbed the fence and where he was headed, and the dogs would soon be brought to the area. Breaking into a run, he began covering the remaining distance with long, thundering strides, crashing through the underbrush with wild abandon in an all out foot race for the border before they had a chance to secure the final stretch of meadow he had to cross. His thighs began to ache and go numb, and his lungs burned and his balance wavered with the tremendous demands placed on his already exhausted body. A third scout car carrying six men, dispatched to help cut him off before he reached the border, now followed close behind the one traveling along the finger of land between the road and the treeline.

Casting desperate glances back toward the fast-approaching vehicles, he realized that the race was lost. He could not reach the border before them, and he would provide an easy target if he ran across the final stretch of open ground. Speeding along the side of the road, the two scout cars were still at least fifty yards behind him; the one that had entered the woods was farther away, traveling much more slowly over the rough-cut track, and not posing an immediate threat. Stopping as he reached the edge of the meadow—the blue-and-white striped border posts in view halfway across—he dropped into a prone position still inside the woods. The Soviet-made submachine gun had a thirty-round banana magazine, enough to stop all three cars and kill the drivers—if his aim was accurate. He had used the weapon before, having fired and dismantled it as part of the ongoing Special Forces foreign-weapons familiarization training.

Mopping the sweat from his brow with the sleeve of his parka, he drew the weapon tight into the cradle of his shoulder.

The lead car was coming toward him at a slight angle, heading for the treeline along the meadow where the guards expected him to emerge. Flipping the selector switch to semiautomatic, he held the sights steady on the windshield and the chest of the driver behind it. He fired two shots in rapid succession. The rounds shattered the windshield, deflecting from their intended trajectory and tearing into the shoulder of the driver. The vehicle swerved violently, turning completely over, pinning three of the men underneath and tossing the fourth out onto the ground, where he staggered to his feet, then toppled over.

The scout car bringing up the rear skidded to a stop as it reached the overturned vehicle, its occupants taking cover behind it on the side away from the woods. Kessler fired again, this time aiming not for the men, but for the front tires, which he flattened with two well-placed shots. None of the border guards laid down suppressing fire or rushed his position or attempted to make it to the woods where they could stalk him. Obviously inexperienced, they stayed under cover of the car and fired blindly, well to the right of their target.

Turning his attention to the area behind him, he saw the headlights of the scout car that had entered the woods. The driver was now moving even slower as two of the guards with him aimed their spotlights in the direction they had seen the muzzle blast from the AKR. Kessler was no longer there. He had rolled off to the side and jumped to his feet, running through the underbrush to where the crude road cut through the forest. Taking a position on the opposite side of the road, he waited for the scout car as it lumbered slowly toward him. Switching to full automatic, he opened up as the car came abreast, killing all four men with a sustained burst of fire that emptied his magazine. Quickly approaching the vehicle where it had crashed into a tree, he grabbed a full magazine from one of the dead guards' weapons and ran toward the edge of the woods, checking to see whether the men who had been hiding behind their car had ventured out. Three of them had—one, obviously an officer or senior NCO, shouted to the others, who moved tentatively toward the treeline, diving to the ground when Kessler wounded the man trying to rally them.

Slinging the submachine gun across his back, Kessler broke from cover, calling upon what remained of his strength and will as he ran across the open area. He fixed his eyes on the blue-

and-white border posts, aware that just before he reached them he would have to leap across the steep banks of the branch of the Regen River that flowed through the meadow. Once on the other side, he would be in West Germany. He had chosen the spot with great care, judging it to be the narrowest point in the river—a sharp bend in its winding course where the current was swift and dangerous and it reached a depth of seven feet but was no more than twelve feet across. The leap to the other side was critical. If he fell short, the current would carry him back into Czech territory and possibly drown him. He sprinted the last ten yards to the water's edge. Over the sound of his labored breathing and the blood throbbing at his temples, he heard the sharp crack of automatic-weapons fire all around him. The muzzle blasts echoed loudly off the surrounding hills and back across the meadow. The guards who had been hiding behind the scout car were up and firing. Ignoring the deadly barrage, he adjusted his stride seconds before he reached the river, and, with a leap born of desperation, his arms and legs flailing like a long jumper's, he was airborne, above the turgid, fast-flowing water and headed for the other side. His heels struck the ground first, digging into the edge of the bank, causing part of the soft earth to give way. Feeling his weight pulling him back toward the river, he threw his body forward and clawed at the ground as he landed face down, grabbing fistfuls of grass and driving with his knees to scramble away from the crumbling bank.

Reaching solid ground, he gulped in great breaths of air and rolled onto his side, unslinging the submachine gun as he turned and faced in the direction of the Czech border guards. Five of the men who had initially taken cover behind their scout car were still firing sporadically as they moved across the meadow, obviously unaware or ignoring the fact that he was now on West German soil. Shouldering the AKR, Kessler fired a long burst of low-level raking fire in a sweeping arc across the top of the grass. The advancing troops dove to the ground. He ceased firing at the sight of a scout car speeding along the narrow strip at the side of the road. The vehicle stopped where the men were pinned down, and an officer jumped out, shouting at the troops and ordering them back in the direction of the death strip.

Kessler felt his entire body go limp with exhaustion as he

watched them retreat. The cold mist that clung to the ground along the banks of the river soothed his grimy, sweaty face, and he envisioned himself sprawling in the grass and sleeping for days. The area around him appeared brighter than it was when he began running from the woods, and for the first time he noticed that the floodlights mounted on the roof of the West German border station had been turned on. The station was on the northern edge of the meadow, eighty yards away, and the flurry of activity around the small guardhouse brought the sudden realization that his private war with the Czech border guards had not gone unnoticed by the West Germans. Spotlights on top of the official cars parked at the station flashed on and moved slowly over the section of the meadow where he had leaped across the river. And forty yards behind him, where the open ground ended at the town of Bayerisch Eisenstein, Kessler saw two cars screech to a halt at the side of a road. Four men dressed in the uniforms of the Bavarian frontier police got out of the cars and entered the meadow. Forcing himself to get to his feet, Kessler crouched in the high grass and watched them approach. Removing his shoulder holster and pistol, he tossed them along with the submachine gun into the river, and began low-crawling away from where the frontier police, aided by the spotlights at the border station, had pinpointed his position. He moved slowly off into the shadows, toward a corner of the clearing where a thinly wooded slope bordered the edge of the town.

Although he had nothing to fear from the West Germans, he had no identification other than the forged internal passport identifying him as a Czech citizen. If taken into custody, as any legitimate defector from the East would be, he could not answer their questions without compromising the mission and bringing the wrath of the West German government down on the CIA and the United States for launching an operation from their territory without their consent.

The narrow beams of the policemen's flashlights swept the ground before them as they spread out and continued toward the bank of the river where they had seen Kessler returning the fire of the Czech border guards. They suspected, because the fleeing man was armed, that the Czechs were pursuing one of their own guards who was defecting to the West, but were curious about why the "defector" had not come running toward them with open arms, unless he had been wounded in the last exchange. The low-lying mist hampered their vision in the tall grass, and by the time they reached the river, Kessler was into the woods on the slope leading up to the railroad station located on a rise overlooking the border area.

The street running parallel to the meadow on the eastern edge of the town was lined with a number of onlookers who had heard the noise, recognized it as gunfire, and rushed to the scene. The area in front of the railroad station had drawn the largest crowd. Since the end of World War II, the station no longer served in its former capacity. The tracks leading into Czechoslovakia had been torn up by the Communist regime and the closest rail crossing into their territory was now located thirty miles north at the town of Furth-im-Wald. The Bayerisch Eisenstein station had been converted to a restaurant, popular with vacationers who visited the modest resort town favored by middle-income families in the summer and fall for its miles of hiking trails through unspoiled forests, and in the winter for the nearby skiing. The small border town consisted primarily of reasonably priced guest houses and pensions and an assortment of shops and restaurants.

The customers who had streamed out of the railroad station restaurant were watching the frontier police comb the banks of the river, and commenting on what had happened to the man they had seen escape across the border. A few suggested that he had been shot by the Czechs and fallen into the river. Others stated with great certainty that he had indeed been wounded, but was still lying in the tall grass. Two American servicemen—members of the army's Eleventh Armored Cavalry Regiment unit that patrolled the border in conjunction with the West German forces—were not so sure. Having reached the southern limit of the sector they patrolled, they had stopped at the restaurant to use the men's room before starting the return leg of their trip. The automatic-weapons fire had brought them charging out of the building ahead of the others. They had seen Kessler's desperate leap across the river and witnessed his subsequent suppressing fire directed at the advancing Czech troops. The American sergeant in charge of the patrol stood away from the crowd, watching the darkened slope below the restaurant. "Keep an eye on the jeep," he told the private first class with him. "I want to check something out."

Walking around to the side of the station that faced toward

Czechoslovakia, he stayed in the deep shadows along the wall and drew his forty-five caliber automatic pistol from its holster on his hip. Cocking the hammer, he stood quietly watching the woods where they ended at the old railroad yard littered with long-abandoned equipment at the rear of the restaurant. Reinforcements from the West German border station had joined the search, and more spotlights had been trained on the meadow, but the slope leading up to the restaurant was illuminated only by the moonlight through the trees.

The sergeant heard a rustling in the underbrush, then saw Kessler appear out of the woods.

"Hold it, mac!" the sergeant said as he stepped out of the shadows, his silhouette barely discernible against the wall of the building.

Kessler did as he was ordered, breathing a sigh of relief at the sound of the unmistakably American voice. Raising his hands, he moved forward to get a closer look at the man holding the pistol on him.

"I said hold it!" the sergeant repeated. "You understand English?"

"Easy, sergeant," Kessler said, noticing the stripes on the sleeve of the man's field jacket. "I'm on your side."

The sergeant's face showed his surprise at the discovery that the man he was confronting seemed to be an American. "Then what the hell were you doing on *their* side," he said, gesturing with the muzzle of the pistol toward the Czech border.

"You don't want to know."

"Try me."

"I need your help," Kessler said. "Are you patrolling this area?"

The sergeant nodded, taking a step back, keeping his distance from the huge man standing before him.

"Then you have a jeep."

"Yeah."

"Get me out of here, fast."

"You're not going anywhere until I radio the duty officer. The procedure is to turn anyone coming across that border over to the Germans. What's your name?"

"You don't want to know that either. And you won't be doing the duty officer any favor if you bring him in on this."

The sergeant stared hard at Kessler. He had been on border

144

patrol duty long enough to have heard stories about some of the strange activities other men in the unit had encountered, and wished they had ignored.

"You in the army?"

Kessler nodded.

"What's your unit?"

Kessler didn't respond to the question. "We haven't got much time, sergeant. The Germans are going to realize pretty soon that I'm not down there. They'll seal off the roads and bring in enough troops to start going house to house. If you turn me over to them, believe me, some people you don't want to mess with are going to have a case of the ass. And when the dust settles, guess who's going to lose his stripes while your duty officer skates."

The sergeant lowered his pistol and carefully uncocked the hammer. He recalled the fate of another sergeant in his unit who had pulled border patrol duty and stumbled onto something he wasn't supposed to see. The sergeant had done his duty and taken the men into custody, having had to rough them up in the process; he lost his stripes and was immediately transferred to a backwater post in the United States for his efforts.

"You just said the magic words. You're either a spook or a Green Beanie, or both. Right? Whatever, I don't need this shit."

"Just get me to a pay phone in the next town," Kessler said. "My people will take care of the rest."

"Where you from? In the States, I mean."

"Jersey."

"Figures. Tony Vacarro," the sergeant said, shaking hands with Kessler, "South Philly."

Vacarro glanced around the side of the building where the crowd was still watching the frontier police combing the meadow. "The jeep's in front of the restaurant, the top's up. Get in the back." Taking off his field jacket, he handed it to Kessler. "Ditch that parka and put this on. If the Germans stop us we'll tell them you're with us."

Kessler struggled into the field jacket that was two sizes too small and tossed the parka into the woods. Following the sergeant to the jeep, he climbed in the back as his benefactor pulled the private first class aside and briefly explained the situation. The PFC glanced toward Kessler then back to the sergeant and nodded.

Kessler had no way of contacting the CIA isolation base, nor did he know where it was located, except that it was near Regensburg, having recognized the city as the helicopter taking him and the team to the base had passed over it. He decided to call the battalion executive officer at Bad Tolz and tell him where he was, asking him to contact Lieutenant Colonel Kitlan and advise him of his location and ask that someone be sent for him.

The young PFC patrolling with Vacarro climbed into the front passenger seat of the jeep and turned to Kessler. "J. D. Swartz, from Johnson City, Tennessee," the broad-shouldered, stocky teenager said, reaching back and shaking Kessler's hand with a firm grip. "The sarge says you're one of us. You an officer?"

Kessler shook his head. Swartz's southern twang reminded him of Shumate and again brought back the painful memory of the ambush at the drop zone.

"Good. Then I don't have to call you sir."

Vacarro got in the jeep and started the engine, driving slowly down the access road and away from the restaurant. As he approached the bridge that crossed the Regen River and led to the main road out of town, he saw a police car partially blocking the intersection at the other side. Two Bavarian frontier policemen were stopping each vehicle and asking the passengers for identification and insisting that they open the trunks of their cars for inspection.

"You ready, hillbilly?" Vacarro said to Swartz.

"Yeah. Let's hope they didn't get a real good look at the Clydesdale in the back when he was runnin' across the field." Swartz flashed a good-natured smile at Kessler and said, "We'll tell them your harness broke and you ran away from the beer wagon. And we're just escortin' you back to the stable."

"They know we usually patrol in two-man teams," Vacarro said. "If they ask, we'll pass him off as a new man we're breaking in."

Vacarro stopped and exchanged greetings with the policeman who flagged them down.

"What's up?" Vacarro said. "Another one of those commie bastards tryin' to make it to the good life?"

146

"There has been an escape across the border," the policeman said as he looked into the back of the jeep and saw Kessler, who smiled and nodded.

"Need any help?" Vacarro asked. "We could call in some of our units."

"No. We will find him," the policeman said, glancing again at Kessler's unshaven face and ill-fitting jacket. His disapproval of Kessler's appearance registered clearly. Stepping away from the jeep, he waved them on and walked to the car behind them.

"Good luck," Vaccaro called out as he pulled away and turned west onto the road leading out of town.

Kessler slumped in the rear seat, and for the first time since the mission began allowed himself to relax completely.

Swartz chuckled softly, then began singing in a low monotone as Vacarro sped along the winding mountain road. "Fooled you. Fooled you. Got all pig iron. Got all pig iron."

Kessler made his call from a pay telephone on the outskirts of the town of Cham, half the distance to Regensburg. It was nine o'clock when the black BMW sedan carrying two men in civilian clothes pulled up to where he was waiting in the woods opposite a mile-post marker on a road west of the town. Kessler got into the car without a word, and the three men rode in silence to the CIA isolation base from which the mission had been launched twenty-four hours before.

9

✂ JOSEF MASEK SAT BEHIND a large metal desk in his cramped and sparsely decorated office inside the walled-in compound at STB headquarters in Prague. He carefully read the report just handed him concerning the discovery of the bodies of two VB officers at the planetarium near the Park of Culture. In compliance with his directive to VB headquarters that all serious crimes and unusual incidents be brought to his immediate attention, a brief note was attached to the last page of the report mentioning that a garage attendant at the Intercontinental Hotel had been found bound and gagged; the man had not seen his assailant, but stated that a car he had been washing at the time of the attack had been stolen. Masek noted that the stolen car was the same vehicle found by a local farmer near the West German border less than an hour ago.

Viktor Rudenko stood impatiently in front of Masek's desk. The KGB adviser had been venting his anger and frustration at the news of the American's escape across the border, accusing Masek of incompetence and negligence. His tirade, including threats of punitive action, had been interrupted by the young woman who had brought the VB report to Masek's attention.

"You did not answer my question," Rudenko said, his arms folded tightly across his chest. "Is there any evidence to indicate that the American did not have Volodin's briefcase in his possession when he escaped?"

Masek calmly placed the report in a file tray off to the side of his cluttered desktop without mentioning its subject matter to Rudenko. The ballistics report stated that the VB officers had been killed by multiple wounds from a twenty-two-caliber weapon, and that the wounds had been inflicted at close range and had entered the heads of the victims within millimeters of each other. The mark of a trained assassin, he thought, a man who only kills when he must. The concealed weapons found on the Americans killed during the parachute infiltration had been silenced twenty-two-caliber pistols; a fact that accorded with the street vendor's statement that he had heard no shots, remembering only that the VB officers had bought their usual snack and walked off toward the planetarium. Masek rose from his well-worn desk chair and, turning his back to Rudenko, crossed the bare wooden floor to the window where he stared across the darkened courtyard at the glow of lights from the detention center where those arrested were being held and interrogated. The bodies of the VB officers had been found not more than a ten-minute walk from where he now stood. He had been right. The briefcase had been brought back to Prague and the American had come after it. But what had he been doing at the planetarium? Perhaps a clandestine meeting in the wooded park with one of the dissidents?

"Do not ignore me, Comrade Masek!" Rudenko snapped.

"I'm sorry, comrade. I did not hear your question."

"The briefcase. Did the American escape with the briefcase?"

"The officer in charge of the roadblock at the border said that he was carrying only a weapon he had taken from one of the guards."

"He could have removed the contents and placed them in a coat pocket," Rudenko said. "Your men have just reported that the CIA case officers have all returned to their embassy; attempts to communicate with their agents here in the city have ceased. That would indicate that the American parachutist was successful in getting the briefcase, would it not?"

Masek slowly turned his massive head away from the window, his dark, fathomless eyes making contact with those of Rudenko. "I don't believe the American parachutist's efforts were successful."

"Are we dealing in intuitive hunches now, comrade, or do you have evidence to support that belief?"

"The American infiltrators did not come here for a briefcase. They came to take your scientist to the West. The surviving American was a professional; he did not kill a garage attendant from whom he stole an automobile, or the sentry at the border —only those who posed an immediate threat to him. A professional would not discard the briefcase and simply retain the contents. Your scientist would surely have taken precautions against accidental discovery of any classified documents he had in his possession. He may have had concealed compartments in the case or have secreted microfilm or microdots inside where only a highly trained specialist would be able to find them. The American would have taken the case with him, had he managed to get it."

Rudenko nodded his agreement, his smug expression falsely conveying that he had considered the same facts and that the conclusion was one he had already reached. "Then why have the CIA activities in Prague ceased?"

Masek shrugged. "I don't know."

"And what are your men doing to find the briefcase?"

"We have increased our surveillance of the CIA case officers and, in the event they leave the embassy and contact someone who can lead them to the briefcase, my men have orders to do what they must to prevent it from falling into their hands. But we have them at a disadvantage—most of their agents will have gone into hiding or will ignore requests for meetings because of the mass arrests. That in itself may be the reason for the CIA inactivity. The location of the briefcase is undoubtedly known by one or more of the people we have in custody. Undercover agents in my department who have managed to infiltrate a number of the dissident cells have also been arrested and placed in detention with those we believe are most likely to have been involved."

"And you have learned nothing."

"The process is slow, comrade. Many of the dissidents belong to different cells and are unknown to each other. We must determine not only the ones who were directly involved in Volodin's defection, but members of other cells who have knowledge of what was done with the briefcase. We have arrested over one hundred people, including all of the dissidents who fled Professor Marcovic's cottage, and their friends and associates. The professor is undergoing intensive interrogation now. The answer lies with them, and we will have it soon."

Rudenko's mouth twisted into a grim smile, his insidious wintry-gray eyes mirroring an icy dispassion. "Sooner than you think, comrade. I have assigned a team of KGB interrogators to take over the questioning of the esteemed professor and those who were at his cottage."

"On whose authority?" Masek asked, the muscles along his prominent jawline twitching as he momentarily considered throwing the Russian through the glass panel in his office door.

"Your immediate superiors, of course," Rudenko said. "I also requested that someone else be placed in charge of the investigation. They refused . . . for now. They seem to have more faith in your abilities than your performance would merit."

Interrogations of Czech citizens were always conducted by STB personnel, allowing the KGB to attend only in situations when the subject being questioned had committed an offense against the Soviet Union. Masek had appealed to the head of his department to keep the KGB out of the interrogation process, but had received only a vague promise that his request would be considered. In the meantime, he was to give the KGB his fullest cooperation in a matter of such vital importance to them.

Masek's broad, Slavic face showed none of the disgust he felt at the thought of what the KGB would do to Marcovic. Their sophisticated methods used to break down a subject psychologically—prolonged intensive interrogation with the subject imprisoned in an isolation cell—were of no use to them in the present situation. Nor were the drugs that altered a subject's personality while causing great pain, paranoia, and anxiety. Immediate results were necessary, requiring the use of more brutal techniques with which most of the KGB were more comfortable: terror and torture. And Rudenko, as Masek had witnessed on previous occasions, was a man who enjoyed being knee-deep in blood and broken teeth.

A knock at the office door interrupted Masek's thoughts. One of his assistants entered the room and stood beside his desk, glancing at Rudenko before he spoke.

"The prisoner . . . Professor Marcovic," the man said, diverting his eyes from Masek's intense stare. "They have taken him to the hospital ward in the detention center. The doctors said he is in a coma. He has suffered a cerebral hemorrhage. They do not expect him to live."

Masek dismissed the man with an angry wave of his hand and glared at Rudenko. "You are defeating your own purpose," he told the Russian, who had shown no reaction to Marcovic's fate. "I want your men out of the detention center. They are to have no further contact with the prisoners. If you do not follow my orders, and your actions result in the failure to locate the briefcase you so highly value, the blame will be yours."

Rudenko's response was quick and forceful. "My immediate superior is in direct contact with the Chairman of the KGB, who has taken a personal interest in this matter. I have complete authority to do whatever I feel is necessary to find Volodin's briefcase. The head of your department has been informed of this and has honored the chairman's wishes. My men will continue to aid in the interrogations, and you, Comrade Masek, will not interfere with our work."

"The majority of those arrested are students or members of the academic community," Masek said, sitting heavily in his desk chair. "They are amateurs, but they are not fools or cowards. They hate us, and that gives them strength. Your methods only make them stronger. You are creating martyrs. My way will take a little longer, but I will eventually find your briefcase. Your methods may result in failure."

Rudenko turned to leave the office. "We shall see, comrade. Fear and pain are great motivators," he said, closing the door behind him.

Masek massaged the back of his thick neck with his hand. He knew better than to attempt to undermine or challenge Rudenko's authority—it would only result in his being removed from the case entirely, leaving him unable to even limit the damage the KGB interrogators were doing. He cared nothing about the Soviet scientist or his valuable documents, but he was deeply concerned with the deaths of the border guards and the VB officers. They were Czech citizens, and he wanted those who aided the American found and punished for their crimes. Leaning back in his chair, he stared at the only personal memento in an otherwise utilitarian office of drab, institutional furnishings: a small framed photograph on a corner of his desk. The picture had been taken by a friend ten years ago. A seven-year-old girl, bundled against the cold, a gleeful smile on her face, the condensation from her breath forming a crystalline vapor in the brittle evening air. She was flanked by her mother and father, and held firmly on to their hands as they guided her, skating slowly, unsteadily across the ice-covered pond in the park near their home. Tassels of light blond hair were visible around the edges of the wool cap pulled down over her ears. She had her mother's eyes, eyes that told of the warmth and kindness within. Masek turned his attention from the photograph and rose abruptly from his chair. Leaving the office, he crossed the darkened courtyard, pausing to watch a car speed through the entrance gate and stop a short distance away. Two of his men pulled an attractive young girl from the rear of the car and, each taking an arm, escorted her up the stairs and into the detention center. Masek stared after them. The girl looked vaguely familiar, but he could not remember where he had seen her, finally attributing her familiarity to the short, light blond hair and the large blue eyes that reminded him of his daughter. His wistful thoughts of his family were replaced with those of the distasteful tasks that awaited him during the long night ahead; a night that he suspected would allow him only a few hours sleep on a cot in his office.

✳ ✳ ✳

Two miles from STB headquarters, on the third floor of the American embassy in the Mala Strana section of the city, Adam Purcell and other case officers of the CIA Prague station were gathered in Jordon Palmer's office listening to the instructions the chief of station had just received in a cable from the Deputy Director for Operations at Langley.

"There will be no more attempts to contact any of our agents until further orders from the DDO," Palmer said. "The surviving member of the Special Forces infiltration team has made it across the border. He is in the process of being debriefed by the deputy chief of station Bonn. We'll be kept advised on a need-to-know basis."

The Prague station had been informed of the Prairie Fire Emergency code shortly after it had been received at the mission support site in West Germany. Adam Purcell had again contacted his principal agent, Anton Nemecek, through the radio-controlled tape recorder in the agent's apartment. He had retrieved a message concerning Volodin's death and the survivor of the ambush at the drop zone and about the STB search for the briefcase. The information had been cabled to Langley, and Palmer had received an immediate reply telling him to pull out all stops to locate the briefcase and to continue relaying any intelligence information gathered from their agents. But under no circumstances were they to attempt to locate or assist the surviving Green Beret.

"Did the man who escaped get Volodin's briefcase out with him?" Purcell asked.

"I don't know," Palmer said. "The STB are still beating the bushes, so my guess is that he didn't."

"Then why is the DDO calling us off?"

"He didn't say." Palmer's tone expressed his impatience with his junior case officer.

"I think the briefcase is here in Prague," Purcell said. "And I'm pretty sure the man who survived the ambush came here looking for it."

Palmer fixed a weary gaze on Purcell. "Would you care to tell us why?"

"Two reasons," Purcell said. "As you pointed out, the STB are still rousting the locals, and just before I got back to the embassy, I checked my principal agent's recorder again. There was a brief message about two VB officers who were killed near the Park of Culture. The weapon used was twenty-two-caliber, and they were both shot in the head at point-blank range. Sound familiar? The Green Beret who escaped may have been trying to make a contact when the VB stopped him. And if he didn't get the briefcase, it could still be in the city, and some of our agents will eventually find out who has it."

"The DDO's orders were explicit," Palmer said. "There will be no individual efforts. All of you will catch up on your paperwork until we receive further orders. Anyone who does otherwise will end up in some forgotten cubicle in the bowels of Langley. You have my word on that."

10

✖ FRANK KESSLER HAD GONE directly into the debriefing room upon arriving at the CIA isolation base. He drank most of a pot of coffee and quickly devoured the tray of sandwiches placed before him. His contempt and total lack of respect for Elliot Simpson was plainly evident in the manner and tone in which he responded to the persistent questions from the CIA deputy chief of station who had exercised command and control of the mission. But he restrained himself from overtly telling Simpson what he thought of him and his mission planners in deference to Lieutenant Colonel Kitlan, who had remained silent throughout most of the debriefing. Kitlan sat opposite him, his face expressing his own sorrow and the empathy he felt for the profound sense of loss he knew Kessler was suffering from the deaths of his teammates.

In response to a summons from a code clerk, Simpson left the room, returning moments later with the hard copy of a cable that had just come in from CIA headquarters. A request for background information on Adrian Dulaney and Hana Cernikova had been cabled two hours earlier, reaching Langley at 3:30 P.M. Washington time. The available information had been quickly garnered from CIA files, their contacts at the IRS, Department of State, and the Marine Corps barracks in Washington.

"We've received some preliminary information on Dulaney and Cernikova," Simpson said.

"Then both of them do work for you," Kessler said.

"I answered that question when you first brought it up, Sergeant Kessler. The answer still holds. Dulaney and Cernikova are completely unknown to us, with one minor exception—which I'll tell you about if you give me the chance."

"If the debriefing is over," Kessler said, "I prefer to leave here and get back to Bad Tolz. I've heard enough bullshit tonight to last me a lifetime."

"If you don't mind, sergeant, I'd prefer that you stay and give me your input on this."

"I've told you everything I know. I have no 'input' that you want to hear. I'd like to leave." He turned to his commanding officer. "Sir?"

Kitlan nodded. "You're here on a voluntary basis, Frank. You can leave when you want."

Simpson directed a hard glance at Kitlan. "I'm still operating under the same authority you were apprised of prior to the mission, colonel. I want your full cooperation in this matter."

Kitlan's temper flared. "I am obligated to stay as long as you need me," he told Simpson. "Master Sergeant Kessler volunteered for this mission. The man obviously needs sleep. If the debriefing is over, I see no further point in his staying."

"The point is that I want him here!"

"I'll stay, colonel," Kessler said, wanting to avoid putting a man he respected in a difficult position.

"For the record," Simpson said to Kitlan. "You were ordered to select your best man for this mission. You selected Kessler and he handpicked the rest of the team. The mission was not voluntary. They would have been ordered on it if they hadn't volunteered. And until I receive orders to the contrary, I am still your commanding officer. Is that clear?"

"What the *fuck* do you want?" Kessler shouted, rising from his chair with a sudden explosive fury that alarmed both Simpson and Kitlan. The mental and physical exhaustion and the stress of his ordeal had gotten the best of him, his outburst triggered by Simpson's arrogance toward his commanding officer. "You aren't fit to polish this man's boots, you incompetent son-of-a-bitch."

Feeling certain that Kessler was about to punch the CIA

deputy chief of station, Kitlan stood and positioned himself between the two men and placed a calming hand on Kessler's shoulder. "Easy, Frank. Unfortunately he's right—he is in command," he said, quickly defusing the situation. "If we can salvage anything from this mess it's the least we can do for the men who didn't make it back."

"Yes, sir," Kessler said, backing off and returning to his chair. He drained the last of the coffee in his cup and continued to glare at Simpson.

"IRS records show that Adrian Dulaney still lives in Chadds Ford, Pennsylvania," Simpson began, consulting the report he held in his hand. "Quite comfortably, it seems. He is a wealthy man with a mid-six-figure, after-tax income, averaging four hundred seventy-five thousand dollars a year, all derived from trust funds provided by his parents, who are now deceased. He is thirty-eight years old, no dependents, and he doesn't file a joint return so he's probably unmarried. Judging from the size of his charitable contributions, I'd say that he's a man with some social conscience.

"The information from the Marine Corps is sketchy. He dropped out of Princeton at the end of his sophomore year and joined the Corps. Qualified for Officer's Candidate School but turned it down. He served in Vietnam for one tour in 1968 with Second Force Recon. Most of that unit's records from Vietnam for the years 1968 and 1969 were lost by the Navy in transit from Da Nang back to the States. But there is a record of a citation awarding him a Bronze Star for valor; he saved his commanding officer's life during a VC mortar attack on the company compound. He had a top-secret clearance . . . that seems unusual . . . but helpful. And he was honorably discharged with the rank of corporal. So, as a former member of Second Force Recon, he's reconnaissance trained, airborne qualified, and has combat experience."

Kitlan immediately sensed what Simpson had in mind, and a glance at Kessler confirmed that he, too, was aware of it. Both men remained silent as Simpson continued.

"Hana Cernikova. Thirty-four years old. Three times European and world women's figure-skating champion, gold medal at the Winter Olympics in 1972. Now a coach for the Czech national team. This is where we got lucky," Simpson said. "We have a report filed by our Prague station in April of 1975. Dulaney came to the Prague embassy for information on the procedures involved in marrying a Czech national and taking her to the United States. He was referred to someone he was told was with the political section; unknown to him, the person he spoke with was one of our case officers. Shortly after the interview, Dulaney ran into some problems with the Czech authorities. It seems they didn't want to lose a national heroine to the West and they started harassing him. He reported the incidents to the case officer he had spoken with earlier; he wanted us to grant Cernikova political asylum at the embassy and get her to the States, but that was out of the question. There was nothing we could do for him. The case officer's report states that he advised Dulaney to leave the country before the Czechs arrested him on trumped-up charges. He refused. A week later the Czech Ministry of Interior filed a formal complaint against him with our embassy. According to them, Dulaney had assaulted two of their citizens. Dulaney's version was that he was defending himself against two STB thugs who had attacked him. They locked him up for a week, then revoked his visa and threw him out of the country."

Simpson flipped through the last two pages of the report. "He's a determined man. One month later he made contact with a group of West Germans who specialize in arranging escapes from the Eastern Bloc. Dulaney paid them fifteen thousand dollars to bring Cernikova out. One of the men in the group was an agent of ours and reported the contract to us. They made the arrangements and contacted her, hand delivering a letter from him . . . it seems the STB was preventing his mail from getting through to her. She read the letter, then refused to leave, offering no explanation. That seems to be where it ended. Ten years ago. As far as we know there have been no further attempts to contact her."

Kessler sat up in his chair, his groggy mind suddenly alert. His thoughts returned to the skating rink in Prague. Having listened to the CIA's background information, and with time to reflect on his brief conversation with Cernikova, he now realized what he had seen in her eyes and heard in her voice that he had been unable to isolate and define at the time. It was not ignorance and stubbornness, or a fear-induced reluctance to trust him as he had first thought. It was a toughness and determination, the spirit and the granite will and character found in all world-class athletes and those who have dedicated their lives to being the best at what they do.

And there had been something calculated in her measured words that had eluded him until now. It was not that she had doubted he was an American, only whether he could be trusted. And her message to Dulaney made sense. She wanted out. She had always wanted out, but had stayed behind despite Dulaney's efforts to bring her to the West, probably to protect her father from almost certain retribution by the STB—the loss of his job, a less desirable apartment; Kessler was aware of the many ways in which they could apply pressure to those they were intent on bending to their will. She had been frightened when he spoke with her, aware of what would happen if the STB learned she had the briefcase. But she had conquered the fear, drawing on the inner strength that had become an integral part of her through years of discipline and relentless training and the stress of competition. She was taking advantage of the situation in an attempt to recapture what had been taken from her ten years ago.

Simpson took notice of Kessler's renewed interest. "Is there something you have to add to this, sergeant?"

"Does Cernikova have any connections to the dissident community?" Kessler asked.

"As far as we can tell, no. And our files are pretty complete," Simpson said. "I believe Raven's assessment was correct. Professor Marcovic's niece panicked when she saw her uncle being arrested by the STB, and with the rest of the dissidents on the run, she didn't know where to turn and went to her skating coach for advice and help. There's usually a close bond between athlete and coach, especially when the athlete's event is an individual effort. I doubt that Cernikova initially thought about anything other than helping the young girl. Friendship and protective instincts overshadowed her better judgment. And I think it's safe to assume that Cernikova didn't turn the briefcase over to the STB because she knew they would eventually force her to give up her student. And consequently she had to realize that the STB might find out that the student had had the briefcase and go to work on her. When you showed up she saw a way out of a no-win situation."

"And you're going to send Dulaney in to get the briefcase?"

"I'm considering it, along with a few other things," Simpson said, carefully studying Kessler's reactions to what he was saying. "Our agents in Prague could toss her apartment and the locker room at the skating rink—we might get lucky and find the briefcase. But on the other hand, if we don't find it, and we make a mistake in the process, we could lead the STB to her." Simpson paused for effect. "There's also the option of a direct approach. We could guarantee to get her out of the country in exchange for the briefcase."

"I told you she was frightened, not stupid. She's already stated her terms, and in my opinion you have no choice but to meet them. She doesn't know any of your people and she'd be a fool to trust them even if she did," Kessler said pointedly. "And believe me, she's no fool. She's not going to deal with anyone other than Dulaney—she made that very clear. She's dancing on the edge, and if you spook her you could damn well push her into taking her chances with the STB."

"If she's as smart as you think she is," Simpson said, "she's got to know that the longer she keeps the briefcase the more she's implicating herself. As it is now, she'd have to talk hard and fast to convince the STB she wasn't involved from the beginning."

"And if you drag your feet on delivering Dulaney and getting her out, the STB are going to get to her first. You said they were picking up every dissident they could lay their hands on. They'll eventually get around to the professor's niece. If they haven't already. And you'd better get to Cernikova before that happens, because when she hears about it she's going to start coming apart at the seams."

"I agree," Simpson said. "We don't have much time. Do you have any suggestions? You seem to have developed more than a professional interest in her."

Kessler resented the tone and implications of the last remark. "I'm a happily married man, Simpson. I love my wife and children. I can see where you might be the type to demand sexual favors from a woman in return for helping her, but that's never been my style. I respect loyalty and people who have the courage of their convictions. Cernikova's out there twisting in the wind. She may have ulterior motives now, but she put her neck in the noose for a friend. It's understandable why you can't relate to that; I seriously doubt that you have a personal frame of reference for any act of altruism."

Kitlan couldn't help smiling. Kessler's knowledge extended far beyond his military expertise, having earned an M.S. degree in political science while in the army. He had a quick, agile mind and was extremely well read; his intellect, hidden behind a regional argot and unpretentious manner, was invariably underestimated by people he did not allow inside.

"I meant no offense, sergeant," Simpson said, uncharacteristically apologetic. "I didn't know you were married."

"There's a lot you don't know about me. You're probably arrogant enough to believe that I don't know where this bullshit conversation has been leading. Well, let me save you some time. Use your own paramilitary people to take your boy Dulaney over the fence. You can count me out."

"As long as you're wearing a uniform it's not your choice to make."

"I'll take my chances at a court martial before I run another mission with you in command. You're not talking to some hard-charging greenhorn. I've been around. And I've been around your kind enough to know that you're bad news. You take unnecessary risks and make avoidable mistakes that get people killed. I remember your brethren from Vietnam; their lousy intel maps and their cavalier attitude and reckless disregard for the lives of the men they sent on reconnaissance missions. It was all a goddamn *game* to them, and we were the pawns. They sat in their air-conditioned offices in Saigon and we pounded the bush. They dealt in politics and we dealt in life and death. And when the three-piece suits in Washington called the game to protect their political asses, your boys took their ball and went home . . . in one piece . . . no scars . . . no grieving families . . . no one to spit on your uniform and hit you in the back of the head with a half-empty beer can as you walked through the San Francisco airport."

"Are you finished?" Simpson asked.

"It doesn't matter to your kind. It never did. Not then. Not now."

"Under the circumstances, we did the best we could on your insertion into Czechoslovakia," Simpson said. "We didn't have the time we needed. I'm sorry about the five men you lost, but—"

"Five damn good men! With wives and children! Five friends of mine!"

"And we lost a good agent."

"He was an incompetent fool. The man led a goddamn company of Czech troops to the DZ and never knew it. We were compromised before we even got there. He was armed with a *pistol,* for Christ's sake. One man with a pistol to secure a drop zone!"

"He wasn't compromised before he got to Marcovic's cottage. The STB had one hell of an advantage—they got there first. We had no control over that. It happens."

"It happens when you put together a half-assed mission in a sloppy, unprofessional manner. You and your people may be good at whatever it is you do, I don't know. But I do know you're not good at what Colonel Kitlan and I do. It was your end of the mission that went wrong, not ours."

Simpson dismissed Kessler's final insult with a wave of his hand. "All right. You've pointed the finger. You've fixed the blame. The pressure of the situation forced us to act in haste. We made mistakes. But the problem still remains. Volodin's briefcase is of vital importance to the security of the United States. Now, what comes first with you, personal grievances against us or your country's welfare?"

Simpson cut him off before he could respond, adding, "I already know the answer to that. I've read your service record. You're a fine soldier. You've served your country well, and despite your previous statement, you're not a man to disobey a direct order. You're a professional. I can order you to take this mission, but I'd prefer that you volunteer."

"Dulaney is the key to Cernikova and the briefcase," Kessler said. "You have time to bring in your own special operations people to take him in. Why do you need me?"

"Continuity, for one reason," Simpson said. "You and Dulaney have a common denominator; he was Force Recon, you're Special Forces. You've shared some of the same experiences: special operations in Vietnam, similar training, combat, 'the brotherhood of the Nam,' for lack of a better term."

"What makes you think he's going to volunteer? It's been ten years since he last saw Cernikova. A lot can happen in ten years."

"You'll have a better chance of recruiting him than any of our people. All we've got going for us is a straight patriotic appeal. And we don't want him told anything about the briefcase or Cernikova until we get him over here in isolation. He might tell us to go to hell and attempt independent action. We can't risk that with the stakes as high as they are."

"If he still cares about Cernikova, that's the best way of getting him to do what you want."

"He's to be told nothing other than that he's needed for a mission for which he has special qualifications. One of our special operations people will go with you to show him his credentials and get him to sign an agreement swearing him to secrecy. You get him to commit to the mission and bring him here. We'll take care of the rest. He may not be in love with Cernikova any longer, but the chances are good he still feels something for her. His actions after being thrown out of the country tell us this wasn't just a romantic fling for him. And there's always the possibility he'll respond to the chance to even an old score with the STB. You've had a face-to-face with Cernikova. Once we have him under wraps you can give him her message about her father. Answer any questions he might have about her. Give the personal touch to what you saw, what she said. Convince him of the seriousness of her situation."

"If I get him over here you can use your own people to take him in. You don't need me."

"We have a lot of highly trained paramilitary people," Simpson said, "but not with your unique blend of qualifications for this particular mission. There's no substitute for in-depth knowledge and hands-on experience. Your focus of training for the last six years has been special operations inside Czechoslovakia in the event of war. You speak the language like a native. You know the country, Prague, the people, and in an emergency situation you know every weak spot in their western border defenses better than they do."

"You have local Czech agents who can work from inside to assist your paramilitary people. Between the two groups you've got what you need."

"We're limited in the use of our operational field agents inside Czechoslovakia; we haven't had time to determine who's been compromised within the last two days. Those we're sure of are support agents and pavement pounders. Without you that puts us in the position of having to pull seven or eight men out of our special operations section to equal what you've got going for you, and most of them wouldn't be field agents, so we'd still come up short in your areas of expertise and experience. You weren't compromised on the hay-ho insertion—the only people who could have identified you were the two VB agents you terminated. The garage attendant and the border guard sentry didn't see you, did they?"

"No," Kessler said. "I took them out before they had the chance."

"As you said, you're good at what you do. Damn good. It all adds up to the fact that you're the best man for the job," Simpson said, "and the importance of the mission demands just that."

"You want me to take Dulaney in alone?"

"Colonel Kitlan and I will work on a detailed mission plan while you're recruiting Dulaney. But you're going to need at least two or three men for security on the mission."

"None of your people," Kessler said emphatically.

"Choose your own."

"I want men I've trained with." Kessler looked to Kitlan, who nodded his approval. Turning back to Simpson he said, "Dulaney's been out of the Corps for fifteen years. We don't know what his physical condition is. And even though he's airborne trained we sure as hell can't insert him on anything as complicated as a hay-ho jump."

Simpson relaxed with Kessler's unspoken commitment. "We'll have something worked out by the time you get back."

"There's a time element to consider," Kessler said, his mind now attuned to the mission. "I've got to get to the States, recruit Dulaney, get back here, prepare him for the insertion—at least refresh his memory on certain tactics and procedures. The STB may get to Cernikova before we're ready."

"We'll give you something to knock you out so you can sleep for five hours," Simpson said. "We had your class A uniform brought here. You can shower, shave, and change clothes before you leave. We'll have one of our aircraft ready for departure at four thirty A.M. With a six-hour time difference in our favor and an eight-and-a-half-hour flight, that will put you at the Dover Air Force Base tomorrow morning at seven A.M. eastern standard time. Chadds Ford, Pennsylvania, is on the Delaware border, a short hop from Dover. We'll have a chopper standing by for your arrival. I want you and Dulaney back here by this time tomorrow night, so you've got to get him to commit fast.

Within two hours. As soon as you return, he'll be briefed on the mission. You'll have all of the following day and half of the next to prepare him. You'll work with him on a one-to-one basis. Colonel Kitlan and I will brief the other men you select for your team. I want to launch the mission no later than nine P.M. on the third day—less than seventy-two hours from now. That's all we can give you to get him ready for a final briefing, and that's pushing our luck."

"If Cernikova is compromised by her student and talks to the STB before my men get there," Kitlan said, "they'll use her to set them up when they make contact with her."

Simpson disapproved of discussing Agency procedure with outsiders, but considering the circumstances he made an exception. "The Company has an Office of Technical Services regional support base in Frankfurt. The DDO has already dispatched our best wireman to Prague, an audio technician, under diplomatic cover. He's taking in some state-of-the-art listening devices that will allow us to monitor Cernikova's conversations from a considerable distance. We can't risk breaking into her apartment to wire it, as I mentioned earlier—we could inadvertently bring her to the attention of the STB if we're spotted. If that happened, or if her student is picked up and talks, and we believed that Cernikova's arrest was imminent, the only option we'd have left, if we had enough lead time, is to get to her before the STB, kidnap her, and try to force her into giving us the briefcase. I don't have to tell you how little appeal that holds for any of us. If that gambit blew up in our faces the fallout would reach all the way to the President."

"If she spots your surveillance," Kitlan said, "she might panic. She has no way of knowing you're not STB."

"It's a chance we have to take. We've got to know what she's doing. We'll use both mobile and fixed surveillance. Depending on the circumstances we'll vary it between loose and close. But we have to stay with her every minute. Needless to say, our case officers at the Prague station can't go anywhere near her. The local agents we're certain haven't been compromised will keep her under twenty-four-hour surveillance. If she has a car, and depending on where she parks it, we might risk putting a directional indicator transmitter in it—that'll make it easier to follow her without any danger of being spotted."

"Do you have any informants inside the Czech government who can let you know what the STB is up to?" Kitlan asked.

Simpson hesitated, but answered the question, deciding not to hold back. "We have a penetration agent inside the Czech Ministry of Interior . . . and a few in other places with knowledge of STB activity. None of them have contact with the dissident community or any other agents who do, so they're in no danger of being compromised by anyone the STB has arrested. They'll all be alerted to the immediacy of the situation. If the STB learns about Cernikova and tries to use her to draw us in, we'll know it. If they don't learn about her before we're ready, we've got the upper hand—this time we know who we're after and they don't."

"Whatever means of insertion you and Colonel Kitlan decide on," Kessler said, "I'm going to need at least one local field agent on the other side for transportation. Where are you going to get him?"

Simpson inferred the unspoken criticism Kessler intended with his question. "I have authority to activate a sleeper agent. A man who has been in place for years and has never been made operational. I assure you, his cover is secure, he's competent, highly trained, resourceful, and unknown to anyone on the other side."

"What's he trained for?" Kitlan asked.

"To organize partisans and work behind the lines with unconventional warfare units like yours in event of war. He was trained at Camp Perry, and he's damn good." Simpson turned to Kessler. "Who do you want to go with you and Dulaney?"

"Sergeants Natalie and Hawke," Kessler said, glancing at Kitlan, who again nodded. Kessler had chosen them not only for their abilities, but for the fact that of the remaining six members of his team they were the only ones who were not married.

"They'll be here when you get back," Simpson said.

"If your sleeper agent turns out to be as unprepared and unqualified as Raven was," Kessler said, "I assure *you,* I'll do a one-eighty and bring my men and Dulaney back over the fence immediately."

"Understood," Simpson said.

✳ ✳ ✳

Kessler stood in the cold predawn air in front of a large hangar at the north end of the CIA isolation base. He had slept soundly for five hours but still felt tired, mentally and physically. Snugly anchoring his beret at a jaunty angle, he watched a sleek Gulfstream G-3 twin jet aircraft—unmarked except for its registration number—taxi up to the tarmac, its engines idling at a high-pitched whine as it swung into position and stopped parallel to the hangar. The plane and its two-man crew had been brought in from Frankfurt where it was operated as a special-mission aircraft under the cover of a CIA proprietary company.

Saluting Lieutenant Colonel Kitlan and nodding to Simpson, Kessler mounted the steps and entered the waiting aircraft. The copilot, a bright-eyed young man dressed in a blue blazer and gray slacks, immediately closed and secured the door behind him. The luxuriously appointed cabin was capable of carrying nineteen passengers, but in its present spacious configuration was fitted to include just six large leather-covered armchairs that swiveled and reclined, and a sofa and two easy chairs arranged in a conversation grouping.

"Make yourself comfortable, sergeant," the copilot said with a sweep of his arm. "You're the only passenger. There's a john at the other end, a fully stocked bar next to the sofa. Sandwiches in the refrigerator."

"I think I'll just try to get some more sleep," Kessler said, admiring the luxury of his surroundings; he had never been in a private jet before.

"The sofa pulls out into a single bed," the copilot said. "When we reach cruising altitude, I'll come back and set it up for you. You can strap yourself in and I'll wake you when we're fifteen minutes out of Dover."

After the copilot had returned to the cockpit, Kessler took off his uniform coat, stuffing his beret through an epaulet, and hung it in the small closet at the entrance to the cabin. Sitting in one of the leather recliners and fastening his seatbelt, he took the extra sleeping pill Simpson had given him and swiveled the chair to face toward the window where he stared at the night sky as the aircraft taxied away from the hangar. He thought of Cernikova and what might happen to her, and of the man he would soon be traveling across an ocean to recruit for a mission he could tell him nothing about. But most of all, he thought about going back in, and the conflicting feelings he had about that. There was no fear or apprehension, no omens of tempting the gods by going over the fence again, rather an anticipation not unlike what he had felt before his missions in Vietnam. The past two days had been the first combat he had experienced since the war, and it evoked a deluge of memories now that it was over. His most privately held thoughts, thoughts that occasionally stirred from the depths of his soul and that he had never confided to anyone for fear of being misunderstood, dominated his mind. He was not a war lover, he harbored no macho blood lust or death wish, nor was he lacking in instincts for self-preservation. He was a loving father and husband, but at times he truly missed what he had found and left behind in the jungles of Southeast Asia. The war still held a fascination for him and always would. His only regrets, then and now, were that they had not been allowed to win and had gambled their lives for men who never had any intentions of letting them win. It had been the greatest adventure of his life. He had performed at his fullest potential, it had brought the best out in him. Weighed on the scales and not found wanting, he had learned things about himself that most men never know. And he believed that nothing would ever equal it again. Nothing, that was, until now.

He mourned the deaths of his teammates and friends, as he had those who had died beside him in the jungle, but deep inside he believed that we all owed God a death and that there were far worse ways to die, less meaningful and less honorable, than in the service of one's country. There had been times when he found himself thinking that he would gladly relive his five years of combat in Vietnam, and he suspected that one of the reasons he had made a career of the army was to be there and ready if the opportunity presented itself again. He had fond memories of the friendship and courage and comradeship, and vivid recollections of the awesome power at their beck and call, the exhilaration of battle and the spine-tingling, nerve-fraying life-and-death challenge of reconnaissance missions behind enemy lines—the ultimate game of hide-and-seek, hunting and being hunted by an elusive, determined enemy who meant to kill you.

But there was the cautious side of his personality warning him that what he was remembering was being viewed at a distance and had gained an illusory retrospective appeal, filtered through the calm and relative boredom of the intervening years and enhanced by a memory that had become selective and self-serving, placing the pride and the glory out of all perspective to the brutality, the terror, the evil, the callousness, and the cost in terms of human pain and suffering and loss. But regardless of his rationalizations, regardless of the rightness or wrongness of his thinking, something that had been missing in his life was now back, and he wondered if he was better or worse for its reemergence.

The roar of the two Rolls Royce Spey engines, responding smoothly to the demand for full power as the G-3 streaked down the runway, was only a faint, distant sound in Kessler's ears. He was asleep, adrift in his memories, before the landing gear was retracted into the belly of the aircraft.

11

✖ THE DIRECTOR OF THE Central Intelligence Agency had been in his office since 4 A.M., carefully monitoring the Deputy Director for Operations' decisions and replies to the heavy flow of cable traffic from Prague and the CIA isolation base in West Germany. His displeasure over the telephone conversation he had just completed with the Secretary of State was evident in his expression.

"Our ambassador to Czechoslovakia is getting wise to us fast," he said to the DDO, who had just entered the office in response to his summons. "He's picked up some rumblings through the diplomatic community and he's beginning to suspect that we're running a paramilitary operation on his turf. Our Prague station chief is stonewalling him, as instructed, but he wants some answers."

"How much does he know?" Tom Dyer asked.

"Nothing concrete," Stevens said. "Just rumors, but he's been around, and there's too much going on to hide it all from him. He sent an eyes-only/NODIS cable to the Secretary of State and asked him to demand the details from me. The secretary's on the Trojan Horse bigot list; the President informed him about the mission when he gave the go-ahead. He's managed to calm the ambassador without telling him anything, but he suggested that in the event the rumors spread, we should at least partially cover our flanks and comply with the law to a limited extent by briefing the chairman of the Senate Intelligence Committee."

"Who else would have seen the no-distribution cable?" Dyer asked.

"Possibly no one. But we have to assume that the insiders and horseholders on the seventh floor at State—four or five people who don't need to know—are aware of it. And they'd take great pleasure in leaking whatever they know to Senator McConnell and his Intelligence Committee staff, especially if it can embarrass us."

"Are you talking about giving the senator a full briefing on Trojan Horse, or just the attempt to get Volodin out?"

"A full briefing. That crusty old warhorse wouldn't settle for anything less," Stevens said. "As DCI I'm required by law to brief both the Senate and the House Intelligence Committees on all covert action. If we take McConnell into our confidence and he's aware of the stakes involved, he'll understand the necessity for utter secrecy. He's the strongest supporter we have in the Congress, if anything about the Special Forces' mission leaks out, he'll keep the rest of the committee in line."

"How are you going to handle the House committee?"

"The chairman and McConnell are close friends. He can help us out there, too."

"When do you want to brief him?"

"I just called him," Stevens said. "He'll be here within the hour."

"I'll contact Jack Stallfort," Dyer said, knowing that the head of the Directorate of Science and Technology would be needed to conduct the technical side of the briefing.

"I've taken care of it. He's on his way. When he gets here tell him what we want and have him bring his charts, graphs, and whatever else he needs to my office."

✳ ✳ ✳

Senator Michael McConnell drove up to the steel door barring the entrance to the VIP garage beneath CIA headquarters. He nodded to the guard who, having been told to expect his arrival, studied the five-term senator's well-known face before allowing him to go on down to the exclusive parking area below.

An Office of Security guard dressed in civilian clothes opened the door of the senator's car as it came to a stop. "The Director is waiting for you in his office, senator. If you will follow me."

"I know the way, son," McConnell growled.

"Just a courtesy, sir."

"Bullshit," McConnell replied good-naturedly. "You're afraid I'll roam around and find out what you're really up to over here in your den of iniquity."

"Yes, sir," his escort said.

Another security guard opened the door to the DCI's private elevator as the two men approached. McConnell nodded a curt greeting to the dour-faced man and stepped inside. Exiting on the seventh floor, he walked briskly past the glass-enclosed guard station and through the anteroom, ignoring the secretary as he knocked once and entered the DCI's office without waiting for a response.

"It's six o'clock in the goddamn morning, John. This better be good," McConnell said, shaking hands with Stevens and sitting in a chair opposite his desk. "Whose harbors did you mine this time?"

"You're close," Stevens said with a smile, handing the senator a cup of coffee—black with three sugars, the way he liked it. The two men had known each other for twenty years and were close friends despite their differing views on the degree of autonomy the Agency should have from the legislative body. Their friendship and shared opinions on most areas of national policy stemmed from a common background: Stevens had served three terms in the House of Representatives early in his government career, and both men were combat veterans of World War II; McConnell with the army in Europe and Stevens with the navy in the South Pacific. The senator, having stayed on with the high commissioner's office in Berlin for three years following the end of the war, had developed an abiding disdain and distrust of the Soviets that bordered on blind hatred, and the Defense Department and the CIA could always count on him as a staunch ally when it came to matters of national defense.

"I'll get right to the point, Mike," Stevens said. "We ran a mission into Czechoslovakia using a six-man team from the

Tenth Special Forces Group at Bad Tolz. We failed to get what we were after. Five of the men were killed. One just got back out. They went in sterile, so they can't be tied to us for propaganda purposes. We're in the process of organizing a second attempt."

McConnell's stunned expression was one seldom seen after his many years of exposure to CIA intrigues. "I take it the President knows about this."

"He gave the go-ahead."

"What the hell is going on? And why wasn't this brought before my committee?"

"The bigot list is severely restricted on this one, Mike."

"Your friendship and trust overwhelm me," McConnell said. "Why didn't you at least keep it in your own arena, use your own people instead of involving hot-war troops?"

"Time element. We needed qualified people ready to go at a moment's notice."

"As you damn well know," McConnell said, "you've violated one of our own laws by not informing both the Senate and House Intelligence Committees, not to mention a flagrant violation of international law that can be easily interpreted as an act of war."

"You'll have to hear me out on this," Stevens said.

"You're goddamn right I will. What was the purpose of the mission?"

"One of our Soviet agents, a scientist, jumped the gun before we were ready for him and defected in Prague. We had to get him out."

"Where is he now?"

"Dead. Heart attack."

"Then why another mission?"

"He had some valuable documents, intelligence information vital to our national security, in his briefcase. We couldn't get to it on the first mission, but we've got it located and are preparing to go back in."

"I think I already know the answer to this," McConnell said, "but humor me. Why am I being honored with this privileged information now?"

"The truth?"

"That would be nice."

"Our ambassador to Czechoslovakia is getting wise to our

operation. He may have stirred up a few people at State trying to get the answers our Prague station chief wouldn't give him. The secretary has him under control, but some of what he said might leak out to your committee. We're going to need your help to keep the lid on if it does."

"Enough of the vague crap, John. I want to know what the hell is going on. What's so important about the scientist and his briefcase?"

Stevens moved to his desk and pressed a button on the intercom. "Have the DDO and Stallfort come in," he told his secretary. When the two men entered, he directed them to the conference table off to one side of the room, where he and the senator joined them.

"You already know my Deputy Director for Operations," the DCI said to McConnell. The two men shook hands. "And this is Jack Stallfort, head of our Directorate of Science and Technology."

At a gesture from Stevens, the austere, soft-spoken scientist pushed his wire-frame glasses farther up on the bridge of his nose and nervously cleared his throat as he began speaking. "As I'm sure you are aware, Senator McConnell, the Soviet Union's technology in electronics, microminiaturization, and computers is at least seven to ten years behind ours."

McConnell nodded, taking a cigar from his coat pocket and lighting it. A puff of blue white smoke curled upward in the morning sunlight now streaming through the large glass wall beyond the DCI's desk.

Stallfort winced at the pungent odor from the cigar and continued his briefing. "The only hope they have of achieving parity and keeping pace with us is to bypass the lengthy and expensive process of research and development, eliminating thousands of man-hours and tens of millions of dollars in development costs. As you well know, the only way they can accomplish that is to steal our technology. Consequently, the KGB has been maintaining a priority emphasis aimed at our key technology centers, primarily the Silicon Valley area in California. Their efforts are coordinated with their weapons-systems design teams who give them what can accurately be described as a shopping list. They place a high priority on both hardware and software, but their main focus is on computer-aided design and automated manufacturing systems."

"I'm familiar with the technology transfer problem," McConnell said impatiently, his gaze shifting to the pigeons fluttering about on the balcony outside the glass wall.

"The Soviet missile guidance systems, while they're steadily improving, are still primitive compared to ours. When you're aiming at a city and you miss by a mile with ten megatons, it doesn't mean very much, but when your target is a hardened missile silo, 'circular error, probable' is all-important in order to assure that your enemy cannot retaliate with any great force." Stallfort paused, shifting positions in his chair to angle his body away from the cigar smoke that was drifting into his face. "So, the area of improvement most important to the Soviet Strategic Rocket Forces continues to be accuracy, followed closely by reliability, reduction in missile-components size allowing for more warheads per missile, along with reduction in overall size, which increases operational flexibility by enabling them to launch from mobile carriers that are extremely difficult, if not impossible to target. Thanks to the laws you helped get passed and the new powers given the Customs Department, we have had some success in stemming the tide of technology transfer, but it is still a serious problem."

"Excuse me . . . Stallfort," McConnell said. The scientist's pedantic delivery was beginning to irritate him. "You'll forgive me if I ask you to gloss over the things that my committee has already been briefed on."

"Yes, sir," Stallfort said, skipping two pages of material he had intended to include in his briefing. "The Directorate of Science and Technology includes, among other things, the Foreign Missiles and Space Activities Center, the Office of Special Projects, the Office of Research and Development, and the Office of Computer Services. Four years ago the heads of these various sections, along with myself, came upon an idea for using the Soviets' needs to our advantage. We presented the idea and thesis to the DDO and the DCI, who agreed with the concept and subsequently got the President's approval to proceed with the developmental stage. Only the development team—which was expanded to include select personnel from IBM's Federal Systems Division in the private sector—and a special group chosen from within the National Security Council were privy to the operation that had been code-named Trojan Horse.

We completed our work in fourteen months and the President approved deployment."

"Who's on the bigot list?" McConnell asked.

Stevens told him the names of the nine members. "That's it, except for the scientists who put it together."

McConnell's bruised ego quickly recovered with the knowledge that people who outranked him in power and prestige, some closer to the President than he was, had not been included. "Okay, tell me about Trojan Horse."

"The concept originated with a discovery we made when the navy recovered a Soviet submarine-tracking ocean buoy they had somehow lost and was adrift at sea. Upon close examination of the buoy, we found that the printed circuit boards inside were identical, pin-for-pin compatible, with those produced by Texas Instruments." Stallfort removed two glossy photographs from his portfolio and handed them to McConnell. "The Soviets had apparently managed to acquire the boards through industrial espionage, despite the fact that they are on a restricted list of defense-sensitive products. Other pieces of Soviet weapons systems we acquired through various means began to reveal a pattern: they were duplicating our technology without any attempt to modify what they had stolen. They had been so meticulous in some cases that they had even copied the manufacturer's mark." Leaning across the conference table, he pointed to the Texas Instruments mark on the photograph of the circuit board taken from the Soviet ocean buoy. "The copies were usually larger, due to their inability to produce them on the same scale as we do, but they were identical in all other respects. Further discoveries told us something else: the Soviets had learned from their past mistakes. They were no longer simply trying to adapt our designs to their systems, which often led to failure, but were now developing their systems around our designs."

"Creative bunch of cretins," McConnell said.

"They do the best they can with what they have, senator," Stallfort said. "In certain areas they're very creative."

"If they don't have the brains and talent to make what they steal from us," McConnell asked, "how can they copy it?"

"They've become very adept at reverse engineering."

"Define the term," McConnell snapped.

"It involves using microphotographic techniques to copy the

176

original schematic design. They strip away the protective coating on the stolen microchip and photograph the successive layers of etched patterns. The masks needed to manufacture the chips are derived from the photographs. It's a tedious process that can take two experienced designers as long as six months to unravel the complexities of a central-processing-unit chip, but that's one sixth of the time it would take the Soviets to design and produce it themselves . . . if they had the technical sophistication to do it . . . which they don't when it comes to our latest technology."

McConnell nodded. "Go ahead."

"We decided to help them with their shopping list without them knowing it," Stallfort said. "We couldn't just give them anything—we had to make sure it was something that would make the hair on the back of their necks stand up. A legitimate espionage coup."

"Why the hell would you want to do that?" McConnell asked.

"To give them enough rope to hang themselves," the DCI interjected.

"Precisely," Stallfort said. "At first we considered using a computer 'virus,' also known as a software 'mole,' to infiltrate and attack their computer system. Once fed into a computer, it can be left dormant for months or years until it is activated by certain preconditions. It would then theoretically spread throughout the entire system, disrupting its operations to the point of rendering it ineffectual. We gave up on that approach due to the uncertainty of whether the Soviets would use the software containing the 'mole' as we intended it to be used. And there were other complications, primarily the lack of intelligence information as to how Soviet military computers are linked. They may or may not be centrally controlled. The computers that serve one ICBM missile launch control center could very well be isolated from those at other launch centers, preventing the 'virus' from spreading throughout the entire system."

Stallfort poured himself a glass of water from the carafe on the table, taking a drink before continuing. "The objective was to affect their first-strike capability, and their ability to retaliate if we exercised the same option—speaking hypothetically, of course. To accomplish that we had to ensure that what we 'gave' them was, technologically, a quantum leap forward, so vastly superior to their existing technology that the Strategic Rocket Forces would put it to immediate use in their missile development program. We decided on high-quality integrated circuits—the basis for all modern weapons systems. Possessing our recent improvements in that area would make it possible for the Soviets to attain accuracy, reliability, reduction in size, and operational flexibility almost equal to what we now have—all the things on their shopping list necessary for them to upgrade their existing missiles and further improve their new ICBMs."

"So what did you give them?" McConnell asked. He was beginning to feel uneasy about what he was hearing.

"In essence, by letting them steal a circuit board designed for the guidance module in our MX missile, we gave them the technology for our new generation gallium arsenide VHSICs— very-high-speed integrated circuits," Stallfort explained. "The VHSICs provide complex guidance system functions in small, ultrareliable packages that, due to the use of gallium arsenide, as opposed to silicon, are more radiation resistant and operate over a wider temperature range that enables them to withstand the severest military operating environments. Their processing speed is one hundred times that of anything the Soviets now have."

The senator shifted uneasily in his chair, casting a disapproving glance at the DCI. "I hope you're getting to the good part real soon," McConnell said. "So far I don't like a damn thing I've heard."

Stallfort smiled confidently and continued.

"Due to the sophistication of the technology involved, reverse engineering the VHSICs would have been useless to the Soviets, and negated our purposes, without their having the ability to duplicate them and manufacture them in large quantities. That left us with no option but to make certain they also got the fabrication techniques and processes, as well as the automated engineering system necessary for computer-aided manufacturing of what they had acquired."

"Goddamn, son," McConnell said. "It sounds like you've given away the store."

"If we did anything less, senator, Trojan Horse wouldn't have worked."

"How did you arrange for all of this to conveniently fall into their hands without them realizing you were making it possible?" McConnell asked.

"The circuit board containing the critical central processing unit—the functions of which I'll explain in a moment—was smuggled out of a defense subcontracting firm by one of the engineers who had worked on the firm's design team for the MX guidance module. The engineer in question had been selling defense secrets to Sovict agents in this country for two years before we caught and turned him. We began operating him as a double agent. We continued to provide him with genuine low-level defense-related intelligence information until we were ready to implement Operation Trojan Horse. At our instruction, he delivered the circuit board to his KGB contact. It was taken immediately to the Soviet consulate in San Francisco and flown to Moscow in a diplomatic pouch the same day."

McConnell shook his head slowly, casting worried glances at Stevens and Dyer. The DCI and DDO remained silent as Stallfort continued.

"Within six months we learned that the Soviets had put the highest priority on obtaining the components for a computer-aided manufacturing system for VHSICs. Every KGB agent involved in the acquisition of defense-related technology in the United States was assigned to the project. That told us they had realized rather quickly the value of the circuit board and that they were elated rather than suspicious about getting their hands on it. The manufacturing system had to come from another source and required more complicated arrangements. The Soviets were offering millions for the components, and the underground network of dummy corporations in this country and West Germany who export restricted state-of-the-art computer technology and smuggle it into the Soviet Union pulled out all of the stops to get them. We made certain they got everything they needed without making it too easy. We even arranged for the Customs Department to confiscate two separate shipments before eventually letting all of it get to West Germany, where it was transshipped through Austria to Vienna and loaded on a Soviet Aeroflot jet that took it directly to Moscow."

McConnell's face finally brightened. "You gave them equipment to manufacture a circuit board for their missile guidance systems, and the design of the circuit board is faulty."

"It's a little more involved and insidious than that, senator,"

Stallfort said, his somber expression relaxing into a small smile. "If we had simply slipped them a faulty design, they would have found that out through testing, and that would have been the end of our operation."

"Then what the hell *did* you do? Get to the point."

Stallfort withdrew an eight-by-ten-inch schematic drawing from his portfolio and placed it on the conference table before the senator. "This is a drawing of the internal architecture of the central processing unit on the circuit board the Soviets now have. With a few exceptions, it is in all respects identical to the CPU that is used in our MX guidance system. The drawing is enlarged for the purposes of this briefing. What you are looking at is not even the size of the nail on your little finger."

McConnell stared at the drawing, understanding nothing of what he saw: a network of small squares and rectangles connected by lines, their functions explained in a technical language that was alien to him.

"The central-processing-unit chip is the key component part, the brains so to speak, of the circuit board in question," Stallfort said. "It is, in effect, the control center for the missile's on-board guidance computer. It executes instructions and puts things into and takes things out of memory; it tells the input and output sections of the computer where to send information and selects the information that is sent. It is interconnected by integrated circuits to the other chips assembled on the board."

Using the tip of his pen, Stallfort pointed to the "instruction decode" section on the drawing of the central processing unit. "This is where their CPU and ours differ. We've added a 'bandit microcode' and a rudimentary receiver that in no way affects the CPU's normal functions, yet it gives us complete control over those functions whenever we want to exercise it."

"When they . . . reverse engineered this CPU chip, why didn't they see your 'bandit microcode'?" McConnell asked.

"They undoubtedly did," Stallfort said, a sly smile spreading slowly across his face. "But they didn't know what they were looking at. The bandit microcode and receiver were designed as an integral part of the CPU and appear no different from the maze of other subminiaturized electronic circuitry imprinted into the chip. Even the power source for the receiver is derived from the internal power of the guidance system. The Soviet scientists didn't understand all of the complexities of the design, but then they didn't have to. All they were concerned with was that it worked. After testing it and discovering that it worked perfectly, they did just what they'd done with the circuit board in the ocean buoy: made exact duplicates of it and designed their guidance system around it, which in this case, considering the tremendous technological gains, they did faster than usual. There's an old Russian proverb: better is the enemy of good enough. In other words, if it works, leave it alone. Fortunately, the Soviets adhere to that questionable piece of wisdom throughout all of their industries."

"What sort of control does this bandit microcode give us?" McConnell asked, leaning forward in his chair, his enthusiasm now evident.

"There are four phases a missile goes through when it is launched: boost, postboost, midcourse, and reentry," Stallfort said. "During the boost phase, the rocket engines propel the missile through the atmosphere into space to a critical speed—where the accelerometers arm the warheads—and place the postboost vehicle that contains the warheads on the proper trajectory. At that point the postboost vehicle separates from the missile and, using its own guidance and propulsion systems, maneuvers itself into position to release its warheads and decoys toward the targets that have been preprogrammed into its on-board computer. During the midcourse phase, the computer in the postboost vehicle has the capability of being reprogrammed in flight, allowing technicians at the launch site to alter defensive maneuvering, decoy deployment, and target selection. During the reentry phase, the warheads are on the way to their targets and there is no further control over them."

"And at what point does your bandit microcode come into play?" McConnell asked.

"The objective of Operation Trojan Horse," Stallfort said, "is the primary guidance system used in the initial boost phase of the missile's flight—the critical part of the flight that puts the postboost vehicle on the proper trajectory for its targets. The bandit microcode affects the inertial navigation element and the flight control systems during the boost phase. The on-board computer that controls those functions makes course corrections up until the second-stage engines end their burn and drop off. Upon receiving a signal from us, the receiver activates the bandit microcode which will, among other things, instantaneously erase the memory in the on-board guidance system computer, leaving the system without instructions. Devoid of its memory, and its preprogrammed instructions, its sensors become confused and search for references, but its 'mind' is blank and there is nothing left to keep the missile on course.

"If we activate the bandit microcode while the second-stage engines are still burning, the engines might stop, causing the missile to lose velocity, pitch over, and drop to the ground, or it might tumble and break up. A number of other things could possibly happen, but one thing is absolutely certain; the missile will not continue on its course. It will be destroyed in some fashion before the nuclear warheads are armed and en route to their intended targets. In order to be successful, our signal must reach the bandit microcode within three and one-half minutes following the launch, after the missile leaves the protective shielding of its silo and before the second-stage engines are jettisoned from the postboost vehicle. But we have more than sufficient time, considering that the infrared warning instruments on our early-warning reconnaissance satellites can detect the exhaust gases from a missile launch within thirty seconds of the first-stage engine burn and beam down an alert to us. Immediately following that, we receive real-time television signals from visible-light sensors on the satellite for further confirmation of the launch."

"How do we send the signal to activate it?" McConnell asked.

"By satellite transmission of an EHF, extremely high frequency, signal," Stallfort said. "The signal is unaffected by electromagnetic pulse and is impossible to isolate and identify, making it immune to jamming. Once activated it is constant— until deactivated—and, due to the positioning of the satellites, covers the entire Soviet and Eastern Bloc land mass and the ocean areas patrolled by Soviet submarines carrying nuclear warheads within striking range of the United States. The signal has a five-year power supply and can theoretically affect every missile launch, from a mobile or fixed site, capable of reaching our borders."

McConnell lit another cigar and sat silently staring across the room, digesting the information. "I'll be goddamned," he finally said. His brow furrowed as another question occurred to him. "How do we know it works? Have we tested it?"

"Yes, sir. Three times, using signal-transmitter instrument packages piggybacked into orbit on reconnaissance satellites. They were launched during space-shuttle missions. The tests were entirely successful and the instrument packages were jettisoned from their host and destroyed. Two months ago the final stage was completed when the actual satellites, and their decoys, dedicated solely to Trojan Horse, were launched into orbit during another shuttle mission. There are four primary and four backup satellites, 'quiet satellites,' orbiting in deep space. They're well hidden among the refuse from other space flights, just like the covert spares we have in the event our primary defense satellites are knocked out. Having never transmitted since being placed in orbit, they have drawn no attention from the Soviets and are probably considered to be space junk or dead satellites. They will remain dormant until they are needed. Trojan Horse is now in an operational mode."

"What confirmation do you have that it works?" McConnell asked, the eager anticipation and excitement he felt evident in his voice.

"We have hard intelligence confirming the positive results of all three tests," Stallfort said confidently, reading from a document he removed from his portfolio. "On July 19, 1984, at the Tyuratam Space Launch Center in Soviet Central Asia, we caused a test launch of the Soviet's new SS-X-24 to be destroyed approximately three minutes into its flight. Using a variety of means we tracked the missile from the moment it was launched from its silo until its behavior became erratic—less than two seconds after we sent the Trojan Horse signal—resulting in the range safety officer activating the on-board explosive charges. Three months later, at the Plesetsk rangehead north of Moscow, we had identical results when we activated Trojan Horse two minutes after the launch of an SS-X-25, the Soviet's version of our MX.

"Our final test was the most rewarding, and an unexpected bonus. We had reason to believe that the Soviets were using our guidance system not only in all of their land-based missiles but also in the SS-NX-21, their new long-range cruise-type submarine-launched missiles. We had no way of verifying that—until we got lucky: our navy sub trackers in the Barents Sea picked up communications traffic to and from a Soviet nuclear submarine located northwest of the Scandinavian Peninsula. The traffic indicated that a test was imminent. We were worried about not having enough time to get things set up to monitor the test and the effect Trojan Horse had on it. We made it in time, but as it turned out we didn't need to go to all the trouble. It was beautiful," Stallfort said with obvious delight. "When our signal went out, the missile went berserk, strayed across Norwegian territory, and headed southwest before crashing in Finland near Lake Inari. The press picked up on it and it got world coverage."

"I remember that," McConnell said. "The inveterate liars finally had to admit it was their missile. But something just occurred to me. How do you know that the failures of the missile tests you used Trojan Horse on weren't the result of something other than the bandit microcode? The Soviets, as well as we, have had any number of failures during the development stages of their missile programs."

"A good question, senator," Stallfort said. "And one to which we gave a great deal of thought. Since we were limited in the number of tests we could conduct without causing the Soviets to suspect that the guidance system was at fault, as opposed to something mechanical, we had to select them with great care. They were all conducted late in the missile's test series, after most of the initial engineering glitches had been worked out. Each of our tests of Trojan Horse was preceded by at least six successful flights of the missile we went after. We also selected three distinctly different types of missiles, and the fact that each missile was affected within two seconds of our transmitting the signal to activate the bandit microcode is simply too timely to be considered a coincidence. We later learned from one of our agents that the Soviets never suspected the guidance system. They attributed the failures to other components that had given them problems during earlier tests. When the remainder of the tests were successful, they had no reason to look any further."

McConnell's face broke into a broad grin. "A pin-down action," he said. "We've got them by the short hairs. How many of their missiles have the Trojan Horse guidance system?"

"Ten months ago we received intelligence information stating that eighty-seven percent of their ground-based ICBMs have converted to the new system," Stallfort said. "And they are heavily dependent on those ground-based missiles. At that time the remaining thirteen percent were in the process of being converted. One hundred percent of their new long-range cruise missiles, and every new ICBM under development, are using it." Stallfort again consulted his briefing papers. "Seventy-five percent of their submarine-launched nuclear missiles have also been converted, along with sixty-five percent of their intermediate-range nuclear missiles, which are primarily theater weapons targeted for Great Britain, Western Europe, and China."

"Oh, I like this," McConnell said. "I like this a lot." He glanced at Stevens and flashed another broad grin. The DCI gestured to Stallfort to continue.

"They are totally committed to the new guidance system. And the irony is, because of the improved accuracy, they are not replacing their old missiles one-for-one. It's taken them two years to make the conversions to date, but with the testing completed they've accelerated the process, and soon all of their nuclear missiles capable of hitting targets in the United States will be converted to the system, with the possible exception of some of the older submarine-launched types that are being phased out."

"What about the mobile ICBM launchers they keep moving around?" McConnell asked.

"They can't hide them from us or the Trojan Horse signal," Stallfort replied. "We know where they are, and we know every time they move them. They may be mobile, but they're not invisible. They have an elaborate support system that emits an electronic and low-level radiation signature wherever they're set up. Our reconnaissance satellites keep them under constant surveillance."

McConnell thought for a moment, then said, "Then all we'd have to concentrate our entire defense force on would be their long-range strike aircraft and the submarines with missiles that don't have the Trojan Horse guidance system?"

"Yes, sir. And they are extremely vulnerable. Our missiles could take out the majority of their long-range bombers before they got off the ground. And with all of our air defense interceptor aircraft homed in on the few that manage to get airborne, they wouldn't stand a chance of getting anywhere near the North American continent. The submarines we'd have to contend with would be few in number—only ten percent of them are operational at any given time, the remaining ninety percent are in port. Our navy's antisubmarine warfare people track all those at sea. Without go-codes from Moscow the submarine commanders won't launch, and we have the capability to jam those codes. Their operational subs would be unsuspecting targets for our attack subs and air-dropped nuclear depth charges. The ones in port cannot launch their missiles without putting out to sea to reach predesignated close-in launch points —ten to twenty miles out of port. We'd spot them leaving the docks and get to them before they reached their launch points."

The DCI turned to McConnell. "You have to remember, Mike, all we have to do is detect one operational missile launch. Once we activate the Trojan Horse signal it can transmit continuously for seventy-two hours before it has to be shut down for ten hours to allow its power source to recharge the transmitter. During those seventy-two hours the signal will immediately activate the bandit microcode of any missile once it clears its silo or launcher. We can effectively neutralize the Soviets' ability to strike the United States for three days while maintaining our entire military capability, both offensively and defensively."

"They're bound to figure out long before that that we've done something to their guidance systems," McConnell said.

"They will," the DCI replied. "They'll know within fifteen minutes. But there's nothing they can do about it."

"They can put in new circuit boards, I would imagine. Or put the old guidance systems back in the missiles."

"As Stallfort just said, they're totally committed to the new system. The circuit board containing the central processing unit with our bandit microcode is designed to be part of a guidance module that can be easily removed and new circuit boards plugged in if there is a malfunction. But all of the backup modules they have stockpiled have circuit boards identical to the ones they would be replacing. The Soviets do the same thing we do when we develop a new weapons system, they scrap the old ones."

"How long would it take them to get all new circuit boards that couldn't be affected by Trojan Horse?"

"A year to eighteen months," Stevens said. "We're talking about an entirely redesigned guidance system to interface with the modifications that were made to the missile's other components to accommodate the performance characteristics of the new guidance module that was built around Trojan Horse. They couldn't simply reproduce the old system. It wouldn't work with the changes that have been made. And it's not only a question of redesigning; they'd have to manufacture it, install it, and run an extensive series of tests on every type of missile in which it was being installed. It's a very long and complicated process. There are no shortcuts. And we'd know about the new system as soon as they began testing it."

"Jesus, John," McConnell said. "You've nailed their hides to the wall without us having to make any concessions or fire one weapon."

"Now you understand why we would do anything to protect Trojan Horse," Stevens said. "We just couldn't take the chance that even a hint of what we were up to would leak out."

"Of course. Of course," McConnell said. He rose from his chair and began pacing in front of the conference table, his mind reeling with the possibilities at hand. "When will you have confirmation of their total conversion to the Trojan Horse system?"

"That's where the defecting Soviet scientist and his briefcase come into play," Stevens said. "Volodin was an expert in microelectronics, a member of the design team at the Zelenograd Center for Microelectronics that reverse engineered the central processing unit and designed the new guidance system for them. We recruited him when he was an exchange student here in 1972. He kept us informed of their progress through the Agency case officer in Moscow who was handling him. Our deal with him was to bring him to the West when he had gotten all of the information we needed about how and when the guidance system was being used. He got nervous and jumped the gun before we were ready for him."

"What's in the briefcase?" McConnell asked.

"The last of the intelligence information we need to make Trojan Horse a fully operational strategic counterforce weapon," Stevens said. "He was bringing out the installation schedule that would tell us when the remaining missiles would be upgraded with the new guidance system, when all the old missiles not receiving the system are slated to be phased out, and when their stockpile of old guidance systems would be scrapped, leaving them totally reliant on the new one."

"Considering Volodin's position," McConnell said, "won't his defection start the KGB looking into everything he was working on?"

"And what will they find?" Stevens asked. "That he worked on their new guidance system? They got the technology from us, remember. From their viewpoint, we stand to gain nothing, and they stand to lose very little. And much of the intelligence information Volodin passed on to us was not directly related to his work with the design team. It concerned the production schedules for the guidance system, his observations, official documents and directives he happened to see, and conversations he overheard between the head of the team and officers from the Strategic Rocket Forces. Without some further delineation of focus, they won't have any reason to look past the obvious inconsequential loss. They'd never suspect we gave them the technology that made Trojan Horse possible; it's alien to their way of thinking. They desperately want Volodin's briefcase because of the position he held at Zelenograd. He had access to a great deal of information unrelated to Trojan Horse, but nevertheless highly classified by the Soviet Defense Ministry."

"And if they get to the briefcase before we do?" McConnell asked.

"There's the rub. We lose. Once the Soviets know precisely what data he was bringing out, they'll have the thread to unravel Trojan Horse. Even if we have a grace period before they discover it, we'll have no way of knowing when the strategy for which Trojan Horse was designed can be implemented. We could make an educated guess about the conversion dates. Extrapolating from the schedule they've been following, that would mean a week, maybe less, before they were finished with everything but the theater weapons, which are no direct threat to us. But there could have been delays, and with the stakes we're playing for we need factual information. If they even suspect what we've done, they'll stop any further conversions, and without Volodin's information we have no idea how many of their ICBMs will be unaffected by our signal."

"You've got to get that briefcase, John," McConnell said. "Send in the whole goddamn Tenth Special Forces Group if you have to. Hell, send in a division. I guarantee you I'll get both my committee and the House committee to give you the green light; we've got some self-righteous jackasses over there, but none of them are fools. If we get that briefcase we've got those psychopaths checkmated. We can annihilate them and they can't touch us."

Stevens braced himself for the reaction he knew would be forthcoming from McConnell. "We have to handle getting the briefcase with more finesse than you have in mind, Mike. We don't want to start a war over something that's intended to prevent one."

McConnell stared blankly for a long moment before speaking. "What the hell are you talking about? What's the purpose of Trojan Horse?"

"It's a replacement for the Strategic Defense Initiative—Star Wars, as the press is fond of calling it," Stevens said. "The President never believed that we could achieve the degree of accuracy and dependability it would require. He regarded it as violating the laws of physics and common sense and thought it would only serve to motivate the Soviets to increase the number of their ICBMs and develop countermeasures that would escalate things to the point of lunacy. The only people who supported it were the defense contractors and their puppets in Congress. The President used the *threat* of its development to bring the Soviets to the bargaining table. The thought of having to counter a Star Wars technology scared the hell out of them; they can't afford to compete on that level any longer without bankrupting their entire economic system."

"Then Trojan Horse *is* an offensive weapon," McConnell said.

"No. It's leverage. For total nuclear disarmament for them and *us*. All missile production will be halted, all existing missiles will be dismantled, and all nuclear weapons stockpiles eliminated. On-site inspection teams will have unlimited access to all suspect areas."

McConnell's expression was one of anger and confusion. "Have you lost your mind? You're going to throw away an opportunity like this for a treaty with those lying bastards?"

"Yes," Stevens said. "A preemptive strike is not and never has been this country's intention. You know that as well as I do."

"And I've always disagreed," McConnell said.

"I'm aware of that. But since the early sixties, we haven't had the will, the world consensus, or the overwhelming superiority necessary to force the Soviets into a sane strategic defense policy. If Trojan Horse becomes fully operational, that is exactly what we will have. A strategic hammerlock on them. And, without embarrassing them on the world stage, we can, in secret meetings, force them to do precisely what we want. We can deal with them in a fair and open way. They have everything to lose if they refuse to go along, and we both share the same calculated loss if they agree. Nuclear weapons have *never* been defensive weapons, Mike, they're weapons of retaliation with no rational application. The use of only one percent of our combined nuclear arsenals would destroy us both as functioning societies."

McConnell crushed what remained of his cigar in an ashtray and glared at the DCI. "John, I'd like to continue this discussion in private, if you don't mind."

Stevens turned to the other two men at the conference table, who had already taken their cue and risen from their chairs. "Thank you for the briefing," he said to Stallfort. "I want all communications concerning Trojan Horse brought to my immediate attention," he said to the DDO as the two men left the room.

With the closing of the office door, McConnell shoved his chair forcefully away from the table and got to his feet. Stevens remained seated, waiting patiently for the tirade he knew was coming and would have to counter if he wanted the senator's full support and cooperation.

12

✖ THE MORNING SUN WAS a bright orange ball on the eastern horizon as the Gulfstream G-3 streaked across the sparkling, whitecapped water of Delaware Bay on a straight-in approach for Dover Air Force Base. Frank Kessler, thoroughly rested after sleeping undisturbed through all but the past fifteen minutes of the flight, sipped the last of a steaming hot cup of coffee and stared out the window as they crossed the coastline and continued their descent to a smooth touchdown on the broad, fifteen-thousand-foot concrete runway.

The aircraft's engines reversed thrust and it turned sharply onto a taxiway leading to an isolated hangar removed from the daily activities of the busy airbase. Kessler spotted a black Ford sedan parked just inside the open hangar doors, a small, telltale antenna protruding from its trunk. A Bell Jet Ranger helicopter sat off to one side of the tarmac, the mirrored sunglasses of its pilot and copilot flashing reflections of the morning light through the Plexiglas cockpit. One of the car's two occupants, a short, sturdy, middle-aged man with close-cropped hair, got out of the Ford as the aircraft rolled up to the front of the hangar. Raising his arm above his head, he twirled his hand in a signal to the pilot of the waiting helicopter. The rotor blades of the Bell Jet Ranger whined to life, churning quickly to a blurred, hazy circle as the G-3 came to a stop. Waiting at the door until

Kessler exited the plane, the CIA special operations man directed him immediately toward the helicopter—the rotorwash flapping his specially cut suitcoat open to reveal a Mini-Uzi submachine gun in a shoulder holster beneath his left arm.

"Jim Monaghan," the man said, shaking Kessler's hand and shouting over the high-pitched whine of the rotor and the idling engines of the G-3. "No time to waste, sergeant. My orders are to get you to Chadds Ford and back ASAP."

Kessler held his beret in place and ducked his head, squinting against the swirling grit as he entered the radius of the rotor blades and climbed into the rear seat of the helicopter. Monaghan jumped in beside him, closing and locking the door as they lifted off. Rising swiftly, they angled away from the base and headed north along the shore of the bay before reaching the broad sweep of the Delaware River, where they turned inland, passing directly over Wilmington. Once clear of the suburban sprawl of the city, a wooded landscape broken by the well-groomed, fenced-in grounds of country estates and horse farms passed beneath them. Within fifteen minutes, the Brandywine River came into view as they approached the Pennsylvania border. The pilot began a slow descent, following a country road and the course of the river as it snaked its way through more of the rolling meadows and wooded, hilly terrain. The copilot, consulting a large-scale road map of the immediate area, pointed off to his right, and the pilot banked sharply in that direction, flying low over a narrow secondary road that cut away from the river.

The copilot pointed again, this time at a black Ford sedan, identical to the one in the hangar at the airbase. The car, with two CIA special operations personnel inside, was parked on the shoulder of the road where twin stone pillars and a wrought-iron gate marked the entrance to a long, curving driveway that descended through a parklike setting of towering maple and sycamore trees. The pilot made a slow pass over the sprawling estate, looking for a place to land.

Kessler glanced at the beautifully landscaped grounds below him. The stone mansion and main buildings of the three-hundred-acre estate were nestled in a small valley of open, rolling fields dotted with stately shade trees and surrounded by wooded hills that rose gently on all sides. Low stone walls, thick hedgerows, and weathered split-rail fences enclosed lush pastures coursed by a stream that ran the length of the property in the trough of the valley. The stream flowed into a series of four large ponds, the largest with an island connected to the shoreline by a footbridge providing access to an ornate gazebo and boat dock set among a stand of weeping willows. A pair of startled Canada geese took flight from the calm water of the largest pond as the pilot hovered briefly, studying the terrain before circling a stable complex where a magnificent Arabian mare cantered across the paddock, her deep chestnut color glistening as she reared and bucked, kicking at the air, protesting the noisy intruder.

The pilot passed over the gabled roofs of the stables and hovered again above a tennis court and an expanse of lawn bordered by a large freeform swimming pool and poolhouse set on a low hill overlooking the main residence. Both he and the copilot scanned the immediate area for wires and other obstacles before settling gently to the ground.

Monaghan exited the aircraft and unclipped a small handheld radio from his belt. Moving away from the dwindling noise of the rotor blades, he keyed the microphone and spoke to the two men stationed in the car on the road outside the estate. As Kessler stepped to the ground, he noticed a man with pruning shears in his hands staring in their direction. The man, his eyes wide with fear and confusion, stood twenty feet away among the manicured shrubs surrounding the pool terrace. He glanced at the helicopter and Monaghan's tough, hardened features, his eyes coming to rest on Kessler's uniform and green beret. He took a few steps backward as Kessler and Monaghan approached him.

"I'm looking for Adrian Dulaney," Kessler said.

The man remained silent, his eyes darting back and forth.

"Can you tell me where I can find him?" Kessler asked.

"Is there a war?" the gardener asked in a slow, halting voice that made Kessler suspect that his intelligence was in some way limited.

Kessler smiled politely. "No. I'm here to see Adrian Dulaney on official business."

The gardener nodded and his startled expression slowly changed to one of childlike innocence. "Mr. Dulaney is up there," he said, pointing to a wooded hill beyond the lawn surrounding the pool area. "He took his bird with him. He won't be back too soon."

"Tell me how to find him," Kessler said.

The gardener hesitated before answering. "He doesn't want to be bothered when he's with his bird."

"It's very important that I talk to him," Kessler said evenly. "Very important."

The gardener thought for a moment, glancing at the helicopter, and the pilot and copilot still in the cockpit, then pointed to a grove of apple trees bordering the edge of the wooded hill. "There's a path through the woods. Mr. Dulaney is in the fields on top of the hill."

"Thank you," Kessler said.

The gardener pointed again, this time to the helicopter. "Don't take that up there. Mr. Dulaney will be real mad. He doesn't like when people scare his bird."

"You go up and find him," Monaghan said to Kessler. "I'll stay here with the chopper. Try to make it fast. The sooner we're out of here, the better." He handed Kessler an enlarged print made from Dulaney's most recent passport photograph. "Make sure you talk to the right guy," he said with a grin. "Five foot ten, one hundred and sixty pounds."

Kessler noted the aristocratic good looks and the deep-set eyes of the man in the photograph.

The gardener flashed an open, friendly smile at Monaghan. "Can I look inside the Airwolf?" he asked, gesturing toward the helicopter.

"You'd better get back to work," Monaghan said firmly.

The gardener frowned. "I told you where to find Mr. Dulaney."

"All right," Monaghan said. "Come on. You can sit in the back for a few minutes."

Kessler walked quickly across the lawn to the grove of apple trees, finding the path that led through the dense woods and rose steadily for a quarter of a mile to the top of the hill. The terrain leveled off and the forest abruptly ended, opening onto what he estimated was a hundred acres of uninterrupted fields left in a natural state. He stopped short of entering the clearing, his eyes fixed on an unfamiliar sight. Not far from where he stopped just inside the treeline, a man he immediately recognized as Adrian Dulaney stood motionless in the open field, his left arm extended outward from his side. Perched on a leather gauntlet covering his hand and wrist was a hawk, dark gray in color with a contrasting white underside. Kessler's attention was drawn to the hawk's head, where a black crown streaked by a line of light gray was dominated by two fiercely intense ruby-red eyes. Farther out into the field, ahead of Dulaney, was another man standing beside an English setter whose rigid black-and-white speckled body quivered with anticipation as she held a classic point directed at a dense thicket of vines and underbrush.

"Flush it," Dulaney called out.

The dog handler snapped a leash on the English setter and moved slowly forward. A young hen pheasant burst from the brush, its wings pounding the air furiously as it gained speed and altitude. The dog strained at the leash, but the handler held her close at his side.

Kessler's eyes caught the flash of movement as Dulaney released his hold on the hawk and cast him into the air. The tercel goshawk exploded into action—the bells on the leather jesses attached to its legs tinkling loudly and clearly in the calm morning air. A few swift, powerful strokes of his short, rounded wings brought the deadly hunter into a smooth effortless glide that silenced the bells. He flew low to the ground, skimming across the top of the high grass, closing the distance to his prey. With the course and angle of flight of the unsuspecting pheasant fixed in his primitive mind, the goshawk applied a sudden burst of speed, then settled into another faster glide as the pheasant flew across a section of split-rail fencing that divided the fields. The goshawk sped toward the fence with reckless abandon, swooping gracefully upward at the last moment, clearing the top rail by inches, only to miss his strike at the pheasant's head as the desperate bird became suddenly aware of his presence and dropped to the cover of a brush pile on the opposite side of the fence.

Kessler felt a chill run through his body as the shrill *kee a-a-a-r-r-r, kee a-a-a-r-r-r* cry of the hawk echoed across the fields and hung in the air as the angry predator rose into a steep climb and perched on the branch of a tree close to the spot where the pheasant had gone to ground. The goshawk sat quietly for a moment before crying out again as though ordering Dulaney to hurry to where he stood watch over his intended victim's hiding place.

The dog handler guided the English setter through the fence, restraining it with the leash until it caught the scent and froze on point. Dulaney moved with unhurried, easy strides toward the goshawk's perch, knowing that the pheasant would not break the relative safety of her cover unless given no alternative.

Kessler left the treeline and entered the open field, walking slowly to a rise in the ground that gave him a clear view of the area around the goshawk and the dog on point.

"Okay," Dulaney called out as he approached the setter and stood on the near side of the fence.

The handler urged the dog forward to the edge of the brush pile. The young hen pheasant again burst into flight, this time with less speed and energy, having tired from the previous flight of over a hundred yards.

The goshawk had lost none of its strength or determination and immediately left its perch thirty feet above the ground, dropping into a steep dive, building up speed before leveling off and swooping into another graceful glide, its wings held motionless as it followed close behind, gaining in a race the pheasant couldn't possibly win. The young hen tired after less than fifty yards and, taking the only option remaining, broke speed in an attempt to enter cover. A few hard, fast strokes brought the goshawk into within twenty feet of his frantic prey. With his wingtips tilted back, he zigzagged in a rapid sideslipping motion, a blocking tactic used to confuse the pheasant and prevent any sudden veering from her course. With precise control over his every move, he closed the distance to ten feet and dropped below her, forcing her to climb. Again increasing his speed— now exceeding forty miles per hour—he rose above the hen and made his strike as she reached the stalling point in her steep angle of climb. A loud *thwack* sounded clearly across the field as he flashed past her delivering a stunning blow to her head with his talons. The pheasant tumbled twice, literally knocked from the air. The goshawk's check and turn for the return strike was made with such blinding speed that he was able to grasp her head firmly in his talons before she hit the ground, where her wings flapped briefly in a spastic reflex before death.

Kessler walked across the field and vaulted the fence, continuing to where Dulaney sat cross-legged on the ground beside the goshawk as it deftly used its beak to eviscerate the pheasant, making a neat pile of its entrails and stomach off to the side before eating the liver and heart.

Dulaney caught sight of Kessler—taking in the green beret, the spit-shined jump boots with the trousers bloused over the tops in paratrooper fashion, and the five rows of ribbons on the left side of his tunic. He recognized some of the decorations: the Distinguished Service Cross, the Silver Star, the Purple Heart with two clusters indicating that it had been awarded three times.

In response to a reaction from the goshawk, Kessler stopped ten feet short of where Dulaney sat in the grassy field. The hawk had assumed a "mantle over" position, splaying his wings to cover his kill. The feathers on his head flared in a sunburst pattern around the glaring dark red eyes; his half-open beak dripped with the pheasant's blood as he hissed and cocked his head back and forth in wary observance of the stranger.

"Let me take a wild guess," Dulaney said to Kessler. "There's a parade in town and you took a wrong turn."

"That's very funny," Kessler said flatly, continuing to watch as the hawk, having determined that he was not a threat, resumed eating, tearing chunks of flesh from the pheasant's chest cavity. "I've never seen anything like that," he said. "That's one hell of a bird."

"His name's Kovar," Dulaney said, studying Kessler's face and glancing at the name tag on his right breast pocket and the stripes on his sleeves. "He's two pounds of murderous intent. A stone killer. What can I do for you, Sergeant Kessler?"

"I need to talk to you. Alone," he said, looking toward the dog and the handler. "It's important."

Dulaney's eyes narrowed as he held Kessler's steady gaze. "You can't be here to recruit me—I'm a little too old for that." Turning to the goshawk, he took hold of the leather jesses attached to its legs and nudged him on to his gloved hand, removing the pheasant from his grasp with some difficulty and a squawk of protest. With a quick twisting motion of his wrist, Dulaney tore off the pheasant's head. Kovar clamped a greedy talon on it and immediately plucked out one of its eyes.

Getting to his feet with the hawk perched on his fist, Dulaney put what remained of the pheasant's carcass in the game bag attached to his belt and began walking toward the path Kessler had taken through the woods. "Stay on my right side, away from Kovar," he instructed Kessler. "He's bold and fearless in the field, but a schizoid who's afraid of everything from his own shadow to imaginary phantoms when he's restrained."

The man with the English setter fell in behind them, preventing Kessler from getting directly to the purpose of his visit.

"He seems to like his work," Kessler said, gesturing toward the goshawk.

"He's obsessed with it," Dulaney said. "Where he comes from the winters can be pretty harsh. A driving snowstorm can keep them from hunting for two or three days, long enough to starve to death if their stomachs are empty. So they've developed some powerful survival instincts; they hunt at every opportunity and fill their crops whether they're hungry or not."

"How long did it take you to train him not to fly away when you release him?"

"As long as it took him to decide I was useful as his servant," Dulaney said with a wry smile. "Once he learned I could help him hunt, he decided to reward me with his companionship. If he gets bored with that, he'll disappear over the horizon in a matter of seconds. He doesn't need me, he tolerates me."

"He seems pretty tame," Kessler said.

"He's still wild at heart, and always will be. He's a passage bird. I trapped him up in Canada last spring when he was a year old. I'll hunt him for the rest of this season then release him into the wild next summer so he can breed."

"Will he come back?" Kessler asked.

"No. I'll trap another one. The enjoyment is in the training. It's a form of conservation," Dulaney added. "There's a seventy-five-percent mortality rate for hawks during their first year of life. They starve to death before they become experienced hunters. It's a trade-off. I keep him until he's strong and mature and his hunting skills are honed, and he allows me the pleasure of his company and some exciting hours in the field."

Kessler glanced at his watch. Fifteen minutes had passed since the helicopter had dropped him off. "I'd appreciate it if you would ask your friend with the dog to leave us alone. I'd like to explain to you why I'm here."

Dulaney turned to the man walking off to his left. "John, this man and I have some personal business to talk over. If you don't mind going ahead, I'll be along shortly."

"Yes, sir," the caretaker of the estate replied and immediately cut across the field to another path leading into the woods.

"Okay, Sergeant Kessler. Why the mystery?"

"What I've been instructed to tell you is highly classified," he said firmly. "It's important that you understand that and respect the conditions it implies."

Dulaney indicated a tacit but wary consent.

Kessler continued. "I'm on active duty with the First Battalion, Tenth Special Forces Group in Bad Tolz, Germany. I've been temporarily assigned to a special unit under the control of the Central Intelligence Agency. They've sent me here to recruit you for a mission for which you have . . . unique qualifications."

Dulaney's expression was one of disbelief. "Are you certain you have the right person?"

"You're Adrian Dulaney?"

Dulaney nodded, casting a suspicious glance at the imposing man walking beside him. The thought crossed his mind that despite appearances, the sergeant might not be who or what he claimed to be. It would not be the first time he had been approached by someone with a bizarre scheme to defraud him of money.

"You've either got the wrong man," Dulaney said, "or the people who sent you don't have both oars in the water. Do you have any identification, sergeant?"

Kessler removed his ID card folder from his coat pocket and handed it to Dulaney. "You're the man they want."

"For what purpose?" Dulaney asked, glancing at the identity card and returning it.

"I can't answer that," Kessler said. "My instructions are to recruit you and get you to Germany immediately. There's a plane waiting at Dover Air Force Base to do just that."

A broad grin spread slowly across Dulaney's face. "You'll forgive me, sergeant, if I don't take this too seriously. As a matter of fact, I think I've seen this very episode on 'Mission Impossible' reruns."

"This is no joke, and I wasn't sent here by fools. There are lives at stake and your country needs your help."

The only thing that kept Dulaney from laughing out loud was the seriousness of Kessler's tone. He read him as a man not given to foolish endeavors.

"Let me make sure I have this right," Dulaney said as they entered the woods and started down the hill. "The CIA sent you here to recruit me for a mission; a mission for which I alone have special qualifications. And you can't, or won't tell me, what that mission is, but I'm supposed to drop everything and go with you. Doesn't this sound at all odd to you, sergeant? Don't you think a little skepticism is in order?"

"I can't argue with that," Kessler said. "But it's true, and we don't have any time to waste. They need you in Germany. Tonight."

Dulaney continued to smile. "Believe me, sergeant, they've made a big mistake. I don't have any special qualifications; I don't even have a job. I fly my hawk, drive my cars, and chase women. I would think the CIA could come up with a few people within their own organization who can do those things equally well if not better."

"I'm at a disadvantage, Mr. Dulaney. I know for a fact that you have one unique qualification for this mission, but I'm not at liberty to discuss that. You'll have to take my word for it."

"Without knowing what I'm getting involved in?" Dulaney halted abruptly and stared at Kessler. "Even if I was tempted to go along with this, I'm not in your league, sergeant," he said, pointing to the rows of ribbons on Kessler's chest. "I don't have any experience in those areas."

"You've served your country before. You saw combat in Vietnam with the Marines. You're Force Recon trained. You were awarded a Bronze Star for valor. You'll do just fine."

"Now I know there's been a mistake. You've got some very garbled information."

"They got it from your Marine Corps service record," Kessler said.

"Well, they got it wrong. I was a rear-echelon clerk typist. What *you* would call an office pinky."

"You never ran recon?"

"I ran for my life," Dulaney said. "To begin with, I wasn't a Marine. I was *in* the Marines. There's a distinct difference. I was flunking out of Princeton in 1967. It was only a matter of time before I was drafted. I decided to choose my own poison. The Marine Corps seemed the best place to get the training I was going to need to keep me alive in Vietnam. I lucked out and got an office job. I never fought in combat; I never shot at anything other than paper targets at boot camp at Parris Island, and I barely hit enough of them to qualify on the rifle range."

"Your record shows you were in Force Recon."

"That information is right, as far as it goes," Dulaney said. "I was transferred from Third Marine Amphibious Force Headquarters to a Force Recon company for the last four months of my tour. I had a top-secret clearance so they assigned me as the intelligence officer's clerk."

"I thought every man in Force Recon had to be airborne and recon trained."

"They are," Dulaney said. "The clerk I replaced started running missions. The company had a lot of casualties, and they needed every combat-trained man, so I was transferred in as a noncombatant to fill the slot."

"How did you get the Bronze Star?" Kessler asked.

Dulaney smiled as though enjoying a private joke. He hadn't thought about the incident since the day it happened. "There was a VC mortar attack on the company compound. Incoming rounds were exploding all over the place. There was a mad scramble for the bunkers; I tripped and fell. Someone fell on top of me. He was covered with blood and he wasn't moving. I thought he was dead, so I used him as a shield. I crawled with him on my back until I got to the bunker and two guys pulled us both inside. It turned out that the man who fell on me was a lieutenant colonel, and he wasn't dead, just wounded. When he came to and was told what happened, he thought I'd intentionally saved his life. I told him that wasn't true, but he chose to see it his way and put me in for the Bronze Star." Dulaney shrugged his shoulders. "Who was I to argue with a light colonel."

Kessler stared at him in silence. He was beginning to have serious doubts about the wisdom of using him for the mission despite Cernikova's demands. By any standards, he wasn't the right material. "Then you have no combat skills or experience?"

Dulaney shook his head. "And apparently that's what you need for your mission. So as it turns out, sergeant, we were both right. You have the right person, but the wrong man for the job."

"Unfortunately that's not my decision to make. But you do

have something they need that has nothing to do with your military experience or lack of it."

"That unique qualification you mentioned earlier?"

"Yes."

"The one you can't tell me about."

"You're just going to have to accept my word that what you're being asked to volunteer for is of vital importance to your country."

"I don't doubt your word, sergeant, but there seems to be some incongruity here. The criteria used to select me was based on faulty information. Yet you still want me to volunteer."

"I've told you, your military background isn't the only reason I'm here. Your importance to this mission doesn't rest on that alone."

"Now we're back to the part you can't tell me about."

Kessler had never disobeyed a direct order, but he briefly considered telling Dulaney about Cernikova despite the order he had been given.

"Are you married?" he asked Dulaney.

"No."

"You live here alone?"

"At the moment," he said, curious about the line of questioning. "I have occasional live-in roommates, 'relationships' I think is the fashionable term. The last one left three months ago. A Bryn Mawr graduate," he said with a roll of his eyes. "A psychology major. Got to learn to stay away from them—always looking for the subconscious reasons, possessive; follow you to the bathroom for no drug-related reasons. I'm sure you know the type."

Kessler smiled. "I've met a few."

"She told me I was 'too deep into my hawk,' and that we would 'never interface,' because I was 'insensitive, exploitive, depersonalized, and not ready for commitment and wholeness.' I think the last two were based on my refusal to consider adjacent burial plots. Anyway, she left me for some granola-breath zealot with bean sprouts clinging to his beard. He had bumper stickers and T-shirts for every cause and worshiped any politician bearing the slightest physical resemblance to a Kennedy. They went off to save the snail darter, or the lungwort, I forget which. It's been all peace and joy since she left. Any other personal questions?"

202

"No. Just curious," Kessler said as they emerged from the woods on to the stretch of lawn leading to the swimming pool.

Dulaney stopped and stared at the helicopter parked nearby. He gripped Kovar's jesses tightly as the goshawk screeched and tried to take wing at the sight of the strange object. "Friends of yours?"

"They brought me up here from Dover."

Dulaney glanced at the pilot and copilot standing beside the helicopter, then turned his attention to Monaghan. "Who's the no-neck in the Brooks Brothers suit?"

"CIA. There are two more of them in a car parked just outside your driveway. They're here for security purposes."

Dulaney gave Kessler a hard look. "I'm sorry, sergeant. I can't agree to what you're asking. Not without a great deal more information than you're willing to give. And even then I can't guarantee anything. I just don't think I'm your man."

"Give me a few more minutes of your time. I'll see if I can get permission to tell you something I think you need to know."

Dulaney began walking across the lawn to where it dropped off in the direction of the stables. "I'll be in the hawk house on the far side of the stables."

Kessler crossed to where Monaghan stood leaning against the rear of the poolhouse. He was squeezing a wrist developer and looking thoroughly bored.

"How much do you know about why I'm here?"

"Nothing," Monaghan said. "My assignment was to get you here and back to the plane within two hours."

"I need to talk to my commanding officer in Germany. I was told if it was necessary someone would patch me through to him."

"I noticed a telephone in the poolhouse," Monaghan said. "I'll get the call through, but when you talk to him keep in mind that it's not a secure line."

Within minutes, Kessler was talking in cryptic, guarded phrases with Simpson at the CIA's isolation base in West Germany. He was given a conditional approval to tell Dulaney about Hana Cernikova, and no more. Hanging up the receiver, he turned to Monaghan. "If I don't leave here with Dulaney, he's to be put on ice until further notice."

"Someone must have anticipated that," Monaghan said. "That's why two of my men are stationed on the road."

Kessler left the poolhouse and descended the grassy slope leading to the stables. He had not been surprised by the response to his report of Dulaney's lack of military experience. As Simpson had succinctly put it, he was all they had. Kessler was aware of the difficult position he was now in: if he could recruit Dulaney, he would have to prepare him for the mission as best he could, and within two days take him over the fence regardless of his state of readiness.

Crossing the courtyard of Belgian paving blocks, he passed the open doors of an immaculately maintained four-car garage and paused briefly to admire the automobiles inside. A Porsche convertible and a Ferrari coupe flanked another expensive-looking, exotic sports car he couldn't identify. The elan of a Jeep Wagoneer parked in their company was reduced to that of a farm tractor. He found Dulaney in a large room connected to the stables by a breezeway. The room was bright and airy and completely empty with the exception of a wooden perch at each end. Kovar sat on one of the perches, stropping his beak on the crossbar. The goshawk momentarily reacted to his presence in the doorway, then relaxed and roused his feathers until he looked like a fluffy ball, rattling them back into place with a sound that reminded Kessler of a wet dog shaking the water from its coat.

"I couldn't help noticing your cars," Kessler said, closing the door behind him. "Nice wheels."

"Toys," Dulaney said as he turned to face him. "My life's full of them. Play is what I do best." Before Kessler could speak, he added, "Don't take this personally, sergeant, but our conversation about your mission is over. I don't want to hear anything more about it, certainly not anything classified that obligates me to you or the people who sent you."

"I think there *is* something you should hear."

"Nothing's going to change my mind. I'm not your man."

"Hana Cernikova asked me to give you a message."

13

SENATOR MCCONNELL FURIOUSLY PUFFED a fresh cigar to life and paced back and forth in front of the glass wall of the DCI's office. With Dyer and Stallfort out of the room, he spoke freely to his old friend.

"I've known you for twenty years, John, and I've never heard such a patently stupid idea in my life!" he fumed. "The President has it within his power to eradicate a cancer that has been eating away at this world since the end of World War Two. We can strike now! Not scotch the snake, but kill it! And he's acting like some peace-at-any-cost, knee-jerk liberal. How the *hell* can you stand by and let this happen?"

"The President's calling the shots, Mike. And it's not just his thinking, but all of his close advisers'. I'm just a good soldier, and I happen to think he's right."

"Then you've all got one wheel up on the curb," McConnell said. "The President can't run for reelection so he's running for the goddamn Nobel peace prize."

"Something's got to be done. What we have now is an unstable balance of terror. Technology has compressed decision time to the point where the deaths of tens of millions of people could result from a single nervous twitch. Trojan Horse will give us some breathing room, slow down the reaction time to where it's manageable. Like it or not, it's a matter of mutual interest in self-preservation. When we have to consider the very real possibility of a nuclear winter that could have disastrous consequences for the entire planet, only madmen still think in terms of limited nuclear war and acceptable losses. We can't talk about 'hard-target-kill capability' and 'postexchange weapons residuals' as though they had any real meaning in human terms. They're numbers, computer projections that don't take into consideration the effect on humanity. No one is sure *what* would happen, but how much certainty do we need before we refuse to find out how right or wrong we are?"

"You're forgetting the inherent violent nature of the human species. There have always been wars, there will always be wars. You don't change a hundred thousand years of tribal instincts with a few hundred years of social change."

"History will never forgive us if we don't use this in a responsible way," Stevens said. "It's an opportunity that can't be squandered on evening old scores."

McConnell remained unmoved and adamant. He walked over to where Stevens stood beside his desk. Their faces now only inches apart, he said, "You're talking about giving up the ultimate strategic advantage for a treaty that won't be worth the paper it's written on. You seem to be conveniently forgetting that they've violated every goddamn meaningful agreement we've ever made with them: the Threshold Test Ban Treaty, the ABM treaty, the Geneva Protocol on Chemical Weapons, the Biological Weapons Convention, the Helsinki Final Act. And at least three provisions of SALT Two that we know of: telemetry encryption, upgrading of existing ICBMs, and the limits on deployment of new types of missiles. And you can add SALT Three to the list. We've confirmed that they've violated that by expanding and improving their battle-management-capability systems with the HEN HOUSE radar for their ABMs. What the *hell* is the point in another treaty if we can't verify their compliance and hold them to it? It's playing poker in the dark, an exercise in futility."

"The disarmament treaty we present to them will mandate extensive and unlimited means of on-site verification of compliance on both sides."

"Damn it, John! Even with on-site verification we could be deceived. They could hide a dozen of the new cruise-type missiles in a goddamn *garage,* or the back of a *truck.*"

"That's an oversimplification," Stevens said. "Without silos, launch sites, or mobile launchers, all of which we can detect with our existing satellite surveillance, they wouldn't be operational. And you seem to forget, we have a variety of other methods to determine if they're cheating. We know what they have, and where they have it."

"But by your own admission, we'd only have to contend with a few submarines and aircraft once Trojan Horse is fully operational. We can get rid of the Soviets in one fell swoop and put them back in the Stone Age where they belong. The President was right when he called them an 'evil empire.' "

"No matter what we do they could still strike countervalue targets in Great Britain and Western Europe with their intermediate-range missiles that haven't been converted," Stevens said. "Only Moscow knows what Moscow will do, but if we launch a preemptive first strike I can guarantee you, even if they can't hit us, they won't just roll over. They'll retaliate with whatever they have left on any free-world target they can reach."

"To hell with Western Europe. What have they ever done for us?"

Stevens shook his head in exasperation. "It's never been my decision to make, Mike. But I agree with the President. The most intelligent man I've ever known, a man who fought in three wars, once told me that you don't solve anything by killing people. We can't even be sure what effect the number of nuclear warheads we'd have to use to destroy the Soviets militarily would have on us and the rest of the world. Even if they never get off one missile we could still end up with a Pyrrhic victory."

"This is wrong. You'll never pull it off," McConnell said. "You have influence with the President. Make him see the light."

"I think he has. He knows that we're never going to eliminate wars, but we can at least limit them to the conventional types that don't involve the deaths of thirty or forty million people in the best-case scenario and the death of the planet in the worst."

"The way of the world is force, John," McConnell said. "A lot of people don't choose to believe that, but it's a fact. Philosophical principles and ethical codes are empty abstractions; they don't mean a damn thing when it comes to defending yourself against a determined aggressor who doesn't share your sense of justice or fair play. Power and the will to use it are what maintain order. The threat of war maintains the peace. That's all diplomacy has ever amounted to. If both countries didn't have nuclear weapons, I can think of at least three times in the past thirty years when we would have been at war with each other. Nuclear weapons are a deterrence to conventional war for fear of escalating into a nuclear exchange. Our 'balance of terror,' as you call it, is the only thing that's kept us from each other's throats."

Stevens poured a cup of coffee for himself and offered one to McConnell, who waved him off. "That's dangerous reasoning, Mike. We can't count on that continuing. One miscalculation and it's all over. You said it yourself. War is inevitable. Eventually one of us would get around to using nuclear weapons, which means both of us would. With Trojan Horse we'd be dealing with them in the only way they understand and respond to—from a position of strength. And we wouldn't be giving up our ability to defend ourselves. Or the ability to help our friends and allies if they need us. The concept is to limit and contain the extent of the damage when a war is inevitable. Our military doesn't want a nuclear war. If for no other reason, there'd be no promotions. They want weapons they can use, wars they can fight and win. In a conventional war we'd be squandering our own lives, not the lives of future generations. And we can direct some of the hundreds of billions of dollars projected to be spent on offensive and defensive strategic weapons systems to conventional forces—enough to match or exceed anything the Soviets have. The military-industrial complex will still have their slice of the pie, and we'll be able to put more into the exploration of space and address some of our economic problems. And it would put the Soviets in the position of being able to divert their own funds to long overdue social improvements and the production of consumer goods and agricultural products so they can feed their people above a subsistence level."

"Now isn't that wonderful? Suddenly we're concerned with helping them solve their internal problems," McConnell said in disgust.

"I have no love of the Soviets. They've got to be kept on a short leash, preferably attached to a choke collar. But we've got to live together on the same planet."

"What if they call our bluff? What if they just tell us to go to hell and take the gamble that we won't do a damn thing about it? That we don't have the resolve or the guts to launch a preemptive strike? Once we've told them about Trojan Horse, if they don't accede to our demands, we have no choice but to knock out their entire nuclear capability. But in the process we've given them a warning and enough time to kill who knows how many millions of Western European civilians before we wipe them out. Is the President willing to take on that responsibility?"

"That's a worst-case scenario that has already been factored in and given the President's approval," Stevens said. "But they won't call our bluff. We're not demanding their surrender. We're not demanding that they dismantle their empire. And we're not asking them to do anything we're not willing to do ourselves. To use one of your favorite expressions, we plan to leave them their balls."

"Listen to yourself," McConnell said, jabbing his cigar toward the DCI. "You sound as if you're talking about dealing with a boy scout troop. If we strike first we don't have to leave them anything."

"Mike, their decisions, like ours, come from the apex of their power structure. We'd be dealing with wizened old men who got where they are by being shrewd politicians," Stevens said. "They aren't going to do anything that threatens to weaken their hold on their country. They'll do what they have to do to hold on to their power and privilege. If they try to call our bluff and it doesn't work, they stand to lose everything. If they agree to our demands it's just a matter of restructuring their defenses. Faced with certain annihilation, they aren't going to risk the fate of their nation against the possibility of destroying a few European cities. Even their god Marx said you should only set yourself such problems as you can solve. History has taught them that the only security available to them was to conquer those neighboring countries who were constantly attacking them, or those who were too weak to prevent other nations from crossing their territory to attack the Soviet Union. They're paranoid, suspicious of anything foreign, and insecure, but the last thing they want is a nuclear war with us. They're more interested in live Russians than they are dead Americans. By agreeing to our demands, they'd still have their conventional forces to secure their empire and defend themselves. And the same old game will go on, but neither one of us will be locked in a suicidal arms race that's become a force in itself."

"And what about their chemical and biological warfare weapons?" McConnell asked.

"They'll be worked into the disarmament agreement. Verifying their compliance in that area will be more difficult, but it can be done. We know where they're manufactured and where they're stockpiled. Face it, Mike, it's going to work."

McConnell shook his head. "Bullshit. Their ideology precludes peaceful coexistence."

"At least we agree on something. We can't stop their attempts to spread Marxism-Leninism every time they see an opportunity. But the future is guerrilla warfare. They know it and we know it. It's been working for them for the past twenty years. We got off to a slow start, but now we have some first-rate unconventional warfare troops. And we're coming on fast to match what the Soviets have."

"What about the French and the British?" McConnell asked. "They have independent nuclear forces. The Soviets aren't going to deal without the Brits and the Frogs as part of the package."

"Once the British and the French understand what's involved and that they'd be included as full partners in the agreement, they'll ratify the treaty without hesitation. They've never considered their nuclear weapons as anything other than a part of their defensive strategy. They'll welcome the opportunity to eliminate billions from their defense budgets, and so will the Chinese; their priorities are directed inward, to economic development. They want an open-door policy with the West for foreign skills and investment. And the same applies to South Africa, India, and Israel."

"You're forgetting the unstable nations and the psychopaths on the verge of joining the nuclear-weapons club: Libya, Iraq, Iran, Pakistan. They all have the capability and the motivation. What's to keep them from telling us to go to hell and continuing in the direction they're headed?"

"Our objective, along with the Soviets', will be to make the United Nations work as it was originally conceived. Under an international nuclear disarmament law, the U.N. will police the nuclear community and control special operations units for surgical application of conventional military force to deal swiftly and decisively to take out any nuclear weapons facilities that appear. The way Israel did with Iraq."

"Pipe dreams," McConnell said.

"There's a precedent," Stevens said. "We did it in 1977 when Brezhnev and Carter jointly brought pressure on South Africa to stop their nuclear weapons testing in the Kalahari Desert. It won't be easy, Mike. But it can be made to work; it's in everyone's national interests."

"And when is this brotherhood-of-man fairy tale supposed to take place?"

"As soon as we have confirmation of complete conversion to the Trojan Horse guidance system. The President will request a summit meeting with the Soviet Premier, give him the bad news, and offer him a demonstration that will remove any doubts he may have of our capability."

"I think the President is going to fall flat on his ass on this, John," McConnell said as he walked to the door. "But if you want me to keep this from the rest of my committee, I want to be kept abreast of the developments on the mission to get the briefcase. When is the team going back into Czechoslovakia?"

"Within the next seventy-two hours."

"If they fail, and the media gets hold of what's going on, friendship be damned. I'll be at the head of the posse that runs you out of town."

"You won't have any problem finding volunteers for that," Stevens said, attempting to close the meeting on a civil note.

"It doesn't end here, John," McConnell said. "When your covert ops people get out of Czechoslovakia, I'm going to have a face-to-face with the President over this."

"I spoke with him this morning when we decided to brief you. He felt certain he'd be hearing from you," Stevens said. "From one old friend to another, Mike. Are you sure you want to pick this bear fight?"

"I'll relish it," McConnell said. "I'll consider it the crowning achievement of my career if I can prevent the disaster he's headed for."

14

✖ DULANEY'S REACTION WHEN KESSLER mentioned Hana Cernikova's name was immediate and pronounced; a startling transformation, as though a mask had fallen from his face, the cynicism and detachment gone. He stared hard at Kessler, then looked away, his eyes focusing on some distant point.

"She said to tell you that her father died last year."

When Dulaney looked back to Kessler, the powerful emotions the name had evoked were clearly evident in his expression. "You saw Hana?"

"Two days ago, in Prague."

"What else did she say?"

"Nothing that directly concerns you at this point."

"Is she well?"

"For the moment," Kessler said. "But without your help that's not going to last."

"She's the unique qualification you couldn't tell me about?"

Kessler nodded. "You seem to be the only one she'll trust in her present situation."

"What situation is that?" Dulaney asked. "I can't imagine Hana being involved with the CIA."

"I can't give you any details. Except that through no fault of her own she's caught in the crossfire between some people who don't give a damn what happens to her. The bottom line is she could end up dead, or in prison for the rest of her life."

"It's been ten years," Dulaney said, more to himself than Kessler. "It took me a long time to get over her."

"I'd say you didn't succeed."

Dulaney made no immediate response, but the truth of Kessler's observation was evident in his eyes. "I made arrangements to get her out," he finally said, "but it all fell through."

"I know."

Dulaney raised a questioning eyebrow. "How do you know that? Hana?"

"No. One of the people in the group you hired was CIA."

"What can I do to help?" Dulaney asked after a long silence.

"It'll all be explained to you in Germany."

"The Czechs aren't going to issue me a visa," Dulaney said. "I had some problems with the STB; they said they'd kill me if I ever came back. They have long memories."

"That's the least of your worries. I'll get you in."

"And then what?"

"I'll get you both out."

"Just like that?"

"No. I'm not going to lie to you," Kessler said. "It won't be easy. But the mission will be well planned and we'll have a lot of support. We'll pull it off. I'll be with you every step of the way."

"Is Hana married?" Dulaney asked.

The question answered the remaining doubts Kessler had about recruiting Dulaney successfully. "I don't think so. Her telephone is listed in her name, she wasn't wearing a wedding ring, and she wants out; more to the point, she wants out with you."

Dulaney crossed the room to a large window overlooking the paddock where the Arabian mare stood against a backdrop of dark green pastures and autumn-colored woods. He thought of Hana and their last days together, and how he had missed her, and still did on occasions, when the memories were stirred by the countless little things that could bring them to life. Six months after the West German group had failed in bringing her out, he realized the senselessness of dwelling on what might have been. Depressed and angry, certain that he would never see her again, he had torn up the letters she had sent when they had first met, and the few photographs he had kept in the desk in his study. But the pain lingered. Her haunting beauty, her gentle touch, the way she, like no one else, made him feel as though he belonged, were captured forever, timeless and indelible, always there to torment him at will.

Even now, ten years later, at this very moment, he could clearly see in his mind's eye the warmth of her shy half smile that occasionally blossomed into fullness; a genuine smile, not overused and never automatic. He could still remember the scent of her hair as they lay together on the bed in her apartment after making love. Prague's golden afternoon light streamed through the open window; a gentle breeze ruffled the curtains and carried the faint sounds of children playing in the park outside. He heard again her soft voice as they talked about what her life in the United States would be like. She had found joy in things that others, more jaded, took for granted, and had no comprehension of his wealth or the privileges and luxuries that awaited her. All she had wanted was to be with him. And for the first time in his life he had found someone who mattered, someone with whom he was comfortable, and, as he finally admitted, someone he loved more than himself. She made bearable, and at times erased, the bitter memories of his youth: the death of his parents in an automobile accident when he was only ten, the loneliness and dislocation of the succession of elite boarding schools and summer camps, and the indifference of a maternal grandmother, his guardian, whose answer to his rebellious nature was to find another school that would take him despite his frequent expulsions for disciplinary reasons.

Images, both pleasant and unpleasant, flashed through his mind. The rainy spring morning in Copenhagen when they met in 1974—he was beginning a motorcycle tour of Europe and she was ending a week's holiday with the other coaches and the skaters of the Czech national team, their reward after a successful season of competition. He had literally bumped into her in Tivoli Gardens, when they both ducked under cover from a sudden, brief cloudburst, and they had gone on from there to spend the day together in the amusement park. They had dinner that evening, and the following morning she was gone from his life, having returned to Prague, her holiday over. A pleasant interlude, he had thought then, a footnote to his memories. But four days later, when he reached Bonn, he changed his itinerary, applying for and receiving a visa from the Czech embassy. He had no explanation for his overwhelming desire to see her again, but then none was needed; he seldom questioned or checked his impulses. She was beautiful and he had never been behind the Iron Curtain; that was enough.

The week he had planned on staying stretched to three months. He returned that winter, to take her skiing in the High Tatras. He followed her to Paris and Geneva where, as a coach, she had traveled with the skating team for competitions. She had captivated him as no other woman had, and with his return to Prague in the spring of 1975 came the realization that he wanted to share the rest of his life with her. But it all fell apart as quickly as it had begun. First there were subtle forms of harassment by the STB: repeated checking and rechecking of his passport and visa whenever he entered or left his hotel or Hana's apartment. He began to see the same men who had examined his papers seated at nearby tables in restaurants and cafés and following at a discreet distance as he and Hana walked through the parks or along the river. The frequency and intensity of their efforts increased in direct proportion to the length of his stay. They began stopping him in the street when Hana was not with him, first questioning him at length, then taking him to a police station where he sat for hours until it was determined that his papers were in order. His complaints to the American embassy did nothing to alleviate the problem which, despite his efforts to keep it from her, had now been brought to Hana's attention by her friends. His refusal to be intimidated into leaving the country was interpreted as a direct challenge to the authority and power of the STB and resulted in their actions escalating to a more dangerous level.

Hana's application for an exit visa proved to be the final straw. Returning to her apartment with her after dining out, he was shoved into an alley and forced to strip naked as she watched. Accused of black-market-currency violations, he was arrested and thrown in jail. Released the next day, he was told to "cease in his attempt to corrupt one of their national celebrities" and strongly advised to leave the country. His complaint to the American embassy brought the same advice. The following morning he was dragged from his hotel room and interrogated for twelve hours at STB headquarters before being released and warned that he would be killed if he did not leave the country immediately. On his way to see Hana that evening, he was assaulted by two STB officers waiting near her apartment. He fought back, breaking the nose of one of his assailants before being subdued and again taken to STB headquarters where he was beaten severely and thrown into a cold, damp cell in the basement of the detention center. One week later, denied any further communications with Hana, his visa revoked for "crimes against the state," he was taken from his cell and escorted to the airport where he was placed on a flight to Munich.

He had known Hana for little more than a year. They had seen each other only half of that time. But when he returned to the United States, the emptiness he felt without her taught him the bitter lesson that it was not the length of time they were together that mattered, but how close it had come to perfection. He had understood why she refused to escape with the men he sent to bring her out. She had been born late in her parents' life and her mother had died years before. She was an only child, and she was all her father cared about or had left in a life that was a constant struggle against the debilitating effects of emphysema. Her prestige and national prominence had resulted in a better life for them both, securing for them a decent apartment and his office job in the Pariz Hotel. He had urged her to go, but refused to come with her when the men, following Dulaney's instructions, offered to bring him out with them. But in the end, she could not desert her father; to go would have meant not only leaving him alone, but at the mercy of the STB. And now he was dead. And she was alone, and in trouble.

There was no question in Dulaney's mind about doing anything he could to help. His life had been empty without her, full of meaningless self-indulgence. He understood all that the brief message she had given to Kessler was meant to convey, telling him that neither time nor distance had taken from them what they once had. His only hesitation was a gnawing fear that he might fail and lose her again.

"I forgot what little Czech I used to speak," he finally said to Kessler, who left him to his private thoughts while keeping track of the time.

"It doesn't matter," Kessler said. "I speak the language as well as they do, and so will the others who are going with us."

"Do I have time for a shower and a change of clothes?"

"Make it fast," Kessler said, glancing at his watch.

"What do I need to bring with me. Passport? Clothes?"

"Nothing. It'll all be provided over there. For security purposes, if there's anyone you have to notify about your leaving, I'll have to listen in on the call."

"How long will I be away?"

"If everything goes according to schedule, a week at the most."

"There's no one," Dulaney said. "The maid is here every day and John and Billy, the gardener, live in the guesthouse behind the stable. They'll take care of things until I get back."

"What kind of shape are you in?" Kessler asked, judging from Dulaney's trim, youthful appearance that he exercised regularly.

"Not bad for thirty-eight. I run four miles a day. I swim ten laps after that. I can do fifty pushups and fifty situps."

"You can't tell anyone where you're going or why," Kessler reiterated. "No outgoing or incoming calls from now until we leave."

"I understand that," Dulaney said as he left the hawk house and headed for the stone mansion at the opposite end of the courtyard.

Kessler had Monaghan monitor the telephone in the poolhouse while they waited until Dulaney had showered and changed. He began mentally outlining a training schedule for the short time they would have. He knew that the method of insertion for the second mission would have to be a parachute jump if the Czech border troops were still on full alert. Dulaney's nonairborne status would limit it to a simple static line jump, something he could be prepared for within the allotted time. If he and the other two men on his team could stay close to him, his lack of expertise with weapons would present no problem. But Kessler was still troubled by the thought of taking a totally inexperienced and untested man into the type of situation they were likely to encounter. There was something about Dulaney, a hint of arrogance he thought, that told him he would not be easy to control. And yet, with the money and the means to avoid the draft, he had voluntarily gone to Vietnam. Something Kessler found out of sync with his initial impression of the man. And despite his lack of experience, Dulaney demonstrated at least a rudimentary sense of responsibility and mission security by what Kessler heard him tell the caretaker as they entered the poolhouse.

"You're not to mention the helicopter, or the men you've seen here to anyone," he told the caretaker, who gave him his solid assurance. "Kovar won't need to be flown until I get back. Just keep him fed. And fix Billy's meals for him and take him to his appointment at the clinic tomorrow."

Dulaney followed Monaghan's instructions and boarded the helicopter as the engine came to life. Kessler turned in response to a tug at his tunic to see Billy giving him a smile and a salute which he returned as he climbed into the back of the Bell Jet Ranger.

Dulaney stared at the ground as they lifted off and passed low over a grassy meadow belonging to one of his neighbors. A young girl riding bareback, her face brightened by a joyful smile, came into his field of vision. His eyes followed her as she galloped a proud, dapple-gray horse across the meadow; her hair blowing in the wind, her arms outstretched, held parallel to the ground as she expertly maintained a delicate balance over the rolling terrain. He was reminded of Hana and the pure sense of joy and freedom she got from her skating. He settled back in the seat as the helicopter climbed higher and the girl disappeared from sight. He studied Kessler's face and again glanced at the rows of ribbons on his tunic. He had seen men like him before. Men who had repeatedly gone deep behind enemy lines in Vietnam. They all had the same look. What they had been through had left them with one thing in common: they could never be intimidated again. They had repeatedly faced death and survived and had gained a rare degree of self-confidence that set them apart.

"Is there anything more you can tell me about the mission?" Dulaney asked.

"That information is on a need-to-know basis," Monaghan said curtly, although the question had not been addressed to him.

"And I don't need to know?" Dulaney asked with a trace of his earlier sarcasm.

"Not at the moment. Normal procedure is to train an agent before revealing the mission," Monaghan said, falling silent after receiving a cold, hard glance from Kessler.

Dulaney's eyes widened at the use of the term *agent*. Turning to Kessler he asked, "Can you give me some idea of what's expected of me?"

"Nothing you can't handle," Kessler said, managing to conceal his total lack of conviction.

15

✖ HANA CERNIKOVA CAST ANOTHER quick, nervous glance to the rear of the crowded tram car as it swayed and clattered into the heart of the Old Town section of the city. He was still there, seated next to a window. His face was partially concealed by a newspaper, but the dark blond hair combed straight back forming a widow's peak on his broad sloping forehead was clearly visible. She was certain she had seen him in the park near her apartment building last evening wearing the same distinct light green, imitation-leather jacket, and he had boarded the tram with her that morning when she went to work.

Forcing her way to the front of the car, she stepped off as it came to a stop near the entrance to the Charles Bridge. Looking back, she saw him get off, disappearing into the crowd of people waiting to board the tram. Crossing the street, she passed beneath the medieval fortification tower of the fourteenth-century sandstone bridge, erected where the Slavic tribes used to ford the river at its most shallow point. The bridge was open only to foot traffic, and she walked quickly across the cobbled surface, stopping at the midpoint to stand at the balustrade among the sightseers taking in the panoramic view of the city as it rose like an amphitheater along the banks of the river. The skyline of Gothic towers and Renaissance spires was silhouetted in the smooth-flowing water, and the soft earth tones of the centuries-old buildings crowned with greenish copper domes and faded red-tiled roofs and chimney pots glowed in the warmth of the afternoon sun. She thought of Adrian Dulaney, and the terrible consequences she would have to pay if the desperate gamble she had taken was lost. She fought back the tears as she watched an elderly couple in a small wooden rowboat drifting slowly with the current below the weirs, floating like a jackstraw past a cluster of mallard ducks bobbing in the shallows along the shoreline.

She turned her attention to a group of tourists and their guide as they moved among the stained and corroded gallery of Baroque statues that lined both sides of the seventeen-hundred-foot expanse of the ancient bridge. She was looking for the man in the green jacket, but he was gone. Perhaps it was her imagination; the constant fear of discovery causing her to distort things beyond their significance. She had never been so frightened. She had not been able to think clearly since her telephone call to Paulina Marcova's mother that morning when her young student had not shown up at the ice rink for her training class. The tearful, confused woman, distraught to the point of incoherence, had managed to tell her that her daughter had been arrested by the STB and she had been unable to find out why, adding that her husband's brother, professor Jan Marcovic, had also been arrested and later found in his apartment dead of an apparent stroke. Hana had dropped the receiver, terrified at the prospect of what would happen to Paulina and knowing that regardless of their friendship the girl would eventually be forced to reveal what she had done with the briefcase. The news of Paulina's arrest had shaken her to the point where it had taken all of her strength and will power to keep from collapsing into tears. Feigning illness, she had canceled her afternoon classes and was on her way home when she had again noticed the man in the green jacket. Perhaps he lived in the same area, and took the same route to work, and as a matter of coincidence had taken off early as many people did on beautiful autumn days. She believed he had been watching her, but now he was nowhere in sight.

Following a group of teenagers as they left the balustrade, she continued across the bridge, passing through the stone archway beneath the fortified tower on the Mala Strana side of the river. Walking along an arcade of shops, she entered a small grocery store and edged her way among the crowd of women picking over what little remained of the fresh fruits and vegetables that had arrived from the countryside after store hours the night before. The store had drawn a block-long queue she had noticed that morning when she left for the skating rink, and those who worked the system and gave their telephone numbers along with a twenty-crown tip to a salesclerk had been first in line, receiving a call the previous night alerting them to the expected delivery of the scarce commodities. Purchasing a few bruised apples left at the bottom of a basket near the door, and a tin of canned beef from atop the butcher's counter that contained only undesirable cuts of overpriced meats, she left the store and walked back toward the bridge in the direction of her apartment.

She drew a sudden silent breath when out of the corner of her eye she saw him again, seated at an outdoor café across the street from the grocery store. He was holding his newspaper pretending to read it, but she had clearly seen him watching her; their eyes had met and he had looked quickly away. It was not her imagination. He *was* following her. They must know she had the briefcase. What had they done to poor Paulina! But why hadn't they arrested *her*. Perhaps they had already found the briefcase in her apartment and now meant to kill her and make it look like an accident. Despite the weakness in her knees and her heart pounding against her chest, she maintained her composure, repeatedly looking over her shoulder as she moved along the arcaded walk. He was no longer seated at the café, and she saw no sign of him as she turned the corner.

Her apartment was on the island of Kampa—a sliver of land separated from the shore by a narrow canal called the Devil's Stream that branched off the main body of the river where it had once served to power an old mill. Descending the stone stairway to the quiet, tree-lined square of former merchants' houses converted to apartments, she entered her building, passing the out-of-order open-cage elevator and running up the four flights of stairs to the top floor. Fumbling for her keys, she unlocked the door to her apartment, leaning against it to catch her breath as she slammed it behind her. Dropping her small bag of groceries, she rushed to her bedroom closet and pulled out the trunk containing her old skating costumes from her days of competition with the national team. Reaching to the bottom of the scarred and battered trunk, she felt the shape of the leather briefcase buried beneath the silk and lace and breathed an audible sigh of relief as she closed the lid. She was still frightened and confused. If they were following her, they had to know that Paulina had given her the briefcase. But why hadn't they searched her apartment, and why had they not arrested her? She had heard stories of their ways of tormenting people, deriving a perverse pleasure from toying with their prey before closing the trap.

Leaving the bedroom, she went to the kitchen. Her hands shook as she filled the tea kettle and placed it on the stove. They continued to shake, rattling the cup and saucer she removed from the cupboard. Moving to the window that overlooked the park and the river, she searched the path leading into the park and what she could see of the benches beneath the trees and along the walks, her eyes finally settling on the spot near the lamppost where she had seen the man in the green jacket the previous evening. He wasn't there. She stared wistfully at two lovers sitting on the low stone wall overlooking the river, leaning against each other in a silent embrace. She continued to watch them until the kettle whistled and startled her into knocking the plant on the window sill to the floor. Taking her cup of tea into the living room, she turned on the small black-and-white television set and sat in her father's chair, curling her legs beneath her as she held the cup with both hands for fear of dropping it. She stared blankly at the screen, hearing nothing the newscaster said.

Her thoughts focused on the events of the past two days. There had never been a choice, she decided. Despite what had happened, she had no regrets over trying to protect Paulina. If nothing else, her contact with the American who had come to the skating rink had provided her with an opportunity she could never have hoped for. And it had crossed her mind that Paulina's telling her that the briefcase had to be gotten to the Americans had subconsciously been part of her decision to help, giving her a way out, a way of seeing Adrian again. The thought suddenly occurred to her that, although she had no friends among the dissidents that she knew of, the STB might be watching her in hopes of being led to others. She decided not to see Pavel. He had called last night and she had broken their date. He must not become involved. They might also be following him. She had been dating him for five years; surely if they suspected her they would be watching him. He was a loyal Party member, one of the unspoken reasons she had refused to marry him, along with the obligation and desire to take care of her father as his condition worsened with age. She did not love Pavel, not in the way she had loved Adrian, but she did not want to be responsible for him being hurt. There was nothing he could do to help, and any involvement with her now could possibly result in the loss of his position with the Federation of Sport, at least that, if he could not convince the STB that he was ignorant of what she had done. She knew what he would tell her to do if she told him about Paulina. He would use what influence he had within the Party to clear her. But it was too late to return the briefcase with impunity, and his efforts would only result in ruining his career and possibly his life. There was no turning back, nowhere to run but to the West, a thought she had entertained since her father's death, and now fate had given her a chance at what she had believed was lost forever.

Compared to most of the citizens of her country, her standard of living was high. She had never joined the Party as many of her friends had—for privileges and promotions rather than belief—but her status as an Olympic champion and as a coach for the national team provided many of the same special privileges. She had her own car, access to the shops selling Western goods, and was allowed to keep her apartment when her father died, exempted from the strict allotment of space caused by the housing shortage that would have required her to share her small three-room apartment—normally allocated for a family of three—with at least one co-tenant. But she was unhappy and unfulfilled. She had applied for an exit permit to visit West Germany after her father had died, with the secret intention of requesting political asylum once there. The permit had been refused as "not in the interests of the state," and she was informed that any future request would be viewed as disloyal and antisocial behavior resulting in the loss of her telephone and driver's license. It was then that she had learned, through Pavel's quiet inquiries, that her file contained a black mark because of her earlier association with Adrian Dulaney.

From that point on she developed a structured pattern of activity to avoid dealing with her emotions, cutting herself off from everyone but her students and Pavel, seeing him only on weekends and further distancing herself from her coworkers on the coaching staff. She spent long hours at the ice rink and her evenings alone in her apartment, reading and choreographing skating routines for her students as she listened to music. She had no choice but to yield to the helplessness of her situation: the sterile convenience of her relationship with Pavel and the banality of her existence, held hostage by a mechanical, inhuman system that made a prison of her life. They still used her on occasion, flaunting her and her Olympic gold medal to visiting Westerners as a triumph of the socialist system. But the occasions when she was required to appear at official Party functions were fewer now; there were new sports heroes and heroines, though none had equaled her accomplishments. Her only remaining joy was found in the progress and achievements of her students. And much of that was now denied her. Shortly after her father's death and her application for the exit permit, the state decided she could no longer be trusted to travel to the skating competitions outside her own country with the exception of the Soviet Union. It had been the final blow to her dignity and self-esteem.

Turning off the television, she put her favorite Mozart string quartet on the stereo and removed her scrapbook from the shelf where she kept her record albums. Returning to the comfortable, well-worn chair, she sat listening to the music in the gathering darkness, paging through the leather-bound scrapbook, stopping to stare at the only picture she had of her and her father together. The photograph had been taken at a banquet given in her honor upon her return to Prague following her Olympic victory. He stood stiffly beside her, uncomfortable in his only suit; a proud smile on his darkly handsome face. Continuing to turn the pages, she gazed fondly at the faded images of a mother she had hardly known and gave only brief attention to the photographs and newspaper articles commemorating her many victories during her years of international competition.

Flipping to the back of the scrapbook, she found what she was looking for: a small envelope of snapshots taken during her skiing trip to the High Tatras with Adrian Dulaney. Believing that that part of her life was over, she had not looked at them since the agonizing day, ten years ago, when, torn between her love for him and for her father, she had refused to go with the West Germans who had come to take her out of the country.

She held the envelope in her lap, afraid to open it; afraid to let herself believe again. She felt a brief tingling sensation, a surge of emotion that flowed through her body with the vivid recollections of Adrian: the way he would gently massage her neck and shoulders, stiff and sore after a day of skating. She smiled inwardly, remembering what she loved most about him. Beneath the aloof, cynical exterior, she had discovered a tenderness and devotion she had never encountered in a man before or since; he had made her feel as though she was the most important thing in his life. He was two men, she had come to realize: considerate and giving with her, yet indifferent and cold to others—only rarely, after some reasoning or test she did not understand, accepting them as being worthy of his trust and friendship. She wondered if he had forgiven her for not going with the men he had sent for her. Was she being unrealistic to think that he still loved her? He had probably married, and had a family. And if he had not, what right did she have to expect that he would come to her or that he would even care, or remember? She smiled at the last thought, feeling a warmth deep within her. When her father died, she had learned that death ends a life, not a relationship; and that absence and time diminished the intensity of emotions, but love, and the memories of cherished moments together and things shared, remained. Circumstances might prevent Adrian from coming to Prague and she might never see him again, but he would remember. However the years had changed him or his life, he had once truly loved her and he would remember, and he would care.

The room fell silent when the music ended. A noise from the hallway outside her apartment startled her, sending the scrapbook and the envelope tumbling from her lap. It had only been the closing of a neighbor's door. Drawing an acquiescent breath, resigned to accept the consequences of her actions, she sat quietly as the fading twilight cast the room in shadows. She began to tremble again and, no longer able to hold back the tears, covered her face with her hands and cried.

※　※　※

Four blocks from the darkened apartment on Kampa Island, on the third floor of the American embassy, Adam Purcell braced himself for the reaction he expected from Jordon Palmer.

The chief of station's face flushed with anger as he thumped his fist on the top of his desk. "What the hell do you mean she burned him? She's a civilian, with no training and no experience. How the hell did it happen?"

"She uses public transportation to get to and from work. Not her car," Purcell said. "When she left the skating rink early, one of the agents working foot surveillance thought she might be contacting someone. The vehicle surveillance backing him up got caught in traffic. He got nervous when she hit the crowds and moved in too close. She spotted him."

"Where is she now?"

"In her apartment. The fixed surveillance team's taken over."

"Did she contact anyone?"

"No. But she may have broken it off when she spotted our man."

"Any update on the STB's progress?"

"I got a message off Nemecek's recorder two hours ago. They're still running round-the-clock interrogations; its getting pretty rough."

"What about the professor's niece . . . Paulina Marcova?"

"According to Nemecek they haven't gotten around to interrogating her. She was only picked up because she was with her boyfriend when the STB grabbed him. Apparently they don't know what they have, yet."

"I'm going to cable the DDO and ask for approval to grab Cernikova if she doesn't keep to her normal routine tomorrow. It's our only chance if she panics and decides to turn herself in, which she may damn well do if she thinks our man was STB."

"Maybe there's a way we can let her know it's us and not them," Purcell said.

"A brush contact?"

Purcell nodded. "We could have someone slip a message into her pocket tomorrow morning. The tram stops are always crowded; it can be easily done while she's boarding or exiting."

"I'll still have to cable the DDO," Palmer said. "His orders were explicit: no contact with her unless the STB makes a move."

"We can use the same agent she burned," Purcell said. "That

way we can really tighten up the surveillance; if she spots him again it'll reassure her instead of spooking her."

"It might work. But the message will have to be carefully worded."

"I'll draft one for your approval while you cable the DDO," Purcell said. "Any news on Adrian Dulaney?"

"He's ours," Palmer said, glancing at his watch. "He should be landing in Germany in three hours."

16

✖ FRANK KESSLER DROVE THE olive-drab army van through the main gate of the Tenth Special Forces Group base at Flint Kaserne and headed north through the Isar River valley on the outskirts of Bad Tolz. Adrian Dulaney sat beside him, stifling a yawn, still tired from the jet lag and the five o'clock wake-up call. The facilities available at the Kaserne were to be used for his training, and he had been brought there by helicopter shortly after landing at the CIA isolation base. Billeted in a private room in the intelligence section on the third floor of the headquarters building, he had gotten little sleep, finally dozing off just as Kessler called advising him that he would pick him up in forty-five minutes. Dressed in camouflage fatigues and cap, his appearance was no different from that of any of the other soldiers, with the exception that his hair was longer than the required military cut.

Dulaney glanced at the picturesque Bavarian countryside as the morning light spread slowly across the deep pine forest and the alpine meadows. He had seen nothing of the surrounding area when the helicopter landed the night before and noticed for the first time the jagged granite peaks of the Alps towering in the distance above the valley. He examined the weapon Kessler had handed him as he climbed into the van. It was the first time he had handled anything like it. The Italian-made Spectre nine-millimeter submachine gun was less than fourteen inches in length with the metal stock folded over the top, and seemed more like a toy than the deadly weapon it was. Kessler reached into the back seat of the van and removed a black, eight-inch-long, cylinder-shaped object from a fitted case, handing it to Dulaney.

"What's that?"

"A sound suppressor," Kessler said. "A two-stage external silencer. The first stage absorbs most of the muzzle blast and the flame; the second stage absorbs the gases. The bolt action of the weapon is also silenced by rubber buffers at the back of the chamber where the bolt makes contact. With subsonic ammunition, the muzzle blast is reduced to the sound of a finger snap, and the bolt action is no more than a click. It can't be heard more than fifteen feet away in most cases, and any background noise like street traffic makes it impossible to hear anything at all. Screw it onto the threads at the front of the barrel."

Dulaney did as instructed, handling the weapon gingerly.

"It doesn't bite," Kessler said. "It's the safest submachine gun made. Unlike a lot of them, it can't discharge accidentally. The first shot is double action."

"If my only purpose is to contact Hana, and you and your men are going to be with me, why do I need a submachine gun? I've never fired one of these things. I can barely hit the proverbial side of a barn with a rifle."

"It's just a precaution; in case we get separated. And before the end of the day you'll be able to hit what you're aiming at." Reaching into his pocket, he handed Dulaney a Walther TPH automatic pistol in a small holster.

"What's this? Another precaution 'just in case'?"

"It's a backup. If you lose your primary weapon it may damn well save your life in a tight situation. It's only twenty-two caliber, so it's not much good for anything except close-up work, but it might come in handy. Strap the holster to your ankle; in five minutes you'll forget it's there."

Dulaney did as he was told, finding that Kessler was right. The slender pistol weighed less than twelve ounces and was unnoticeable beneath his trouser leg, doing nothing to restrict his movement.

"If you have to use it," Kessler added, "never fire just one shot. Get close to your target and fire two or three shots into his head in rapid succession."

"Makes sense to me," Dulaney said. "When do I get the flame thrower and the rocket launcher in case the civilians turn on us?"

Kessler ignored the remark. Two miles north of the base, he turned off the main road and pulled into the restricted area where the rifle range was located. Dulaney followed him onto the range where a long row of human-silhouette targets had been set up at distances from ten to fifty feet. Kessler took the Spectre from him, inserted a full magazine, and extended the folding metal stock.

"This isn't an assault weapon," he told Dulaney. "It's for self-defense at close range. That's all you're going to be concerned with. Used properly it'll provide you with the capability for multiple hits that will instantly terminate your opponent."

Dulaney's eyes widened as he stared at Kessler. He was beginning to understand what was expected of him on the mission. "Why do I need a silencer if I'll be firing at close range? If they can see me, what difference does it make if they can't hear me?"

"You may only be up against one or two men. Without the silencer in an urban area you'll bring every cop within two miles down on you. And if we get into a firefight at the extraction site the silencer won't give away your position. But we're getting ahead of ourselves," Kessler said. "Our mission plan is to avoid contact, not to eliminate people. The submachine guns are for laying down suppressing fire until we can break out of an ambush situation, and for self-defense in case we run into any unexpected situations.

"Now, forget everything you've ever seen in the movies," Kessler continued, tucking the stock of the submachine gun into his shoulder. "The stock is only folded for purposes of concealment—you always extend it and fire from the shoulder. Never fire from the hip; the garden-hose school of firing only wastes ammunition and tells your opponent that you're a fool or an amateur, or both. You'll have five spare thirty-round magazines with you, but you can't afford to blast away. This weapon can fire nine hundred rounds per minute, fifteen rounds a second. Which means you can empty a magazine in two seconds and be out of ammo in twelve seconds if you fire indiscriminately. And while you're changing magazines you're vulnerable. Sustained bursts only waste ammo and move you off target—most of your rounds will miss. You can't afford to empty a magazine on one man, so use only what it takes to bring him down. Practice firing in short bursts until you get the feel of the trigger, so that you can get off controlled, well-aimed, three-shot bursts. That's enough to contaminate a large area if the rounds are accurately placed. The object is to create a burst pattern so dense that your target can't avoid being hit. If he's running, start your bursts just behind him, overtake him, then come back across him in a figure-eight pattern. Aim for his center mass and track him as you fire. Shoot only as fast as you can hit."

Kessler dropped into a crouch and fired off five three-round bursts, making direct hits on the five targets he had aimed for. Rising to his feet, he moved quickly, dropping again into a crouch and firing with the same results. Dulaney stood in awe of Kessler's accuracy and the lack of noise made by the weapon.

"Fire and move. Fire and move," he told Dulaney, returning to where he stood. "If we run into trouble in the city and you have to open fire, make maximum use of available cover and move quickly from one covered position to another to outflank and eliminate your opponent. Never turn your back on an area you haven't cleared, and be aware of what's around you. Keep the stock to your shoulder and the weapon in position to shoot as you move, and don't fix your attention on just one opponent. Direct your fire from one to the other and keep them pinned down until you can effect your escape. Go through a doorway or any funnel area quickly and get under cover on the other side; if there's no cover, drop into a crouch and keep your back to the wall. The crouch position I just used lowers your target profile, it's a stable firing platform, and you can get up and move quickly."

Dulaney remained silent as Kessler handed him the submachine gun and walked back to the van, returning with a box full of magazines for the weapon and a leather contraption that Dulaney recognized as some sort of holster.

Kessler helped him into the custom-designed shoulder holster made especially for the Spectre, adjusting the straps until it fit snugly along his left side beneath his arm. Taking the weapon from him, he demonstrated how to holster it and draw it into a ready position.

The submachine gun with the silencer threaded onto the barrel weighed less than seven pounds, but extended down Dulaney's side to the top of his thigh, it caused him to move awkwardly as he followed Kessler's instructions and walked around with the Spectre in position and practiced drawing and reholstering it.

"You'll get used to it," Kessler said. "In a little while you'll walk normally. The parka you'll be wearing will conceal it. Just get comfortable with drawing and firing. And remember, when you perceive a threat, use it. Don't hesitate, don't think. Just react immediately and take out your opponent. If we run into the STB, we're up against people who know how to use their weapons and won't hesitate to shoot you. Shoot first with well-aimed fire and don't stop until you've dropped them. They have the edge in experience over you, but you've got the edge in firepower, and a psychological advantage with a submachine gun against the pistols they carry."

"Eliminate. Terminate. Take out. Bring down. Drop," Dulaney said sarcastically. "Why don't you just say what you mean? You want me to kill people."

"I don't want you to kill anyone. I want you committed and prepared to carry out the mission, and to get your ass back here in one piece—with Cernikova."

"I don't feel qualified for this," Dulaney said. "You're putting me in a position where I could jeopardize Hana's life as well as your mission."

"This isn't a marriage made in heaven," Kessler said. "If I had my way you wouldn't be here. I don't like your attitude; it makes you about as useful as a car-chasing seeing-eye dog. But I'm stuck with you, and so is Cernikova if she wants to stay alive. My job is to get you to her and get both of you back out. I want you as prepared for that as I can possibly make you in two days. If you pay attention and do what you're told you'll have the basics of what you'll need by the time we launch the mission."

Dulaney made no reply and began firing the weapon, the majority of his shots impacting in the ground or wide of the targets. His hands shook as he ceased firing at Kessler's command.

"Let the weapon ride easy in your hands," Kessler said. "Don't fight it, and you'll do away with most of the muzzle climb and stay on target."

Taking the submachine gun from Dulaney, he demonstrated the technique as he talked. "Don't use the sights unless you're firing on semiautomatic. Just look over the top of the weapon with both eyes open, fire low, and correct visually when you see where the rounds are impacting."

Dulaney tried again. The first few rounds again impacted in the dirt, but the remainder hit the target in a widely dispersed pattern.

"That's better," Kessler said, noticing the jeep that pulled into the parking area. He nodded to Lieutenant Colonel Kitlan then turned back to Dulaney. "Keep at it," he said. "Practice your trigger control. You're getting off six- and seven-shot bursts. Get it down to three. When you feel comfortable, move from target to target. Don't try to shoot and move at the same time. When you shoot, shoot carefully, when you move, move quickly. Don't hesitate, but don't panic, and don't break visual contact with your target while you're moving. And fire a few magazines from the pistol until you get a feel for it."

Kitlan stood at the entrance to the range, watching as Dulaney's fear of the weapon diminished and his accuracy improved. He returned Kessler's salute as he reached his side.

"How's he doing?" Kitlan asked.

Kessler shook his head. "I think it's beginning to dawn on him that this isn't Dungeons and Dragons or something he can walk away from once we're over the fence and things get rough. He's a little rattled and he's got a bad attitude."

"That's better than someone who's seen too many James Bond movies."

"I'd rather have someone closer to the middle ground, sir," Kessler said. "I don't know if it's a lack of courage or self-confidence, but there's an undercurrent of fear that's going to make him difficult to control."

"You don't make it through Marine Corps boot camp unless you can tough it out under stress," Kitlan said. "He may be more than he thinks he is."

"His only motivation is the girl," Kessler said. "And he's a little too intelligent and perceptive to think this is going to be a cakewalk. He hasn't said anything yet, but I think he's having second thoughts."

They continued to watch as Dulaney gained confidence with the submachine gun and began moving and firing along the line of targets.

"He seems to be getting the hang of it," Kitlan said.

"I don't understand why the Agency insisted on giving him weapons," Kessler said. "We can cover him while he contacts Cernikova. And we have no way of knowing how he'll react under fire. If we get into it with the STB in the middle of the city he's liable to take out innocent civilians."

Kitlan nodded. "I argued that point with them. But they insisted."

"Why?"

"They said the submachine gun and the backup pistol would bolster his confidence," Kitlan said. "Give him a false sense of security. I think it's for their own security purposes. If he doesn't have a weapon he's more likely to throw up his hands and surrender if he thinks he's trapped. Then the Czechs have one live, untrained prisoner they can make talk and put on trial. That's the last thing the Agency wants. If he's got a weapon, chances are he's going to use it and draw fire; the possibilities of him getting killed in an exchange are excellent."

"My heroes," Kessler said. "Always the high road."

"Have you told him about the jump?"

Kessler shook his head. "I'm saving that until this afternoon."

"We've worked out the mission plan," Kitlan said. "One of the Agency's special-mission aircraft flying beneath the radar coverage will take you about seven or eight miles over the fence, beyond the Czech troop concentrations. You'll be going out at three hundred feet using the new cluster canopy chute."

"I was afraid of that," Kessler said, familiar with the Low-Altitude Parachute System. "I don't like that chute, colonel. The speed of the aircraft is critical to proper deployment."

"I'll personally select and brief the pilots," Kitlan said. "You've jumped the chute before, and it's the best way to get a novice like Dulaney on the ground; he won't have time to think, let alone make any mistakes."

"I hope they're not insisting on giving him a practice jump,"

Kessler said. "I was planning on just letting him take a few jumps off the mock tower in the riggers' shed at the base."

"I think that would be best. A practice jump might scare the hell out of him, and if he injures himself he's useless to them."

"I have him scheduled for the riggers' shed after lunch," Kessler said. "I'll make sure the warrant officer in charge understands that the object is to build up his confidence. After that I thought I'd give him a few more hours on the range, then a skull session in his room: some instructions in urban operations and small unit tactics, familiarization with the radio he'll have to use in the event we get separated, and make sure he understands how to use his map to reach the extraction site if he ends up on his own. Then more of the same tomorrow."

"They want you and Dulaney back at the isolation base by sixteen hundred hours tomorrow for the final briefing. I'm going back in an hour. They'll send a chopper for you. Do the best you can with him."

"Yes, sir."

Dulaney was silent during the ride from the rifle range back to the base, and said very little as he and Kessler grabbed a quick lunch in the mess hall. Kessler left him to his private thoughts, making only occasional attempts at small talk, avoiding discussing any aspects of his training or the mission within earshot of the men seated nearby.

Kessler tensed with the approach of a man who pulled out a chair and joined them at their table. The man's name was Butler, a staff sergeant assigned to one of the Special Forces SCUBA teams. He and Shumate had been close friends. Kessler quickly realized his mistake in bringing Dulaney to the mess hall, but could do nothing to avoid what he knew was coming.

"What the hell happened, Frank?" Butler said, his face showing the grief and concern he felt over the loss of his friend. "I just got the word. They said Walt and four other guys from your team all bought it in a chopper crash two days ago. I thought you were with them."

"No," Kessler said awkwardly. "I was on another assignment."

"The sergeant major said you all left together on a classified training exercise. Cut out of here in a hurry."

"The sergeant major's got it wrong."

"Where did it happen?" Butler asked, glancing at Dulaney,

trying to place him. Dulaney was watching Kessler closely, curious about his reaction to Butler's presence, noticing that he was extremely uncomfortable.

"I don't know any more than you do."

"I just can't believe it. A field exercise. What a goddamn waste," Butler said, shaking his head sadly. "A bunch of us are getting together tonight at Walt's place. His wife's taking it pretty hard. Why don't you come over about eight o'clock."

"I'll try," Kessler said. "But the colonel's got me tied up with some work for the next few days."

Butler rose from his chair, placing a consoling hand on Kessler's shoulder. "He was one of the best, Frank, and a good friend. I'm gonna miss him."

"Yeah. Me, too."

When Butler had left the table, Dulaney stared hard at Kessler. "When did you say you saw Hana? Two days ago?"

"Not here," Kessler said sharply. "This isn't the place to discuss it."

"You never mentioned anything about how you got in and out of Czechoslovakia," Dulaney said. "Your friends weren't killed in a helicopter crash, were they? They were killed on that mission."

"I said, not here, *goddamn it!*"

Kessler rose abruptly from the table and motioned for Dulaney to follow him. Leaving the mess hall, they walked through the archway leading out of the quadrangle and proceeded in the direction of the parachute riggers' shed.

Dulaney took two steps to Kessler's one in an effort to keep pace as he stomped toward the entrance to the building that had served as a tank repair shop when the Kaserne was the home of the SS officers' training school.

"Nothing I can't handle, Kessler? Isn't that what you said? Five Green Berets are killed doing the same thing and it's nothing I can't handle?"

"You don't know what you're talking about."

"I think I know a hell of a lot more than you want me to."

"Drop it!" Kessler said as he opened the door to the riggers' shed. "It's got nothing to do with this mission. So just let it lie and concentrate on what we've got to do to get you ready."

Dulaney followed Kessler into the building and shook hands with the leather-faced warrant officer he was introduced to.

Sunlight streamed through the skylights in the high-ceilinged, cavernous building highlighting rows of nylon suspension lines hanging along the walls. The floor on one side of the building was lined with stacks of recently packed parachutes, and dominating the interior of the building, looming thirty feet above the floor, was a platform fronted with a camouflage-painted partition resembling an aircraft door. Dulaney's attention was drawn first to the tower, then to a small area divided from the rest of the building by a row of wall lockers. The area contained a four-foot-high table placed at the end of a padded gymnasium mat. Large posters depicting the cartoon character Snoopy giving basic instructions for safety procedures during a parachute jump were affixed to the backs of the lockers behind the table. While Kessler spoke privately with the warrant officer and one of his assistants, Dulaney walked around the lockers for a closer look at the mock tower and the empty harness attached to a steel cable in the doorway.

"I'm going to start you off on the table with some PLFs," Kessler said, when he'd finished talking with the warrant officer.

"PLFs?" Dulaney said.

"Parachute landing falls," Kessler said. "You stand on the table and jump down onto the mat."

Dulaney stiffened and glared at Kessler.

"It's a simple procedure," Kessler said. "Just do exactly what I tell you."

Climbing up on the table, Kessler stood on the edge. "Keep your feet and knees together, your knees slightly bent, point your toes downward, look down at a forty-five-degree angle, put your hands over your head and your elbows in. When you hit the mat rotate your body in the direction of the fall. Make contact with the balls of your feet, then your calf, thigh, butt and shoulder. Just relax, hit, and roll into it."

Jumping off the table in a demonstration, Kessler did a perfect PLF, following through to a stand-up position. "It's easy. Give it a try."

Dulaney stared in disbelief, shrugging Kessler's hand from his shoulder. "Are you out of your mind! I'm not jumping out of an airplane. I never even went off the high diving board when I was a kid. I'm afraid of heights—I always have been."

Kessler pulled him aside to where they couldn't be overheard by the warrant officer and his assistant. "It's the way we're going in, Dulaney. You've got to learn the basics. Believe me, there's nothing to it."

"You're not listening, Kessler. I'm *not* jumping out of any goddamn airplane! You figure out some other way to get me in there."

"There is no other way. We'd never get through on foot—the Czechs have tripled their border patrols and have them on full alert."

"You mean they're expecting us?"

"They're expecting someone to break out. Not in."

"Out is exactly what we have to get once we're in," Dulaney said.

"We've got that covered."

"How?"

"Once we get you and Cernikova to the extraction site a chopper will be sent in to bring us out."

"If a helicopter can bring us out, why can't it take us in?"

"If a chopper is spotted it immediately tells them that they're dealing with a military mission, and when it lands to put us out everyone in the immediate area will know exactly where we are. We'd be nailed before we got anywhere near Prague. We don't care if they know we've left when the mission's completed, but we can't take the chance of being compromised on the way in. A small twin-engine civilian aircraft can fly nap-of-the-earth, beneath the radar coverage, and drop us without even decreasing its airspeed. Even if it's picked up on radar it could pass for a civilian flight off course. The pilot will be crossing the border at one point and flying a semicircular course inside their territory before he crosses back over. They won't have any way of knowing if we bailed out, or where we bailed out. The drop zone for the jump will be in a remote area well behind their border defenses."

"If he's going to be flying at treetop level, they'll be able to see him, and us, from the ground."

"They might hear the aircraft, but they won't see anything, not at night."

Dulaney shook his head vigorously. "You can count me out, Kessler. I'm not geared for this."

Kessler pointed to the thirty-foot platform. "If you can make a jump off that mock tower, you can do what's required for the mission. It's that simple."

Dulaney glanced up at the tower and back to Kessler. "Don't insult my intelligence. I'm not completely ignorant. I know that you have to steer parachutes."

"We'll be going out at three hundred feet. Your chute will be deployed by a static line. You'll be on the ground in less than ten seconds. You won't have to do anything, you'll be nothing but a bundle." Kessler kept his own doubts about the experimental nature of the triple-canopy low-exit parachute they would be using to himself. "Do a few PLFs off the table—then you can try the tower. Give it a chance."

Dulaney's eyes were riveted on the platform high above him as he slowly shook his head.

"At least try a PLF," Kessler said, leading him to the table. "The only difference between a jump from the table, the tower, or an aircraft is distance. The landings are all the same."

Dulaney smiled grimly as he climbed up on the table. "You should sell used cars when you retire from the army, Kessler. You've got the knack."

Dulaney made six jumps off the table, landing with some semblance of a PLF, but Kessler offered only encouragement and no criticism.

"Now we'll try the tower," he told Dulaney. "I'll show you how it's done."

Unlike the mock tower used at the army's airborne training school at Fort Benning, Georgia, where the jumper is suspended from guy wires and descends at an angle, the tower in the riggers' shed was designed so a jumper descended straight down, the velocity of his fall determined by the resistance set on the mechanism that controlled the release of the steel cable attached to his harness. The tower was used by men reporting to the unit whose jump status wasn't current and who had to reinforce the basics they had learned at airborne school before making an operational jump. Kessler climbed the ladder leading to the platform on top of the thirty-foot tower and slipped into the harness. Standing in the doorway, he jumped, dropping to the padded mat below and landing with only slightly more force than when he had jumped off the four-foot table. He rolled out of his PLF and unfastened the harness, which was retracted back to the top of the tower.

"Your turn," he said to Dulaney. "I'll go up with you to make sure you get the harness on right."

Dulaney hesitated, then climbed the ladder ahead of Kessler, keeping his eyes straight ahead, afraid to look down. Kessler helped him on with the harness when they reached the platform, making certain the straps were secured and in the proper position.

"Nothing to it," Kessler reassured him. "Just do the same thing you did when you jumped from the table."

Dulaney glanced downward and froze in the doorway. The row of wall lockers appeared to be directly in his line of fall. "I'll land on the damn lockers," he said, backing away from the door.

"I didn't hit them, did I?" Kessler said, guiding him back to the door. "It just looks that way. If it makes you feel more comfortable, sit on the edge of the platform and shove yourself out from that position."

Dulaney did as Kessler instructed, closing his eyes as he sat, rigid from sheer terror, on the edge of the platform, finally summoning the will power to launch himself into the air. He landed gently, but forgot to execute a PLF and simply flopped backward onto his rear end. Kessler quickly descended the ladder and helped him out of the harness.

"What did I tell you? Nothing to it. Do a few more for good measure and you're ready."

Dulaney shrugged off the harness and turned to Kessler. He was visibly shaken. "I've gone as far as I can with this. I'm not jumping out of any goddamn airplane."

"All right. Relax. That's enough for now. We'll go back to your room and go over some other things."

Dulaney said nothing in response to Kessler's words of encouragement as they walked back through the quadrangle and entered the headquarters building. Closing the door to his room when they were both inside, he finally spoke. "You either don't understand, or choose not to understand," he said. "It's over. I'm not going on the mission and that's final. And please, no more of your condescending bullshit."

"You're going to quit?" Kessler said. "You're going to leave Cernikova twisting in the wind?"

"I'm going to hire someone. Professionals who specialize in getting people out. They got to her before, they can do it again."

"There's no time for that," Kessler said. "We're dealing with hours here, not days. And they wouldn't stand a chance of getting her out with the border troops on full alert. They wouldn't even attempt it until the alert is over, and by then it'll be too late."

"Judging from what your friend let slip at lunch, five highly trained men were killed trying this same type of operation a few days ago," Dulaney said. "I don't want to be the sixth. And I'm not doing Hana any favor by putting her in a situation that could get her killed."

"I'm not at liberty to discuss that operation with you. Someone screwed up. It's not likely to happen again. But if we don't get you to Cernikova damn soon she's going to end up dead, or worse; she'll spend the rest of her life in a Czech prison. I can't guarantee you that we'll come out on top, but I can guarantee you that Cernikova will pay the price if we don't get to her first."

"I'll get her out my own way."

"It won't work, sport. You've got to get off the fence and make a commitment. This time you have to put your ass on the line, not your checkbook."

"I'm not you, Kessler. I spent most of my life drifting downstream, bouncing off the rocks, with a lot of money to cushion the blows. I can't pretend to be something I'm not. I'm no hero and I'm no tough guy."

"All the tough guys I know are dead," Kessler said. "And the difference between a hero and a coward isn't lack of fear, it's the will to overcome it and do what has to be done, and hope you can pull it off even though you're scared shitless. You go forward, one step at a time, and do the best you can."

"What's the point if all I succeed in doing is getting us both killed."

"If there's nothing worth dying for, then there's nothing worth living for."

"Who dangled those noble prepositions, Rod McKuen?"

"It might be a cliché, Dulaney, but whether you care to own up to it or not, it's true. Cernikova had other options, but she put her life in your hands; that took guts. A hell of a lot more than it seems you have."

"You haven't lived my life, so don't criticize my choices."

"You do what your heart tells you," Kessler said, going to the door. "I'll be back in an hour. If you still feel the same way . . . if you can't hack it, no one can force you to go. You can go back to your gentleman's farm and fly your goddamn hawk and drive your fancy cars and make your smart-ass remarks and keep your distance from the real world. But some day you'll learn that it doesn't work that way. Sooner or later you've got to climb into the ring with the rest of us. I don't know what the hell Cernikova ever saw in you, but she deserves better. A whole hell of a lot better."

⚒ ⚒ ⚒

Kessler contacted Lieutenant Colonel Kitlan on the secure line he had been instructed to use in the colonel's office, apprising him of the situation. He spent the balance of the hour in his on-base apartment with his wife and three-year-old daughter. His mind was on the mission, grappling with the possibilities left to him to make a success of it without Dulaney. If he could convince Cernikova that he would get her out of the country, she might give him the briefcase. He dismissed the thought. It was her only leverage, and he believed she would see the folly in trusting a stranger who could throw her to the wolves. With the briefcase in her possession, she at least had something to give to the STB if all else failed, claiming to have been confused or paralyzed with fear, or whatever excuse she could invent for her delay in turning it over. He tried to force the mission from his mind and switched on the television, watching the delayed satellite telecast of the "Today Show" as his daughter fell asleep at his side. His wife, Janet, sat beside him trying unsuccessfully to hide the fear she felt after hearing about the deaths of his teammates, knowing that her husband had been with them when it happened. Kessler put his arm around her and held her close. She knew he could not talk about whatever it was he was doing, and she had learned through the years not to ask; not to make it any more difficult for both of them.

"You'll be careful, Bear," she said, raising her head to kiss him, holding on tightly as he embraced her.

"I'll be back in a few days. I promise," he said, lingering in her arms. Getting to his feet, he leaned over and kissed his sleeping daughter lightly on the forehead before leaving the apartment.

The colonel had instructed him to inform the provost marshal to place an MP on guard outside Dulaney's room. He was not to be allowed out until further notice. Kessler returned to the third floor of the headquarters building and knocked on Dulaney's door to tell him of the restriction. There was no answer. He knocked louder; the door was ajar and swung open to reveal an empty room. Kessler stepped inside and checked the bathroom. He was gone. Running down the hallway and taking the stairs two at a time, he left the building and sprinted the distance to the main gate, startling one of the guards on duty as he grabbed him by the shoulder. The guard assured him that he had seen no one matching Dulaney's description leaving the base since he came on duty four hours before. Kessler was about to return to the headquarters building to get the van and continue his search when he heard a familiar voice call out to him. It was the warrant officer from the riggers' shed; he was parked in the outbound lane at the gate waiting for the traffic light to turn green. Leaning out the window of his car, he motioned to Kessler. "Your greenhorn's not as dumb as you thought he was."

"What are you talking about? Do you know where he is?"

"Yeah. He's at the riggers' shed," the crusty veteran said with a grin. "He told me to knock off the crap and set the tension on the cable the same as it would be for a real jump."

Kessler ran the short distance to the riggers' shed and entered to see Dulaney standing in the doorway of the mock tower: his face white with fear, his eyes fixed straight ahead. He spotted Kessler standing next to the young sergeant who the warrant officer had left in charge and called down to him. "Don't read more meaning into it than it can support, Kessler. I'll try. That's all I can promise."

"It's his eleventh jump," the young sergeant said. "He lands in a heap every time, but he goes back for more. Keeps mumbling something about the obstacle strengthening the will."

Dulaney closed his eyes and jumped, landing with a bone-jarring jolt that sent him tumbling off the mat. Getting slowly to his feet, he started back up the ladder to the top of the tower.

"Don't lie to me anymore, Kessler," he shouted from the doorway as he strapped on the harness. "I think I can handle it if you just don't lie to me."

17

THE LARGE HOLDING CELL on the basement level of the detention center inside the STB headquarters compound was packed with more than one hundred fifty men and women. Teenage students, middle-aged professors, writers and artists, known and suspected members of the dissident community—a few guilty of nothing more than being in the presence of others when they were arrested—all were crammed into a space meant to accommodate less than half their number. Some leaned against the cold stone walls while others sat huddled on the concrete floor or peered through the bars at the front of the cell, their faces drawn and sallow in the glare of the naked light bulbs dangling from the ceiling in the hallway outside. The vacant stares and silent resignation of those who had suffered previous visits to the detention center set them apart from the young and inexperienced whose urgent whispers and darting eyes reflected their fear and dread of the unknown. An occasional scream of pain echoed throughout the basement—an electrifying jolt that heightened the anxiety and unbearable tension as they waited their turn in the interrogation rooms occupied by the KGB at the end of the hallway.

No closer to locating the scientist's briefcase than when they had started, Rudenko's frustration and innate cruelty had driven him, and consequently his men, to extremes that served only to abuse and terrorize their subjects into revealing worthless rumors and giving false confessions in hopes of avoiding further torture. In contrast to Rudenko's narrow selection of victims, Josef Masek's STB interrogators, following his orders, used less brutal and more intelligent methods. They had worked in shifts around the clock in a systematic attempt to single out and concentrate on those who were closely associated with the student dissident who had been identified when fleeing the professor's cottage and arrested shortly after his return to Prague. The student had revealed nothing under interrogation, but through his friends and acquaintances Masek's men had pieced together enough information to identify the others who were seen leaving the cottage with him. Their progress beyond the initial stages of interrogation of the three student dissidents had been limited by Rudenko's untimely demands to have them turned over to his men in an attempt to get immediate results.

One of the students had died while being tortured, and another had been beaten to the point of incoherence and had been subsequently thrown into an isolation cell. Both of them had denied any knowledge of the briefcase. Eduard Antos, the third student who had been at the cottage and the only one remaining with direct knowledge of the events following the defector's death, had been dragged to the KGB interrogation room despite Masek's protests to allow him to continue his own interrogation. Antos was strong and defiant, and his resistance and determination did not waver despite the brutal punishment he was enduring. Masek believed the young man's resolve and courage lay in the fact that he was protecting someone—possibly someone who had been at the cottage and left prior to the arrival of his men—and he had suggested that Rudenko delay any further physical torture of Antos until it could be determined who his close friends were. They could then be isolated and interrogated in a more productive manner and any information gotten from them used to convince Antos that the discovery of the person he was protecting was inevitable and any further resistance would only prolong his agony to no purpose. Rudenko had refused to release him to Masek's men, steadfast in his conviction that Antos had himself hidden the briefcase and would eventually tell them where it was.

Masek left the interrogation room in anger and disgust, certain that Rudenko's gruesome methods would get nothing from the young man. Continuing up the hallway, he paused before the crowded holding cell. His eyes moved slowly over the faces of those inside, revealing no hint of recognition as he spotted the two undercover agents who had been arrested with the dissidents. His attention was drawn to a young girl he judged to be no more than eighteen. She had light blond hair and was dressed in a bright red sweater and jeans and sat in a corner near the iron grille. Her knees were tucked under her chin and she stared blankly at the floor. She looked familiar to him and he recalled seeing her being brought into the detention center two nights ago, or was it the previous night—he was too tired to remember. He attributed her familiarity, as he had before, to the fact that she bore a slight physical resemblance to his daughter and was approximately the same age. Turning away, he continued to the end of the hallway and slowly climbed the stairs, leaving the detention center, and walking toward his office building. As he crossed the inner courtyard, the cold morning mist that hung in the air served to revive him while the gray dawn light reminded him that he had lost track of time and had been up the entire night.

Pouring himself a cup of thick, black coffee, he settled into his office chair and propped his feet up on the desk. He unwrapped one of the sandwiches his wife had sent over the previous evening, but he was too exhausted to eat and placed it back in the paper bag. He had had less than seven hours of sleep in the past three days, and drank a second cup of coffee in an attempt to fight off the mental fatigue. A trace of a smile creased his weary face as his gaze settled on the photograph of the family outing at the skating pond near their home. The smile was slowly replaced with a pensive stare. His onyx eyes hardened, fixed and unfocused as he searched his memory for the name and association that were eluding him. With a sudden movement born of inspiration, he swung his legs from the desk and reached into the top section of his file tray, pulling out a stack of arrest reports as he pressed the button on his intercom.

"There is a young blond girl in a red sweater in the holding cell," he told the assistant who answered the intercom. "I believe her name is Marcova. Bring her to my office immediately, along with our complete file on Professor Marcovic. And say nothing of this to our KGB friends."

Paging quickly through the stack of papers, he found Paulina

Marcova's arrest report. A smile of satisfaction returned to his face as he read the brief entry under the heading "Reason for Arrest and Detention": *"Subject and two other students were seated at café table in company of Eduard Antos at the time of his arrest. Subject has no record of affiliation with dissident community."* The hastily written report gave no biographical information, due to the peripheral nature of her arrest, and she had been given low priority for interrogation. Her name, and the fact that she knew Antos, had not consciously registered during his initial perusal of the arrest reports and had not been what jogged his memory, though it now confirmed his growing suspicions. He now knew why she had looked so familiar to him. She was a member of the Czechoslovak national figure-skating team —a promising skater, an Olympic hopeful who had won the Prague Skates competition the previous winter. He had seen her perform on a number of occasions when he had accompanied his wife and daughter to the competitions. With the recollection of her name—the feminine derivative of Marcovic used by all female members of the family as was the Czech custom—came the realization that she might be related to the professor who had died at the hands of the KGB. Removing another stack of papers from the lower section of the file tray on his desk, he sorted through them until he found the copy of the report on the murder of the two VB officers at the planetarium just outside the Park of Culture where the skating rink was located. The ties were tenuous at best, but held promise given Paulina Marcova's association with Eduard Antos. And the coincidences of location and the synchronicity of events could not be ignored. The American parachutist could have been meeting a contact in the wooded park near the planetarium, but he could also have been en route to the skating rink.

The door to his office opened and Paulina Marcova was escorted in by one of his assistants, who left at Masek's command after handing him the file on Professor Marcovic. The young girl stood stiffly before Masek's desk. She was short and small boned with a compact figure of well-conditioned muscles defined and toned from within by the rigors and demands of her training. Her facial features, framed in the soft natural curls of her short-cut hair, were fine and delicate, possessing the exquisite, fragile beauty of a porcelain figurine and dominated by large, expressive blue eyes full of the innocence of youth and inexperience. She nervously shifted her weight as she stared into the coarse, brooding face of the squat, heavily muscled man who occasionally glanced up at her in silence as he flipped through the pages of the file.

"I have seen you skate many times," Masek said as he closed the file folder. "You are very good. My daughter tells me you will be our next Olympic champion."

"Thank you," Paulina said. "I train very hard."

"You are related to Professor Marcovic?"

"Yes." Her voice was weak and nearly inaudible. "He is my uncle."

Masek saw her struggle to maintain her balance as she began to sway. Her alabaster skin paled and her eyes drifted about the room. Rising from his desk, he pulled a chair over to where she stood.

"Please. Be seated," he said in a soft, consoling voice.

"Thank you," she said, dropping into the chair as if she were about to collapse.

"Have you had anything to eat since you were arrested?"

Paulina slowly shook her head.

Masek poured her a cup of coffee and reached into the brown paper bag on his desk, offering her one of his sandwiches. "You will feel better if you eat something."

Paulina hesitated, then took the sandwich from his outstretched hand. Quickly unwrapping it, she bit hungrily into the first food she had had in three days.

"Do you know why you were arrested?" Masek asked, keeping his tone as soft and avuncular as his deep gruff voice would allow.

"No one has told me," she replied, avoiding Masek's penetrating gaze. "I would like to call my mother. She will be very worried."

"Your mother has been notified," Masek said. "You were arrested because you were in the company of a young man who has committed a very serious crime against the state."

"I have done nothing," Paulina said, her eyes rising to meet Masek's. "I am a student. I was having coffee with friends at a café near the university."

"With Eduard Antos."

Paulina directed her eyes downward, taking another bite of

the sandwich. After a long pause she answered. "Yes. I know him from school."

"He is your boyfriend?"

Paulina's expression was none too convincing. "No. He is a fourth-year student; I am only in my first year."

"He is a student of your uncle's?"

Paulina nodded and again looked away.

"Your friend Antos is in a difficult situation," Masek said. "The KGB are interrogating him at this very moment. I do not approve of our Soviet advisers' methods, but without your co-operation I can do nothing to help him."

"I don't know how I can help you."

"Were you at your uncle's cottage at the lake four nights ago?"

Paulina shook her head.

"Was Eduard Antos there?"

"I don't know."

"How long have you been involved with your uncle and Antos in their activities with the dissident community?"

"I know nothing about the dissidents," Paulina said, her voice gaining strength with the denial. "I am a student and a figure skater. I am not political."

"I believe that Eduard Antos is indirectly responsible for the deaths of two VB officers," Masek said. His tone had turned angry despite his efforts to remain calm. He wanted to spare her the treatment she would receive from the KGB when her significance was discovered, and he knew his time was limited. There were those within his department who would soon learn that he had singled her out and would inform Rudenko.

"Eduard is not a murderer!"

"Why do you think the American CIA parachutist was going to the skating rink? Were you to meet him there and give him the defector's briefcase?"

Paulina's head jerked suddenly upward. Tears welled in her eyes as she vigorously shook her head. "Please, you are confusing me. I know nothing about the CIA or a briefcase, or the murder of the policemen. I don't know what you want from me."

"I want you to tell me the truth, and save the life of Eduard Antos," Masek said, again softening his tone. "The KGB knows that he was at your uncle's cottage the night of the Soviet defector's death. And I know that neither he nor the others with him had the briefcase when they left. Someone removed it from the cottage before my men arrived. I believe it was you."

Paulina's body trembled as tears streamed from her eyes. Her hands gripped the arms of the chair as she stared at the floor. "I was not at my uncle's cottage," she said in a halting voice. "Please don't let them hurt Eduard anymore . . . I heard him scream."

"I can do nothing unless you tell me where the briefcase is."

"I don't know." She was sobbing now and began to shake uncontrollably, wrapping her arms around her body in an effort to gain control. "I don't know."

18

�֍ LT. COL. PAUL KITLAN retracted his telescoping pointer and turned away from the large-scale map of the Czech–West German border.

"Any questions?" he asked, looking into the tense faces of the men seated before him in the briefing room at the CIA isolation base.

Frank Kessler, along with Arnie Natalie and Jim Hawke— the two other Green Berets selected for the operation—remained silent, having completed their briefback of the mission plan prior to Kitlan's final comments.

"Yes," Adrian Dulaney said, looking up from his small folding map of the border area on which he had carefully marked the location of the extraction site. "I don't understand why I can't simply take Hana to the embassy in Prague. If I'm supposed to hand the briefcase over to the CIA when I contact her, why can't we just go with them instead of exposing her to the dangers involved in getting her out your way?"

Elliot Simpson, the CIA's deputy chief of station from Bonn, fielded the question. "This is a covert operation," he said. "You're entering the country illegally and she's attempting to leave it illegally. The State Department would in all probability be left with no alternative but to turn you both over to the Czechs. We'd be unable to help you and would have to deny any knowledge of your activities. So under no circumstances are you to go to our embassy. You will adhere to the mission plan. Is that understood?"

Dulaney nodded. The information and instructions he had absorbed during his training and the briefings were forced to the back of his mind as his thoughts again returned to the parachute jump and the raw fear that had been with him since he first learned about it. The only reprieve had been the sleeping pill that allowed him to get six hours of uninterrupted rest before the 1 A.M. wake-up call for the final briefing. The emphasis Kessler had placed on his being prepared in the event he and Hana were separated from the three-man team or any of them were captured or killed had rattled him further, but the instructions he had received in the use of the sophisticated radio to contact them or the mission support site on the border in the event of such an emergency had helped calm him.

"Then that's it, men," Kitlan said, consulting his watch. "It is now oh-two-thirty hours. You will board the aircraft in exactly thirty minutes."

Dulaney followed Kessler and his two teammates out of the briefing room and down a narrow corridor to the supply room where the CIA stored their weapons and equipment for covert operations. They had already been given and were wearing the sterile civilian clothing of Czechoslovakian and East German manufacture; all that remained was to be issued their weapons and ammunition and the equipment for the parachute jump.

Dulaney felt an arm drape over his shoulder. It belonged to Arnie Natalie. The short, wiry staff sergeant had a perpetual mischievous glint in his eyes and an engaging sense of humor that occasionally surfaced from beneath his stern, professional manner. Natalie gave him a smile and wink. "Relax," he told Dulaney. "You're in good hands. I've seen every movie John Wayne made. Twice."

Dulaney forced a nervous smile as he strapped on the shoulder holster Kessler handed him along with the sound-suppressed submachine gun. Inserting a full thirty-round magazine of ammunition into the weapon and placing it in the holster, he pulled on a parka that concealed its presence. He felt relatively comfortable with the weapon in place; he was aware of its weight and bulk but had become accustomed to it to the point where his natural movement was no longer obviously restricted.

He placed three spare magazines of ammunition in the cargo pockets of his parka and two more in the slim leather pouches attached to the shoulder-holster strap on his left side beneath his arm. Pulling up his trouser leg, he wrapped the Velcro strap of the small holster containing the twenty-two-caliber automatic pistol around his ankle and struggled into the one-piece jumpsuit that would be discarded once they were on the ground. Slipping into his parachute harness and pack tray, he fumbled with the adjustment straps, and Jim Hawke, the second man Kessler had chosen for the mission, helped him, checking to make sure the straps were secured and in the proper position.

"I thought we were supposed to have a reserve parachute in case the first one doesn't work," Dulaney said.

Hawke, a tall, handsome, soft-spoken man, exuded the same calm self-assurance as the others and gave Dulaney a friendly pat on the back. "A reserve won't do you any good from three hundred feet. It wouldn't have time to deploy." Noticing that his comment had unnerved Dulaney, he quickly added, "The cluster parachutes we're using have three separate canopies— we checked them all out carefully and packed them ourselves. There won't be any malfunctions." Hawke was aware of the critical relation of the aircraft's speed to the safety of the jump, as were Kessler and Natalie, but said nothing, not wanting to add to Dulaney's already shaky condition. Unlike conventional jumps from an altitude of twelve hundred fifty feet that utilized the descent speed of the jumper to fully deploy the parachutes, the low-exit jump was dependent upon the forward thrust of the jumper upon leaving the aircraft for proper deployment and full inflation of the canopies. The colonel had made certain that the pilot of the mission aircraft was well schooled in the precision flying necessary to avoid the parachute's deadly idiosyncrasies, and the copilot had been instructed to closely monitor and call out the airspeed when they reached the release point for the jump.

"Where do I put my radio and transponder?" Dulaney asked.

"Frank will jump them in," Hawke said. "He'll give them to you once we're on the ground."

Kessler stood off to the side, arranging the equipment in the chest pack he would attach to his harness for the jump. Along with his and Dulaney's radios and transponders, he put in six mini-grenades and two claymore mines and the balance of the gear he had drawn for the mission. Despite Kitlan's assurances that the Agency had taken extraordinary measures to make certain their agent on the ground wasn't compromised, Kessler still felt uneasy about again jumping into a drop zone secured by one man, but he kept his thoughts to himself.

With the completion of a final equipment check, Kitlan joined the men in the supply room and led them outside to a van, driving them the short distance to the airstrip where they stood on the tarmac under the clear night sky as the aircraft was pulled out of the hangar.

Kessler was familiar with the small, single-engine, high-wing Helio Courier, having jumped from it into Laos and North Vietnam on Special Operations Group reconnaissance missions during the war. Modified and specially equipped for low-level infiltrations beneath radar coverage, it was the perfect aircraft for the mission into Czechoslovakia. Its three-bladed propeller was redesigned to drastically cut down on tip noise, and the engine, modified to reduce the RPMs, was equipped with an exhaust system with an elongated muffler that concealed the exhaust flames and lowered the sound level to that of an automobile engine at idle when heard from a distance of more than thirty-five feet. Any protruding rivets in the exterior metal skin of the fuselage had been countersunk, the antennas removed, and the nonretractable landing gear fitted with aerodynamic farings, all serving to decrease wind resistance and noise. The sound made in flight was not identifiable as that of an aircraft, and at altitudes above fifty feet anyone on the ground would hear nothing more than a low hum, if anything at all, depending on the background noise in the immediate area.

Dulaney had stood silently watching the aircraft being rolled into position in front of them. "I've never been so damned scared," he finally said to Kessler. "I don't know if I can jump."

"Take it one step at a time," Kessler said reassuringly, "and you'll be all right."

"Have you ever watched a rabbit when it breaks cover?"

Kessler gave him a questioning look.

"I think I know the terror it must feel when it's caught in the open and sees the shadow of a hawk the instant before it strikes."

Kessler hesitated before putting on his helmet as the aircraft engine broke the night silence, coughing and sputtering then settling into a low rumble. Turning to Dulaney he asked, "What made you change your mind back at the base?"

A thin smile creased Dulaney's tightly drawn face. "As you said, Hana deserves better. But part of it is selfish. I've had a good life; gone everywhere I wanted to go and done everything I wanted to do. The rest is repetition. Fun, sometimes, but repetitious. If I die on this operation I don't stand to miss much. But if we pull it off, I get to live the best part of my life over again, with Hana, through her eyes."

"My kids give me that same feeling," Kessler said, extending his hand to Dulaney, who grasped it firmly. "Let's do it."

Following Kessler's lead, Dulaney pulled on his helmet and boarded the aircraft. The seats had been taken out of the narrow six-passenger cabin and the team sat cross-legged, shoulder to shoulder on the floor, leaning back against the bulkhead. The cargo door on the starboard side had been removed to facilitate a quick exit, and the cold air rushed into the cabin space, obscuring the sound of the muted engine as they began their take-off roll. Taking advantage of the aircraft's short-takeoff and landing capability, the pilot used only a fraction of the runway as he pulled into a steep climb and quickly gained altitude. The bright lights of Regensburg were visible below in the distance, disappearing as the pilot banked and turned to a heading that took them over the dark rounded shapes of the wooded hills of the Bavarian forest.

Unlike the high-altitude jump on the previous mission, civilian airline traffic, had there been any at that time of night, would have been of no help in masking their mission, considering the low altitude and the course they were flying. The jump had been scheduled for the predawn hours not only to take advantage of the cover of darkness, but more precisely because it was a time of night when the Czech radar operators and border guard sentries—anyone working the graveyard shift—would be most tired and least attentive. No military flights had been scheduled to provide a deception capability for the mission—any unusual activity at that hour would only have served to draw attention to the area of infiltration, alerting the Czechs rather than deceiving them. The aircraft was to fly a quick low-level penetration into Czech territory, drop the team behind the border defenses, and return immediately to West Germany. The team would be on the ground and linked up with the agent on the drop zone shortly after 4 A.M., allowing ample time to reach the CIA safehouse on the outskirts of Prague before daylight.

"We're coming up on the border," the copilot shouted back to Kessler, who had moved to the opposite side of the aircraft to kneel by the open door.

The pilot was a CIA contract employee, a former Luftwaffe fighter pilot who had flown countless special missions for the Agency and knew the terrain below him well. Easing back on the throttle to slow his airspeed and decrease his altitude, he shut off the outside navigation lights and dimmed the instrument lights in the cockpit to a soft red glow. Dropping down perilously close to the ground, he began to fly nap-of-the-earth with a precision that testified to his experience and expertise.

Kessler pulled his goggles into position and peered outside, watching the ground for the reference points burned into his memory. The force of the wind stretched his skin tight across his face and made his eyes water behind the goggles. The aircraft flew low and slow, just above the tops of the dense pine forest, maintaining an airspeed of eighty knots that further reduced the engine noise from that of its normal cruising speed. Short stretches of roads and rivers reflected the moonlight, and the lights of small, isolated villages appeared and disappeared as the pilot weaved his way through the narrow, winding valleys, rising quickly above low mountain ridges to descend into yet another remote valley.

"Six minutes!" the copilot shouted back to the men in the cabin, holding up six fingers as further confirmation of the time remaining to the release point.

Kessler nodded to Natalie and Hawke, who checked to make certain the static lines used to deploy the parachutes as the men exited the aircraft were securely fastened to the overhead cargo tie-downs in the cabin. Dulaney sat rigid and immobile as Hawke once again checked his harness straps and gave him a thumbs-up for encouragement. Dulaney, wide-eyed and chalk-faced, returned the gesture none too convincingly as he saw Kessler motion to him to move into position at the open door. Sliding across the deck of the cabin, he gripped the handholds on either side of the door and knelt at Kessler's side.

"Two minutes!" the copilot called out, holding up two fingers.

"Sit in the door and put your feet outside the aircraft," Kessler shouted above the rush of the wind.

Dulaney hesitated, closing his eyes and taking a deep breath before edging slowly into position, his fingers locked in a death grip on the handholds. The wind flapped at the legs of his jumpsuit as he kept his eyes straight ahead on the horizon and felt his stomach tighten and sour.

Natalie got into position behind him, sitting on the deck and straddling him with his legs while gripping a handhold with one arm and placing the other around Dulaney's waist as further insurance against a premature fall-out of the aircraft during the pop-up maneuver they knew was coming, a maneuver they had briefed Dulaney about but had understated—describing it simply as an elevator making a quick stop—in deference to his already substantial reservations about the jump. Hawke got into position as Kessler again stuck his head out the door, spotting the distinctive reference points that told him the drop zone was on the other side of the approaching ridgeline.

All four men were grouped at the open door as the copilot called out the one-minute warning.

"Let go of the handholds," Kessler shouted to Dulaney.

Dulaney didn't respond.

"Let go!" Kessler shouted again. "We've got hold of you."

"I can't!"

Kessler released his own grip on one of the handholds and grabbed the collar of Dulaney's jumpsuit with his free hand. He motioned with his head to Hawke, who reached over and pried Dulaney's hands loose. Natalie quickly pinned them against Dulaney's sides as he wrapped his arm tighter around his waist.

"You won't fall out," Hawke shouted above the noise of the wind. "Just sit tight."

"There's your man," the copilot called out as the aircraft rose above the ridgeline that dropped steeply off into a low-lying valley of sparse woodlands and open meadows.

Kessler spotted the flashing strobe light at the edge of a large grassy field a mile ahead; the narrow beam was hooded so it could only be seen from above. The light reminded him of the muzzle flash from ground fire, and thoughts of the disaster on the drop zone for the HAHO jump flashed through his mind, but he forced himself to concentrate on the terrain below.

"Hang on!" the copilot shouted to the four men huddled near the open door in the narrow cabin.

Kessler and Hawke made a quick check of the static lines, making certain they were not tangled or encumbered in any way, then gripped the handholds firmly as Natalie further tightened his hold around Dulaney's waist and prepared himself for the violent maneuver he knew was coming.

The pilot applied full throttle and pulled into a steep climb. The aircraft rose swiftly from treetop level to an altitude of four hundred feet, one hundred feet above the required altitude for the release point. The pop-up maneuver created a positive force three times that of gravity, forcing the team firmly onto the deck.

At the apex of the maneuver, with the airspeed decreased to seventy knots, the pilot abruptly pushed the yoke forward and nosed the aircraft into a steep dive, this time creating a negative force three times that of gravity that caused the men to cling to the handholds to keep from being tossed about the cabin. Dulaney felt light-headed and queasy, as though his stomach had risen to his throat. He struggled frantically to reach for the handholds, but Natalie kept his arms pinned to his sides. The aircraft dropped rapidly to an altitude of three hundred feet while increasing its airspeed to one hundred thirty knots before leveling off with a second positive three-G force precisely over the release point.

"One hundred twenty knots!" the copilot shouted.

Natalie shoved Dulaney out the open door, following immediately behind him. Kessler and Hawke bailed out a split second before the aircraft again nosed down to fly nap-of-the-earth. The pop-up maneuver had limited its exposure to enemy radar to less than twenty seconds, an exposure the pilot hoped had gone unnoticed or ignored by the Czechs during the two twelve-second sweeps when the aircraft would have appeared as a blip on their screens.

Dulaney had fallen one hundred and eighty feet in three seconds when his harness straps dug into his groin from the series of three sharp jolts as the cluster canopies blossomed in rapid succession. His next sensation was one of floating briefly in the moonlit sky before he saw the ground rising swiftly toward him. The parachute-landing-fall procedures he had so carefully memorized were quickly forgotten and seven seconds later he hit the ground, having only managed to remember to keep his feet and knees together as he tumbled forward into a somersault and came to a sudden stop in a shallow depression in the middle of the field. Recalling Kessler's instructions, he jumped to his feet, astonished and elated that he had survived intact and uninjured, and began collapsing the air from his canopies and gathering them in. Spotting Kessler as he landed twenty feet away, he ran toward him, dragging the half-collapsed canopies with him.

"I did it, Frank!" he shouted. "I did it."

Kessler pulled him to the ground and clamped a hand over his mouth to quiet him, but couldn't help smiling at Dulaney's "first jump" euphoria, an experience shared by every airborne soldier. "Congratulations, you're no longer a 'leg,' " he said, using the term those who have jumped apply to those who haven't. "Now shut the hell up and pull yourself together—we've got work to do."

Helping Dulaney out of his harness, they carried their parachutes to the edge of the clearing where Natalie and Hawke already knelt in the underbrush with the tall, gangly CIA agent who had used only his code name, Alex, to identify himself. When Kessler reached them, Natalie and Hawke moved further into the woods, their eyes and weapons trained on the deep shadows of the forest.

"How secure is the immediate area?" Kessler asked the stranger kneeling beside him as he scanned the perimeter of the open field.

Alex's voice was as calm as his sharp-featured face. For the past two days he had carefully scouted the area around the drop zone and his reply left no doubt in Kessler's mind that he was dealing with a man who was at least prepared for his mission.

"The regular army troops, both Czech and Soviet, have been recalled to their units," Alex replied in near perfect English. "The border guards are still on alert and have been reinforced by units from the Polish and East German frontiers, but they are now concentrated along the death strip. The closest patrols are three miles from the border; four miles west of our present position. All roadblocks and checkpoints have been relocated to major intersections in that area. There are none to the east between us and the safehouse."

"Where's our transportation?" Kessler asked.

Alex pointed toward a barely visible path through the woods. "One kilometer. I have a small Skoda station wagon, but it is adequate for five people."

Kessler got to his feet and stripped off his jumpsuit. The others did the same, carrying them along with their parachutes and helmets to a shallow trench the thorough CIA agent had prepared in advance. After burying the now useless equipment and covering the freshly disturbed earth with underbrush and leaves, they proceeded along the overgrown path toward the car. Kessler took the point while Hawke and Natalie stayed in the woods, paralleling his course, providing flank security. Dulaney fell behind Alex, covering the rear as Kessler had taught him at Bad Tolz during their evening cram course in patrolling and small-unit tactics.

The compact Skoda station wagon that had seen better days was parked on a deserted farm track off a secondary road that led northeast through the Bohemian countryside. Alex had taken great care in rehearsing the route he would take from the drop zone, and the team reached the outskirts of Prague without incident as the first traces of predawn light appeared on the horizon. The safehouse selected for the mission was a warehouse among a row of similar storage and maintenance buildings adjoining the grounds of a huge coal-burning power plant in an industrial suburb west of the city. It was located in an alley behind Alex's home—an unremarkable single-story stucco house encrusted with soot and grime emitted from the smokestacks of the power plant. A row of identical homes on postage-stamp-size lots lined both sides of the narrow alley.

"Has the Agency used this place before?" Kessler asked.

"Never. Nor have they used me since I received my training," Alex told Kessler as they turned off the street into the darkened alley. "I lease the warehouse from the state for use as an automobile repair shop. The neighbors are accustomed to seeing me coming and going at irregular hours to pick up and deliver customers' cars. And due to the nature of my business the sight of strangers does not arouse their curiosity."

"Are you aware that my instructions are to take you across the border with us once we've completed our mission?" Kessler asked.

Alex nodded solemnly. "It is probably best."

Pulling up to the front of the warehouse, Alex got out of the car, quickly sliding open the door to one of the three bays and driving inside. Kessler closed the open bay behind them as Alex switched on a single light fixture over a workbench cluttered with tools and grease-stained rags.

Kessler glanced about the warehouse. A small truck and a car, their engines and transmissions in various stages of disassembly, filled the other bays. "What's out back?" Kessler asked, gesturing toward the rear door.

"A fenced-in yard," Alex replied.

"Can the neighbors see over the fence?" Kessler asked.

"No," Alex replied. "It is solid wood, eight feet high. It is where I keep the discarded auto parts. They are returned to the state for scrap metal whenever they get around to collecting them."

Natalie and Hawke took up positions at windows where they could observe the alley and the neighboring houses as Kessler opened the rucksack he had kept strapped to his chest during the jump. Removing one of the compact, dictionary-size radios, he walked to the back of the warehouse and went outside into the yard where he knelt on the ground in a corner where the fence joined the building. Placing a piece of equipment that resembled a small folding umbrella on the ground in front of him, he extended its legs, spreading them apart for stability, and opened it into a dish-shaped antenna sixteen inches in diameter. Connecting one end of a coaxial cable to the antenna and the other to the radio, which he switched on, he typed in DANIEL BOONE on the keyboard. The two-word code was his scheduled Initial Entry Report to advise the mission support site on the West German border that the team had arrived at the safehouse and were fully operational. The MSS was maintaining a "guard net"—a constant twenty-four-hour monitor on the primary frequency and the alternates assigned for the mission. In addition to the Initial Entry Report, Kessler had two other required transmissions on his schedule of communications: after they had made contact with Cernikova and were en route to the extraction site, and again upon reaching the extraction site to call in the helicopter.

Having been given the exact location of the safehouse during the final briefing, Kessler had no need to consult the Equatorial Satellite Antenna Pointing Guide—a flat, graphlike map printed on a plastic strip ten inches long and three inches wide

—that gave the elevation angle and azimuth relative to his position, information that was necessary to orient the radio's antenna to the satellite that would relay his message to the mission support site. He had memorized the azimuth and angle before leaving the isolation base, and he quickly oriented the antenna to the proper elevation and direction. The preselected frequencies were stored in the radio's memory, and Kessler simply pressed the designated number on the keyboard to select the primary frequency. The HST-4 satellite radio had burst-transmission capability, and with the touch of a single switch the brief message was transmitted in a split second. Any enemy direction-finding equipment sweeping the frequencies would acquire a fix that would tell them only the direction from which the transmission had originated, limiting their knowledge to the fact that the radio operator was somewhere within a hundred miles along a given line—knowledge that would do them no good unless repeated transmissions were made from the same location.

Going back inside the warehouse, he returned to the workbench where he removed the second satellite radio and a miniature radar transponder from among the contents of his rucksack. Calling Dulaney to his side, he handed him the equipment along with a padded nylon camera bag. "Put these in the bag and don't let them out of your sight," he told him. "They're your only way out if anything happens to us."

"I wish you wouldn't keep saying that," Dulaney said. "As far as I'm concerned, the parachute jump was the worst of it. If I'm wrong, leave me some illusions."

"Just covering all the bases," Kessler said, motioning for Alex to join them as he went over the details of Dulaney's part of the mission: details it had been decided were best withheld from him until they had reached the safehouse.

"Alex will drive you into the city to contact Cernikova. Arnie will go along as security. If she doesn't have the briefcase in her apartment, take her to the car and Alex will drive you to wherever she has it hidden. There will be CIA agents and at least one case officer from the Prague station on your tail at all times —you won't see them until you get the briefcase or unless you get jammed up, but they'll be there. As soon as the case officer sees that you have possession of the briefcase he will approach you and use your code name, Hickory. Give him the briefcase and go immediately back to the car with Arnie. Alex will bring you and Cernikova back here where we'll regroup and proceed to the extraction site."

"Where are you going to be when I go into the city?"

"Hawke and I will stay here at the safehouse."

"You said you'd be with me every step of the way," Dulaney protested. "Those were your exact words."

"We all can't go into the city," Kessler said. "There'd be five of us in a small car, six once you get Cernikova. And we can't lurk in alleyways or sit in a parked car while you make contact; we've got to keep a low profile to avoid drawing attention. There's a hard-and-fast rule for this type of operation: don't deploy until the last possible moment, and when you do, commit the smallest number possible. You're the only person necessary for the contact with Cernikova; we're of no use to you. You're the only one she'll deal with. Arnie can help you if a couple of local police get curious for some reason and stop you. He's all you need."

"What if we run into serious trouble—more than just a few local police?"

"If we've been compromised, and the STB have set us up, there's no safety in our numbers against what they'll have waiting for us. Whether there's two, three, or five of us, it doesn't matter—we've all had it if we're together."

"We'd have a better chance of getting away if we're all there," Dulaney said.

Kessler shook his head. "The fewer the number when you're on the run, the better, especially in an urban environment. If you and Cernikova were to break free from an ambush setup, you could hide a lot easier than all six of us. With Hawke and me here, you have someone to contact if things fall apart."

"How do I get back here if anything happens to Alex?" Dulaney asked, his voice tense and strained from the thought of leaving the man whose guidance he had come to depend on.

"You don't," Kessler said, pointing to the telephone on the wall above the workbench. He wrote the number down on a slip of paper and handed it to Dulaney. "If you run into any snags or delays, Alex will call me. If I don't hear from him within thirty minutes after your scheduled contact with Cernikova, I'll know something is wrong. If you're separated from Alex and Arnie, call me here and give me a situation report along with your location. If you're outside the city and can't get to a pay phone, use your radio. I'll be monitoring the primary frequency until I hear from you and can direct you to a rally point where we can link up. And remember, if you have to use the radio you'll be using voice transmission and not burst, so think out what you want to say first, then transmit your message and keep it short. Use the code I gave you for the grid coordinates when giving me your position on the map, and change locations immediately after transmitting and head in the direction of the extraction site. If Hawke and I have to leave the safehouse for any reason, we'll be headed in the same direction."

"How will I know when to contact you if you leave here?" Dulaney asked.

"I'll come up on the primary frequency every half hour until we make contact. Just get into a concealed position and set up your radio. Turn it on, use the handset, and listen. Don't key the microphone or transmit on any of the frequencies until I contact you. You can listen as long as you want without giving away your position, but the moment you key the mike and transmit, the Czech direction-finding equipment is going to start zeroing in on you. Listen for five minutes. If I don't make contact, continue toward the border and set up in another thirty minutes. No matter what happens, keep heading for the extraction site. If I haven't contacted you by the time you reach it, call in the chopper to get yourself and Cernikova out."

"What about you and the other men?"

"We can take care of ourselves. We'll get out later," Kessler said. "If we aren't there at the scheduled time, you don't wait."

Dulaney put his equipment in the nylon bag, lengthening the strap so it hung at waist level when he slung it around his neck on the side opposite his submachine gun. "I don't like the idea of splitting up, Frank."

"It's the way it has to be," Kessler said, reaching over and unzipping Dulaney's parka. "Keep the zipper open—the weapon isn't visible and you've got ready access. If you're on the run and anyone tries to stop you, remember what I told you. Don't hesitate to take them out. Act instantly and get away from the scene immediately."

He paused before giving Dulaney one final instruction at the risk of rattling him further, but finally did as he had been ordered and pointed out two switches on the radio, the function of which he had not previously explained. "If you think you're going to be captured and you can see no way out, activate the destruct switches for the radio and get the hell away from it in a hurry."

"Oh, shit," Dulaney said. "I really needed that."

"I've got to prepare you for worst-case scenarios," Kessler said. "That doesn't mean they're going to happen. In all probability everything will go according to plan; if it doesn't, you'll know what to do."

"I'm surprised they didn't issue me a cyanide capsule."

"I'm sure it entered their minds," Kessler said, recalling what the colonel had said about why the Agency had insisted on arming Dulaney. Glancing at his watch, he turned to Alex.

"I've got oh-six-thirty hours," Kessler said.

Alex confirmed the time. He had been informed of Cernikova's daily routine and had planned the drive into the city to coincide with the increase in traffic as the city came to life.

"We will leave here in exactly thirty minutes," he told Kessler. "It is a fifteen-minute drive to Cernikova's apartment. She leaves for the skating rink between seven thirty and seven thirty-five each morning."

"You never told me what's in the briefcase," Dulaney said to Kessler.

"I don't know."

"You don't know or you can't tell me?"

"I don't know," Kessler said. "Just remember. Don't remove the contents. They want the entire briefcase, intact. And Cernikova's got to be able to travel fast and light; she can't lug a suitcase full of mementos. The clothes she's wearing and a purse. That's it."

"Anything else I need to know? Any more *comforting* surprises?"

"Yeah," Kessler said. "You're holding up a hell of a lot better than I thought you would."

"Praise from the master," Dulaney said with a grim smile. "Don't be deceived by external appearances. Inside I've got all the composure of a goddamn gerbil on Benzedrine."

19

JOSEF MASEK'S BROAD FRAME took up most of the space in the tiny bathroom adjoining his office at STB headquarters. Splashing cold water on his freshly shaven face, he used a paper towel to remove the splotches of shaving cream from behind his ears and ran a comb through his thinning silver-blond hair. It was 6:35 A.M. when he glanced at the wall clock above the rumpled cot crammed into a corner beside his desk. Refreshed and alert after allowing himself four hours of sleep, he put on a clean, starched shirt and carefully knotted his tie before leaving the office. The day had dawned bright and clear, and he breathed deeply of the crisp fall morning air as he pulled on his wrinkled suitcoat and crossed the deserted inner courtyard to the detention center, his heavy footsteps on the smooth cobblestones echoing off the surrounding buildings.

Frustrated and angry after personally questioning Paulina Marcova to no avail late into the night, he had left her in the hands of his two most experienced interrogators, giving them explicit instructions not to use any physical violence as a means of extracting information. Entering the detention center, he turned a corner and walked to the end of a long corridor on the first floor where he partially opened the door to a stuffy room smelling strongly of stale cigarette smoke.

Paulina Marcova sat slumped in a simple wooden chair in the

center of the room while one of Masek's officers slowly paced the floor in front of her. The second man in the room, resting as his comrade conducted the interrogation, responded to Masek's silent summons and joined him outside in the hallway.

"Has she told you anything?" Masek asked.

The STB officer shook his head. "Nothing, comrade. We have not let her sleep; she has been awake now for more than twenty-four hours. She is physically weak and tired, but she does not fear us. She has said little since you left. When she speaks it is only to repeat her denial of any knowledge of the briefcase or the dissidents' activities."

"Why does she continue to resist us when she knows we have her boyfriend in custody?" Masek said, more to himself than the man standing before him. "She has no political motivations and she must realize that it is only a matter of time until Rudenko breaks the boy, or kills him. She is only causing him to suffer needlessly."

"If you will allow me, comrade," the STB officer said, looking to his superior for permission to offer his opinion.

"By all means."

"I do not think that Eduard Antos is resisting because he believes he is protecting her. He knows she has been arrested, and he knows that the professor and the other students who were at the cottage with him are dead . . . the one in the isolation cell died early this morning," he added, realizing that Masek had been asleep when it happened. "There is no one left who was directly involved with the Soviet defector for Antos to protect. It is my opinion that he does not know where the briefcase is. We have learned from others that Marcova is indeed his girlfriend and has been his constant companion for the past year. If he knew what she had done with the briefcase after she left the cottage he would surely tell us, if for no other reason than to spare her what he is going through. I believe she is the only one who knows where it is. She may not have hidden it—it is possible she gave it to someone else and is protecting that person. It is the only explanation for her behavior. Perhaps a visit to the KGB interrogation room where her boyfriend is being tortured would shock her into being more cooperative."

Masek scowled at the suggestion. "If our KGB comrade becomes aware of our interest in her," he said, "he will demand that we turn her over to him, and I cannot stop him."

"I believe it is the only way, comrade. I am convinced she knows where the briefcase is. Whatever her reasons are for resisting us, they are strong, and will require strong measures to overcome."

After a long silence Masek said, "Unfortunately you may be right. If we don't succeed shortly, I can do nothing to spare her her boyfriend's fate. It is inevitable that Rudenko will discover we have singled her out. I am surprised that he does not already know. I will take over the interrogation," he said, dismissing the man with a compliment for his good work.

Masek entered the room and motioned for his other officer to leave. Paulina Marcova raised her chin from her chest and gazed at the familiar face through tired, bloodshot eyes.

"Come with me!" Masek said.

Paulina rose slowly on legs that were stiff and cramped from sitting hours on end. "May I go home now?" she asked in a meek and shaky voice.

Masek looked away from her pleading eyes and delicate beauty. "No, you may not! You have continued to lie to us; I want you to fully understand the suffering your lies are causing others. Suffering you could prevent by simply telling us the truth."

Paulina said nothing more, following Masek along the corridor and down the steps into the basement level of the detention center. She paused as they reached the large holding cell and had to be taken by the arm when she realized that her destination was not the cell but the dreaded rooms at the end of the hallway. Masek swung open the door of one of the rooms the KGB interrogators were using to torture their victims. A vile odor fouled the air in the damp, dimly lit, confined space—an odor Masek recognized as a mixture of perspiration and human excrement. Viktor Rudenko stood just inside blocking the doorway; his suitcoat removed and the sleeves of his sweat-stained shirt rolled up. He nodded to Masek, then looked beyond him to where Paulina stood in the hallway. His eyes lingered on her firm breasts and shapely thighs. Paulina felt a sudden chill in his presence, intuitively understanding the nature of the man from the hard, unyielding look in his cold, gray eyes.

"And who is this?" Rudenko asked, stepping aside to let them enter, his eyes still moving slowly over Paulina. He had been blocking her view of the room as she stood in the hallway.

270

Once inside, she covered her mouth with her hand and cried out in horror at the scene before her.

In the center of the bleak concrete-walled room, near a large drain set in the tile floor, two burly KGB officers, their clothing drenched with sweat and spotted with blood, stood beneath the spot where Eduard Antos hung from the ceiling, grotesquely twisting his tightly bound body in a desperate effort to keep from suffocating to death. He was stripped naked, his chest and torso streaked and crusted with dried blood from his shattered mouth. A pool of urine had collected on the tiles directly below him, and the backs of his thighs were covered with his own excrement. His wrists and ankles were bound together behind his back and one end of the rope was slipped over a pulley attached to a support beam in the ceiling. Hoisted into the air with a force that had dislocated his shoulders, he hung suspended in a horizontal position six feet above the floor—the ropes knotted in such a manner as to stretch the nerves in his arms and cause temporary paralysis. A clear plastic bag had been pulled over his head and tied tightly around his neck. His face, badly swollen and disfigured from repeated beatings, was turning reddish blue; his eyes bulged and his chest heaved as his mouth opened and closed in an attempt to breathe what little oxygen remained in the bag. He was emitting a low, almost inhuman moan that changed to a muffled scream of pain as one of Rudenko's men grabbed his testicles and squeezed them in the palm of his hand. The other man, holding the end of the rope, jerked it suddenly upward with a force that popped the joints in his victim's elbows.

Paulina's scream momentarily startled the two torturers who looked in her direction. Exchanging comments she couldn't hear, they grinned and returned their attentions to Antos.

"Please make them stop!" Paulina pleaded with Masek, who stared in revulsion at the sight before him.

Masek was familiar with the brutal, primitive methods Rudenko had instructed his men to use. He had been exposed to them during a brief stint in Santiago as an administrative adviser to the secret police when Chile was ruled by the Marxist Allende government. The use of the plastic bag to bring the victim close to the point of suffocation was known as the "Dry Submarine," and the rope suspension, known as the "Hook," inflicted hideous, often unbearable pain.

Taking Paulina by the arm, he pulled her out into the hallway and shook her by the shoulders.

"I cannot stop them! Only you can do that—by telling me what you did with the briefcase. These men will torture your boyfriend to death if necessary, and then they will do the same to you. They have already killed your uncle and the other students who were at the cottage. You cannot allow this to continue. There is nothing to be gained. They will eventually find the briefcase."

Paulina had been unaware of the deaths of her uncle and the other students. Her body shook convulsively as she began to cry and collapsed against Masek's chest where he supported her to keep her from falling. Escorting her to an empty interrogation room across the hall, he sat her down at a bare wooden table, taking the chair opposite her. Before he could speak, the door to the room was flung open and Rudenko entered, his eyes again fixed on Paulina.

"Who is she?" Rudenko demanded.

"I am conducting an interrogation, comrade. You will be advised if I learn anything of interest to you."

Rudenko glanced suspiciously from Masek to Paulina, then back to Masek. He recalled Masek's earlier speculation that Antos did not have possession of the briefcase but was protecting the person to whom he had given it. "Is this who you believe our dissident friend in the other room is protecting?"

"I will keep you informed of my progress, Comrade Rudenko."

"We shall soon find out if you were correct," Rudenko said, grabbing Paulina roughly by the wrist and pulling her to her feet.

Masek moved with surprising quickness for a man of his bulk. Rising from his chair, he reached across the table and dug his fingers deep into Rudenko's throat, causing the startled Russian to let go of the terrified girl. Gasping for breath as Masek increased the pressure on his windpipe, Rudenko found himself being lifted from his feet and slammed onto the top of the table with a force that momentarily knocked the wind out of him.

Masek's face was florid with rage. Releasing his hold on Rudenko's throat, he grabbed him by his shirt collar and threw him like a rag doll from the table onto the floor. Gaining control over his emotions, he let him get to his feet.

"You will pay dearly for this, Comrade Masek," Rudenko said in a raspy, half-choked voice as he brushed fastidiously at his clothing.

"You will kill no more of my people!" Masek shouted. *"No more!"*

"Your superiors have given me—"

"I will answer to my superiors for my actions. Not to Russian swine. You will leave this room and you will not interfere with my work again. If you attempt to do so I will instruct my men to lock you and your KGB comrades up until I have completed my investigation."

Rudenko opened his mouth to speak, but thought better of it as Masek moved toward him. Backing away, not wanting to provoke the anger of the bull-like man again, he retreated to the door and left the room without uttering another sound.

Masek turned to Paulina, who stood against the wall immobilized with fear. Gently taking her by the arm, he led her back to the chair and again sat across from her.

Lowering his tone, he spoke softly. "He will win in the end. If you do not tell me what I need to know, I cannot prevent that from happening."

Paulina looked up, staring into Masek's eyes, but said nothing.

"The American parachutist was going to the skating rink. Yes?"

Paulina slowly nodded her head.

"You were to give him the briefcase."

"No."

"You had hidden it there for him?"

"No." She began to cry again, this time looking pleadingly into Masek's eyes. "Please. Please, don't make me do this."

"You have given it to someone else. Who?"

"Please. No."

"You must tell me," Masek said gently.

Paulina again fell silent, staring at the floor.

Masek leaned across the table and spoke in a persuasive, fatherly voice. "I give you my word that no harm will come to the person you are protecting. The KGB does not have to know. It will not be necessary. I will have my men retrieve the briefcase; your friend will not be arrested. The Russians will have what they want and the matter will be forgotten. They will stop torturing Eduard Antos and I will personally see that he receives the medical attention he needs."

Paulina looked up, wanting to believe, but torn between loyalties and afraid to trust a man she saw only as a member of the STB.

Masek saw her indecision, recognizing it as a wider breach in what had once been an impenetrable defense. His mind reached for a plausible explanation for the depth of loyalty she was exhibiting—a loyalty that went beyond her relationship with Eduard Antos. It came to him with the recollection of his own daughter's deep friendships and strong bonds; how close she had been to her teammates and trainers when she had been an aspiring figure skater, a promising first-year member of the national team before a knee injury ended her career at the age of thirteen.

Continuing his questioning in the same manner and tone, he said, "You gave the briefcase to one of your friends on the national team, didn't you, Paulina?"

"No," she whispered, the tears again streaming down her face.

"To your trainer."

"Please," she said without looking up. "Hana is my dear friend. I love her."

Masek leaned back in his chair; a flicker of recognition showed in his dark eyes. "Hana Cernikova?"

"Please don't hurt her. She did it only to help me," Paulina said. Then, exhausted and tormented, she began to sob uncontrollably.

Masek used the in-house telephone on the wall near the door. Dialing the office of his chief assistant, he instructed him to dispatch four of his officers to the skating rink and four to Hana's residence.

"She is to be brought to my office unharmed," Masek said firmly. "If she denies knowledge of the briefcase, she is to be asked no further questions. Have the men search her apartment and her locker at the skating rink and report back to me immediately."

20

✖ ADRIAN DULANEY STARED NERVOUSLY out the window from the front passenger seat of the Skoda station wagon. Arnie Natalie sat in the back, his eyes constantly scanning the people and the cars as Alex weaved his way through the early morning traffic on the narrow winding streets of the Mala Strana section of the city.

Prague appeared to Dulaney much as it had ten years ago, only worse. He had never liked it, seeing it only as a bankrupt city in inexorable decline, with Hana as its only saving grace. He could never see beyond the shabby elegance of its ancient buildings, many of them marred and obscured by scaffoldings of rusted steel pipes and warped planks erected in a futile attempt to keep up with unending repairs for which there were inadequate funds and even less concern from a government with more pressing problems. He saw the scaffoldings as representative of the failure and deceit of the Communist system. Empty of workmen, they were intended to give the appearance of restoration in progress, but in reality served primarily to route pedestrians around sagging archways and cracked and decaying masonry that frequently dislodged and dropped to the sidewalks. With the exceptions of a few showplaces like the National Theater, the once elaborate and detailed façades were now indistinct remnants, discolored and crumbling from neglect and the combined effects of the ever present industrial emissions and pollution from the near gridlock traffic conditions. Sulfurous fumes penetrated and corroded, and on windy days, when the city was trapped in the grips of frequent high-pressure systems and temperature inversions that sometimes lasted more than a week, the people had to cover their faces with handkerchiefs against the acrid sting of the gritty air.

Dulaney remembered only one occasion when he had seen a brief glimpse of its former medieval beauty: during the winter when he had come to take Hana skiing. Unable to sleep, he had walked alone through the Old Town section in the predawn hours as a blizzard blanketed the city with a mantle of pure white crystals. The grime and decay had been blurred and hidden by the heavy wind-driven snow that clung to the steeply sloping tile roofs and gables and swirled about his feet as it drifted knee high in the narrow streets. In the cold silence and the glow of the lamplights, he felt as though he had stepped back four hundred years in history, but within a few hours, after the city had awakened, the snow had turned to a black, ugly slush and the illusion was gone.

The spires and ramparts of the Prague Castle came into view as Alex crested a steep hill. Dulaney's pulse quickened as they reached the bottom and turned into a cobbled lane he recognized as the approach to the rear of Hana's apartment building in the small square on Kampa Island adjacent to the Charles Bridge. Alex made a U-turn in the cul-de-sac at the end of the lane and pulled into an alley before parking. The alley was the only other way out of the lane that dead-ended where the square bordered on a large wooded park that stretched along the banks of the river.

Natalie quickly studied his surroundings; the first thing he noticed was that none of the apartment buildings had rear exits other than windows.

"Where's Cernikova's apartment?" he asked Dulaney.

"Top floor," Alex answered, pointing to the corner apartment in the building closest to the park. It was almost directly across the street from the alley.

"Time to go to work," Natalie said, getting out of the car and opening Dulaney's door.

Dulaney stepped out and followed Natalie's lead as they exited the alley and crossed the cul-de-sac to the park. Taking a footpath that angled through the open woods toward the river, they stopped at a bench beneath a lamppost just off the square. The vantage point allowed Natalie a clear view of the entrance to Hana's apartment building and most of the others. The small square, divided by a narrow strip of grass and trees in the center, was approximately forty yards wide and twice as long with five four-story buildings on each side facing each other. There was no access available for any vehicle with more than two wheels. The tenants' cars were all parked behind the buildings on the side of the square away from the river.

Natalie's trained, wary eyes slowly swept the area, coming to rest on a middle-aged woman who left one of the buildings at the far end of the square. Unlocking her bicycle and removing it from the rack on the sidewalk, she disappeared around the corner, pedaling beneath the archway where the stone steps led down from the entrance to the bridge on the street above. The square was again deserted, and with a quick look around the park Natalie was satisfied. Reaching inside his unbuttoned knee-length raincoat, he undid the snaps securing his sub-machine gun in its holster. He kept his hand inside the coat to hold the weapon in place but ready to be brought instantly into play.

"You're on," he said to Dulaney. "And make it fast. I don't want to see you dragging the stereo, the TV, and the bed out with you. Get in, get the briefcase and the broad, and get out. No kissy-face-huggy-bod; there's plenty of time for the cheap physical stuff later."

"You're not coming in with me?"

"I'll be covering the street," Natalie said, recognizing the bad case of premission jitters Dulaney was exhibiting. "Hey," he said with a broad grin, "if you want to play with the big boys you've got to learn to piss in the high weeds."

"Your mind's a treasure trove of folk wisdom, Arnie," Dulaney said, taking a few deep breaths to calm himself.

"Ain't it the truth." Natalie glanced at his watch. It was seven fifteen. "Now go to it. And remember there's no rear exit from any of these buildings, so you've got to come out the way you go in. Don't look for me. Go around the corner and straight to the car."

"Where will you be?"

"Hopefully where you, or nobody else will see me." He gave

Dulaney a gentle shove. "Move it. And don't look back like some goddamn amateur."

As Dulaney left, Natalie moved away from the bench, paralleling the boundary where the park joined the square, pausing every few yards until he found the site he was looking for—a place of concealment with an unobstructed view of the building Dulaney had entered, the cul-de-sac, and the alley where Alex was parked.

Dulaney passed the out-of-order open-cage elevator and started slowly up the steps. People were getting ready for work and the sounds of muted voices drifted out onto the landings. Reaching the top floor, he stood before the door to Hana's apartment, hesitating before pressing the buzzer. He realized now that part of his nervousness was due to seeing her again. Ringing once, he glanced down the empty hallway and waited. He rang again just as the door opened.

The woman who stood facing him through the half-open door was more beautiful than he had remembered. The fresh-faced ingenuousness and youthful beauty of her early twenties were gone, replaced with a maturity that intensified and deepened what had always been a stunning handsomeness. She was barefoot, the smooth, olive tone skin of her strong, shapely calves visible below the white terrycloth bathrobe cinched tightly around her small waist and clutched about her neck; her other hand held a hairbrush, stopped midway through a stroke of her dark, silky shoulder-length hair.

Because of the tension and anxiety of the past few days, Dulaney had given no thought to what he was going to say when he saw her. He was speechless, captivated as he had been when they first met and fell in love. The mission, the briefcase, the waiting car, all were forgotten in the emotions of the moment. Lost in the haunting gaze of her deep chestnut-brown eyes, he detected a subtle difference. The shy gentleness was still there, but there was something else, something that hadn't been there before. It was a sadness he could not have known; an accommodation with harsh realities, a dissolution of hopes and dreams that brought with it the unwelcome but accepted knowledge and understanding that not everything was possible.

"Hanka," he said softly, using the diminutive form of her name when he found his voice, a voice filled with more emotion than he could ever remember feeling.

Her face glowed with a warm, inviting smile that bridged the years. Dropping the hairbrush, she reached out, her hand gently touching his cheek. "Oh, Adrian. How many summers. How many winters."

He smiled in recognition of the words from her favorite poem —a poem she had tried to teach him in her native language. He stepped inside and closed the door. It had been ten years since he held her, but she came easily into his arms, her head against his cheek, her arms around his neck. A brief hesitation, a moment of self-consciousness, and she relaxed in his embrace. He felt her trembling as he pressed his lips to her forehead. There were fond remembrances with the scent of her hair and he found comfort in the warmth of her body as she pressed against him. Placing his hand beneath her chin, he raised her head to look into her eyes. Using the back of his hand, he brushed away a single tear and kissed her on the mouth, a kiss she passionately returned, clinging to him with the strength of the memories of what they had shared.

Resting her head on his shoulder, she kissed him lightly on the neck. "I thought you would not come. That I would never see you again."

"I'm here, Hanka. I'm here." He felt her body tense as she lowered her arms to embrace his chest. She had felt the submachine gun beneath his parka and looked up.

"We've got to hurry," he said, the spell broken by the thoughts of what lay ahead.

"Yes. The briefcase?"

"Is it here in the apartment?"

Hana nodded and started down the hall to her bedroom. Dulaney followed, standing in the doorway as she threw open the closet door and pulled out the trunk. His eyes were drawn to the bed beneath the window. The covers were tossed back and the impression of her body remained where she had slept. Something stirred deep inside him with the vivid recollections of the long nights of lovemaking, the endless conversations about her new life, and her smoky, melancholy voice in crescendos of laughter as she tried in vain to teach him a language he had found impossible to speak, let alone retain. His brief reverie ended as she pulled the briefcase from the trunk and got to her feet. She approached him hesitantly, handing it to him, a strange conflict of emotions in her eyes, a wavering disparity that suggested both joy and apprehension.

"Get dressed," he said. "There are people outside waiting for us. We've got to leave immediately."

"You are taking me with you? To America?"

"Your message about your father," he said. "I assumed it meant you . . ."

"Yes. I do. I do."

"You thought I came here for this?" he said, holding up the briefcase.

"I didn't know. I hoped, but . . ."

Dulaney smiled and held her tightly. "I don't even know what's in it." Gripped by a sudden tension, his mind returned to the mission. "Wear jeans and a heavy sweater," he said, remembering what Kessler had told him about the terrain they would have to cross on foot to get to the extraction site. "And a windbreaker . . . and hiking boots if you have them."

Dulaney stepped out into the hallway to allow her her privacy as she began taking the clothes she would wear from her closet and dresser.

"It is all right," she called to him as she stuffed the bottom of a cotton turtleneck into her jeans and pulled on a thick wool sweater, "you can come in."

Dulaney entered the bedroom as Hana slipped on a lightweight nylon jacket and sat on the edge of the bed to lace up a pair of tennis shoes.

"I do not have hiking boots," she said.

"Tennis shoes are fine."

There was an awkward silence before she spoke again. "You are not married?"

Dulaney shook his head. "And you?" he asked, having assumed Kessler's assessment had been correct.

"No." She kissed him tenderly, lingering in his arms. The intervening years paled to insignificance, as though they had never existed. No further accounting was necessary or desired.

Dulaney held her at arm's length and looked at his watch. It had been ten minutes since he left Natalie in the park. "If you do that again, we'll never get out of here."

Hana smiled and returned to the closet, bringing out a suitcase.

"No," Dulaney said. "You can't take anything with you."

"Nothing?"

"Only what you can carry in a purse."

Leaving the bedroom, Hana quickly covered the short distance to the living room. Taking her scrapbook from the record shelf and the frame containing her Olympic gold medal from the wall above the sofa, she tried to force them into her shoulder bag but they wouldn't fit.

"Give them to me," Dulaney said, unzipping the expandable nylon flight bag and just managing to get them inside with his radio equipment and transponder.

He followed her into the kitchen where she had left the small purse she usually carried. Emptying its contents into the shoulder bag, she checked to make certain her internal passport and money were there.

"You won't need them," Dulaney said, reaching for her hand to lead her to the door.

"Oh, God!" she cried out. "Oh, no!" She had glanced out the kitchen window that overlooked the park and the cul-de-sac and had seen a black Tatra sedan come to a sudden stop at the rear of the building.

"What's wrong?" Dulaney said, coming to her side. He looked out the window and saw four men exit the car. One of them consulted a small street map and pointed to Hana's apartment building. Dulaney's first thought was that they might be the CIA agents Kessler had told him about, but he knew better. The black Tatra sedan and the actions of the man with the map told him they were STB.

Hana began to cry. "Not now. Please. Not now."

Dulaney took her by the hand; it was shaking and he held it tightly, hoping to reassure her—but he did little more than transmit his own fear like an electrical discharge.

"I didn't come alone," he said in as calm a voice as he could manage. "There are others outside waiting for us." He knew he had to act immediately, but action was beyond him. He was near the point of panic. Struggling to get hold of himself, he tried to remember all that Kessler had taught him, but it only came to him in a rush of tangled thoughts that added to his confusion.

"We've got to get out of the building," he finally said, pulling her with him as he ran to the door and out onto the landing.

"Take the briefcase." His voice was sharp and high-pitched,

but calmer than before as he handed it to her and reached inside his parka. He struggled with the snaps on the shoulder holster before managing to withdraw the silenced submachine gun. He felt better now. More in control. He was reacting, doing something, fighting off the paralysis of fear.

Hana stared at the strange-looking weapon. "I'm frightened, Adrian."

"So am I," he said, but his voice was growing steadier. Extending the folding stock of the submachine gun, he flipped the selector to full automatic and tucked the stock into his shoulder, placing one hand on the trigger and the other on the grip forward of the magazine as Kessler had instructed him.

"Stay behind me," he told Hana. "If there's any shooting, lie flat on the floor until we get outside and can get under cover." Moving quickly down the steps, he peered around the corners on each landing before descending to the next level, hoping to get to the street before the STB trapped them in the building.

Reaching the foyer, he peered around the entryway, ducking back just as three of the STB officers came around the corner and entered the square. Beyond them, at the entrance to the park, he had also caught a fleeting glimpse of Arnie Natalie as he crouched low and darted from behind a tree to kneel at a clump of shrubs near the edge of the park.

Dulaney closed his eyes and took a deep breath. "We're going to walk out of here as though we don't know who those men are," he said to Hana. "I'm going to put my arm around you and I want you to walk on the inside, close to the building. Don't look at them. Rest your head on my shoulder, kiss me on the cheek, anything, but ignore them."

Hana nodded, her eyes wide with fear.

Dulaney held the small submachine gun in one hand, the hand he placed behind Hana's back. Pulling her against him, they stepped out onto the sidewalk and moved slowly toward the corner. Hana rested her head in the crook of his neck and looked at the ground. Dulaney turned to kiss her on the forehead just as the three men came abreast of them in single file to avoid stepping off the curb. Two of the men gave only a passing glance, the third man slowed his pace, his eyes fixed on Hana's face as he continued past.

Dulaney turned his head so that he could watch them out of the corner of his eye. He felt a cold chill run through his body as the inquisitive STB officer stopped to look back, immediately spotting the submachine gun as Dulaney removed his arm from around Hana to carry the weapon in front of him where they couldn't see it. The STB officer's hand reached inside his coat and quickly withdrew a machine pistol as he shouted to his comrades.

"Get down!" Dulaney heard someone shout in English, and he pulled Hana to the pavement.

It was Natalie who had shouted and then fired, his silent shot striking the STB officer in the head, knocking him against the wall where he slid to the sidewalk. A spasm shook his body before he lay still.

Getting to his feet, Dulaney pulled Hana up with him and held her hand tightly as they ran for the corner of the building, only ten yards away.

Natalie fired again, his weapon on semiautomatic. The only sound heard was the chipping of the masonry wall at the point of the round's impact on the edge of the archway near the entrance to the building. He had pinned down the two other STB officers who, unable to locate his position, were afraid to venture out into the open square.

Dulaney dragged Hana out of the line of fire as they turned the corner. He leaned against the wall and brought his weapon into the ready position. Fifteen feet from where he stood, he saw Natalie take careful aim from behind the clump of bushes at the edge of the park, squeezing off another round that again hit the archway, causing one of the STB officers to pull his head back inside.

"Get to the car," Natalie shouted, rising to his feet and beginning to move in that direction. The words were no sooner out of his mouth than a rapid, ear-shattering burst of automatic-weapons fire followed. Natalie staggered backward, a look of surprise and pain on his face as he spotted the man who had shot him. His attention had been on the men approaching Dulaney and Hana, and he had lost track of the man who had stayed with the car. He placed a hand over the area where the rounds had ripped into his chest, removing it to stare at the bright red blood before dropping his weapon and falling over backward.

Dulaney spun in the direction from which the shots had come. The fourth STB man stood at the rear of the building, the wire stock of a machine pistol to his shoulder. He ducked out of sight as Dulaney dropped into a crouch, yanking Hana down with him before squeezing off a short sound-suppressed burst that was both high and wide, smashing a window in a building on the other side of the cul-de-sac, twenty feet from his intended target. Kessler's words came back to him: "Fire and move. Fire and move."

Hana was terrified. Dulaney, forcing himself to take the initiative, dragged her to her feet and held on to her hand as he ran across the narrow strip of pavement separating the building from the park. Another burst from the Czech machine pistol split the air as he reached the woods and took cover behind a large tree partially surrounded by waist-high shrubs. His first thought was of Hana and he knelt beside her, making certain she hadn't been shot. But the man had not been aiming at them. Dulaney glanced at Natalie, who lay dead in the grass only a few feet away, the blood seeping through the holes in his coat. He turned from the gruesome sight and looked toward the alley where Alex had parked the car.

"They're only supposed to have regular pistols, goddamn it!" Dulaney muttered under his breath. Hearing two single shots, his eyes searched for Alex, spotting him behind the open door of the Skoda station wagon. He was firing his revolver at the man who had killed Natalie. Looking back toward the square, Dulaney saw the two STB officers who had been pinned down in the building run from the entrance and hide behind the trees in the center strip in the square. Both were carrying Czech-made machine pistols capable of high rates of fire. They began moving from one tree to another in the direction of the park. They had seen Natalie fall, but had not yet located Dulaney and Hana.

Dulaney's attention was drawn back to the cul-de-sac by another volley of fire. His heart sank as he saw Alex fall forward, hanging limply over the open car door. The STB officer remained concealed, waiting for Dulaney to reveal his position.

Focusing his thoughts on the techniques he had practiced at the rifle range at Bad Tolz, Dulaney settled into a stable position and prepared to fire at one of the men moving toward the park from the square. Sighting over the top of the weapon, he concentrated on trigger control and fired two short bursts as the man sprinted across the open area for the woods. The first burst was short and low but ricocheted off the pavement and struck the STB man in the legs below the knees. The second burst tore into his chest and neck as he fell, killing him instantly and sending his comrade scurrying back behind a tree.

"Do you have a car?" Dulaney asked Hana.

"Yes. It is parked at the end of the alley, not far from where your friend was shot," she said, pointing to where Alex lay slumped over the door of the Skoda.

"Do you have the keys?"

She thought for a moment, then remembered that they had been in the small purse she had emptied into her shoulder bag. "Yes."

"I've got to get to a telephone," Dulaney said, his eyes watching the cul-de-sac for the other STB man—without knowing the man's exact position, he was afraid of being caught in the open if he tried to get to the station wagon. Looking behind him, he saw that the park continued for no more than a hundred yards, ending at a low brick wall that enclosed a large, ornate building.

"What's that building?" Dulaney asked.

Hana turned to look. "It was a conservatory, but it is no longer in use."

"What's beyond it?"

"That is where the park ends. There is a street of shops and apartments."

"We'll have to go that way and double back to your car. You'll have to lead the way through the park. Take the briefcase and run as fast as you can. But not in a straight line. Use the trees for protection. Once you get to the other side of the wall, stop and wait for me."

"No. Please, Adrian. I want to stay with you."

"I'll be right behind you," Dulaney said. "I've got to keep them from getting too close to us or we'll never lose them."

Hana got to her feet behind the tree. "Please, Adrian. I don't want to leave you."

"You have to. It's our only chance." Dulaney said, turning his attention to the cul-de-sac, watching for any sign of the STB agent who had killed Arnie and Alex. The one man remaining in the center strip in the square occasionally glanced from behind a tree. Unsure of where Dulaney was, he was reluctant to move.

Holding the briefcase tightly to her side, Hana ran through

the park, making quick, short changes of direction as she headed for the wall that surrounded the conservatory.

Dulaney spotted the profile of the STB man in the cul-de-sac. He had risen from behind a car and was sighting his weapon on Hana, moving it back and forth in a slow arc, trying to anticipate her next change of direction. Dulaney fired a sustained burst that emptied his magazine. The rounds penetrated the windshield and hood of the car, sending the man diving for cover.

The man in the square had also caught sight of Hana and made his move, darting across the open area and dropping behind a row of hedges at the entrance to the park. Dulaney's eyes were on him, marking the spot. Taking a full magazine of ammunition from his pocket, he quickly slapped it into place and chambered a round—he was functioning smoothly now, calmly; the things he had practiced and Kessler's instructions were all coming back to him. He glanced first to the cul-de-sac, then to the spot where the man lay beside the hedges. Neither of the STB officers knew where he was. Getting to his feet, he lay down a short burst of covering fire at the hedges, then at the car where the other man was raising his head above the fender, a radio microphone to his mouth as his eyes scanned the park. Dulaney's intention was to keep their heads down as he broke from cover to follow Hana. The impact of the rounds from the sound-suppressed weapon again caught them by surprise. Both men hit the ground and Dulaney started to run, catching sight of Hana halfway to the opposite end of the park.

The benches along the wooded paths were empty with the exception of an old couple sitting ahead of Dulaney in the direction of the conservatory. They had seen Hana run past and now turned to watch him. They had either not heard the shots fired by the STB and Alex or had not recognized them for what they were. Their deeply lined faces had expressions of amusement that changed instantly when they noticed what Dulaney was carrying in his hand. On the far side of the park, fifty yards away, a young woman pushing a baby carriage strolled along the wall overlooking the river. She was headed in the direction of the square. In his peripheral vision, Dulaney caught a flicker of movement through the trees in front of her. Slowing his pace, he continued to watch over his shoulder and saw it again. The STB man who had taken cover in the hedges had seen him bolt from behind the tree and was following, his machine pistol held in both hands as he paced his quarry, waiting for a clear shot.

Dulaney stopped running and hid behind a small maintenance building next to a sandpit and children's playground in the center of a sweep of open lawn just off the wooded path. An old man with a small dog approached him from the rear and startled him. Swinging his weapon in their direction, he eased his pressure on the trigger within a split second of firing. The dog barked and snapped at his heels as the old man tugged at the leash and hurried away around the opposite side of the building, his rheumy eyes fixed on the submachine gun.

Dulaney's sudden change of direction had caused the STB man to lose sight of him, but he had heard the disturbance and seen the old man glancing backward, restraining the barking dog. Stepping out from among the trees, he walked slowly through the playground area.

Dulaney saw him coming. Peering around the edge of the building, he took aim from a standing position, revealing only a partial profile as he braced himself against the wall. The STB officer didn't see him; his attention was on the opposite corner where he had first noticed the old man and the dog. Dulaney fired. All four rounds of the short burst hit their target just above the waist, doubling him over and sending him tumbling to the ground. Making certain that the man who had been in the cul-de-sac was nowhere in sight, Dulaney immediately turned and continued running through the park, holding the nylon flight bag to his side with his free hand and looking back every few seconds until he reached the brick wall enclosing the conservatory. Vaulting the four-foot wall in stride, he dropped to the ground in the midst of an untended, overgrown garden and saw Hana sitting only a few yards away, the briefcase clutched to her breasts, a look of terror on her face.

"There's still one left," Dulaney said as she rushed to his side. "But I don't see him anywhere."

The wail of sirens could be heard in the distance, the sound growing louder with each passing moment.

"VB," Hana said, recognizing the distinctive klaxons of the Prague city police cars.

"I saw the STB man in the cul-de-sac using his car radio," Dulaney told her. "This place is going to get awfully crowded in a hurry." Rising to his knees from where he sat leaning against the wall to catch his breath, he glanced about the grounds of the conservatory. "It wasn't supposed to happen this way; it's all going too fast," he said. "Which way to the street?"

"On the other side of the conservatory," Hana said. "There is a footbridge leading to a lane that will take us to Karmelitska. It is a busy street. There will be many people on their way to work. It will lead us back to my car."

"Can your car be seen from the cul-de-sac?" Dulaney asked, his eyes constantly moving about the immediate area.

"I don't think so. It is parked on the hill at the top of the alley."

Dulaney raised his head above the wall just enough to see into the park. There was no sign of the fourth STB man. Getting to his feet, he extended his hand to Hana. Her eyes widened, staring beyond him to where the wall was covered with thick vines at the edge of the woods.

"Adrian!" she shouted.

Releasing his hold on her hand, Dulaney spun around, swinging the submachine gun into position to fire. His shots struck the ground at the feet of a man who had climbed over the wall.

"Hold your fire, Hickory!" Adam Purcell shouted as he dove off to the side.

His code name for the mission registered immediately and Dulaney lowered his weapon, only to swing it back into position at the sight of another man in a green leather jacket coming over the wall from the same direction.

"He's with me!" Purcell called out.

"Jesus!" Dulaney said, lowering the submachine gun. With all that had happened he had forgotten about his CIA contact. "Where the hell have you people been? I need some help here."

"I believe you have something for me, Hickory," Purcell said as he reached Dulaney's side. Glancing at Hana, he spotted the briefcase and held out his hand.

Hana hesitated and looked to Dulaney.

"It's okay. Give it to him. They're CIA."

Purcell took it by the handle and turned to leave, the man in the green leather jacket following him.

"Where the hell are you going?" Dulaney said. "Everything's gone wrong. We need help."

"I'm sorry," Purcell said, his face showing genuine concern.

"The briefcase is my primary responsibility. Weren't you given a contingency plan in the event this happened?"

"Yes, but—"

"You're on your own," Purcell said, his eyes studying Hana's face. He felt a twinge of guilt. "You'd better move out of here fast. This place will be swarming with VB and STB in a matter of minutes."

"You could have fooled me." Dulaney watched them retreat toward the woods beyond the vine-covered wall. "Thanks for nothing, you *bastards!*" Getting to his feet, he pulled Hana up with him, taking one last sweeping glance around the park. "Lead the way," he told her.

They had taken no more than a few steps when the now unmistakable clatter of a Czech machine pistol stopped them in their tracks. Dulaney shoved Hana down and dropped to his knees, turning in the direction Purcell and his agent had gone.

The man in the green jacket was shot as he swung over the wall. Purcell caught the second burst in his chest and head before he was able to react. Dulaney saw the muzzle blast from the fourth STB man's weapon; he was standing behind a tree on the far side of the wall a few yards into the woods. Dulaney fired just as the man stepped into the open to get a clear shot at him, emptying the rest of his magazine with surprisingly accurate fire, the majority of the rounds impacting in his target's upper body. Tearing open the pocket of his parka, he quickly replaced the spent magazine with a full one and moved cautiously toward the spot where he had seen the STB man fall. A quick glance told him that the man was dead—one of the rounds had struck him in the forehead just above his eyes. Kneeling beside Purcell, he saw that he had suffered the same fate. His face was covered with blood and a large skull fragment from the left side of his head lay on the ground beside him.

Dulaney turned away, taking a few deep breaths to keep from retching. Grabbing the briefcase, he returned to where Hana stood silently staring at the carnage. Placing the submachine gun in his shoulder holster, he left the snaps partially undone and his hand inside his parka as they ran from the walled-in grounds. They slowed to a fast walk as they followed a maze of lanes and alleys before emerging onto a busy thoroughfare. The noise of the heavy traffic diminished the sound of the sirens, and the crowded sidewalk offered anonymity. Keeping pace with the people on their way to work, they headed back toward the alley and Hana's car.

A sudden screech of tires ahead of them on the opposite side of the street caused Dulaney to pull his weapon partway out of his parka before he realized they had not been spotted. Two VB patrol cars had swerved to a stop, blocking access to the entrance to Trziste Street where the American embassy was located halfway up the block, less than a hundred yards away. The VB jumped out of their cars and stood in the middle of the narrow side street. Stopping a delivery truck that tried to drive around the obstruction, they pulled its driver out of his seat and flung open the rear doors of the vehicle and began searching it. As Dulaney and Hana came abreast of the street, they saw that it was also blocked in the same manner at the upper end across from the embassy.

They heard more sirens, and an ambulance sped past them as they drew nearer the main street leading down to the river's edge. Reaching the top of the alley, Dulaney switched to the inside of the sidewalk, taking Hana's hand and purposely walking past their intended destination, glancing down the steep hill to the small section of the cul-de-sac that was visible. The area was jammed with VB patrol cars and he could see men running toward the park. Alex's body had been removed and no one was standing in the alleyway.

Pausing to stare in a store window midway through the next block, they changed direction and walked back toward the alley.

"Which car is yours?" Dulaney asked.

"The second one on the left," Hana said. "The red Skoda."

Dulaney realized that she had been wrong when she had told him that it could not be seen from below. It was partially hidden by other vehicles parked on the hill, but they could still be seen by anyone looking in their direction.

"You drive," he told Hana. "Get me to an outside pay phone as far away from here as we can get in ten minutes." He was conscious of the time, remembering Kessler's statement that if he had not heard from Alex within thirty minutes of the scheduled contact with Hana at seven thirty, he would know something had gone wrong. It was seven fifty. He wanted to reach Kessler before he left the warehouse, afraid that radio contact might be difficult, and he needed desperately to rejoin him and

Hawke. The automatic responses required when the STB were trying to kill him had given him little time to think; he was now feeling trapped, the fear again beginning to take over—he needed reassurance and direction.

Entering the alley, Dulaney saw nothing at the bottom of the hill but the cars crammed into the cul-de-sac. Hana quickly unlocked the doors, fumbling with the ignition key as she tried to start the car.

Dulaney reached across and took her hand, squeezing it gently. "We'll get out of this," he said, his voice less than steady. "I promise you."

Hana pressed his hand against her cheek. "We are together," she said. "At least I have that."

The car started smoothly and Hana pulled slowly out of the alley into the flow of traffic. Dulaney placed the briefcase at his feet and took the submachine gun from the holster and lay it across his lap, covering it with the bottom of the parka, his hand on the trigger as they drove south and then west, heading out of the city.

21

✖ FRANK KESSLER STOPPED PACING the floor of the warehouse and stared out the window above the workbench. The alley was quiet; most of the people in the nearby houses had left for work. He glanced impatiently over his shoulder at the telephone on the wall beside him.

"It's five after eight," Hawke reminded him, watching the opposite end of the alley from another window.

Kessler nodded. "I'll give him a few more minutes. If he hasn't called by then, we'll relocate and set up the radio." The telephone rang as he finished his sentence. Picking up the receiver, he waited for Alex to speak.

"Hello? Hello?" Dulaney said. "Frank, is that you?"

With the sound of Dulaney's strained voice, Kessler knew immediately that something had gone wrong. "Where's Alex?"

"He's dead," Dulaney said. "So is Arnie, and the CIA people."

"How long ago?"

"What?"

"How long ago was Alex killed?"

"I don't know . . . . ten minutes after we got to Hana's apartment. Maybe a half hour ago."

"Are you all right?"

"I haven't been shot, if that's what you mean."

"And Cernikova?"

"She's with me. She's okay."

"Did you get the briefcase?"

"Fuck the briefcase! People are trying to kill us."

"Do you have the briefcase in your possession?"

"Yes. Goddamn it! I have it with me." Dulaney began to relate what had happened outside of Hana's apartment and at the conservatory, but Kessler cut him off.

"Where are you?"

"I don't know where the hell I am."

There was a long silence, and Kessler could hear Dulaney talking to Hana in the background.

"We're near the train station in the Radlice section of the city."

"Do you have Alex's car?"

"No. Hana's," Dulaney said. "I'm going to put her on the phone so you can tell her how to get to the warehouse."

"No. You can't come back here."

"You said we would meet somewhere if things went wrong," Dulaney said, the tension in his voice increasing. "They couldn't be more wrong!"

"This place has probably been compromised," Kessler said, realizing that even if Alex was not carrying any identification papers his car would give the STB what they needed to find the warehouse. "If Alex was killed a half hour ago they've had time to run a check on his license plate. It'll lead the STB right to us."

"Frank," Dulaney said, his tone almost pleading. "I need help. I can't think straight. I don't want to get Hana killed."

"You've done fine so far," Kessler said. "Just calm down and do it by the numbers. Follow the instructions I gave you. Keep heading toward the extraction site. Hawke and I are leaving now. Get to a rural area and get under cover. Set up your radio on the half hour. When we make contact, give me your grid coordinates and we'll come to you. Don't try to bluff your way through any roadblocks. If you see any and you can't detour around them, ditch the car and head for the woods. Use the compass and the map I gave you and you'll have no trouble finding the extraction site."

"Frank," Hawke called softly from the opposite side of the warehouse. "We've got company."

"Get moving," Kessler said to Dulaney. "Just do what I told you." He hung up the phone without waiting for a reply and crossed to the window where Hawke was watching the alley.

"Arnie and Alex are dead," Kessler said. Hawke nodded, continuing to stare out the window.

A military scout car with four uniformed STB soldiers was parked at the rear entrance to Alex's house. A black Tatra sedan pulled in behind it. Two STB officers in civilian clothes climbed out of the sedan and instructed the soldiers to break down the door. Kessler saw one of the men watching the windows at the side of the house, and he assumed that there were more men sealing off the front entrance.

An old woman came out of the house directly across the alley. One of the STB men approached her and began asking questions. Kessler saw her point toward the warehouse.

"The back door," Kessler said, slipping his arms through his rucksack.

Hawke responded immediately. Running to the rear of the building, he threw open the door and dove into a forward roll, taking cover behind an engine block as his eyes swept the small, fenced-in yard. Kessler followed, rolling into position a few feet away. Seeing no one in the immediate area, they got to their feet and ran toward the back section of the fence, darting and weaving among the clutter of rusted car frames and engine parts. Slinging their weapons across their backs, they both scrambled over the top of the fence, landing hard and dropping into a crouch on the opposite side, immediately unslinging their weapons and training them in opposite directions, covering both ends of a broad access road used by coal trucks unloading at the power plant behind the warehouse. A short distance away on their left was the rear entrance gate to the plant. An old man stepped out of the gatehouse and squinted in their direction. To their right, where the chain-link fence enclosing the grounds of the power plant ended, another row of dingy houses lined both sides of the road up to its exit onto a main street a hundred yards from their position.

Kessler spotted a narrow passage between the first house and the chain-link fence. It appeared to lead to another street lined with similar houses continuing along the boundary of the plant. Motioning to Hawke, he rose to his feet and sprinted for the passageway. Halfway there, he saw a scout car enter the road from the street beyond. The two soldiers in the rear of the vehicle shouted for them to stop and fired warning shots over their heads.

Kessler and Hawke opened fire shattering the windshield and wounding the driver. The scout car swerved up onto the sidewalk and crashed into the front steps of one of the houses. The two men in the rear seat jumped out and ran toward them, firing wildly from the hip. Hawke brought one of them down with a short burst and swung toward the other who had taken cover behind the concrete steps of another house.

Kessler reached the passageway just as the soldier behind the steps fired again. Hawke was caught in the open, only a few yards from where Kessler stood around the side of the house. Kessler's attempt at covering fire was too late. The Czech soldier was armed with an assault rifle and his shots were accurate. Kessler's first burst caught him in the head and neck, but not before the man's rounds struck Hawke, killing him and knocking him off his feet into the chain-link fence. Glancing quickly around the corner of the house, Kessler saw that the wounded driver had not moved, nor had the man in the front passenger seat. Rushing to Hawke's side he confirmed that he was dead, and ran back around the corner of the house just as three soldiers on foot entered the access road from the street.

Running down the passageway, he followed it through to the next row of houses that backed on an alley similar to the one in front of the warehouse. A young man caught his eye. He had just come out of the rear door of one of the houses carrying a small satchel that he was attaching to a luggage rack behind the seat of his motorcycle. The alley was otherwise deserted, and the three soldiers he had seen entering the access road had not reached the passageway behind him. Putting his submachine gun in its shoulder holster, he walked slowly toward the young man, who turned and nodded when he saw him approaching.

"I need to borrow your motorcycle," Kessler told him, glancing over his shoulder and then up the alley to the street as he spoke.

The young man stared at him in disbelief. "I don't know you."

With no time to waste, Kessler, outweighing his opponent by at least sixty pounds, caught him flush on the jaw with a short powerful right hand, knocking him unconscious. Taking the keys from his pocket, he tossed the satchel from the luggage rack and put his rucksack in its place. Slinging his weapon across his chest, where it was partly concealed by his parka yet readily available, he swung onto the seat. The CZ motorcycle sputtered twice then started, the two-cycle engine giving off a high-pitched whine as he spun it around and headed for the street at the end of the alley where he nearly turned it over as he banked sharply and sped away in the opposite direction from Alex's house.

* * *

Eleven miles west of where Jim Hawke's body was being tossed in the back of a Czech army panel truck, Frank Kessler knelt in the woods where he had driven the motorcycle off a country road near the town of Cernosice and set up his radio. Using a one-time pad, he encrypted his situation report for the mission support site. He reread the SITREP carefully before typing it out on the keyboard and entering it in the satellite radio's memory.

> DANIEL BOONE EMERGENCY. NATALIE, HAWKE AND DZ AGENT KIA. CIA CONTACT KIA. DULANEY AND CERNIKOVA EN ROUTE EXTRACTION SITE WITH BRIEFCASE. NOT UNDER MY CONTROL. WILL ATTEMPT CONTACT AND RENDEZVOUS.

By using a one-time pad—a different code for each message—and keeping his messages brief, Kessler ensured that even if they were intercepted by the Czechs there would not be enough identically encrypted text for decoding. With the SITREP typed into the radio's memory, and the burst transmitter activated, he sent the supercompressed message to the communications satellite to be relayed and received within seconds at the mission support site, where it was recorded, and played back at normal speed. Changing to the primary frequency, he glanced at his watch. It was eight thirty-one. Connecting the handset to the radio and switching to voice transmission, he attempted to contact Dulaney. "Hickory, this is Papa Bear. Do you read? Over."

Kessler heard nothing but a low static hiss through the earpiece. Waiting another thirty seconds, he tried again.

"Hickory, this is Papa Bear. Over." Again there was no answer. He tried three more times within five minutes with the same results. Cursing softly under his breath, he gathered his equipment into the rucksack and secured it to the luggage rack on the motorcycle. Rather than returning to the road and the danger of the roadblocks that would soon be in place, he followed a series of farm tracks that led southwest in the general direction of the extraction site. Using all the power the two-hundred-fifty-cc engine had, he bounced and skidded up a wooded footpath to the top of a steep hill, stopping as he reached the crest to survey the panoramic view of the fields and intersecting roads below. He saw no signs of troop movements in the direction he was heading. But he knew they would soon be swarming into the area.

"Where the hell are you, Dulaney?" he muttered to himself. "Where the hell are you?"

22

✖ DULANEY STRUGGLED WITH THE immobilizing fear that lurked behind each conscious decision. He thought that once they had reached the Bohemian countryside, with its maze of secondary roads and farm tracks, his tension and anxiety would lessen, leaving him more calm and clear-headed—but the opposite had happened. What had seemed uncomplicated and precise when Kessler had given him his instructions became confused and chaotic when he missed his scheduled radio contact by ten minutes. The roadblock Hana had spotted on the outskirts of Pribram had forced her to drive a circuitous route over back roads and through small villages. Dulaney's preoccupation with the road map, keeping track of the direction in which they were traveling, and his fear of stopping to set up the radio until they were well clear of the danger area, had kept them from reaching a suitable hiding place until it was too late.

He felt isolated and inept without Kessler's guidance, but derived some sense of accomplishment from the fact that they had covered forty-seven miles, more than half the distance to the border from where they had stopped to call the warehouse. But the knowledge that the heaviest concentration of troops searching for them would be in the area they were approaching did nothing to instill confidence that they would reach the extraction site. He glanced repeatedly at his watch. Fifteen minutes remained before his next scheduled contact with Kessler. As they skirted the town of Strakonice, the terrain ahead of them began to change from gently rolling hills and meadows to the densely wooded foothills of the Sumava Mountains that rose in the middle distance toward the West German border. The less open and more remote area bolstered Dulaney's spirits; he would have no difficulty finding a concealed location to set up his equipment.

Hana turned up the volume on the car radio and listened intently to a news bulletin that had interrupted the music.

"What is it?" Dulaney asked, understanding nothing the announcer was saying.

"He said I have been kidnapped by an American," Hana said. She listened to the rest of the bulletin before speaking again. "That you are a dangerous murderer who has killed four officials of our government and that you have taken me hostage in your flight to the border. He has given our physical descriptions and the license number and make of my car."

"Great!" Dulaney muttered. "That's all we need."

"We must stop for fuel," Hana said, glancing nervously at the gauge. "There is not enough to get us to the border."

"Stop at the next station you see," Dulaney said. "We're going to have to stick to the back roads. Every civilian who heard that broadcast will be watching for us."

A few miles from the village of Tazovice, Hana braked hard as they rounded the final bend of a long S curve, raising a cloud of dust as she pulled into a tiny rural gas station. An old man came out of a small, weathered clapboard building beyond the two fuel pumps at the side of the road and slowly approached the car.

Dulaney reached in his pocket and handed Hana the Czech money Kessler had given him at the warehouse. "Just have him put in enough to get us to the border. We've got ten minutes before I have to set up the radio."

Dulaney held his submachine gun inside his parka and got out of the car with her. He watched a woman dressed in a peasant skirt and blouse walking along the side of the road. She was carrying a gas can in each hand. Two small children trailed behind her. Upon reaching the station, she stopped in front of the diesel pump and began to fill the cans. Dulaney smiled as the woman stared blankly at him and then Hana before turning her attention back to her task. The children stood silently watching Hana as she paid the old man and insisted that he keep the change rather than wait until he went back inside to get it.

A small white sedan pulled off the road and parked at the side of the building, immediately drawing Dulaney's attention. Two provincial policemen in army-style uniforms got out of the car. The taller of the two began walking toward the outdoor toilet facilities behind the gas station. The other leaned against the car, his arms folded across his chest as he gazed admiringly at Hana. She pretended not to notice as she quickly shoved the money into the old man's hand. The taller man, noticing his partner's interest, glanced at Hana and the car and then at Dulaney. The expression on the policeman's face changed from casual interest to one of alarm.

Dulaney quickly withdrew the submachine gun from beneath his parka as the taller officer reached for the pistol holster on his belt and shouted to his partner.

"Get down!" Dulaney told Hana.

The policeman behind her had drawn his weapon. Frightened and confused, she failed to respond, staring into the barrel of the officer's revolver.

Dulaney stood behind one of the gas pumps and raised the submachine gun to his shoulder. He prepared to fire, but hesitated with the realization that the woman and the two children were between him and the taller officer, and Hana and the old man stood directly in front of his partner. The woman screamed and gathered the children to her side, but Dulaney could still not get a clear shot at the man behind her. A moment of panic gripped him as both policemen pointed their revolvers in his direction. Neither fired, holding their weapons and reacting in a manner indicating that, like most small-town cops in Eastern Bloc countries, they seldom encountered situations that required them to use their weapons. They were faced with the same dilemma, unable to shoot without risking hitting the people in front of them, and reluctant to move off to the side where Dulaney would have a clear field of fire from a concealed position behind the gas pump.

Dulaney kept the submachine gun to his shoulder, swinging the barrel from one policeman to the other. He saw only one way out of the situation. If he moved to his left, away from the pump, he would be in position to get the officer without hitting the woman and children, but in doing so he would leave himself open to the man behind Hana, unless he could get her to move away and give him a clear shot. It was a slim chance, but all he had, and it hinged on his ability to get the first man with a quick, short burst and swing immediately to his partner, firing perilously close to the old man, who stood frozen in position.

He caught Hana's eye and motioned with his head for her to move behind the car. She took a few tentative steps in that direction, but the officer behind her ordered her to stop, eliminating the only possibility Dulaney had.

Dulaney spoke to Hana in English, hoping that no one would understand what he was saying.

"Ask them to help you," he said. "If they know who we are, they believe you've been kidnapped."

Hana stared at him with a confused and frightened expression.

"Do it! Now!" Dulaney shouted, watching the faces of the two policemen. Their expressions gave no indication they understood what he had said.

Hana turned to face the man behind her. "Please help me," she said, speaking in her native language. "He has threatened to kill me if I do not help him escape."

The taller officer shouted at Dulaney, aiming his revolver over the shoulder of the woman.

Dulaney slowly lowered the submachine gun and placed it on the roof of Hana's car.

The officer behind Hana quickly pulled her out of the line of fire and approached Dulaney, jerking his revolver upward. Dulaney clearly understood the gesture and raised his hands above his head.

"Tell them you speak English and will translate for them," Dulaney said to Hana, who stood by helplessly as the taller man came over to the car and glowered at Dulaney.

She did as Dulaney asked. The shorter officer smiled and spoke to her in a consoling voice. Hana forced a grateful smile, and answered his question about what Dulaney had said to her. "He said to tell you not to shoot him."

The taller man, the one Dulaney decided was senior in rank, took possession of the submachine gun, recognizing it for what it was, but unsure of the purpose of the extension tube screwed onto the end of the barrel. During his required military service he had handled automatic assault rifles but nothing as exotic as the weapon he now held in his hand. Returning to his patrol car, he placed it in the front seat. Rummaging through the glove compartment, he brought a pair of handcuffs back with him. Dulaney held out his hands, hoping that the nervous and inexperienced man would not have the presence of mind to frisk him or tell him to put his hands behind his back. He did not, simply snapping the cuffs over his wrists in front of his body.

The shorter man, gaining in confidence and assuming an air of authority, looked inside Hana's car and removed the nylon flight bag and the briefcase. Opening the flight bag, he proudly showed the contents to his partner and cast a disinterested glance inside the briefcase before putting them both in the patrol car with the submachine gun.

The taller man issued an order. Hana translated. "He said to get in the back of their car."

Dulaney did as he was told. The shorter man climbed in with him, holding his revolver to Dulaney's ribs.

Hana nodded understandingly as the other officer apologetically explained to her that she would have to accompany them to the police station to issue a statement. He assured her that he would personally bring her back to her car once the necessary formalities were completed.

Hana sat in the front passenger seat, looking over her shoulder at Dulaney as they pulled onto the road.

"Tell them exactly what we heard on the radio," Dulaney said. "That's obviously the official government line." Hana winced as the officer in the rear seat jabbed the barrel of his revolver into Dulaney's ribs.

"What did he say?" the driver of the car asked.

"He said he was sorry." Realizing that the translation of Dulaney's English into Czech required more she added, "And asked me to forgive him."

"Did he hurt you in any way?" the driver asked.

"No," Hana said. "He only wanted me as a hostage."

"You are Hana Cernikova? The Olympic champion?" the officer guarding Dulaney asked.

"Yes," Hana replied.

"It is an honor to meet you," he said. The driver of the car confirmed the sentiment and told her that they had just heard the radio broadcast about what had happened to her.

The drive to the police station, a tiny half building on the main street in the village of Tazovice, took less than five minutes. With the exception of an elderly man who stood night duty, the two officers who arrested Dulaney were the only members of a village police force that concerned itself primarily with disorderly drunks, domestic squabbles, and the occasional theft of a pig.

Drawing curious looks from the few local citizens on the street—those too young or too old to work on the district collective farm—the policemen each took an arm of their handcuffed and docile prisoner. Escorting him into the one-room stationhouse, they shoved him onto a wooden bench inside a holding cell—a six-by-eight-foot cubicle enclosed with iron bars that occupied one corner of the room. Locking the door of the cell and putting the key in his pocket, the officer who had sat beside Dulaney during the drive holstered his revolver and went outside, returning with the submachine gun, the nylon flight bag, and the briefcase. Placing them on a table across from the cell, he continued to stand guard, leaning against the wall a few feet from where Dulaney sat staring through the bars and studying the room.

The taller officer, serving his first year as chief of police, pulled a chair up to the side of his desk and asked Hana to please be seated. Picking up the telephone, using his most officious voice, he told the local operator to get him the number for STB headquarters in Prague.

23

✕ JOSEF MASEK CLOSED THE file folder he had requested on Hana, placing it in his desk drawer as Viktor Rudenko entered his office.

"We have found your briefcase," he told Rudenko. "The American and the girl who was with him are being held at a police station in the village of Tazovice."

"The girl . . . Cernikova, she was a willing accomplice?" Rudenko asked.

"An unwitting and frightened accomplice," Masek said. "She has no connection with the dissidents."

"Your release to the journalists described her as a hostage?"

"She is a national heroine," Masek said. "There are political considerations. It is a matter to be handled with proper discretion."

"Where is this village?"

"An hour's drive."

"Get a helicopter," Rudenko said. "It will be quicker."

"All of our available helicopters have been deployed to the border area. They are now aiding in the search for the man who escaped from the warehouse. I can have two of my men drive to the village and back in less time than it would take to get one from another source."

"No!" Rudenko said. "The briefcase is believed to contain

top-secret information. I will personally take possession of it. You will call the police who have it and instruct them not to open it or remove any of its contents."

Masek picked up the telephone. "I will drive to the village myself."

"And I will come with you," Rudenko said. "I want the briefcase in my hands as soon as possible. And I insist on taking custody of the American. He will prove useful."

"I care nothing about the American," Masek said.

"The young girl you were interrogating. She was the one who had given the briefcase to Cernikova?" Rudenko asked.

Masek nodded. "An unfortunate victim of her relationship with the prisoner Antos."

"Of course," Rudenko said. "A pity she did not confess sooner. She might have spared her boyfriend's life."

"You killed him?" Masek said. "He was still alive when I told you we had the information you needed. My men had orders to take him to the hospital."

"A young man of shallow character," Rudenko said. "My men left the room for only a few minutes, and they returned to find that he had hanged himself from the rafters."

Masek had to restrain himself from again attacking the hated Soviet adviser. "I am telling you now that Hana Cernikova is the responsibility of the STB. She is a Czech citizen and will not be subjected to interrogation by the KGB. You will have your briefcase. The matter will then be in our hands."

"I want the briefcase and both Americans, if your people manage to catch the one still missing," Rudenko said. "That is all I want." Moving closer to the desk as Masek dialed the telephone, he smiled and added, "Perhaps our altercation in the interrogation room can be forgotten if the part I played in your investigation is presented in a favorable light in your report to my superiors."

"Perhaps," Masek said. The thought of covering up the stupidity and brutality of a man he detested repulsed him, but it would not be the first time circumstances had caused him to put personal convictions and animosities aside to assure his own survival within the system.

24

✖ FRANK KESSLER DOWNSHIFTED THE motorcycle into first gear and crept slowly along the narrow opening through the trees to the edge of a steep dropoff. Below him, at the bottom of the hiking trail he had followed through the foothills for the last fifteen miles, the forest opened to a natural clearing. In the distance, a few hundred yards on the other side of the clearing he could see a roadblock at the intersection of two secondary roads leading into the mountains. The terrain he was crossing was becoming increasingly more difficult to negotiate. From his present location the mountains began to rise steeply toward the border. The woods were dense and the ground rocky and thick with undergrowth. Letting the engine idle, he sat watching the soldiers on the road below. He counted six of them, armed with assault rifles that were slung over their shoulders. Two scout cars were blocking all but one lane, through which they funneled the traffic they had checked.

Unable to make radio contact with Dulaney on his second attempt, his thoughts were on getting to the extraction site as quickly as possible to be there when Dulaney arrived, if he was still operational, which, despite his failure to keep his schedule of communications, Kessler believed he was—basing his belief on the observation that the helicopter traffic and troop movements in the direction of the border had not decreased and the roadblocks he had seen from a distance were still stopping cars and not singling out motorcycles. Consulting his map, he determined that he was two miles south of the town of Susice, twelve miles from his destination. If he had to proceed on foot from his present location, and Dulaney and Hana were still traveling by car, he would never reach the designated area in time. Keeping the motorcycle and using the roads were his only chance of linking up with them before Dulaney called in the helicopter as he had been instructed to do immediately upon reaching the extraction site.

The ground on the other side of the clearing in the direction he had to go rose almost vertically. The motorcycle would be useless unless he doubled back and tried to find an easier route. A quick glance at the terrain features and elevations on his map told him that he would only be forestalling the inevitable by backtracking. He would gain little in forward progress before he would have to abandon the motorcycle and hike a considerable distance over rough terrain. If he could get past the roadblock below, he estimated he could get within three miles of the site before running into another. At that point he could cover the remaining distance on foot in a short time, something Dulaney and Hana would also be forced to do, given the lack of roads or farm tracks into the remote area of the extraction site.

His instincts told him there was a chance that if Dulaney and Hana had not been captured, the STB's primary concern would still be the briefcase, and the border guards would be on the alert for her car and might not yet have been informed about the theft of the motorcycle. Given the alternatives, he decided to attempt to bluff his way past the roadblock. Following the trail back in the direction from which he had come, he found a section that branched off and led to a more gentle slope that descended to the road around a curve where he could not be seen by the troops at the intersection.

Waiting until a farmer's truck had passed, he emerged from the woods and headed toward the roadblock. As he entered the border guards' field of vision, he watched for any indications that they were looking for a man on a motorcycle. They showed no sign of alarm: two of the guards stood in the open lane, three leaned against the side of one of the scout cars smoking, while the sixth man sat in the back of the vehicle, his feet propped up on the seat in front of him. None of them had bothered to unsling their weapons. As he came to a stop, a closer look at the scout cars told him the reason for his good fortune. Neither of the vehicles were equipped with field radios. If the guards had been dispatched when the alert first went out for Dulaney and Cernikova, before his escape from the warehouse, they would have no way of knowing about his theft of the motorcycle. The remote location of their roadblock, still twenty miles from the border and off the primary routes west and south, had probably been given low communications priority due to a shortage of equipment in their unit.

The two guards on the road approached the truck and asked for the driver's identification papers. Kessler guessed from what he heard of the conversation that followed that the farmer did not have any papers with him; he was en route to work at a local collective. One of the guards walked around to the back of the truck and peered inside. Returning to the cab, he dismissed the farmer with a wave of his hand.

Kessler pulled between the two men and handed his forged identity papers to the man on his left while casting a quick glance at the other guards.

"Where are you going?" the soldier asked, looking curiously at the rucksack attached to the luggage rack.

"Nowhere," Kessler said. "I have a day off from work. It is a beautiful day for a tour."

"I suggest you go east," the guard said. "All the roads toward the border are blocked."

"What's the problem?" Kessler asked.

"There has been a kidnapping," the man on his right said.

"A kidnapping?" Kessler said with genuine surprise. "I thought only rich capitalists were kidnapped."

"An American has kidnapped one of our citizens," the man replied. "A famous Olympic champion."

Kessler frowned and nodded solemnly. "I hope you catch him" he said, turning his attention back to the man on his left.

"There is a national alert," the man with his papers said, handing them back to him. "He will not escape." Stepping aside, he motioned with his hand for Kessler to proceed.

Without thinking, Kessler unzipped his parka to reach inside to the pocket where he had kept his papers. The parka opened wide enough for the guard on his right to see the submachine gun in its holster.

Immediately realizing his mistake, Kessler gave the motorcycle full throttle, leaning forward as the rear tire squealed and the front wheel rose off the ground. He saw the guards unsling their weapons as the man who had seen the submachine gun cried out. Bending low over the handlebars, forcing the front wheel back onto the pavement, he sped past them through the open lane, his eyes quickly scanning the area ahead.

The road continued in almost a straight line for the next half mile, and Kessler looked back to see all six guards with their rifles to their shoulders. With a large open field on his left, the only available cover was the steep wooded hillside on his right that led back into the mountains. A split second before he swerved off the road and headed for the woods, he heard the faint sound of automatic-weapons fire above the hollow whine of the two-cycle engine. A sharp searing pain struck at his side, followed by a powerful blow to his knee that nearly threw him from his seat. Reaching the woods, he took the slope at an angle, bouncing and skidding over the uneven ground at full throttle, nearly passing out from the pain in his leg as he reached the top where the ground leveled off. He felt sick to his stomach and his eyes blurred, but he pressed on, slowing down as he weaved among the rocks and trees. A dark void where the forest floor seemed to end came into vision. He applied the brakes in a panic stop, letting the motorcycle slide out from under him. He hit the ground with a solid thud and rolled into the trunk of a tree with a force that knocked the wind out of him. The motorcycle lay on a rock ledge above a granite-walled dropoff that plummeted a hundred feet or more down into a ravine where the waters of a swift-flowing river churned and swelled through a narrow passage.

Fighting off the dizziness after catching his breath, Kessler struggled to his feet, only to cry out from the excruciating pain in his knee. He dropped to the ground and sat with his back against the tree and used his knife to cut open his trouser leg. Small shards of bone had broken through the skin around his kneecap where a bullet had shattered the joint, expanding and fragmenting, embedding itself in the cartilage. The wound was not bleeding badly, but a burning sensation and a wet stickiness on his right side reminded him of the first round that had struck him. He opened his shirt and saw that the wound was in and out, the round having passed through the flesh just above his waist, shredding tissue and rupturing blood vessels. It was bleeding profusely and needed to be treated.

Gritting his teeth, he fought off another wave of unconsciousness and crawled out onto the ledge where he removed his rucksack from the luggage rack of the motorcycle. He peered over the dropoff and decided on a ploy that might deceive the troops he knew would soon be combing the woods for him. Using his uninjured leg, he placed his foot on the frame of the motorcycle and shoved it over the ledge. It fell into the ravine and crashed on the rocks below, where it lay battered and broken, clearly visible at the edge of the river. Crawling back off the ledge, he concealed himself in a tangle of thick underbrush, and opened the rucksack, and removed the first-aid kit. He cleaned the wound in his side and applied a pressure bandage that stopped the bleeding. There was little he could do for his shattered knee. Cleaning and dressing it, he broke a fallen branch into two sturdy braces and taped them on either side of the useless joint, wrapping it tightly with an elastic bandage in an attempt to immobilize it. The effect of the hydrostatic shock, stunning and traumatizing his central nervous system, was beginning to take its toll. He needed a place to hide and lie quietly until he could recover from the mind-numbing pain and its side effects.

The distant sound of fast-approaching scout cars reached him. The engines stopped, and shouted commands told him that, unable to drive up the steep slope, the troops had left the vehicles and were proceeding on foot. He glanced quickly about the area from where he sat in the underbrush. Something caught his eye. A broad rock shelf that could not be seen unless the observer was at ground level and viewing it from an angle jutted out from beneath the ledge where the motorcycle had been. He slung the rucksack over his shoulder and crawled toward it, using what remained of his waning strength to hold on to a thick sapling as he lowered himself over the side and onto the shelf, out of sight of anyone above. He could hear the cracking of small limbs and the sound of voices as the men approached. He elevated his feet by placing the rucksack beneath them and lay flat on the hard rock surface with his submachine gun across his chest, his finger on the trigger. His breathing was shallow and his muscle response sluggish, but the dizziness and weakness were beginning to pass.

The men from the roadblock were standing on the ledge directly above him now. He could hear their conversation. They had seen the skid marks and spotted the motorcycle at the bottom of the ravine and were discussing the possibility of Kessler's body having been carried downstream by the swift current of the river. The consensus was that it had been and that they would return to their roadblock assignment and dispatch one of the men in a scout car to report the incident to their immediate superior. As they retreated through the woods they wondered aloud who the motorcyclist was. Two of the men argued over whose shots had inflicted the wounds that had sent him to his death.

As their voices faded in the distance, Kessler checked the time. He had missed the five-minute time frame for his scheduled communication with Dulaney by three minutes. He considered contacting the mission support site and reporting his location and condition, advising them that he would be unable to reach the extraction site. But the fact that he had not made a scheduled attempt to contact Dulaney would alert them to the fact that something had gone wrong. He decided to wait thirty minutes for his next attempt to contact Dulaney when he would have to tell him that he was on his own. The MSS, monitoring the frequency, would hear it, making a separate transmission to them unnecessary.

25

✖ ADRIAN DULANEY STOOD AT the bars of the tiny cell in the corner of the one-room police station. The clock on the wall read nine thirty-six, reminding him that he had missed another radio contact. Time was running out, and he focused his attention on the chief of police and his partner, summoning the courage to attempt what he had been planning since he had been arrested a half hour ago.

Hana sat across the room watching him, drinking the cup of coffee offered her by the man who had grown tired of staring at Dulaney and was now helping the chief tidy up the office for the expected arrival of the STB officer who had telephoned from Prague. The chief was confused by the importance placed on the briefcase as opposed to the murderer he had captured and the national heroine he had risked his life to save from being kidnapped. He had told Hana as much and asked her what she knew about the contents of the briefcase, wanting to know how valuable a service he had performed for his country. She had used the opportunity to talk to Dulaney in English, telling him about the STB officer who was due to arrive at ten o'clock, and giving the chief another erroneous translation, explaining that Dulaney refused to tell her what was in the briefcase.

Dulaney glanced nervously at the wall clock. "Ask them if

they'll remove my handcuffs," he said. "Tell them they're cutting off my circulation."

"What did he say?" the chief asked, eying Dulaney suspiciously.

Hana told him. Then she added something of her own: "He said if you do he will tell you what is in the briefcase."

The chief, eager for the information, and considering the handcuffs unnecessary with his prisoner locked in the cell, motioned to his partner, who went over to where Dulaney stood with his hands through the bars.

"When he starts to take off the handcuffs," Dulaney said to Hana, "I want you to go to the table and pick up the submachine gun. Point it at the ceiling and pull the trigger and release it quickly. Then point it at the chief."

"I have never fired a gun. I don't think I can shoot anyone."

"After you shoot into the ceiling, hold it at your side and keep your finger lightly on the trigger. It won't fire unless you apply pressure. You won't have to shoot him."

The chief gave Hana a questioning look, waiting for an explanation of the conversation.

"He said he is grateful for your consideration," Hana said. "And that the briefcase contains extremely valuable documents."

"What kind of documents?"

Hana told Dulaney what she had promised the chief.

Dulaney motioned to the officer who held the key to the handcuffs, indicating he would answer the question once the handcuffs were removed.

The officer inserted the key and released the cuffs. Dulaney began rubbing his wrists and turned his back to the two men. Out of the corner of his eye, he saw Hana cross the room and pick up the submachine gun. He reached inside his parka to the waistband of his trousers where he had placed the twenty-two-caliber pistol when he removed it from the ankle holster shortly after being locked in the cell.

Hana held the submachine gun awkwardly in her hands and jerked the trigger, failing to release it immediately as she flinched at the recoil. She almost dropped the weapon as the uncontrolled burst shattered a light fixture in the ceiling and tore holes in the plaster halfway down the wall.

Dulaney reacted instantly, reaching through the bars and

grabbing a fistful of the officer's hair as he turned in the direction of the breaking glass and the unfamiliar noise made by the silenced automatic weapon. Pulling him back against the cell door, he pointed the pistol at his temple as he repeatedly banged his head forcefully against the bars, knocking him unconscious.

The chief stared at Hana in utter confusion and disbelief. He placed his hand on his holster and Dulaney shouted. "Tell him I'll kill his partner if he draws his gun!"

Hana told him, stepping back toward the cell, her hands shaking as she steadied the weapon against her side. The chief kept his hand on his holster but made no attempt to remove the pistol.

Dulaney bent down to where the unconscious officer lay against the outside of the cell door and pressed the barrel of the twenty-two to the back of his head.

"Give me the submachine gun."

Hana did so with obvious relief, placing it in his free hand.

Dulaney raised the weapon to his shoulder and pointed it at the chief. "The key to the cell is in his pocket," he said, gesturing to the officer on the floor.

Hana quickly retrieved it and unlocked the cell. Dulaney kept his weapon trained on the chief as he leaned against the door with his shoulder, sliding the unconscious officer out of the way as he opened it wide enough to get through.

"Tell the chief to come over here and get in the cell," he said to Hana, who translated immediately.

The chief glared at him and stood his ground, his hand now on the grip of his pistol, having managed to release the safety strap on the holster unnoticed.

In a further demonstration of the overwhelming fire power at his disposal, Dulaney fired a short burst into the coffee pot on the desk, splattering the contents across the room. The chief raised his hands over his head and moved quickly, stepping over his partner as he entered the cell.

"Tell him to drag his buddy inside with him," Dulaney said to Hana.

The chief did as instructed. Dulaney glanced again at the wall clock. His intentions had been to tie up the two men and gag them, but time was running short.

"Turn around and face the wall," he ordered the chief, who did so immediately upon hearing Hana's translation.

Dulaney entered the cell and raised the submachine gun over his head and brought it down forcefully, striking a vicious blow with the butt of the forward hand grip to the base of the chief's skull, knocking him against the wall where he slid face down onto the floor on top of his partner. Dulaney closed the cell door and locked it, putting the key in his pocket. He crossed the room to the chief's desk and took the key ring containing the keys to the patrol car and the front door of the stationhouse. Hana grabbed the briefcase and the flight bag from the table and they left the building, locking the door behind them.

Dulaney concealed the submachine gun beneath his parka as they walked casually to the unmarked patrol car, drawing no attention from the few passers-by. Hana took the wheel and pulled slowly away from the curb, following the main street out of the village and back onto the road they had been traveling before they were arrested.

"Pull into the first side road," Dulaney said. "I've got ten minutes to set up the radio."

*   *   *

"Hickory, this is Papa Bear, do you read? Over."

Dulaney felt the tension drain from his body at the sound of Kessler's voice. He quickly keyed the microphone and spoke into the handset. "Papa Bear, this is Hickory. We're okay. Where are you?"

"Give me your coordinates," Kessler said, ignoring Dulaney's question.

Dulaney looked at the note pad on which he had encoded the grid coordinates prior to Kessler's transmission and read them off to him.

Kessler decoded them and located Dulaney's position on the map, smiling grimly at the irony—Dulaney was in the mountains west of the village of Strasin, nine miles northeast of the extraction site and thirteen miles from the border, only a few miles south of where Kessler had crawled off the shelf and sat propped against a tree near the edge of the ravine.

"Continue to the extraction site and contact the MSS on the primary frequency immediately upon arrival," Kessler said, his voice shaky and weak.

"Where are you?" Dulaney asked. "You said we'd meet at a rally point."

"Acknowledge the instructions I just gave you," Kessler said.

Dulaney hesitated, sensing something was wrong. "Where are you going to meet us?"

"I'm unable to continue," Kessler said, deciding to tell Dulaney what had happened in order to get him off the radio as soon as possible. "I've been wounded. Proceed to the extraction site."

"Where's Hawke?"

"He's dead. Goddamn it, Dulaney, do what I told you."

"How far away are you? We can come and get you."

"Don't turn hero on me—I wouldn't know how to handle it. Your mission has priority. Proceed to the extraction site!" he repeated emphatically. "You're on your own. Just stay calm and remember what I taught you. Do not attempt to contact me again. I'm destroying my radio. Out."

Dulaney continued to hold the headset to his ear, hearing only the background static, his face clearly showing the disappointment and consternation he felt. He recalled what the CIA officer at the isolation base had said during the final briefing. There would be no further assistance for anyone who was not at the extraction site when the helicopter was sent in to pick up whoever arrived first with the briefcase. He stared blankly at Hana—it was now solely up to him to get them safely to the extraction site, and he could feel the immobilizing fear beginning to take hold.

"Unless we find a back road through the woods, we can't use the car much longer," he said, staring at the map. "We'll chance it until we get to the next intersection, but then we'll have to get rid of it."

"Where do we have to go?" Hana asked.

Dulaney showed her on the map. She had never been to the area, but had friends who had. It was an area of small farming communities in the remote valleys, and modest resorts in the mountains with facilities for boating and fishing in the lakes in the summer.

"There are many hiking trails through the mountains," she told Dulaney. "We should be able to reach it without much difficulty."

Dulaney saw no point in alarming her further by telling her

that the area would be swarming with patrols searching for them. He checked the time. It was five minutes after ten. The STB officer from Prague was due at the police station in Tazovice at any moment.

Gathering his equipment into the flight bag, they returned to the car and continued in the direction of the border. Two miles from where he had set up the radio the road wound up the face of a mountain in a series of sharp curves. As they reached the top and started down the other side they could see the brake lights of another car in front of them. Drawing closer to the slow-moving vehicle they saw the reason for its hesitation. There was a line of cars in front of it that were creeping slowly around a curve. Dulaney didn't need to see past them to determine why they had stopped. The map showed they were approaching an intersection at the bottom of the mountain, a likely location for a roadblock. The decision of when to leave the car had been made for them. With the terrain rising at a severe angle on their right and dropping off steeply on their left, there was no option but to continue straight ahead. He told Hana to pull off to the side and stop on the shoulder. Taking the briefcase and the flight bag, they got out of the car and entered the woods. Once out of sight of the traffic on the road they stopped while Dulaney took out his map and compass. Orienting himself to his position on the map, he led the way down the steep forested slope, beginning a trek across what he estimated to be at least seven miles of rough terrain before they reached the extraction site.

26

THE SOMBER MOOD IN the operations room at the CIA isolation base in West Germany had changed rapidly when Dulaney's voice came up on the primary frequency in response to Kessler's transmission. The situation report Kessler had sent after escaping from the warehouse had left them with some hope, but the inability of Dulaney to keep his communications schedule, and the cable from the Prague station chief, sent when one of his case officers had learned through an agent in the Czech Ministry of Interior that Dulaney and Cernikova had been caught, had left them with no choice but to write off the mission as a total disaster. Kessler's radio contact with Dulaney, monitored only minutes after receiving the cable from Prague, had been accompanied by a short, spontaneous cheer and a flurry of activity from the radio operators and other CIA personnel in the room.

"We're back in the ball game," the deputy chief of station from Bonn said, elated with the confirmation that Dulaney was still alive and operational. Lt. Col. Paul Kitlan shared only part of Simpson's enthusiasm; his thoughts were of Kessler, wondering how badly he was wounded and if he would be able to make it out on his own.

Having decoded Dulaney's grid coordinates, Kitlan placed a pin in the map on the display board at the front of the room.

"That's where Dulaney and Cernikova were when Kessler contacted them," he told Simpson.

Simpson stared at the terrain features and network of roads in the immediate area of the pin. His eyes followed the road leading west from the town of Strasin toward the border.

"They're probably on foot by now," he said, tapping his finger where the road intersected with another at the bottom of a mountain pass. "There's got to be a roadblock here. And there's no way off that mountain in a car without going through it. Let's hope they spotted it in time."

"If they did, that leaves at least seven or eight miles of rough terrain to cross on foot," Kitlan said, glancing at his watch. It was ten thirty. "If they don't get lost or run into any patrols it's going to take them at least five or six hours."

"If they ditch the car near that intersection, the Czechs will have no trouble determining the general area of the extraction site once they start tracking them," Simpson said.

Kitlan agreed. "And they'll know we're coming in after them and that we wouldn't chance having them try to get through the death strip, which narrows it down even further." Pointing to the map, he added, "Their troops and helicopters are spread all along the West German border from East Germany to Austria, but they'll probably pull in as many units as they can and concentrate them along a ten-mile corridor on the far side of the death strip running northwest and southwest from where they find the car."

"Why northwest?" Simpson asked. "Dulaney's inexperienced; he'll follow a course straight to the site."

"They don't know that," Kitlan said. "They'll know we wouldn't put the extraction site too far east of the death strip, but they'll have to consider the possibility that Dulaney and Cernikova might double back and head north instead of south; that'll disperse them a little."

"If you're right about how long it's going to take Dulaney to reach the extraction site, the Czech troops are still going to be as thick as flies in that area by the time we have to go in and get him."

"If you give me what I need, I can make them dance to our tune."

"I've got the authority for anything you want," Simpson said. "Just say the word."

"I'll need some fast movers to fly at high altitude along the entire Czech–West German border area."

"I can get some F-15s out of Bitburg."

"And as many helicopters as you can get to fly at low altitude along a fifteen-mile strip of the border that parallels the extraction site."

"What else?"

"MC-130H Combat Talons. The Air Force Seventh Special Operations Squadron has four or five of them at the Rhine-Main airbase. I want two of them on station along the border when we're ready to go in."

"Do you plan on having them cross into Czech territory?" Simpson asked, familiar with the Talon's use for "black flights" —clandestine missions across international borders that had earned it the nickname "Blackbird." "If you do, I'll have to get approval from Langley."

"Quick in and outs," Kitlan said. "Just long enough to make it look like they're headed over the fence. Their terrain-following radar can keep them down on the deck where they can give the Czechs fits. Their primary purpose will be the use of their electronic-countermeasures capability. When we head for the extraction site they can start jamming the enemy radar."

"The minute the Czechs see all this activity on our side they're going to scramble their combat air patrol MIGs," Simpson said.

"We can make sure the MIGs concentrate on the F-15s. They'll keep them away from our penetration point."

"When do you want to start?"

"In four hours," Kitlan said. "Before Dulaney's estimated time of arrival at the extraction site. We'll rotate aircraft and keep them in the air until he makes contact. We can keep the Czechs so busy they won't know whether they're coming or going. Every time we have a chopper or a Blackbird probe the border and duck back across they'll have to check it out. Presented with enough diversions they'll have no way of knowing which one is the real thing. They may know we're coming, but we can give them a hell of a lot more to look at than they ever expected."

27

✖ DULANEY IGNORED THE THORNS that scratched his face and hands as he parted the thick tangle of scrub and vines. Hana crawled into the thicket and he pulled her tightly against his side, poking the muzzle of the submachine gun partway through the undergrowth in the direction of the ridgeline.

The sounds of heavy footsteps and voices drew nearer as the six-man patrol rose out of the hollow where Hana had spotted them. Cresting the ridge, they spread out at twenty-yard intervals on the level ground and began walking slowly through the woods. Dulaney and Hana lay motionless, their eyes fixed on a Czech soldier who had stopped to light a cigarette only a few yards away. The patrol had not seen them, climbing the ridge only to get to the high ground to continue their search. They passed by without incident, dropping out of sight as the ground sloped away in the direction they had gone.

The scent of the forest deepened in the cool, crisp air as the sun sank slowly behind the mountains, and Dulaney and Hana stayed under cover until the distant voices faded and the only sounds heard were those of the birds and the mountain breeze rustling the dying leaves. They had been walking for six hours, with only brief rest stops, and had seen other patrols in the distance and heard the Czech helicopters passing low overhead, occasionally seeing them swoop down into the valleys and hollows to circle and hover before rising again to continue toward the border.

Dulaney was hopelessly lost. The sighting of the patrols had caused him to change directions so often that he had strayed far from the course he had plotted on the map. His compass still told him he was headed southwest, in the direction of the extraction site, but he had no idea how far it was to the left or right of his present position. The prominent terrain feature, a distinctive ridgeline, on which he had taken a bearing, was no longer in sight. In his haste to find a place to hide from the patrol that had just passed, he had taken a number of turns and failed to keep track. The terrain features that surrounded him now were enough alike that he could not distinguish them from the countless others on the map. His best estimate was that he was at least a mile off course, but he did not know in which direction. The trails shown on the map were of no use, intersecting with other trails not on the map, and crossed by trodden paths that looked like hiking trails but had turned out to be paths where deer had traveled along the ridges and moved down into the valleys.

He decided they could no longer continue in the direction they had been heading for fear of running into the Czech patrol in front of them. Descending into the hollow where Hana had first seen the soldiers, they climbed to the ridge on the opposite side, but again saw no terrain feature they could identify on the map. Confusion and panic overruled Dulaney's better judgment, causing him to doubt his compass. Sitting beneath a tree and forcing himself to calm down, he remembered what Kessler had told him to do in the event he got lost: "Most hiking trails in that area parallel streams; go downhill until you find one. The stream will eventually flow into the Otava River; the river will give you a bearing on the extraction site."

Hana forced a brave smile and kissed him on the cheek, resting her head on his shoulder as they sat on the soft bed of pine needles beneath the tree. They were both exhausted from the grueling forced march; a monotonous climb up and down an endless series of steep slopes—the narrow valleys in between giving little relief before they had to begin climbing again. Resting for a few minutes, they followed the broadest trail traversing the ridge to the southwest. After a mile or so the trail led to a gentle slope that descended into a thinly wooded valley. Pausing frequently to watch for patrols, they moved slowly down-hill. A few hundred yards from where they stood the valley broadened and the forest ended. They heard an unfamiliar sound, and on the other side of the treeline they saw a large field of uncut rye, and to the right of it, separated by a hedge-row, another clearing where a man drove a horse-drawn hay rake, gathering the freshly cut field into windrows. Behind him were a dozen women in coarse peasant dresses and brightly colored aprons and babushkas. The women, wielding large wooden rakes, meticulously combed the rows into small rounded stacks.

Reaching the edge of the field, they stayed under cover as Dulaney took out his map and studied the terrain features in the surrounding area. He saw a road in the distance on the far side of the uncut field, and a short bridge spanning what he felt certain was the Otava River. Beyond the road, barely visible above the tops of a distant stand of trees, he saw sections of red tile roofs and corners of buildings and the ubiquitous onion dome of a village church.

"Sokol," he whispered to Hana, pointing to the village on the map. The small farming community lay only a few miles from the death strip—less than five miles from the West German border. "We're about two miles from the extraction site. On the other side of the field there's another ridge to cross, then the rest of the way through the forest is across level ground."

Hana squeezed his hand and smiled, refraining from embrac-ing him for fear of making any noise that could be heard by an old woman working not far from where they knelt just inside the treeline.

Using the village as a reference point, Dulaney took a bearing from his position. Quickly folding the map and putting it back in his pocket, he led the way as they skirted the clearing, stay-ing inside the woods and out of sight of the farmworkers.

Near the end of the field, where they made a slight change in direction to climb a slope at an angle, Dulaney stopped sud-denly and dropped into a crouch, pulling Hana down with him. But he had reacted too late. Two women sitting at the edge of the woods, taking a rest break, had seen them approaching. They stared silently for a long moment, then whispered ur-gently to each other and got to their feet, returning to the field and hurrying off in the direction of the road.

Josef Masek and Viktor Rudenko sat inside the guardhouse listening to the young captain explain how he had deployed the border guards in his sector of the death strip. The telephone rang, interrupting his briefing, and the expression on his face changed as he listened to the local policeman on the other end of the line. Dropping the receiver, he turned back to the map spread across his desk and pointed to an area approximately two miles east of the guardhouse.

"They have been sighted here," he said excitedly.

"How long ago?" Masek asked.

"Twenty minutes."

"In which direction were they headed?"

"Northwest," the captain said, indicating the contour lines of a low mountain rising north of the river.

"How accurate is the description?"

The captain picked up the receiver and asked the question, nodding his head as he listened. "They sound like the people we are looking for. The woman with the man was wearing a light blue jacket over a yellow sweater; the same as the woman who escaped with the American from the police station."

"Where are your closest patrols to that area?" Masek asked.

"I have one six-man patrol seven or eight kilometers north of where they were sighted."

"That is all?"

"In the immediate area, yes, sir. The American helicopters have made three incursions across our border in the last half hour. Four during the half hour before that. They all returned immediately to West German territory, but each one had to be investigated. We had to determine if they had inserted more troops."

Masek studied the map. His eyes came to rest on the representation of the low ground where Dulaney and Hana had been sighted. "What is this?" he asked, pointing to a small square indicating a building at the end of a narrow valley.

"A farmhouse. But it is deserted. The people were moved into the village years ago."

"Are there still fields and clearings around it?" Masek asked.

"Yes. They have not been farmed in years, but it is still open ground."

A trace of a smile creased Masek's broad, scowling face. The road leading east from the guardhouse on the death strip passed within a few hundred yards of the deserted farm. "How long will it take your patrol to reach the farmhouse?"

The captain glanced at the terrain features of the map before answering. "Twenty to twenty-five minutes . . . it is difficult terrain."

"We can drive there in ten," Masek said.

"There is just myself and my radio operator, and the guards in the towers," the captain said. "I cannot leave my post—I must stay in contact with my troops on patrol. I can have two scout cars with eight men here in approximately fifteen minutes," he offered.

"Comrade Rudenko and I will leave immediately," Masek said. "Have your radio operator contact all patrols in the area and have them proceed to the farm. And alert the commander of the border guards to the sighting and the possibility of the extraction site being located at the deserted farm."

Masek removed two assault rifles from the weapons room, handing one to Rudenko as they rushed from the guardhouse to the car. "What makes you believe they are at the deserted farm?" Rudenko asked.

"It is the only open ground in an otherwise remote area," Masek said. "The American will not attempt to cross the death strip, and there are no other suitable landing sites between here and there. In the direction they were seen heading, the farm is the only place within a five-kilometer radius where a helicopter can pick them up without being observed."

"There have been four false sighting reports in the past three hours," Rudenko said. "If this is another we could be drawing troops from where they may be needed."

"The American incursions have all been north and south of this sector, purposely scattering our troops and helicopters over a wide area, away from where they intend to cross the border. It is them," Masek said with conviction. "And the farmhouse is the site where they will come in to get them."

28

✘ GASPING FOR BREATH AFTER running the last mile through the forest, Dulaney and Hana stopped abruptly and dropped to their knees at the edge of a clearing. The shadows in the woods grew deeper in the gathering twilight and the surrounding hills began to merge with the landscape in the cold, bluish light. The fallow, dun-colored field before them still smelled of summer; an eerie stillness and silence hung in the evening air, broken only by a gentle breeze coming down off the mountains that swayed the slender stalks of waist-high wild grass.

Dulaney's eyes moved slowly across the open area, pausing to stare at an abandoned farmhouse and equipment shed on the far side. He didn't recall the house being mentioned during the final briefing at the isolation base, but the clearing lay directly in line with the azimuth he had taken from the village. Continuing to watch the house, he could see that it was deserted. There were no signs of people or dogs or livestock. The porch sagged and remnants of shutters hung at odd angles from the frames of broken windows. What had once been a small lawn around the immediate area of the house had now grown as high as the field grass. Boards were missing from the walls of the equipment shed and the garage-style doors were torn from their rusted hinges and lay on the ground, revealing the barren interior.

"This has to be it," he said to Hana, who was still breathing heavily as she clutched the briefcase to her side.

With one last look about the field, they left the woods and sprinted across to the other side, taking cover in the open bay of the equipment shed. Placing his submachine gun on the ground beside him, Dulaney quickly unzipped the flight bag and removed his radio equipment. He read his notes on the angle of elevation and azimuth for transmitting from the extraction site and set the antenna in place, connecting it to the radio.

"Adrian!" Hana whispered, her eyes peering through a gap in the wall of the shed.

Dulaney turned in the direction she was looking and saw the black Tatra sedan moving slowly through the trees along the deeply rutted track that had once been the access road to the farm. Grabbing the submachine gun and checking to make certain he had a full magazine, he watched as the car came to a stop at the front of the house. A short, heavyset man wearing a leather trenchcoat got out from behind the wheel, followed by his passenger who walked around the rear of the car, his head moving back and forth as he surveyed the area. Both men carried assault rifles, and Dulaney had no doubts they were STB.

"Son-of-a-bitch," he muttered, as the two men disappeared around the far side of the house, reappearing a few moments later as they walked along the edge of the rear porch and stopped to look at the field before continuing in the direction of the equipment shed.

Rudenko held his assault rifle at his hip, his finger on the trigger, the muzzle sweeping the area in front of him. Masek followed a few steps behind and off to the right, carrying his rifle with the muzzle pointed at the ground.

Dulaney had hoped they were simply making a random spot check of the farm and would leave without making a thorough search, but the way the two men moved told him they were there for a specific purpose. Considering Rudenko the more immediate threat, Dulaney chose him as his first target. Aware that shots from their weapons would be heard by any patrols in the area, he decided not to chance having them see him first, leaving him no option but to open fire before they reached the shed. His eyes darted from Rudenko to Masek. They were both in his line of fire from where he sat cross-legged behind the narrow opening in the wall. If he reacted quickly after killing the first man, he was certain he could get his companion before he could fire his assault rifle.

Rudenko was only ten feet from the shed when Dulaney squeezed the trigger. The short accurate burst cut across the Russian's torso from his waist to his shoulder, dropping him to his knees before he fell face forward into the grass.

"Hold your fire!" Dulaney heard the other man shout as he swung the muzzle of the submachine gun in his direction.

Hearing only the rapid clicking sound made by the bolt of the sound-suppressed weapon, and unable to locate Dulaney's exact position behind the wall of the shed, Masek had quickly realized that any attempt to return fire or reach cover would be futile. He had immediately dropped his rifle and raised his hands high in the air.

"Don't shoot," Masek called out again in heavily accented English.

Dulaney released his pressure on the trigger, momentarily confused by the man's surrender. He hadn't anticipated taking a prisoner.

"Walk away from the rifle," he shouted to Masek, who did as he was ordered.

Dulaney kept his weapon to his shoulder, unsure of how to handle the situation. Getting to his feet, he stepped from inside the shed and faced the squat, barrel-chested man standing in front of him. The look on Masek's face puzzled him; there was no fear or surprise, only a calm, steady gaze that changed to an enigmatic expression as he glanced at Rudenko's lifeless body sprawled on the grass a few yards from where he stood.

"Who are you?" Dulaney asked.

"Josef Masek. I am a State Security officer." His eyes looked beyond Dulaney as Hana came out of the shed.

"Did you know we were here?"

"You were seen heading in this direction," he said, nodding his huge head toward Hana in acknowledgment of her presence.

"Who else knows we're here?" Dulaney asked.

"No one," Masek answered, his dark, steady eyes now fixed on Dulaney. "I remembered the clearing and decided to check on it."

"My ass," Dulaney said, having noticed the special antenna on the car. "You've got a police radio in that car, and you didn't come in here on any hunch." He gestured with the muzzle of the submachine gun toward a tree a few feet away at the edge of the field. "Sit over there with your back against the tree and keep your hands clasped behind your neck."

Masek did as he was told as Dulaney sat on the ground beside the radio and switched it on. Selecting the primary frequency, he kept his eyes on Masek as he plugged in the handset. Holding his weapon in one hand at his side, his finger on the trigger, the muzzle pointed dead center at Masek's chest, he keyed the microphone on the handset and transmitted. "Blue Light, this is Hickory. Over."

The response was immediate. "Hickory, this is Blue Light. Are you at the site?"

"I think so," Dulaney replied.

There was a brief pause, then, "Are you at the preselected extraction site?" It was Kitlan's voice now and not that of the radio operator.

"Yes. I think so. I just don't remember you mentioning a deserted farmhouse."

"There is no farmhouse at the site," Kitlan said. There was another pause and then Dulaney heard Kitlan's voice again. "Keep your radio on and do not transmit until I contact you."

"Don't take too long," Dulaney said, his voice wavering with a nervous tremor. "I have a prisoner. They know where I am and there's got to be more on the way."

"Stand by," Kitlan said.

Elliot Simpson stared at the map on the display board. "Where the hell is he! There's no goddamn farmhouse anywhere near the site."

"He's got to be close to it," Kitlan said. "He's oriented his radio antenna according to the instructions we gave him at the briefing. If he was more than three miles off in any direction we wouldn't be receiving him."

Simpson picked up an in-house telephone and spoke to one of his area specialists. "Bring me the reconnaissance satellite photographs for a five-mile radius of the extraction site," he told the man. Turning to Kitlan he said, "We've got closeup high-resolution photos of every inch of the border. If there's a farmhouse we'll find it."

"We can't waste any time while you're looking," Kitlan said. "He doesn't know how to code his messages for burst transmissions, so we're going to have to talk to him in clear voice on the primary frequency. If he's right, and the Czechs are on the way to his location, it won't make any difference if we ask him to describe his surroundings. Get the rescue chopper in the air," he said to one of the radio operators who immediately relayed the command on another frequency to the Black Hawk helicopter standing by on the border.

"Hickory, this is Blue Light," Kitlan said. "Put on your radar transponder and leave it on. Acknowledge."

Dulaney removed the miniature transponder from the flight bag and turned it on, informing Kitlan that he had done so.

"If he's within three miles of the extraction site," Simpson said, "he's got to be surrounded by mountains. That transponder is line-of-sight. If we can't narrow down his position the chopper's going to have to get up to at least seven thousand feet and fly parallel to the border until they pick up his signal."

"I'm aware of that," Kitlan said. He spoke again to Dulaney. "Describe the terrain features in the immediate area of your position."

"I'm at the edge of a clearing about half the size of a football field and I'm surrounded by mountains," Dulaney said.

"From where did you shoot your last azimuth?" Kitlan asked.

"The village of Sokol," Dulaney replied.

"Did you see the Otava River?" Kitlan asked, his eyes locating Sokol on the large map on the display board.

"Yes. I saw a bridge crossing it . . . west of the village."

"What was the azimuth you followed from the village?"

Dulaney told him.

"Was the river on your right or left as you followed the azimuth you shot?"

"On my right," Dulaney answered.

"He didn't see the village of Sokol," Kitlan told Simpson. "He saw Modrava. It's about a mile southwest of Sokol."

Kitlan keyed his microphone and spoke to Dulaney again. "How many ridgelines did you cross before you reached your present position?"

"One," Dulaney said. "Then about a mile and a half of level ground through the forest."

Kitlan ran his finger along the map bringing it to rest at the base of a group of closely drawn contour lines. "He's only about a mile in from the death strip. Three miles from the border. Somewhere near the middle of this valley."

Simpson's border area specialist entered the operations room with a large file of photographs and placed them on the table in the center of the room. Kitlan showed him on the map where he thought Dulaney was, and the specialist quickly flipped through the photographs, pulling out a series of four and placing them side by side on the table.

* * *

"What is he saying?" Dulaney asked Hana, aware that Masek had been speaking to her in Czech while he had been talking to Kitlan.

"He said he saw me skate many times when I was in competition," Hana answered. "He said I was the best he had ever seen, and I thanked him."

"I will speak in English if you like," Masek said.

Dulaney glanced nervously back toward the farmhouse and the dirt road leading to it; the house was becoming a silhouette in the failing light. It had been ten minutes since Masek had arrived. "What the hell am I supposed to do with you?" Dulaney said to Masek, who simply shrugged and continued to stare with a directness that unnerved Dulaney further.

"You were my daughter's trainer when she was a junior member of the national team," Masek said to Hana in English. "She always spoke fondly of you."

"Your daughter?"

"Maria Maskova."

"Maria," Hana said. A warm smile spread slowly across her face. "She was one of my best students. Her injury was unfortunate."

"Why are you doing this?" Masek asked.

Hana quickly took the smile away. "That is a very foolish question, Mr. Masek. Especially from someone with the STB."

"If you return with me to Prague, I have the authority to assure you that this matter will be overlooked. You can continue with your life as it was before."

"My life was not my own, Mr. Masek. I will miss my work and my students. Nothing else."

"Shut up!" Dulaney shouted, his sudden anger startling both

Hana and Masek. "You took her away from me once. But not this time. You talk to her again and I swear I'll kill you." Dulaney released his pressure on the trigger of the submachine gun, a pressure he had inadvertently increased in response to Masek's words to Hana.

"You have done very well for an amateur," Masek said to Dulaney. "But I am afraid your luck has run out."

"Well, if it has, you're the first son-of-a-bitch I'll shoot when I see your people coming," Dulaney said. "I have a long memory, Masek."

"Ah, yes. Ten years ago," Masek said. "When I read Cernikova's file and saw that your photograph matched the description of the man who had fled with her, I knew you had not come for the briefcase."

Kitlan's voice came over the radio, ending the conversation.

"Hickory, this is Blue Light. Guardian Angel is on its way. Estimated time of arrival is five minutes. What is your present situation on the ground?"

There was still anger in Dulaney's voice as he keyed his microphone and responded. "Still the same," he said, glaring at Masek, intimidated by his size and tough, hard face. "What do you want me to do with the prisoner."

"Who is your prisoner?"

Dulaney told him.

Kitlan looked to Simpson who shook his head emphatically. "Leave him," Kitlan said.

"I don't know how much longer it's going to take the Czech troops to get here," Dulaney said. "What should I do if they arrive before the helicopter does?"

There was little Kitlan could say. If Dulaney's location was known, the Czech troops would be closing in from all points on the compass. If they got to him first there was nothing he could do. "Guardian Angel is on its way. Sit tight."

"I guess that answers my question," Dulaney said.

"Hang in there, Hickory," Kitlan said, detecting the fear in Dulaney's voice. "The opera isn't over until the fat lady sings."

"Colonel," the radio operator in contact with the air force Combat Talons said to Kitlan, "the Blackbirds report three Czech helicopters headed in the direction of Hickory's position."

"How far out?" Kitlan asked.

"Five or six minutes at their present speed. Their infrared has also picked up scout cars on a road headed in the same direction."

Kitlan and Simpson sat quietly waiting to hear from the rescue helicopter. The aircraft was on its own once across the frontier. The mission of the air force F-15s and Combat Talons, and the army helicopters flying along the border, was to provide a deception capability under the guise of training maneuvers. They were under explicit orders not to cross into Czech airspace except to briefly probe the border, and under no circumstances were they to fire on any Czech aircraft or ground troops. The border incursions they had already committed would be officially explained and apologized for as unfortunate mistakes during training exercises.

※ ※ ※

The CIA's Black Hawk helicopter had risen like a great prehistoric beast from the small, isolated clearing just inside the West German border. Its fuselage was painted with a camouflage pattern devoid of any identifying numbers or unit insignia. The three-man crew on the flight deck, as well as the gunners manning the side-firing M60 machine guns on both sides of the forward area of the cabin, were former military personnel, now civilian contract employees of the Agency and as such carried no personal identification on the mission. Climbing to an altitude of seven thousand feet, the combat assault transport helicopter headed for the sector of the border where the radio operator in the operations room at the isolation base had told them Dulaney was located. Flying at cruising speed, they paralleled the frontier as one of the flight crew watched the radar screen while the system interrogated the frequency on which Dulaney's transponder was transmitting the coded signal. The mountains to their east rose to four thousand feet, and the helicopter had to reach an altitude and position that would put them in line-of-sight with the signal before it would appear on the screen. They had been airborne no more than four minutes when the tiny blip appeared.

"Blue Light, this is Guardian Angel," the copilot said. "We've got him." Checking the distance to the site and seeing it was less than three miles, he added, "Estimate under two minutes to site."

Quickly losing altitude, the Black Hawk dropped down to the deck, flying at treetop level, skimming the tops of ridges and descending into valleys as it headed directly toward the signal at its maximum speed of one hundred eighty miles per hour.

Five miles south of the rescue helicopter, an electronic warfare officer on board one of the air force Combat Talons activated his esoteric equipment, sending out a signal to jam the Czech radar along the border. The Czechs reacted immediately, changing frequencies, and the highly sophisticated electronic cat-and-mouse game was on. The Talon's electronic warfare officer began to sweep-jam the Czech radar: sending nanosecond bursts over a broad spectrum of frequencies. The Czech radar operators and equipment were no match for the Talon's electronic countermeasures and soon were lost in a confusion of interrupted signals.

Fifteen miles north of the area where the rescue helicopter had crossed into Czech territory, the F-15s began a series of breathtaking maneuvers intended to draw the Czech MIGs north toward the East German border, while a few miles away at a lower altitude, the second air force Talon concentrated on jamming the communications between the Czech ground control and the MIGs.

✳   ✳   ✳

One moment the edge of the field where Dulaney and Hana knelt beside the radio was silent, and the next it was filled with the powerful throbbing sound of the Black Hawk helicopter as it appeared out of nowhere, rising above the ridge at the end of the valley and descending at a steep angle toward the clearing.

"Signal, come up voice," the copilot of the helicopter transmitted over the primary frequency on Dulaney's radio. "Hickory, this is Guardian Angel, come up voice."

"I see you," Dulaney said, his voice filled with relief. "I'm on the north side of the clearing. Twenty yards past the farmhouse, in front of the equipment shed."

"Are there any bad guys around?" Guardian Angel asked.

Dulaney glanced back toward the access road leading to the house and wished he hadn't. He saw three sets of headlights flashing through the trees. They had just turned off the main road and were still a half mile from the house. "They're on the way," Dulaney said.

The pulsating beat of the helicopter grew in volume and intensity, resonating off the surrounding mountains as it passed directly overhead, looming menacingly like the dark shadow of death as it hovered briefly, flailing the air, before settling into the center of the field, its four huge rotor blades flattening the grass around it. The side doors were thrown open, sliding rearward to reveal the interior of the cabin. Two men, facing in opposite directions and covering both sides of the field, hunched over swivel-mounted M60 machine guns; the man facing Dulaney spotted the fast-approaching scout cars and trained his weapon where the road ended at the house.

"Go!" Dulaney shouted to Hana. Cradling the briefcase in her arms, she raced toward the helicopter thirty yards away.

Dulaney's eyes shifted rapidly from the cars on the road to Masek, who had also seen them. Keeping the muzzle of the submachine gun pointed at the curiously calm STB officer, Dulaney disconnected the antenna, leaving it behind as he stuffed the radio into the flight bag. Slinging the bag over his shoulder, he got to his feet and paused at the edge of the field. Leveling the muzzle of his weapon at Masek's chest, he slowly applied pressure to the trigger, releasing it just short of firing. Masek's expression remained impassive.

Looking toward the helicopter, Dulaney saw one of the crew pull Hana into the cabin. The man's shouts for him to hurry reached him above the noise of the twin turbine engines and the swirling blades. Leaving Masek sitting at the tree, his hands still clasped behind his neck, he ran backward into the field, looking from Masek to the scout cars that were now within fifty yards of the house. Halfway across the open area, he turned to face the waiting helicopter and began to sprint the remaining distance. His foot sank into a soft mound of earth and he fell. Scrambling to his feet, he saw Masek standing a short distance from where he had left him, an assault rifle to his shoulder.

Glancing quickly about the darkening field, Dulaney searched frantically for the submachine gun he had dropped when he fell. The door gunner behind the M60 in the helicopter shouted for him to hit the ground; the gunner could not get a clear shot at Masek. Dulaney froze in position, staring at the barrel of the rifle aimed at his chest, too frightened to move, waiting for the shot that would end his life. He again heard the shouts from the helicopter, but could not bring himself to respond. The voice that reached him next was not that of the door gunner. It was Masek. He had called out his name and had lowered the assault rifle from his shoulder without firing when he had it within his power to kill him. Tossing the weapon off to the side, he cupped his hands around his mouth and called out again. Dulaney heard the words clearly above the roar of the helicopter as it prepared to lift off.

"Not for you, Dulaney," Masek shouted. *"Not for you. For Cernikova."*

Dulaney turned and ran as fast as he could to the helicopter, diving inside the cabin as the Black Hawk applied full power and rose from the clearing just as the Czech scout cars reached the farmhouse.

The pilot saw the soldiers rushing toward the field; the helicopter was still within range of their ground fire. Rotating the nose of the aircraft in their direction, he hovered ten feet off the ground. The copilot fired a rocket from one of the pods on the exterior of the fuselage, its fiery tail streaking through the growing darkness. The rocket impacted where intended, releasing a thick cloud of tear gas with a vomit injector that stopped the advancing soldiers, their eyes and throats burning, their stomachs heaving from the effects of the gas.

Dulaney knelt in the open door of the cabin. He saw Masek standing in the shadows away from the cloud of gas, his hands deep in the pockets of his trenchcoat, staring after the helicopter as it rose swiftly and climbed out of sight. The doors were pulled shut as the aircraft crossed the ridge, and Dulaney strapped himself into one of the troop seats beside Hana.

"Is it over?" she asked Dulaney. "We are free?"

Dulaney put his arm around her shoulder and held her tightly. "It's over."

The flight deck was open to the cabin, and Dulaney listened to the radio transmissions and the conversations of the crew. He understood little of the jargon, but enough to realize that the pilot had taken some evasive maneuvers and was being aided by assets on the West German side, and that they would be safely across the border before any of the Czech aircraft in pursuit reached them.

Dulaney and Hana sat in the deep, comfortable leather chairs around the heavy oak table in the debriefing room at the CIA isolation base. Still tense and needing to unwind from the events of the past twelve hours, they ignored the plates of sandwiches and drank only the coffee that was offered. They sat, holding hands, listening to Simpson's short speech congratulating them on a successful mission and warning them of the importance of revealing nothing of what they had done to anyone outside the debriefing room.

"All I want you to do is take us home," Dulaney said. "You people dance too close to the edge for me." His eyes were drawn to Kitlan, who stood in a corner of the room staring out a window.

"We'll need you here for two days of debriefing," Simpson said. "During that time we'll make the necessary arrangements with the State Department to get Hana's travel documents and temporary papers."

"You mean we have to stay here?"

"It's a necessary inconvenience," Simpson said. "We'll take you back to Chadds Ford the same way we brought you here. Until then we need your full cooperation. We've arranged comfortable quarters, there are toilet articles and clean clothing. If you need anything, just ask one of the men assigned to your security detail."

"I'd like to make a telephone call to the States," Dulaney said.

"Not until after the debriefing," Simpson said firmly. "I suggest you get some sleep—we'll begin first thing in the morning."

One of Simpson's assistants escorted Dulaney and Hana from the room and down the hallway to the apartment that had been prepared for them.

"I'm sorry about your men," Simpson said, turning to Kitlan. "I know the importance of the mission doesn't lessen the sense of loss, but they didn't die in vain."

"Anything more on Frank Kessler?" Kitlan asked.

"We intercepted some radio traffic among the Czech border guards. It seems Kessler had stolen a motorcycle during his escape. According to their reports he lost control of it and plunged into a ravine just north of the village of Strasin. They found it smashed on the rocks below. It makes sense if he was wounded badly. They searched for his body most of the day; they haven't found it. Apparently there was a river with a pretty strong current at the bottom of the ravine. It may never be recovered." Simpson placed a consoling hand on Kitlan's shoulder. "I'm sorry. I know you two go back a long way, but there's nothing more we can do."

"Are the Czechs still looking for him?"

"No," Simpson said. "When we got Dulaney and Cernikova out they lifted the alert status and pulled back the troops they brought in as reinforcements in the border area."

"Are you through with me?" Kitlan asked.

"Yes, of course," Simpson said. "I know you didn't want any part of this mission, colonel. I understand and appreciate that. But nonetheless, your cooperation and expertise were greatly appreciated. They won't go unrewarded."

"I'd like transportation back to Bad Tolz," Kitlan said.

"There's a helicopter waiting for you at the airstrip."

Kitlan opened his mouth to speak, but instead simply nodded and left the room.

29

THE COLD NIGHT WIND swept the rain in solid sheets
across the grassy clearing between the fences along the death
strip. The Czech guards in their open-sided towers huddled
miserably beneath ponchos, their hoods obscuring most of their
peripheral vision; the beams of their spotlights, diffused and
deflected in the heavy downpour, reached only partway to the
opposite fence.

Behind the towers, beneath the canopy of the deep pine forest
bordering the eastern side of the strip, the rain dripped heavily
through the trees to where Frank Kessler sat on the sodden
ground, shivering and exhausted, racked with unbearable pain
from a knee that had swelled to four times its normal size. After
spending most of the day he had been wounded on the rock
shelf above the ravine, watching the troops a hundred feet below comb the woods and the banks of the river, he had left
under the cover of darkness, using a sturdy branch fashioned
into a crude crutch for support as he began his journey toward
the death strip. Traveling the open, level terrain off the roadbeds at night and entering the wooded mountains during the
daylight hours, it had taken him the better part of three pain-
filled, occasionally delirious days to cover the nine miles to
where he had chosen to attempt his escape across the border.

The location he had selected was the nearest weak spot in the

339

Czech border defenses from where he had been wounded—one of the weak spots his team had designated for use as an entry or exit point during a hot-war situation. Once through the two fences, the West German border was less than a mile away. But the task before him seemed impossible. His shattered knee was not his only handicap; the fever he had been suffering for the past two days, caused by the infection of the wound in his side, had at times weakened him to the point of immobility. Eliminating the guards in the towers on either side of him was the least of his problems. As soon as he cut through the first wire fence the alarm would sound in the guard station three quarters of a mile away and bring at least one scout car full of troops to the area, possibly two or three, considering that many of them would be taking shelter in the station against the weather as opposed to patrolling their usual sectors of the strip. Under normal circumstances, he could cut through the first fence, cross the strip, and cut through the second and be well into the woods on the other side before the scout cars reached the site. But he had no illusions about things being that uncomplicated in his present condition.

Low-crawling to the edge of the forest, he pulled himself into a sitting position against the trunk of a tree, equidistant between the two towers. Raising his submachine gun to his shoulder, he flipped the selector switch to semiautomatic and sighted on the guard in the tower on his right. His aim was unsteady and his vision blurred as he tried to hold his sights on the silhouetted figure. Lowering the weapon to his side, he slumped against the tree and fought off the unconsciousness that promised relief and peace. He reached for the reserves of strength and will that had always been there for him, but there was nothing left. Slowly raising the submachine gun to his shoulder again, he found he had even less control than before. The weapon dropped from his hands and he sat listlessly looking up into the tower on his right where his intended target stood hunched against the weather.

Unable to move, Kessler continued to stare blankly at the tower. A sudden, violent reaction by the guard registered in his half-conscious mind. At first he thought he was hallucinating, seeing in his mind's eye what he had to do. He watched in a dreamlike trance as the guard was knocked backward, tumbling over the side of the tower and somersaulting twenty feet to the ground, landing with a solid thud in the rain-soaked grass. Glancing quickly to the tower on his left, Kessler squinted through the cold, driving rain that pelted his face. He could barely distinguish the outline of the second guard within his field of vision—he was still standing upright, looking in the opposite direction from where his comrade lay dead on the ground. Kessler was at first confused, then worried that he was no longer coherent. Then he understood, and a smile slowly etched the corners of his mouth.

On the far side of the death strip, at the edge of the forest, a man sat in the crotch of a tree a few feet higher than the top of the wire fence. He wore camouflage fatigues and a black wool watch cap and his face was streaked with black greasepaint; he was all but invisible to even the five identically dressed men who knelt near the base of the tree, their weapons and eyes trained on the death strip and the surrounding woods. Again taking care not to expose the optics of his sensitive instrument to the harsh glare of the spotlights angling down and away from the towers on the opposite side of the clearing from where he sat, the man in the tree swung the barrel of his sound-suppressed sniper rifle with swift precision to his second target. Bracing himself into a stable platform, the eye cup seated firmly in position, he gazed steadily at the rain-distorted green-tinted image in his lens and held the crosshairs of the passive night-vision telescopic sight on the chest cavity of the guard in the second tower as he slowly squeezed the trigger. The deadly subsonic round killed the unsuspecting guard instantly, knocking him onto the floor of the tower with the force of its impact. Slinging the rifle across his back, the sniper dropped silently from his perch to the ground, where he rejoined the other men.

Kitlan led the way as the team cut through the wire and ran across the clearing, quickly cutting through the second fence directly in front of where the man with the night-vision scope had spotted Kessler. Two of the men from the Tenth Special Forces Group mountain team spread open a litter and placed Kessler in it while the rest of the men provided security as they carried him back in the direction they had come. With Kitlan taking the point, the litter bearers moved Kessler through the gaping hole they had cut in the first fence and entered the woods, followed by all but one member of the team who remained behind, his M60 machine gun aimed at the two sets of headlights that had just come into view over a distant rise in the clearing. The rest of the team continued toward the border, deployed in a manner to secure their retreat.

The members of the mountain team had been in the woods inside the Czech border for two days. Kitlan, having said nothing to Simpson of his intentions, had asked for volunteers immediately upon returning to Bad Tolz. Every man in the battalion had come forth, despite the knowledge of the personal risks to their lives and careers inherent in the unauthorized mission. Kitlan had chosen five men from one of the mountain teams and they had crossed into Czech territory on foot only seven hours after the extraction of Dulaney and Hana. There was no doubt in Kitlan's mind where Kessler would attempt to cross the border. Knowing approximately where he had been when he was wounded, he knew it was the most logical place for him to make his escape if he was still alive.

Having watched and avoided the Czech vehicle and foot patrols in the wooded area between the death strip and the actual border for the past two days, they knew their routines and from which directions they would converge once the alarm was sounded. The man with the M60 opened fire on the scout cars as they came into range, putting the vehicles out of commission and killing the troops inside before they had time to react. Providing rear security for the rest of the team, he ran through the opening in the fence and followed behind as the litter bearers raced toward the van parked in the woods off a dirt road on the West German side of the border. One of the men providing flank security stopped at a trail that intersected with the one the team was using. Dropping to his knees, he quickly set an antipersonnel mine in place, stringing a trip wire across the trail. The man providing flank security on the opposite side stopped at the next intersecting trail and set up an identical booby trap. The roar of the explosions ripped through the forest within seconds of each other as the team crossed the border. The rear doors of the van were thrown open by the medic who had stayed with the driver waiting for the return of the insertion team. With Kessler and the men safely inside, the van backed out onto the road and sped away in the opposite direction from which they knew the Bavarian frontier police would be rushing to the area.

Kessler swung gently in the litter that now hung from straps suspended from the roof of the van. The interior lights were turned on and he flinched as the medic began removing the dirt-encrusted bandage from his knee.

"Did Dulaney and Cernikova make it out?" he asked Kitlan.

"With the briefcase and without a scratch."

"I thought Simpson's orders were no second efforts."

"Simpson's not one of us," Kitlan said. "He's a spook. We take care of our own."

Kessler smiled through the pain and exhaustion as he glanced at the familiar grease-stained faces of the men crammed in beside him. Moments later he lapsed into unconsciousness as the morphine injection took effect.

Epilogue

✖ DULANEY AND HANA SAT in the small lounge inside the International Air Charter Service building. Located away from the main commercial terminal of the Frankfurt airport, the CIA proprietary company functioned as a legitimate charter service as well as fulfilling various needs for the Agency.

Hana's eyes were on the tarmac outside the plate-glass windows of the lounge, watching eagerly for the private jet that would take them to the United States. She saw the reflection in the window at the same time Dulaney did and turned to look into a face she remembered from the night she had arrived at the CIA isolation base.

Kitlan was an imposing figure in his Class A uniform and green beret, drawing glances from the employees behind the counter and a group of West German businessmen seated close by. He stopped beside Dulaney's chair and nodded a greeting.

"Colonel," Dulaney said, eying Kitlan suspiciously. "I hope you're not here for any official reason. I've had enough of the cloak-and-dagger business to last the rest of my life."

"There's a small complication with Cernikova's travel documents," Kitlan said.

"Simpson said everything was in order until we got home."

"Something about a health certificate. I didn't ask for details. I'm here to take you to get it and bring you back."

"I didn't know there were any health certificates required for travel between the United States and West Germany."

"I guess it only applies to people coming out of the Eastern Bloc countries."

"Our plane's due any minute," Dulaney protested.

"We just have to go into Frankfurt. We'll be back within an hour," Kitlan said. "I'll tell them where you're going. You're the only passengers; the plane won't leave without you."

Dulaney shook his head in resignation. "All right. Let's get it over with."

Kitlan filled most of the twenty-minute drive into the heart of the city with small talk, asking Hana about her life in Czechoslovakia. Dulaney listened impatiently, curious as to why Kitlan had been assigned to do something any staff driver could have done. They turned off a busy street and entered a driveway leading to a fenced-in complex of buildings dominated by a large brick structure. The sign at the entrance to the grounds read: UNITED STATES ARMY 97TH GENERAL HOSPITAL. Kitlan showed his identification card to a military policeman at the gatehouse, returned his salute, and drove through to the parking lot. Dulaney and Hana followed him into the hospital, where they took the elevator to the fourth floor and continued down a long corridor to a room near the end. Kitlan held open the door and ushered them inside.

Dulaney stared at the man in the bed, taking in the full-length cast on his leg, and smiled. "I should have known you were too mean to die," he said.

It took Hana a moment to recognize Kessler as the man who had first contacted her at the skating rink. She crossed the room with Dulaney and stood beside the bed.

Dulaney clasped Kessler's outstretched hand and shook it firmly. "I'm glad you made it out, Frank."

In a gesture that surprised Kessler, Hana leaned over and kissed him on the cheek. "Thank you for bringing Adrian back to me."

"You brought him back—I just delivered the message," Kessler said, embarrassed by the display of affection. Turning to Dulaney he flashed a broad grin, "I hear you were busted by some local-yokel cops, got lost, missed the extraction site by a few miles . . . you made me look bad."

Dulaney took the remarks in the spirit in which they were intended. "I'm not the one laid up with my leg in a cast."

Kessler laughed and took something from Kitlan's hand, which he in turn handed to Dulaney. "You paid your dues for an honorary membership," Kessler said.

Dulaney examined the silver-dollar-sized object. It was the unit coin carried by those who served with the Tenth Special Forces Group. He smiled and closed his fist around it, the pride he felt evident in his face.

"I just wanted a chance to say good-bye," Kessler said, "and to wish you both a long, happy life together."

"Make sure you come to see us when you get back to the States," Dulaney said.

"Only if I can drive that Ferrari of yours."

"Anytime," Dulaney said, acknowledging Kitlan's gesture as he glanced at his watch and motioned with his head toward the door.

"Hey," Kessler called out just as Dulaney stepped into the hallway. "You done good. For a Marine."

> *Warm summer sun, shine brightly here.*
> *Warm southern wind, blow softly here.*
> *Green sod above, lie light, lie light.*
> *Good-night, dear Hana, good-night, good-night.*